"THE FROG IN THE WELL
KNOWS NAUGHT OF THE OCEAN. . .

"We have no more reason to believe that we will be visited by super-intelligent, super-enlightened social workers from Outer Space, a la Close Encounters of the Third Kind, than to fear that some Darth Vader and his space-borne legions will inflict their star wars on us here at home.

"No more, and no less . . ."

—Reginald Bretnor
From his *Introduction*

For Poul and Karen Anderson

THE FUTURE AT WAR, VOL. 2

The Spear of Mars

Edited by
Reginald Bretnor

SF

ace books

A Division of Charter Communications Inc.
A GROSSET & DUNLAP COMPANY
360 Park Avenue South
New York, New York 10010

THE FUTURE AT WAR VOL II: THE SPEAR OF MARS

Copyright © 1980 by Reginald Bretnor

An ACE Book

Cover art by Vincent di Fate
First Ace printing: March 1980

2 4 6 8 0 9 7 5 3 1
Manufactured in the United States of America

ACKNOWLEDGMENTS

The Screwfly Solution, by Raccoona Sheldon
Copyright © 1977 by Raccoona Sheldon. First published in *Analog Science Fiction/Fact,* June 1977. Reprinted by permission of the author.

The Sword, by Frank Quattrocchi
Copyright © 1953 by Quinn Publishing Co., Inc. First published in *Worlds of IF,* March 1953. Reprinted by permission of the author's agent, Forrest J. Ackerman, 2495 Glendower Avenue, Hollywood, CA 90027.

Temple Guardian, by Kevin O'Donnell, Jr.
Copyright © 1979 by Kevin O'Donnell, Jr. First published in *Analog Science Fiction/Fact,* June 1979. Reprinted by permission of the author.

Mirror, Mirror, by Alan E. Nourse
Copyright © 1967 by Alan E. Nourse. First published in *Psi High and Others* by Alan E. Nourse. Reprinted by permission of the author and of the publishers, David McKay Co., Inc., New York.

Balaam by Anthony Boucher
Copyright © 1954 by Henry Holt & Co. First published in *9 Tales of Space and Time,* edited by Raymond J. Healy. Reprinted by permission of the author's agent, Curtis Brown Ltd., 575 Madison Ave., New York, NY 10022.

This Faithful Soldier's Life, by James Stevens
Copyright © 1979 by James Stevens. Published by arrangement with the author.

Cold Victory, by Poul Anderson
Copyright © 1957 by Fantasy House, Inc. First published in *The Magazine of Fantasy and Science Fiction,* May 1957. Reprinted by permission of the author.

CONTENTS

Reginald Bretnor, *Introduction*..1

Stories:
Raccoona Sheldon, *The Screwfly Solution*......................8
Frank Quattrocchi, *The Sword*....................................40
Kevin O'Donnell, Jr., *Temple Guardian*......................101
Alan E. Nourse, *Mirror, Mirror*.................................113
Anthony Boucher, *Balaam*...171
Poul Anderson, *Cold Victory*.....................................196
James Stevens, *This Faithful Soldier's Life*..................248
Orson Scott Card, *Ender's Game*...............................298
Robert Sheckley, *Fool's Mate*....................................357
Fred Saberhagen, *Wings Out of Shadow*....................378

Articles:
L.J. Stecher, Jr., *Invasions of Earth*............................59
Joseph F. Goodavage, *UFOs and Stranger Intruders*.......82
Carl Sagan, *Man: A Transitional Animal*....................162
Vicki Ann Heydron, *Women Under Fire*....................229
T.R. Fehrenbach, *The Ultimate Weapon*....................271

Poem:
Robert Frazier, *Encased in the Amber of Death*.............194

INTRODUCTION

The Spear of Mars is the second volume of *The Future at War*. The first, *Thor's Hammer*, dealt with war on Earth and in near space; the third, *Orion's Sword*, will explore warfare between the stars and galaxies.

This present volume is concerned primarily with invasions of Earth by extraterrestrials and with war within the solar system—and only at its very end with the next step further out. As I explained in my introduction to *Thor's Hammer*, the fact that *The Future at War* deals entirely with war in the future does *not* mean that it is an argument *for* future warfare, and similarly the fact that *The Spear of Mars* contemplates invasions of Earth by extraterrestrials does not mean that it argues for the sort of gibbering paranoia evoked by too many Lovecraftian fantasies and Orson Wellsian broadcasts . . .

However . . .

There is a wise old Japanese proverb: *The frog in the well knows naught of the ocean.* It applies equally to frogs in ordinary wells and to humankind at the bottom of the gravity well in which all but a handful of us have spent, and will spend, our entire lives. The frog, if his well is near the sea, can hear its surf. We, with our radio telescopes and other instruments, can listen to the surf of space. But, at present, we *know* literally nothing about other forms of life *out there*. We do not even *know* that they exist. Indeed, we have only recently started to discover that certain life-forms who share our earth also share the once-thought-to-be-unique gift of intelligence. Dolphins do—and so do killer whales.

In short, we have no more reason to believe that we will be visited by super-intelligent, super-enlightened social workers from Outer Space, à la *Close Encounters of the Third Kind,* than to fear that some Darth Vader and his space-borne legions will inflict their star wars on us here at home. No more, and no less.

Our myths and legends are full of visitations and invasions out of space, some beneficent, some hostile or punitive, some seeking to seed the Earth with intelligent life (often with their own progeny), some demanding worship and obedience. In addition, we have numerous reports—of widely varying credibility—indicating that mysterious visitors on mysterious missions still are coming here; and none of these should, in my opinion, be dismissed out of hand, even though most explanations for them may hold little water. Many of the "scientific" arguments trying to explain them *away* have just as many holes in them. For example I, not a trained observer, have never mistaken the planet Venus for anything but a celestial object, and I find it hard to believe that military pilots who *are* trained observers have been deluded into trying to chase it down. Therefore we must discriminate between well-reasoned arguments against such theories (like L. D. Stecher's) and the flat denial, the absolute refusal to examine evidence. (Is there anyone more credulous than a dedicated debunker, whether he happens to be an accredited expert on UFOs or a member in good standing of the Flat Earth Society?)

The literature, from Charles Fort on (and of course even before his time), reports many phenomena which we can at least accept as having some basis in reality; various UFO reports, accounts of mysterious appearances and disappearances, unknown objects and curious happenings in our seas, livestock mutilations—you name it. Discount all but a fraction of one percent of these, and we still have quite enough to be disquieting—and tantalizing. Let us grant, for the moment, that this is so. Immediately we are confronted by two related, but contradictory, human drives: that which tells us that we must *discover* order in the Universe, and its counterpart which seems to dictate that we must define order in the Universe whether we actually discover it or not. A good example of the latter is Dr. Haushofer's hollow earth theory; another is the Marxist dialectic, explaining all social phenomena, past, present, and future, in terms of "laws" derived from pseudo-scientific mid-nineteenth century observations and deductions. Our "social sciences" today are full of examples quite as ripe as these.

Hence on the one hand we have our alleged visitors and their asserted motives explained to us with a religious fervor by people who know no more about them than we do ourselves, and on the other hand explained away as nonexistent by people who, because their minds are closed to

evidence, may know even less. (Our local newspaper, here in Southern Oregon, recently ran a
syndicated item about an astronomy professor
somewhere in Texas who had come to the conclusion that man was unique in the Universe,
which could hold—and he was apparently
ready, like a Flat or Hollow Earth believer, to
prove it logically—no other intelligent life. The
story, naturally, referred to him as an "expert.")

We seem to have exchanged the Frog Prince of
fairy tale for the frog expert of today. Actually,
where incontrovertible knowledge about extraterrestrial life is concerned, we really aren't
much better off than Bernard de Fontenelle was
when he wrote *A Plurality of Worlds* in 1686:

> *I have fancied nothing* [he wrote] *concerning
> the inhabitants of the many Worlds, which is whol-
> ly fabulous; I have said all that can be reasonably
> thought of them, and the Visions which I have
> added have some real foundation; what is true and
> what is false are mingled together . . . I will not
> undertake to justifie so fantastical and odd a
> Composition . . .* *

Unfortunately, our own concern with the plurality of worlds is, because we are beginning to
adventure into space, rather more immediate
than M. de Fontenelle's, and so, while we still
cannot undertake to justify our own fantastical
and odd compositions, we must take them more
seriously. Either there are extraterrestrials, or
there are not—and considering the vastness and
complexity of the Universe, I would bet on their

---

*Bernard de Fontenelle (1657-1757), *Entretiens sur la Pluralité des
Mondes*, 1686; John Glanvill's translation, 1688.

existence. Either they know about us, or they do not. Do they resemble us in any way? Their evolutionary paths may have been completely different, and—still in our well—we can only guess, basing our guesses on scraps of knowledge and much supposition. Are they more advanced than we? Suppose they have FTL spacecraft, but have no poetry, no music, no graphic arts, no carved gems or tea ceremony vessels or flutes or harpsichords? We can probably grant them technological superiority, or they would have been as planet-bound as we ourselves have been. We can probably grant them, at least from a purely pragmatic standpoint, sociological superiority, for if they can cross the seas of space between the stars the chances, in my opinion, are high that they have managed to control the toys and tools of war in the only way they can be controlled, by controlling whatever aggressive and self-destructive drives they have not outgrown.

What their attitudes toward us may be when finally we erupt into interplanetary and extraplanetary space, that we have no way of knowing. Perhaps the convention is that you simply refuse to know the neighbors down the hall. Perhaps space-faring beings compete for *lebensraum* and for resources very much as we do here on Earth, in which case, compared to those already there, we will be starting with a handicap. Or perhaps it's just a matter of restricting membership in the club to those who, culturally and socially, are qualified.

In that case, at our present levels of development, and with our present behavior patterns, we may be told (gently but firmly?) that space travel is a no-no.

Finally, perhaps in space we may, as so many science fiction writers have imagined, find both friends and enemies. If so, then we may witness the fulfillment of the prophecy in Revelation:

> *And there was war in heaven: Michael*
> *and his angels fought against the dragon;*
> *and the dragon fought and his angels.*
> *And prevailed not; neither was their*
> *place found any more in heaven.*

Reginald Bretnor
Medford, Oregon
June 5, 1979

Any number of scenarios for invasions of Earth are, of course, conceivable; and science fiction writers already have explored a great many of them, starting with H. G. Wells's Martians in The War of the Worlds, *and continuing with legions of Bug-Eyed Monsters, variations on the theme of Ming the Merciless, homicidal robots, advanced societies to whom we are disgusting primitives, and just plain miscellaneous nasties.*

Any of these, however, has to have (at least for story purposes) some sort of reasonable motivation. Invaders may want us to worship them. Or they may be planning to enslave us. Or they may want certain of our resources. (Who knows? Perhaps planets capable of supporting any form of life are rareties in the Universe?) Or possibly—as more than one story has suggested—they may just want to eat us.

Whatever their motivation, our invaders must employ a method at once dramatic and plausible; and in my own reading I have encountered no motive or method as plausible and as frighteningly believable as those presented here by Raccoona Sheldon.

Racoona Sheldon

THE SCREWFLY SOLUTION

The young man sitting at 2° N, 75° W sent a casually venomous glance up at the nonfunctional shoofly *ventilador* and went on reading his letter. He was sweating heavily, stripped to his shorts in the hotbox of what passed for a hotel room in Cuyapán.

How do other wives do it? I stay busy-busy with the Ann Arbor grant review programs and the seminar, saying brightly "Oh yes, Alan is in Colombia setting up a biological pest control program, isn't it wonderful?" But inside I imagine you surrounded by nineteen-year-old raven-haired cooing beauties, every one panting with social dedication and filthy rich. And forty inches of bosom busting out of her delicate lingerie. I even figured it in centimeters, that's 101.6 centimeters of busting. Oh, darling, darling, do what you want only come home safe.

Alan grinned fondly, briefly imagining the only body he longed for. His girl, his magic Anne. Then he got up to open the window an-

8

other cautious notch. A long pale mournful face looked in—a goat. The room opened on the goatpen, the stench was vile. Air, anyway. He picked up the letter.

Everything is just about as you left it, except that the Peedsville horror seems to be getting worse. They're calling it the Sons of Adam cult now. Why can't they do something, even if it is a religion? The Red Cross has set up a refugee camp in Ashton, Georgia. Imagine, refugees in the U.S.A. I heard two little girls were carried out all slashed up. Oh, Alan.

Which reminds me, Barney came over with a wad of clippings he wants me to send you. I'm putting them in a separate envelope; I know what happens to very fat letters in foreign POs. He says, in case you don't get them, what do the following have in common? Peedsville, Sao Paulo, Phoenix, San Diego, Shanghai, New Delhi, Tripoli, Brisbane, Johannesburg, and Lubbock, Texas. He says the hint is, remember where the Intertropical Convergence Zone is now. That makes no sense to me, maybe it will to your superior ecological brain. All I could see about the clippings was that they were fairly horrible accounts of murders or massacres of women. The worst was the New Delhi one, about "rafts of female corpses" in the river. The funniest (!) was the Texas Army officer who shot his wife, three daughters, and his aunt, because God told him to clean the place up.

Barney's such an old dear, he's coming over Sunday to help me take off the downspout and see what's blocking it. He's dancing on air right now, since you left his spruce bud-worm-moth antipheromone program finally paid off. You know he tested over 2,000 compounds? Well, it seems that good old 2,097 really works. When I asked him what it does he just giggles, you know how shy he is with women. Anyway, it seems that a one-shot spray program will save the forests, without harming a single other thing. Birds and people can eat it all day, he says.

Well sweetheart, that's all the news except Amy goes back to Chicago to school Sunday. The place will be a tomb, I'll miss her frightfully in spite of her being at the stage where I'm her worst enemy. The sullen sexy sub-teens, Angie says. Amy sends love to her Daddy. I send you my whole heart, all that words can't say.

Your Anne

Alan put the letter safely in his notefile and glanced over the rest of the thin packet of mail, refusing to let himself dream of home and Anne. Barney's "fat envelope" wasn't there. He threw himself on the rumpled bed, yanking off the lightcord a minute before the town generator went off for the night. In the darkness the list of places Barney had mentioned spread themselves around a misty globe that turned, troublingly, briefly in his mind. Something . . .

But then the memory of the hideously para-sitized children he had worked with at the clinic that day took possession of his thoughts. He set himself to considering the data he must collect. *Look for the vulnerable link in the behavioral chain—* how often Barney—Dr. Barnhard Braithwaite— had pounded it into his skull. Where was it, where? In the morning he would start work on bigger canefly cages . . .

At that moment, five thousand miles North, Anne was writing:

Oh, darling, darling, your first three letters are here,

they all came together. I knew *you were writing. Forget what I said about swarthy heiresses, that was all a joke. My darling, I know, I know . . . us. Those dreadful canefly larvae, those poor little kids. If you weren't my husband I'd think you were a saint or something. (I do anyway.)*

I have your letters pinned up all over the house, makes it a lot less lonely. No real news here except things feel kind of quiet and spooky. Barney and I got the down-spout out, it was full of a big rotted hoard of squirrel-nuts. They must have been dropping them down the top, I'll put a wire over it. (Don't worry, I'll use a ladder this time.)

Barney's in an odd, grim mood. He's taking this Sons of Adam thing very seriously, it seems he's going to be on the investigation committee if that ever gets off the ground. The weird part is that nobody seems to be doing anything, as if it's just too big. Selina Peters has been printing some acid comments, like When one man kills his wife you call it murder, but when enough do it we call it a lifestyle. I think it's spreading, but nobody knows because the media have been asked to downplay it. Barney says it's being viewed as a form of contagious hysteria. He insisted I send you this ghastly interview. It's not going to be published, of course. The quietness is worse, though, it's like something terrible was going on just out of sight. After reading Barney's thing I called up Pauline in San Diego to make sure she was all right. She sounded funny, as if she wasn't saying everything . . . my own sister. Just after she said things were great she suddenly asked if she could come and stay here awhile next month. I said come right away, but she wants to sell her house first. I wish she'd hurry.

Oh, the diesel car is okay now, it just needed its filter changed. I had to go out to Springfield to get one but

*Eddie installed it for only $2.50. He's going to bankrupt
his garage.*

*In case you didn't guess, those places of Barney's are
all about latitude 30° N or S—the horse latitudes.
When I said not exactly, he said remember the equatorial
convergence zone shifts in winter, and to add in Libya,
Osaka, and a place I forget—wait, Alice Springs, Australia. What has this to do with anything, I asked. He
said, "Nothing—I hope." I leave it to you, great brains
like Barney can be weird.*

*Oh my dearest, here's all of me to all of you. Your
letters make life possible. But don't feel you have to, I
can tell how tired you must be. Just know we're together,
always everywhere.*

Your Anne

*PS I had to open this to put Barney's thing in, it wasn't
the secret police. Here it is. All love again. A.*

In the goat-infested room where Alan read this,
rain was drumming on the roof. He put the letter
to his nose to catch the faint perfume once more,
and folded it away. Then he pulled out the yellow flimsy Barney had sent and began to read,
frowning.

PEEDSVILLE CULT/SONS OF ADAM SPE-
CIAL. Statement by driver Sgt. Willard Mews,
Globe Fork, Ark. We hit the roadblock about 80
miles west of Jacksonville. Major John Heinz of
Ashton was expecting us, he gave us an escort of
two riot vehicles headed by Capt. T. Parr. Major
Heinz appeared shocked to see that the NIH
medical team included two women doctors. He
warned us in the strongest terms of the danger.
So Dr. Patsy Putnam (Urbana, Ill.), the psychol-

ogist, decided to stay behind at the Army cordon. But Dr. Elaine Fay (Clinton, N.J.) insisted on going with us, saying she was the episomething (epidemiologist).

We drove behind one of the riot cars at 30 mph for about an hour without seeing anything unusual. There were two big signs saying SONS OF ADAM—LIBERATED ZONE. We passed some small pecan packing plants and a citrus processing plant. The men there looked at us but did not do anything unusual. I didn't see any children or women of course. Just outside Peedsville we stopped at a big barrier made of oil drums in front of a large citrus warehouse. This area is old, sort of a shantytown and trailer park. The new part of town with the shopping center and developments is about a mile further on. A warehouse worker with a shotgun came out and told us to wait for the Mayor. I don't think he saw Dr. Elaine Fay then, she was sitting sort of bent down in back.

Mayor Blount drove up in a police cruiser and our chief, Dr. Premack, explained our mission from the Surgeon General. Dr. Premack was very careful not to make any remarks insulting to the Mayor's religion. Mayor Blount agreed to let the party go on into Peedsville to take samples of the soil and water and so on and talk to the doctor who lives there. The mayor was about 6′ 2″, weight maybe 230 or 240, tanned, with grayish hair. He was smiling and chuckling in a friendly manner.

Then he looked inside the car and saw Dr. Elaine Fay and he blew up. He started yelling we had to all get the hell back. But Dr. Premack talked to him and cooled him down and finally the Mayor said Dr. Fay should go into the warehouse office and stay there with the door closed. I had to stay there too and see she didn't come out, and one of the Mayor's men would drive the party.

So the medical people and the Mayor and one of the riot vehicles went on into Peedsville and I took Dr. Fay back into the warehouse office and sat down. It was real hot and stuffy. Dr. Fay opened a window, but when I heard her trying to talk to an old man outside I told her she couldn't do that and closed the window. The old man went away. Then she wanted to talk to me but I told her I did not feel like conversing. I felt it was real wrong, her being there.

So then she started looking through the office files and reading papers there. I told her that was a bad idea, she shouldn't do that. She said the government expected her to investigate. She showed me a booklet or magazine they had there, it was called *Man Listens to God* by Reverend McIllhenny. They had a cartonful in the office. I started reading it and Dr. Fay said she wanted to wash her hands. So I took her back along a kind of enclosed hallway beside the conveyor to where the toilet was. There were no doors or windows so I went back. After a while she called out that there was a cot back there, she was going to lie down. I figured that was all right because of the no windows, also I was glad to be rid of her company.

When I got to reading the book it was very intriguing. It was very deep thinking about how man is now on trial with God and if we fulfill our duty God will bless us with a real new life on Earth. The signs and portents show it. It wasn't like, you know, Sunday-school stuff. It was deep.

After a while I heard some music and saw the soldiers from the other riot car were across the street by the gas tanks, sitting in the shade of some trees and kidding with the workers from the plant. One of them was playing a guitar, not electric, just plain. It looked so peaceful.

Then Mayor Blount drove up alone in the cruiser and came in. When he saw I was reading the book he smiled at me sort of fatherly, but he looked tense. He asked me where Dr. Fay was and I told him she was lying down in back. He said that was okay. Then he kind of sighed and went back down the hall, closing the door behind him. I sat and listened to the guitar man, trying to hear what he was singing. I felt really hungry, my lunch was in Dr. Premack's car.

After a while the door opened and Mayor Blount came back in. He looked terrible, his clothes were messed up and he had bloody scrape marks on his face. He didn't say anything, he just looked at me hard and fierce, like he might have been disoriented. I saw his zipper was open and there was blood on his clothing and also on his (private parts).

I didn't feel frightened, I felt something important had happened. I tried to get him to sit down. But he motioned me to follow him back down the hall, to where Dr. Fay was. "You must see," he said. He went into the toilet and I went into a kind of little room there, where the cot was. The light was fairly good, reflected off the tin roof from where the walls stopped. I saw Dr.

Fay lying on the cot in a peaceful appearance. She was lying straight, her clothing was to some extent different but her legs were together. I was glad to see that. Her blouse was pulled up and I saw there was a cut or incision on her abdomen. The blood was coming out there, or it had been coming out there, like a mouth. It wasn't moving at this time. Also her throat was cut open.

I returned to the office. Mayor Blount was sitting down, looking very tired. He had cleaned himself off. He said, "I did it for you. Do you understand?"

He seemed like my father, I can't say it better than that. I realized he was under a terrible strain, he had taken a lot on himself for me. He went on to explain how Dr. Fay was very dangerous, she was what they call a cripto-female (crypto?), the most dangerous kind. He had exposed her and purified the situation. He was very straightforward, I didn't feel confused at all, I knew he had done what was right.

We discussed the book, how man must purify himself and show God a clean world. He said some people raise the question of how can man reproduce without women but such people miss the point. The point is that as long as man depends on the old filthy animal way God won't help him. When man gets rid of his animal part which is woman, this is the signal God is awaiting. Then God will reveal the new true clean way, maybe angels will come bringing new souls, or maybe we will live forever, but it is not our place to speculate, only to obey. He said some men here had seen an Angel of the Lord. This was very deep, it seemed like it echoed inside me, I felt it was an inspiration.

Then the medical party drove up and I told Dr. Premack that Dr. Fay had been taken care of and sent away, and I got in the car to drive them out of the Liberated Zone. However four of the six soldiers from the roadblock refused to leave. Capt. Parr tried to argue them out of it but finally agreed they could stay to guard the oil-drum barrier.

I would have liked to stay too the place was so peaceful but they needed me to drive the car. If I had known there would be all this hassle I never would have done them the favor. I am not crazy and I have not done anything wrong and my lawyer will get me out. That is all I have to say.

In Cuyapán the hot afternoon rain had temporarily ceased. As Alan's fingers let go of Sergeant Williard Mews's wretched document he caught sight of pencil-scrawled words in the margin. Barney's spider hand. He squinted.

"Man's religion and metaphysics are the voices of his glands. Schönweiser, 1878."

Who the devil Schönweiser was Alan didn't know, but he knew what Barney was conveying. This murderous crackpot religion of McWhosis was a symptom, not a cause. Barney believed something was physically affecting the Peedsville men, generating psychosis, and a local religious demagog had sprung up to "explain" it.

Well, maybe. But, cause or effect, Alan thought only of one thing: eight hundred miles from Peedsville to Ann Arbor. Anne should be safe. She *had* to be.

He threw himself on the lumpy cot, his mind going back exultantly to his work. At the cost of

a million bites and cane-cuts he was pretty sure
he'd found the weak link in the canefly cycle.
The male mass-mating behavior, the com-
parative scarcity of ovulant females. It would be
the screwfly solution all over again with the sexes
reversed. Concentrate the pheromone, release
sterilized females. Luckily the breeding populations were comparatively isolated. In a couple
of seasons they ought to have it. Have to let them
go on spraying poison meanwhile, of course;
damn pity, it was slaughtering everything and
getting in the water, and the caneflies had
evolved to immunity anyway. But in a couple of
seasons, maybe three, they could drop the canefly populations below reproductive viability. No
more tormented human bodies with those stinking larvae in the nasal passages and brain . . . He
drifted off for a nap, grinning.

Up north, Anne was biting her lip in shame
and pain.

*Sweetheart, I shouldn't admit it but your wife is
~~scared~~ a bit jittery. Just female nerves or something,
nothing to worry about. Everything is normal up here.
It's so eerily normal, nothing in the papers, nothing anywhere except what I hear through Barney and Lillian.
But Pauline's phone won't answer out in San Diego; the
fifth day some strange man yelled at me and banged the
phone down. Maybe she's sold her house—but why
wouldn't she call?*

*Lillian's on some kind of Save-the-Women committee,
like we were an endangered species, ha-ha—you know
Lillian. It seems the Red Cross has started setting up
camps. But she says, after the first rush, only a trickle*

are coming out of what they call "the affected areas."
Not many children, either, even little boys. And they have
some air-photos around Lubbock showing what look like
mass graves. Oh, Alan . . . so far it seems to be mostly
spreading west, but something's happening in St. Louis,
they're cut off. So many places seem to have just vanished
from the news, I had a nightmare that there isn't a woman left alive down there. And nobody's doing anything.
They talked about spraying with tranquilizers for a
while and then that died out. What could it do? Somebody at the U.N. has proposed a convention on—you
won't believe this—femicide. It sounds like a deodorant
spray.

Excuse me, honey, I seem to be a little hysterical.
George Searles came back from Georgia talking about
God's Will—Searles the lifelong atheist. Alan, some-
thing crazy is happening.

But there aren't any facts. Nothing. The Surgeon
General issued a report on the bodies of the Rahway Rip-
Breast Team—I guess I didn't tell you about that. Anyway, they could find no pathology. Milton Baines wrote
a letter saying in the present state of the art we can't
distinguish the brain of a saint from a psychopathic
killer, so how could they expect to find what they don't
know how to look for?

Well, enough of these jitters. It'll be all over by the
time you get back, just history. Everything's fine here, I
fixed the car's muffler again. And Amy's coming home
for the vacations, that'll get my mind off faraway problems.

Oh, something amusing to end with—Angie told me
what Barney's enzyme does to the spruce budworm. It
seems it blocks the male from turning around after he
connects with the female, so he mates with her head
instead. Like clockwork with a cog missing. There're

*going to be some pretty puzzled female spruceworms.
Now why couldn't Barney tell me that? He really is such
a sweet shy old dear. He's given me some stuff to put in,
as usual. I didn't read it.*

Now don't worry, my darling, everything's fine.

I love you, I love you so.

Always, all ways your Anne

Two weeks later in Cuyapán, when Barney's
enclosures slid out of the envelope, Alan didn't
read them either. He stuffed them into the
pocket of his bush jacket with a shaking hand
and started bundling his notes together on the
rickety table, with a scrawled note to Sister
Dominique on top. The hell with the canefly, the
hell with everything except that tremor in his
Anne's firm handwriting. The hell with being
five thousand miles away from his woman, his
child, while some deadly madness raged. He
crammed his meager belongings into his duffel.
If he hurried he could catch the bus through to
Bogotá and maybe make the Miami flight.

He made it, but in Miami he found the planes
north jammed. He failed a quick standby; six
hours to wait. Time to call Anne. When the call
got through after some difficulty he was un-
prepared for the rush of joy and relief that burst
along the wires.

"Thank God—I can't believe it—Oh, Alan,
my darling, are you really—I can't believe—"

He found he was repeating too, and all mixed
up with the canefly data. They were both laughing hysterically when he finally hung up.

Six hours. He settled in a frayed plastic chair
opposite Aerolineas Argentinas, his mind half
back at the clinic, half on the throngs moving by

him. Something was oddly different here, he perceived presently. Where was the decorative fauna he usually enjoyed in Miami, the parade of young girls in crotch-tight pastel jeans? The flounces, boots, wild hats and hairdos, and startling expanses of newly tanned skin, the brilliant fabrics barely confining the bob of breasts and buttocks? Not here—but wait; looking closely, he glimpsed two young faces hidden under unbecoming parkas, their bodies draped in bulky nondescript skirts. In fact, all down the long vista he could see the same thing: hooded ponchos, heaped-on clothes and baggy pants, dull colors. A new style? No, he thought not. It seemed to him their movements suggested furtiveness, timidity. And they moved in groups. He watched a lone girl struggle to catch up with others ahead of her, apparently strangers. They accepted her wordlessly.

They're frightened, he thought. Afraid of attracting notice. Even that gray-haired matron in a pantsuit resolutely leading a flock of kids was glancing around nervously.

And at the Argentine desk opposite he saw another odd thing: two lines had a big sign over them, MUJERES. Women. They were crowded with the shapeless forms, and very quiet.

The men seemed to be behaving normally: hurrying, lounging, griping and joking in the lines as they kicked their luggage along. But Alan felt an undercurrent of tension, like an irritant in the air. Outside the line of storefronts behind him a few isolated men seemed to be handing out tracts. An airport attendant spoke to the nearest man; he merely shrugged and moved a few doors down.

To distract himself Alan picked up a *Miami Herald* from the next seat. It was surprisingly thin. The international news occupied him for a while; he had seen none for weeks. It too had a strange empty quality; even the bad news seemed to have dried up. The African war which had been going on seemed to be over, or went unreported. A trade summit-meeting was haggling over grain and steel prices. He found himself at the obituary pages, columns of close-set type dominated by the photo of a defunct ex-senator. Then his eye fell on two announcements at the bottom of the page. One was too flowery for quick comprehension, but the other stated in bold plain type:

THE FORSETTE FUNERAL HOME REGRETFULLY ANNOUNCES IT WILL NO LONGER ACCEPT FEMALE CADAVERS

Slowly he folded the paper, staring at it numbly. On the back was an item headed "Navigational Hazard Warning," in the shipping news. Without really taking it in, he read:

AP/NASSAU. The excursion liner *Carib Swallow* reached port under tow today after striking an obstruction in the Gulf Stream off Cape Hatteras. The obstruction was identified as part of a commerical trawler's seine floated by female corpses. This confirms reports from Florida and the Gulf of the use of such seines, some of them over a mile in length. Similar reports coming from the Pacific coast and as far away as Japan indicate a growing hazard to coastwise shipping.

Alan flung the thing into the trash receptacle and sat rubbing his forehead and eyes. Thank God he had followed his impulse to come home. He felt totally disoriented, as though he had landed by error on another planet. Four and a half hours more to wait . . . At length he recalled the stuff from Barney he had thrust in his pocket, and pulled it out and smoothed it.

The top item seemed to be from the *Ann Arbor News*. Dr. Lillian Dash, together with several hundred other members of her organization, had been arrested for demonstrating without a permit in front of the White House. They had started a fire in a garbage can, which was considered particularly heinous. A number of women's groups had participated; the total struck Alan as more like thousands than hundreds. Extraordinary security precautions were being taken, despite the fact that the President was out of town at the time.

The next item had to be Barney's, if Alan could recognize the old man's acerbic humor.

UP/VATICAN CITY 19 JUNE. Pope John IV today intimated that he does not plan to comment officially on the so-called Pauline Purification cults advocating the elimination of women as a means of justifying man to God. A spokesman emphasized that the Church takes no position on these cults but repudiates any doctrine involving a "challenge" to or from God to reveal His further plans for man.

Cardinal Fazzoli, spokesman for the European Pauline movement, reaffirmed his view that the Scriptures define woman as merely a temporary companion and instrument of Man. Women, he states, are nowhere defined as human, but merely as a transitional expedient or state. "The time of transition to full humanity is at hand," he concluded.

The next item appeared to be a thin-paper Xerox from a recent issue of *Science:*

SUMMARY REPORT OF THE AD HOC EMERGENCY COMMITTEE ON FEMICIDE

The recent worldwide though localized outbreaks of femicide appear to represent a recurrence of similar outbreaks by groups or sects which are not uncommon in world history in times of psychic stress. In this case the root cause is undoubtedly the speed of social and technological change, augmented by population pressure, and the spread and scope are aggravated by instantaneous world communications, thus exposing more susceptible persons. It is not viewed as a medical or epidemiological problem; no physical pathology has been found. Rather it is more akin to the various manias which swept Europe in the 17th century, e.g., the Dancing Manias, and like them, should run its course and disappear. The chiliastic cults which have sprung up around the affected areas appear to be unrelated, having in common only the idea that a new means of human reproduction will be revealed as a result of the "purifying" elimination of women.

We recommend that (1) inflammatory and sensational reporting be suspended; (2) refugee centers be set up and maintained for women escapees from the focal areas; (3) containment of affected areas by military cordon be continued and enforced; and (4) after a cooling-down period and the subsidence of the mania, qualified mental health teams and appropriate professional personnel go in to undertake rehabilitation.

SUMMARY OF THE MINORITY REPORT OF THE AD HOC COMMITTEE

The nine members signing this report agree that there is no evidence for epidemiological contagion of femicide in the strict sense. *However,* the geographical relation of the focal areas of outbreak strongly suggest that they cannot be dismissed as purely psychosocial phenomena. The initial outbreaks have occurred around the globe near the 30th parallel, the area of principal atmospheric downflow of upper winds coming from the Intertropical Convergence Zone. An agent or condition in the upper equatorial atmosphere would thus be expected to reach ground level along the 30th parallel, with certain seasonal variations. One principal variation is that the downflow moves north over the East Asian continent during the late winter months, and those areas south of it (Arabia, Western India, parts of North Africa) have in fact been free of outbreaks until recently, when the downflow zone moved south. A similar downflow occurs in the Southern Hemisphere, and outbreaks have been reported along the 30th parallel running through Pretoria and Alice Springs, Australia. (Information from Argentina is currently unavailable.)

This geographical correlation cannot be dismissed, and it is therefore urged that an intensified search for a physical cause be instituted. It is also urgently recommended that the rate of spread from known focal points be correlated with wind conditions. A watch for similar outbreaks along the secondary downwelling zones at 60° north and south should be kept.

(signed for the minority)
Barnhard Braithwaite

Alan grinned reminiscently at his old friend's name, which seemed to restore normalcy and stability to the world. It looked as if Barney was on to something, too, despite the prevalence of horses' asses. He frowned, puzzling it out.

Then his face slowly changed as he thought how it would be, going home to Anne. In a few short hours his arms would be around her, the tall, secretly beautiful body that had come to obsess him. Theirs had been a late-blooming love. They'd married, he supposed now, out of friendship, even out of friends' pressure. Everyone said they were made for each other, he big and chunky and blond, she willowy brunette; both shy, highly controlled, cerebral types. For the first few years the friendship had held, but sex hadn't been all that much. Conventional necessity. Politely reassuring each other, privately—he could say it now—disappointing.

But then, when Amy was a toddler, something

had happened. A miraculous inner portal of sensuality had slowly opened to them, a liberation into their own secret unsuspected heaven of fully physical bliss ... Jesus, but it had been a wrench when the Colombia thing had come up. Only their absolute sureness of each other had made him take it. And now, to be about to have her again, trebly desirable from the spice of separation—feeling-seeing-hearing-smelling-grasping. He shifted in his seat to conceal his body's excitement, half mesmerized by fantasy.

And Amy would be there, too; he grinned at the memory of that prepubescent little body plastered against him. She was going to be a handful, all right. His manhood understood Amy a lot better than her mother did; no cerebral phase for Amy ... But Anne, his exquisite shy one, with whom he'd found the way into the almost unendurable transports of the flesh ... First the conventional greeting, he thought: the news, the unspoken, savored, mounting excitement behind their eyes; the light touches; then the seeking of their own room, the falling clothes, the caresses, gentle at first—the flesh, the *nakedness*—the delicate teasing, the grasp, the first thrust—

—A terrible alarm-bell went off in his head. Exploded from his dream, he stared around, then finally down at his hands. *What was he doing with his open clasp-knife in his fist?*

Stunned, he felt for the last shreds of his fantasy, and realized that the tactile images had not been of caresses, but of a frail neck strangling in his fist, the thrust had been the plunge of a blade seeking vitals. In his arms, legs, phantasms of striking and trampling bones crackling. And Amy—

Oh God. Oh God—

Not sex, bloodlust.

That was what he had been dreaming. The sex was there, but it was driving some engine of death.

Numbly he put the knife away, thinking only over and over. It's got me. It's got me. Whatever it is, it's got me. *I can't go home.*

After an unknown time he got up and made his way to the United counter to turn in his ticket. The line was long. As he waited, his mind cleared a little. What could he do, here in Miami? Wouldn't it be better to get back to Ann Arbor and turn himself in to Barney? Barney could help him, if anyone could. Yes, that was best. But first he had to warn Anne.

The connection took even longer this time. When Anne finally answered he found himself blurting unintelligibly; it took awhile to make her understand he wasn't talking about a plane delay.

"I tell you, I've caught it. Listen, Anne, for God's sake. If I should come to the house don't let me come near you. I mean it. I mean it. I'm going to the lab, but I might lose control and try to get to you. Is Barney there?"

"Yes, but, darling—"

"Listen. Maybe he can fix me, maybe this'll wear off. But I'm not safe, Anne, Anne, I'd kill you, can you understand? Get a—get a weapon. I'll try not to come to the house. But if I do, don't let me get near you. Or Amy. It's a sickness, it's real. Treat me—treat me like a fucking wild animal. Anne, say you understand, say you'll do it."

They were both crying when he hung up.

He went shaking back to sit and wait. After a time his head seemed to clear a little more. *Doctor, try to think.* The first thing he thought of was to take the loathsome knife and throw it down a trash slot. As he did so he realized there was one more piece of Barney's material in his pocket. He uncrumpled it; it seemed to be a clipping from *Nature*.

At the top was Barney's scrawl: "Only guy making sense. U.K. infected now. Oslo, Copenhagen out of communication. Damfools still won't listen. Stay put."

COMMUNICATION FROM PROFESSOR MACINTYRE, GLASGOW UNIV.

A potential difficulty for our species has always been implicit in the close linkage between the behavioural expression of aggression/predation and sexual reproduction in the male. This close linkage involves (a) many neuromuscular pathways which are utilized both in predatory and sexual pursuit: grasping, mounting, etc., and (b) similar states of adrenergic arousal which are activated in both. The same linkage is seen in the males of many other species; in some, the expression of aggression and copulation alternate or even coexist, an all-too-familiar example being the common house cat. Males of many species bite, claw, bruise, tread, or otherwise assault receptive females during the act of intercourse; indeed, in some species the male attack is necessary for female ovulation to occur.

In many if not all species it is the aggressive

behaviour which appears first, and then changes to copulatory behaviour when the appropriate signal is presented (*e.g.*, the three-tined stickleback and the European robin). Lacking the inhibiting signal, the male's fighting response continues and the female is attacked or driven off.

It seems therefore appropriate to speculate that the present crisis might be caused by some substance, perhaps at the viral or enzymatic level, which effects a failure of the switching or triggering function in the higher primates. (Note: Zoo gorillas and chimpanzees have recently been observed to attack or destroy their mates; rhesus not.) Such a dysfunction could be expressed by the failure of mating behaviour to modify or supervene over the aggressive/predatory response; *i.e.*, sexual stimulation would produce attack only, the stimulation discharging itself through the destruction of the stimulating object.

In this connection it might be noted that exactly this condition is a commonplace of male functional pathology, in those cases where murder occurs as a response to and apparent completion of sexual desire.

It should be emphasized that the agression/copulation linkage discussed here is specific to the male; the female response (*e.g.*, lordotic reflex) being of a different nature.

Alan sat holding the crumpled sheet a long time; the dry, stilted Scottish phrases seemed to help clear his head, despite the sense of brooding tension all around him. Well, if pollution or whatever had produced some substance, it could presumably be countered, filtered, neutralized. Very very carefully, he let himself consider his life with Anne, his sexuality. Yes: Much of their loveplay could be viewed as genitalized, sexually gentled savagery. Play-predation . . . He turned his mind quickly away. Some writer's phrase occurred to him: "The panic element in all sex." Who? Fritz Leiber? The violation of social distance, maybe; another threatening element. Whatever, it's our weak link, he thought. Our vulnerability . . . The dreadful feeling of *rightness* he had experienced when he found himself knife in hand, fantasizing violence, came back to him. As though it was the right, the only way. Was that what Barney's budworms felt when they mated with their females wrong-end-to?

At long length, he became aware of body need and sought a toilet. The place was empty, except for what he took to be a heap of clothes blocking the door of the far stall. Then he saw the red-brown pool in which it lay, and the bluish mounds of bare, thin buttocks. He backed out, not breathing, and fled into the nearest crowd, knowing he was not the first to have done so.

Of course. Any sexual drive. Boys, men, too.

At the next washroom he watched to see men enter and leave normally before he ventured in.

Afterward he returned to sit, waiting, repeating over and over to himself: *Go to the lab. Don't go home. Go straight to the lab.* Three more hours; he sat numbly at 26°N, 81°W, breathing, breathing . . .

* * *

Dear diary. Big scene tonite. Daddy came home!!! Only he acted so funny, he had the taxi wait and just held on to the doorway, he wouldn't touch me or let us come near him. (I mean funny weird, not funny Ha-ha.) He said, I have something to tell you, this is getting worse not better. I'm going to sleep in the lab but I want you to get out. Anne, Anne, I can't trust myself anymore. First thing in the morning you both get on the plane for Martha's and stay there. So I thought he had to be joking, I mean with the dance next week and Aunt Martha lives in Whitehorse where there's nothing nothing nothing. So I was yelling and Mother was yelling and Daddy was groaning, Go now! And then he started crying. Crying!!! So I realized, wow, this is serious, and I started to go over to him but Mother yanked me back and then I saw she had this big KNIFE!!! And she shoved me in back of her and started crying too Oh Alan, Oh Alan, like she was insane. So I said, Daddy, I'll never leave you, it felt like the perfect thing to say. And it was thrilling, he looked at me real sad and deep like I was a grown-up while Mother was treating me like I was a mere infant as usual. But Mother ruined it raving Alan the child is mad, darling go. So he ran out the door yelling Be gone, Take the car, Get out before I come back.

Oh I forgot to say I was wearing what but my gooby green with my curltites still on, wouldn't you know of all the shitty luck, how could I have known such a beautiful scene was ahead we never know life's cruel whimsy. And mother is dragging out suitcases yelling Pack your things hurry! So she's going I guess but I am not repeat not going to spend the fall sitting in Aunt Martha's grain silo and lose the dance and all my summer credits. And Daddy was trying to *communicate* with us, right? I think their relationship is obsolete. So when she goes upstairs I am splitting, I am going to go over to the lab and see Daddy.

Oh PS Diane tore my yellow jeans she promised me I could use her pink ones Ha-ha that'll be the day.

*   *   *

... I ripped that page out of Amy's diary when I heard the squad car coming. I never opened her diary before but when I found she'd gone I looked ... Oh, my darling girl. She went to him, my little girl, my poor little fool child. Maybe if I'd taken time to explain, maybe—

Excuse me, Barney. The stuff is wearing off, the shots they gave me. I didn't feel anything. I mean, I knew somebody's daughter went to see her father and he killed her. And cut his throat. But it didn't mean anything.

Alan's note, they gave me that but then they took it away. Why did they have to do that? His last handwriting, the last words he wrote before his hand picked up the, before he—

I remember it. *"Sudden and light as that, the bonds gave   And we learned of finalities besides the grave. The bonds of our humanity have broken, we are finished. I love—"*

I'm all right, Barney, really. Who wrote that, Robert Frost? *The bonds gave* ... Oh, he said, tell Barney: *The terrible rightness.* What does that mean?

You can't answer that, Barney dear. I'm just writing this to stay sane, I'll put it in your hidey-hole. Thank you, thank you, Barney dear. Even as blurry as I was, I knew it was you. All the time you were cutting off my hair and rubbing dirt on my face, I knew it was right because it was you. Barney, I never thought of you as those horrible words you said. You were always Dear Barney.

By the time the stuff wore off I had done everything you said, the gas, the groceries. Now I'm here in your cabin. With those clothes you made me put on I guess I do look like a boy, the gas man called me "Mister."

I still can't really realize, I have to stop myself from rushing back. But you saved my life, I know that. The first trip in I got a paper, I saw where they bombed the Apostle Islands refuge. And it had about those three women stealing the Air Force plane and bombing Dallas, too. Of course they shot them down over the Gulf. Isn't it strange how we do nothing? Just get killed by ones and twos. Or more, now they've started on the refuges . . . Like hynotized rabbits. We're a toothless race.

Do you know I never said "we" meaning women before? "We" was always me and Alan, and Amy of course. Being killed selectively encourages group identification . . . You see how sane-headed I am.

But I still can't really realize.

My first trip in was for salt and kerosene. I went to that little Red Deer store and got my stuff from the old man in the back, as you told me—you see, I remembered! He called me "Boy," but I think maybe he suspects. He knows

I'm staying at your cabin.

Anyway, some men and boys came in the front. They were all so *normal*, laughing and kidding. I just couldn't believe, Barney. In fact I started to go out past them when I heard one of them say "Heinz saw an angel." An *angel*. So I stopped and listened. They said it was big and sparkly. Coming to see if man is carrying out God's will, one of them said. And he said, Moosenee is now a liberated zone, and all up by Hudson Bay. I turned and got out the back, fast. The old man had heard them too. He said to me quietly, "I'll miss the kids."

Hudson Bay, Barney, that means it's coming from the north too, doesn't it? That must be about 60°.

But I have to go back once again, to get some fishhooks. I can't live on bread. Last week I found a deer some poacher had killed, just the head and legs. I made a stew. It was a doe. Her eyes; I wonder if mine look like that now.

* * *

. . . I went to get the fishhooks today. It was bad, I can't ever go back. There were some men in front again, but they were different. Mean and tense. No boys. And there was a new sign out in front, I couldn't see it; maybe it says Liberated Zone too.

The old man gave me the hooks quick and whispered to me, "Boy, them woods'll be full of hunters next week." I almost ran out.

About a mile down the road a blue pickup

started to chase me. I guess he wasn't from around there, I ran the VW into a logging draw and he roared on by. After a long while I drove out and came on back, but I left the car about a mile from here and hiked it. It's surprising how hard it is to pile enough brush to hide a yellow VW.

Barney, I can't stay here. I'm eating perch raw so nobody will see my smoke, but those hunters will be coming through. I'm going to move my sleeping bag out to the swamp by that big rock, I don't think many people go there.

. . . Since the last lines I moved out. It feels safer. Oh, Barney, how did this *happen?*

Fast, that's how. Six months ago I was Dr. Anne Alstein. Now I'm a widow and bereaved mother, dirty and hungry, squatting in a swamp in mortal fear. Funny if I'm the last woman left alive on Earth. I guess the last one around here, anyway. Maybe some holed out in the Himalayas, or sneaking through the wreck of New York City. How can we last?

We can't.

And I can't survive the winter here, Barney. It gets to 40° below. I'd have to have a fire, they'd see the smoke. Even if I worked my way south, the woods end in a couple hundred miles. I'd be potted like a duck. No. No use. Maybe somebody is trying something somewhere, but it won't reach here in time . . . and what do I have to live for?

No. I'll just make a good end, say up on that rock where I can see the stars. After I go back and leave this for you. I'll wait to see the beautiful color in the trees one last time.

I know what I'll scratch for an epitaph.

HERE LIES THE SECOND MEANEST PRIMATE ON EARTH

Good-bye, dearest dearest Barney.

* * *

I guess nobody will ever read this, unless I get the nerve and energy to take it back to Barney's. Probably I won't. Leave it in a Baggie, I have one here; maybe Barney will come and look. I'm up on the big rock now. The moon is going to rise soon, I'll do it then. Mosquitoes, be patient. You'll have all you want.

The thing I have to write down is that I saw an angel too. This morning. It was big and sparkly, like the man said; like a Christmas tree without the tree. But I knew it was real because the frogs stopped croaking and two bluejays gave alarm calls. That's important; it was *really there*.

I watched it, sitting under my rock. It didn't move much. It sort of bent over and picked up something, leaves or twigs, I couldn't see. Then it did something with them around its middle, like putting them into an invisible sample-pocket.

Let me repeat—it was *there*. Barney, if you're reading this, THERE ARE THINGS HERE. And I think they've done whatever it is to us. Made us kill ourselves off.

Why! Well, it's a nice place, if it wasn't for people. How do you get rid of people? Bombs, death-rays—all very primitive. Leave a big mess. Destroy everything, craters, radioactivity, ruin the place.

This way there's no muss, no fuss. Just like

what we did to the screwfly. Pinpoint the weak
link, wait a bit while we do it for them. Only a
few bones around; make good fertilizer.

Barney dear, good-bye. I saw it. It was there.
But it wasn't an angel.

I think I saw a real-estate agent.

------◆·◆——◆·◆------

*Raccoona Sheldon = James Tiptree, Jr. = Alice
Sheldon
&*
*James Tiptree, Jr. + Raccoona Sheldon = a great deal
of excellent science fiction.*

*Alice Sheldon (née Bradley) came into this world in
1915, and her Uncle Harry introduced her to her first
copy of* Weird Tales *when she was nine, following it
up with* Amazing *and* Wonder Stories *and others.
Her mother was a world traveller, and as a child she
travelled in Africa. She became an artist, and art editor
of the Chicago* Sun, *and travelled in Mexico. During
World War II, she served in the Army Air Force, end-
ing up a captain; so did her husband, a colonel; they
were in Germany together during the Occupation. She
has been a teacher, a research psychologist, and—as we
know—a science fiction writer.*

*Alice Sheldon invented her two alter-egos, James and
Raccoona, for reasons of her own (which is really all we
need to ask or know,) James making his first appearance
(in* Astounding) *in 1968, and Raccoona arriving (in*
Worlds of IF) *much more recently. Both of them have*

been very much alive, much more so, I think, than most pseudonyms—and they deserve it, for their stories, like "The Screwfly Solution," are wonderfully conceived, beautifully structured, and very strong indeed.

Many years ago, the late Alan Nelson wrote a lovely story called "Narapoia"—about a man obsessed with the idea that people were plotting, not to persecute him, but to do him good; and the notion perhaps isn't as farfetched as it first may seem. Certainly, as I pointed out in the foreword to this volume, our speculations regarding extraterrestrial visitors range from the downright paranoid to what, at this point, we can perhaps term the "narapoid."

Either attitude, as accepted doctrine, could endanger us in any future close encounters, but as science fiction— because science fiction must consider all possibilities— each is perfectly legitimate.

Frank Quattrocchi's story has something in it of both extremes, for his extraterrestrials definitely are plotting to do mankind good—or else.

Frank Quattrocchi

THE SWORD

George Harrison noticed the flashing red light on the instrument panel as he turned onto the bridge to Balboa Island. Just over the bridge, he pulled the car to the curb and flipped the switch with violence. "Harrison," he muttered.

"How's the water, fella?" asked the voice of Bob Mills, his assistant.

There was a beautiful moon over the island.
The surf lapped at the tiers of the picturesque
bridge. Soft music was playing somewhere.
There was a tinkle of young laughter on the light
sea breeze.

Harrison was vacationing and he viewed the
emergency contact from Intersolar Spaceport
with annoyance.

"What do you want, Bob?"

"Sorry, George," Bob Mills said more seriously. "I guess you got to come back."

"Listen—" protested Harrison.

"Orders, George—orders from upstairs."

Harrison took a long look at the pleasant island street stretching out before him. Sea-cor-
roded street lamps lit the short island through-
fare. People in light-blue jeans, bronzed youths
in skipper caps, deep-tanned girls in terry-cloth.

"What the hell is it?"

"Don't know, but it's big. Better hurry." He
clicked off.

Harrison skidded the car into a squealing
turn. Angrily, he raced over the bridge and onto
the roaring highway. Thirty minutes later Intersolar Spaceport, Los Angeles, blazed ahead of
him.

The main gate guards waved him in immediately and two cycle guards ran interference
for him through the scores of video newsmen
who lined the spaceport street.

Bob Mills met him at the entrance to the Administration building.

"Sorry, George, but—"

"Yeah. Oh, sure. Now what the hell is it all
about?"

Mills handed him a sheaf of teletransmittals. They bore heavy secret stamps. Harrison looked up quizzically.

"You saw the video boys," Mills said. "The wheels think there might be some hysteria."

"Any reason for it?"

"Not that we know of—not that *I* know of anyway. The thing is coming in awfully fast—speed of light times a factor of at least two, maybe four."

Harrison whistled softly and scanned the reports frowning.

"They contacted us—"

"What?"

"— *in perfect Intersolar Convention code*. Said they were coming in. That's all. The port boys have done all they could to find out what to expect and prepare for it. Somebody thought Engineering might be needed—that's why they sent for you."

"Used Intersolar Convention code, eh," mused Harrison.

"Yes," said Mills. "But there's nothing like this thing known in the solar system, nothing even close to this fast. Besides that, there was a sighting several days ago that's being studied.

"One of the radio observatories claims to have received a new signal from one of the star clusters . . ."

The huge metal vessel settled to a perfect contact with its assigned strip. It hovered over the geometric center of the long runway and touched without raising a speck of dust.

Not a sound, not a puff of smoke issued from

any part of it. Immediately it rose a few feet above the concrete and began to move toward the parking strip. It moved with the weightless ease of an ancient dirigible on a still day. It was easily the largest, strangest object ever seen before at the spaceport.

A team of searchlight men swivelled the large spot atop the tower and bathed the ship in orange light.

"What's that mean?" asked Mills paging his way through a book.

" 'Halt propulsion equipment,' I think," said Harrison.

"It's a good thing the code makers were vague about that," smiled Mills. "It's a good thing they didn't say jets or rockets—'cause this thing hasn't got any."

"Attention!"

That single word suddenly issued from the alien ship.

"The Races of Wan greet you."

It might have been the voice of a frog. It was low, guttural, entirely alien, entirely without either enthusiasm or trace of human emotion.

"Jesus!" muttered Mills.

Scores of video teams focused equipment on the gleaming alien.

"The Races of Wan desire contact with you."

"In English yet!" amazed Mills.

"The basis of this contact together with its nature are dependent upon *you!"*

The voice had become ugly. There was nothing human about it save only the words, which were in flawless English.

"Your system has long been under surveillance by the Races of Wan. Your—progress has been noted."

There was almost a note of contempt, thought Harrison, in the last sentence.

"Your system is about to reach others. It therefore becomes a matter of urgency that the Races of Wan make contact.

"Your cultural grasp is as yet quite small. You reach four of your own system's planets. You have attempted—with little success—colonization. You anticipate further penetrations.

"You master the physical conditions of your system with difficulty. You are a victim of many of the natural laws—natural laws which you dimly perceive.

"But you master yourselves with greatest difficulty, and you are infinitely more a victim of forces within your very nature—*forces which you know almost not at all.*"

"What the hell—" began Mills.

"Because of this disparity your maturity as a race is much in doubt. There are many among the cultures of the stars who would consider your race deviant and deadly. There are a very few who would welcome you to the reaches of space.

"But most desire more information. Thus our visit. We have come to gather data that will determine your—disposition—

"Your race accepts the principle of extermination. You relentlessly seek and kill for commercial or political advantage. You live in mistrust and envy and threat. Yet, as earthlings, you have power. It is not great, but it contains a threat. We wish now to know the extent of that threat.

"Here is the test."

Suddenly an image resolved itself on the gleaming metal of the ship itself.

It was a blueprint.

A hundred cameras focused on it.

"Construct this. It is defective. Correct that which renders it not useful. We shall return in three days for your solution."

"Good God!" exclaimed Harrison. "It's a—sword!"

"A what?" asked Mills.

"A sword—people used to chop each other's heads off with them."

Almost at once the metal giant was seen to move. Quickly it retraced its path across the apron, remained poised on the center of the runway, then disappeared almost instantaneously.

The Intersolar Council weathered the storm. The representative of the colony on Venus was recalled, his political life temporarily ended. A vigilante committee did for a time picket the spaceport. But the tremendous emotional outbursts of the first day gradually gave way to a semblance of order.

Video speakers, some of them with huge followings, still denounced the ISC for permitting the alien to land in the first place. Others clamored for a fleet to pursue the arrogant visitor. And there were many fools who chose to ignore the implications of the strange speech and its implied threat. Some even thought it was a gigantic hoax.

But most men soon came to restore their trust in the scientists of the Intersolar Council.

Harrison cast down the long sheet of morning news that had rolled out of the machine.

"The fools! They'll play politics right up to the last, won't they?"

"What else?" asked Mills. "Playing politics is as good a way as any of avoiding what you can't figure out or solve."

"And yet, what the hell are *we* doing here?" Harrison mused. "Listen to this."

He picked up a stapled sheaf of papers from his desk.

" '*Analysis of word usage indicates a complete knowledge of the English language*'—that's brilliant, isn't it? '*The ideational content and general semantic tone of the alien speech indicates a relatively high intelligence.*

" '*Usage is current, precise . . .*' Bob, the man who wrote that report is one of the finest semantics experts in the solar system. He's the brain that finally broke that ancient Martian ceremonial language they found on the columns."

"Well, mastermind," said Mills. "What will the *Engineering* report say when you get around to writing it?"

"Engineering report? What are you talking about?"

"You didn't read the memo on your desk then? The one that requested a preliminary report from every department by 2200 today."

"Good God, no," said Harrison snapping up the thin yellow sheet. "What in hell has a sword got to do with Engineering?"

"What's it got to do with Semantics?" mocked Robert Mills.

Construct this. It is defective. Correct that which renders it not useful.

Harrison's eyes burned. He would have to quit pretty soon and dictate the report. There wasn't any use in trying to go beyond a certain point. You got so damned tired you couldn't think straight. You might as well go to bed and rest. Bob Mills had gone long before.

He pored over the blueprint again, striving to concentrate. Why in hell had he not given up altogether? What possible contribution could an engineer make toward the solution of such a problem?

Construct this.

You simply made the thing according to a simple blueprint. You tried out what you got, found out what it was good for, found out then what was keeping it from doing that. You fixed it.

Well, the sword had been constructed. Fantastic effort had been directed into producing a perfect model of the print. Every minute convolution had been followed to an incredible point of perfection. Harrison was willing to bet there was less than a ten-thousandths error—even in the handle, where the curves seemed to be more artistic than mechanical.

It is defective.

What was defective about it? Nobody had actually tried the ancient weapon, it was true. You didn't go around chopping people's heads off. But experts on such things had examined the twelve-pound blade and had pronounced it "well balanced"—whatever that meant. It would crack a skull, sever arteries, kill or maim.

Correct . . .

What was there to correct? Could you make it

maim or kill better? Could you sharpen it so that it would go through thick clothing or fur? Yes. Could you make it a bit heavier so that it might slice a metal shield? Yes, perhaps. All of these things had been half-heartedly suggested. But nobody had yet proposed any kind of qualitative change or been able to suggest any kind of change that would meet the next admonition of the alien:

Correct that which renders it not useful.

What actually could be done to a weapon to make it useful? Matter of fact, what was there about the present weapon that made it *not* useful. Apparently it was useful as hell—useful enough to cut a man's throat, pierce his heart, slice an arm off him . . .

What were the possible swords; what was the morphology of *concept sword?*

Harrison picked up a dog-eared report.

There was the *rapier,* a thin, light, extremely flexible kind of sword (if you considered the word "sword" generic, as the Semantics expert had pointed out). It was good for duels, man-to-man combat, usually on what the ancients had called the "field of honor."

There were all kinds of short swords, dirks, shivs, stilettos, daggers. They were the weapons of stealth men—and sometimes women—used in the night. The assassin's weapon, the glitter in the darkened alley.

There were the *machetes.* Jungle knives, cane-cutting instruments. The bayonets . . .

You could go on and on from there, apparently. But what did you get? They were all more or less useful, Harrison supposed. There was nothing more you could do with any kind of sword that was designed for a specific purpose.

Harrison sighed in despair. He had expected vastly more when he had first heard the alien mention "test." He had expected some complex instrument, something new to Terra and her colonies. Something involving complex and perhaps unknown principles of an alien technology. Something appropriate to the strange metal craft that traveled so very fast.

Or perhaps a paradox. A thing that could not be constructed without exploding, like a lattice of U235 of exactly critical size. Or an instrument that must be assembled in an impossible sequence, like a clock with a complete, single-pieced outer shell. Or a part of a thing that could be "corrected" only if the whole thing were visualized, constructed, and tested.

No, the blueprint he held now involved an awareness that must prove beyond mere technology, or at least Terran technology. Maybe it involved an awareness that transcended Terran philosophy as well.

Harrison slapped the pencil down on his desk, rose, put his coat on, and left the office.

". . . we are guilty as the angels of the Bible were guilty. Pride! That's it, folks, pride. False pride . . ."

Harrison fringed the intent crowd of people cursing when, frequently, someone carelessly bumped into him in an effort to get nearer the sidewalk preacher.

"We tried to live with the angels above. We wanted to fly like the birds. And then we wanted to fly like the angels . . ."

Someone near Harrison muttered an

"Amen." Harrison wove his way through them wondering where the hundreds of such evangelists had come from so suddenly.

"Ya know, folks, the angels themselves got uppity once. *They* wanted to be like Gawd himself, they did. Now, it's us."

There was a small flutter of laughter among the crowd. It was very quickly suppressed—so quickly that Harrison gained a new appreciation of the tenor of the crowd.

"That's right, laugh! Laugh at our folly!" continued the thin-faced, bright-eyed man. "It was a sword that the angel used to kick Adam and Eve out of the garden. The sword figures all through the Bible, folks. You ought to read the Bible. You ought to get to know it. It's all there. All there for you to read . . ."

By Christ, thought Harrison. Here was an aspect of the concept, sword, he had not considered. Morphological thinking required that *all* aspects of a concept be explored, all plotted against all others for possible correlation . . .

No. That was silly. The Bible was a beautiful piece of literature and some people believed it inspired. But the great good men who wrote the Bible had little scientific knowledge of a sword. They would simply describe the weapon as a modern fiction writer would describe a blaster— without knowing any more about one than that it existed and was a weapon.

Surely the ISC's weapons expert could be trusted to know his swords.

"Go on home," Mills pleaded. "You're shot and you know it. You said yourself this isn't our show."

"You go home, Bob. I'm all right."

"George . . . you're acting strange. Strange as hell."

"I'm all right. Leave me alone," snapped Harrison, becoming irritable.

Mills watched silently as the haggard man slipped a tablet into his mouth.

"It's all right, Bob," smiled Harrison weakly. "I know how to use Benzedrine."

"You damn fool, you'll wreck yourself . . ."

But the engineer ignored him. He continued paging his way through the book—the Bible, no less. George Harrison and the Bible!

Mills was awakened by the telephone. Reaching in the dark for it he answered almost without reaching consciousness.

It was Harrison.

"Bob, listen to me. If an angel were to look at us right now, what would he think?"

"For God's sake!" Mills cried into the instrument. "What's up? You still at the office?"

"Yeah, answer the question."

"Hold on, George. I'll be down and get you. What have you been drinking?"

"Bob, would he—she—think much of us? Would the angel figure we were . . ."

"How the hell would *I* know?"

"No, Bob, what you should have asked is 'how the hell would *he* know.' "

In a daze Mills heard the click as the other hung up.

"Mr. Harrison, your assistant is looking for you."

"Yes, I know, Kirk. But will you do it?"

"Mr. Harrison, we only got one of them. If we screw it up it'll take time to make another and today's the day, you know."

"I'll take the blame."

"Mr. Harrison, you look kind of funny. Hadn't I better . . ."

Harrison was sketching a drawing on a piece of waste paper. He was working in quick rough strokes, copying something from a book.

"They'll blame us both, Mr. Harrison. Anyway, it might hold up somebody who's got a real idea . . ."

"*I* have a real idea, Kirk. I'm going to draw it for you."

The metal worker noticed that the book Harrison was copying from was a dictionary, a very old and battered one.

"Here, can you follow what I've drawn?"

The metal worker accepted it reluctantly, giving Harrison an odd, almost patronizing look. "This is crazy."

"Kirk!"

"Look, Mr. Harrison. We worked a long time together. You . . ."

Harrison suddenly rose from the chair.

"This is our one chance of beating this thing, no matter how crazy it seems. Will you do the job?"

"You believe you got something, eh," the other said. "You think you have?"

"I have to have."

"Gentlemen," said the president of the Intersolar Council. "There is very little to say. There can be no denying the fact that we have exhausted our efforts at finding a satisfactory solution.

"The contents of this book of reports represents the greatest concentration of expert reasoning perhaps ever applied to a single problem.

"But alas, the problem remains—unsolved."

He paused to glance at his wristwatch.

"The aliens return in an hour. As you very well know there is one action that remains for us. It is one we have held to this hour. It is one that has always been present and one that we have been constantly urged to use.

"Force, gentlemen. It is not insignificant. It lies at our command. It represents the technology of the Intersolar alliance. I will entertain a motion to use it."

There were no nay votes.

The alien arrived on schedule. The ship grew from a tiny bright speck in the sky to full size. It settled to a graceful landing as before on the strip and silently moved into the revetment.

Again it spoke in the voice of the frog, but the tone was, if anything, less human this time.

"Earthmen, we have come for your solution."

At that instant a hundred gun crews stiffened and waited for a signal behind their carefully camouflaged blast plates and inside dummy buildings. . . .

Harrison was running. The Administration building was empty. His footsteps echoed through the long, silent halls. He headed for an emergency exit that led directly to the blast tunnel. All doors were locked.

The only way was over the wall. He paused

and tossed the awkward, heavy object over the ten-foot wall. Then, backing toward the building, he ran and jumped for a hold onto the wall's edge. He failed by several inches to reach it.

"Earthmen, we have come for your solution."

He ran at the wall once more. This time he caught a fair hold with one hand. Digging at the rough concrete with his feet he was able to secure the hold and begin pulling his body upward.

Quickly he was over the wall and onto the apron, a hundred yards from the shining metal ship.

"Wait!" he shouted. "Wait, for God's sake!"

Picking up the object he had tossed over the wall, he raised it above his head and ran toward the alien ship.

"Wait! Here is the solution," he gasped.

Somehow the command to fire was not given. There was a long moment of complete silence on the field. Nothing moved.

Then the voice of the frog boomed from the alien ship.

"The solution appears to be correct."

The alien left three days later. Regular communications would begin within the week. Future meetings would work out technical difficulties. Preliminary trade agreements, adequately safeguarded, were drafted and transmitted to the ship. The Races of Man and the Races of Wan were in harmony.

"It was simply too obvious for any of us to notice," explained Harrison. "It took that streetcorner evangelist to jar something loose—even then it was an accident."

"And then the rest of us—" started Mills.

"While *all* of us worked on the assumption that the test involved a showing of strength—a flexing of technological muscle."

"I still don't see—"

"Well, the evangelist put the problem on the right basis. He humbled us, exalted the aliens—that is, he thought the alien was somehow a messenger from God to put us in our places."

"We were pretty humble ourselves, especially the last day," protested Mills.

"But humble about our *technology*," put in Harrison. "The aliens must be plenty far beyond us technologically. But how about their cultural superiority? Ask yourself how a culture that could produce the ship we've just seen could survive without—well destroying itself."

"I still don't understand."

"The aliens developed pretty much equally in *all* directions. They developed force—plenty of it, enough force to kick that big ship through space at the speed of light plus. They must also have learned to control force, to live with it."

"Maybe you better stick to the sword business," said Mills.

"The sword is the crux of the matter. What did the alien say about the sword? 'It is defective.' It *is* defective, Bob. Not as an instrument of death. It will kill a man or injure him well enough.

"But a sword—or any other instrument of force for that matter—is a terribly ineffectual tool. It was originally designed to act as a tool of social control. Did it—or any subsequent weapon of force—do a good job at that?

"As long as man used swords, or gunpowder, or atom bombs, or hydrogen bombs, he was doomed to a fearful anarchy of unsolved problems and dreadful immaturity.

"No, the sword is not useful. To fix it—to 'correct that which renders it not useful'—meant to make it something else. Now what in the hell did that mean? What can you do with a sword?"

"You mean besides cut a man in two with it," said Mills.

"Yes, what can you do with it besides use it as a weapon? Here our street-corner friend referred me to the right place: The Bible!

They shall beat their swords into ploughshares, and their spears into pruning-hooks; nation shall not lift up sword against nation, neither shall they learn war any more.

"The aliens just wanted to know if we meant what we said."

"Do we?"

"We better. It's going to take a hell of a lot more than a silly ploughshare to convince those babies on that ship. But there's more to it than that. The ability of a culture finally to pound all of its swords—its intellectual ones as well as its steel ones—into ploughshares must be some kind of least common denominator for cultures that are headed for the stars."

————◆—◆—◆————

Frank Quattrocchi was born in Hannibal, Missouri, fifty-six years ago, and as a boy he played in the caves

Mark Twain wrote about. (However, he didn't read Twain until many years later.)

As an Air Force officer, he served as a bombardier during World War II, and he began writing shortly after the war was over, selling his first science fiction story in 1949. In the ensuing years, he published stories in Astounding Science Fiction, Worlds of If, and other magazines in the field, and wrote three motion pictures, including The Projected Man. With his present wife—who is herself a writer, anthropologist, and college professor—he also wrote a book on the problem of drug misuse entitled Why Johnny Takes Drugs.

A public relations man for about twenty years, Mr. Quattrocchi worked for the J. Walter Thompson advertising agency, for NBC, and for other well-known organizations. Now a father and grandfather, he lives with his wife in Los Angeles.

These two articles, the first by Lewis J. Stecher, Jr., the second by Joseph F. Goodavage, both discuss invasions of our Earth. They do so from very different viewpoints and offer largely contradictory arguments. In spite of this, they are to a great extent complementary, for the subject is so ramified, and so much evidence and alleged evidence has been offered to support one thesis or another, that no one-sided, simplistic discussion can really shed much light on the many problems it poses.

It is a subject so important that we should consider every side and every rational argument pro and con. I myself, for instance, have never made up my mind completely even with regard to such dubious propositions as visiting "Gods from Outer Space" or the imminent arrival of cosmic do-gooders, their picnic baskets overflowing with peace and plenty, love and wisdom. But of one thing I am certain: some very strange things happen on our Earth, things which only tortuous reasoning can explain away; and when we try to explain them in fresher terms the picture suggests itself of a Universe infinitely more complex than the one handed down to us by the science of the nineteenth century.

Perhaps, in order adequately to explain such phenomena as the 1908 Siberian impact and the whole array of those now generally known as Fortean, we will eventually have to elaborate on Hamlet's "There are more things in heaven and earth, Horatio . . ." and ask, "In which heaven and which earth? And in what dimension? And on which time-line?"

L. J. Stecher, Jr.

INVASIONS OF EARTH

It is probable that most of the people who have lived on Earth have believed in the reality of invasions from outside of it: that this Earth has been, is being, or will most probably be invaded from space.

Of course, it is easy to count almost everyone among the believers when within the class of invaders we include even the inanimate—anything that arrives at Earth from outside of it and which may kill. In fact, the most deadly warfare waged by man, as by all other life forms, has been the continuing war for survival against the forces of nature.

By that rule we have indeed been invaded, and are still being invaded. Let us choose to call these devastations by the inanimate "Invasions of the First Kind." The 1908 destruction of an area of Siberia as large as the state of New Jersey by a fall from the sky is only one incident in this ongoing assault.

A look at the moon through even a small telescope shows the vast extent of damage that is the cumulative effect of such falls. The shield that is provided the earth by its atmospheric blanket gives very little comfort to anyone who contemplates the Mare Imbrium—the Sea of Showers—in photographs of the moon. The enormous collision recorded by that lunar feature must have come close to cracking the moon. No amount of atmosphere would noticeably have lessened that crash.

Similarly, the photographs of Mars that have been sent back by our space exploration vehicles clearly demonstrate that an atmosphere is a feeble defense against this type of invasion. Of course, the atmosphere of Mars is far less dense than that of Earth, but Earth too, in spite of rapid erosion, shows the scars of collision craters.

The accidental invasion of Earth by a cometary body significantly larger than that of the 1908 Siberian strike is entirely plausible and possible. Larry Niven and Jerry Pournelle, in *Lucifer's Hammer*, have given careful consideration to the mechanics of such a collision, and their work is convincing. Such a catastrophe is but a moderately extreme variant of the type of invasion of Earth that is going on now, as it has been since the Earth was formed.

Not all writings dealing with invasions of Earth by non-living menaces have received the careful treatment offered by Niven and Pournelle, even when such works do not purport to be fiction. For example, the contrived and contorted constructions by Immanuel Velikovsky of the scenario of a cometary invasion from Jupiter is quickly shredded by Occam's

Razor. Carl Sagan and others have wielded scalpels on this concept that are fully as sharp.

There is another possible example of an Invasion of the First Kind. It involves the bombardment from space by particles far smaller in size than comets or meteors, or even meteoric dust: radiation from space.

Solar radiation must not be considered as an invasion, although it can cause harm. At one extreme, it can give vacationers painful sunburn. Near the other extreme, minor variations in its output can bring on ice ages or the massive floods that result from the thaws following such ice ages. Nevertheless, looking on solar radiation as an invader and successfully repelling it might be considered to do more harm than good, since it would result in the end of all—or nearly all—life on Earth.

Normal levels of cosmic radiation will also not be described as an invasion. Processes resulting from such radiation result in damage to germ plasm, with almost invariably lethal or otherwise harmful results. However, the occasional survivors appear to be an important part of the raw material on which natural selection operates in evolving the species to match changes in the environment, permitting life to wage war successfully on the inanimate forces of nature.

There is, however, a possible radiation attack from space that could be classed as a true invasion—that resulting from the creation of a supernova anywhere in space within a few dozen light years of our sun. Ordinary novas, though more than adequate in levels of catastrophe to destroy all life on any planets that might circle them, are very modest in size compared to supernovas. We would be little affected by the explosion into a nova of even our nearest neighbors among the stars. A single supernova, however, may outshine an entire galaxy of many millions of stars, and there are several hundred stars within supernova invasion range of Earth, at the level of the total destruction of man.

Fortunately, supernovas are a rare phenomenon. Five have been recorded in our galaxy during the past thousand years. The famous supernova of 1054, reported by the Chinese astronomers as brighter than Venus, was at a safe range of about 5,000 light years from Earth.

There is a second possible type of casual or accidental invasion that has been given serious consideration. This "Invasion of the Second Kind" is the contamination of Earth by seeds or spores from space.

Perhaps the most distinguished proponent of this type of invasion was the Nobel laureate Svante Arrhenius. In 1907, in his *Das Werden der Welten,* he offered *inter alia* the idea that spores, emitted from life-bearing worlds and transported interstellar distances by light pressure, could colonize worlds that had not yet felt the touch of life.

When it is considered that natural and customary processes not involving living things can create a wide variety of organic compounds, including amino acids which are a building block of life, and that they can do this in an environment like that believed to have prevailed on Earth before the appearance of life, and that they have probably been doing so since the wa-

ters which were under the firmament first began
to condense, this invasion-by-spores theory of
Arrhenius becomes easy to believe. Over eons,
the conjoined waters of Earth can be imagined to
have become gradually a vast sea of nutrients—
of organic compounds—a rich broth waiting to
be consumed by burgeoning life, and thereby
transformed into life. Suitable spores, wafted
from space and falling into such a broth, would
find no enemies and no competitors, and might
be expected to reproduce explosively to the limits of the environment.

If the creation of life, given an appropriate environment, is still an enormously improbable
event, then Arrhenius provides a probable mechanism for broadcasting life widely throughout
the firmament. However, present ideas about the
initiation of life make it seem nearly inevitable
rather than nearly impossible, and if they are
correct, the probability of successful spore invasion becomes extremely low.

The arrival of spores on an Earth without life
would form a true invasion—one directed
against the established environment of Earth.
Later arrivals of spores would, on the other
hand, be invaders against this newly established
life and their chances of succeeding would be
vanishingly thin. Once the adults derived from
the early arrivals among the spores had finished
their banquet of free soup, they would be forced
to turn on each other for nutriment. Gene variation induced by radiation would inevitably
have been occurring, and the process of natural
selection would favor the survival of those vari-
ants best suited to the environment of Earth at

that time. Invading spores arriving after this process had begun, and not themselves having had the opportunity to adapt to the environment, would prove not to be a menace to their predecessors, but rather a meal.

As billions of years have passed since the inception of life on Earth, however it began, this advantage of the established residents over microscopic invaders has inevitably increased. It is a truism that the winners have survived, and they have survived through continued adaptation to a changing environment including changing competitors. That life on Earth in its myriad forms has itself been a major force in changing the environment to which it must continually adapt has served merely to reinforce the formation of a closed-loop adaptive system that casually rejects non-conforming invaders.

Michael Crichton's fascinating and popular novel, *The Andromeda Strain,* was enhanced, therefore, by its appearance of plausibility rather than by its actuality. Whether alien microscopic life arrives naturally, by way of light pressure, or is brought back by man from space, either deliberately or through contamination, it will expire so quickly as not to be noticed.

Even when these two kinds of accidental invasion are removed from consideration, a general belief persists in the reality of invasions of Earth from space.

Myths, legends, and theology frequently allude to the arrival of malevolent (or at least harmful) non-human creatures from outside of Earth. We can label such arrivals as "Invasions of the Third Kind." Milton's account of the fall of Lucifer from Heaven was a statement of belief, not a mere literary invention.

These myths and legends give evidence as to the *belief* of many in past invasions of Earth; evidence of the *actuality* of such past invasions is much harder to come upon.

The confused ramblings and contorted evidence of such popularizers of visitation theories as Erich von Däniken are entirely unconvincing, but are readily embraced by wide audiences who apparently are eager to believe.

Perhaps at the basis of this ready belief is the idea that our own ancestors of a few thousand years ago were too ignorant and too brutish to have been capable of performing the vast deeds whose archaeological remains we find on earth. We humans moved with improbable—even impossible—speed from nakedness and cowering in caves, these Believers assert, to such splendors as the pyramids of Egypt. We must have had help.

And yet, the dry climate of Egypt has preserved the evidence that even such incredible structures as the pyramids are the work of man alone. From mud-brick mastabas—great platforms covering the remains of pharaohs who preceded the pyramid builders—through the multi-tiered mastaba of Zoser constructed of rough-cut stones, through experimental pyramids of strange shapes, to the precision of the massive structures at Giza, it is possible today to follow all the steps of pyramid development.

From Zoser's step pyramid to the Great Pyramid of Khufu at Giza took a very short time—about the same as the time from the end of the American Civil War to the present. The learning process was swift, but it did not require help from the stars.

It is not necessary to seek in the past for evidence of Invasions of the Third Kind. Unidentified Flying Objects—Flying Saucers—are frequently cited as evidence of the continuing presence of visitors from outer space. Not everyone who believes in UFOs considers them the precursors to invasion. Some think that they are probably passive observers, merely curious about those alien beings—the human race—and their curious way of life.

The more popular concept, however, seems to be that these are scouts of a stellar civilization, examining and testing us for some stronger (and perhaps more sinister) reason than mere curiosity. After all, there are reports of the kidnapping of humans, and of the use of devices that prevent engines from operating and that cause strange effects in electric and magnetic equipment. Spies could be learning the effectiveness of a variety of potential weapons for ultimate use against us.

It is a popular point of view that much solid evidence exists of the reality of these extraterrestrial visitors, but that this information has been systematically suppressed by the military for some reason which the "brass" conceives to involve military security. This military aberration must, of course, include all technologically advanced nations in its cabal, because spies from space could hardly be expected to observe national boundaries.

This theory of an international conspiracy to suppress information concerning UFOs is ludicrous. It was perhaps barely credible during a time when our security organizations were assumed to be enormously capable, more than a little paranoid, and essentially out of the control of civil authority.

This is no longer true. What would formerly have been easily kept secret is now just as easily broadcast. Today we are told the details of official attempts to assassinate Cuba's dictator. Even the private scatological conversations of a former president are widely disseminated. The idea that firm knowledge of visitors from space could remain successfully suppressed is no longer tenable.

There can be no such secrets. Information is not being hidden. The evidence is no better or more convincing than what has already been published. And that evidence is not at all convincing. It should be far better documented if the supposed visitants are not trying to maintain secrecy. And if spies from an advanced civilization are in fact trying to scout us and remain hidden, they should be expected to be able to succeed well enough to avoid such flying saucer sightings as have been reported.

This does not in itself give any reason to believe that there are no extraterrestrial visitors; it merely indicates that the cult of UFO believers is not providing such evidence. There are a number of debunkers who, in informal opposition to the UFO cult, advance the claim that, as the result of statistical analysis, it can be proved that the probability is vanishingly small that there has been, during the entire history of mankind on Earth, any visit by aliens from the stars. Their argument proceeds something like this:

What might be reasonable, when applied to the star-filled center of the galaxy, about the ability of the civilizations of one star to contact those of others, does not make sense when applied to the neighborhood of Earth, far out on one of the sparsely populated spiral arms, with our nearest neighbor farther away than it takes light to travel in four years. Distances are great, and travel-time is long.

Of all the time that higher life forms have lived on this planet, *Homo sapiens* has been present perhaps one-tenth of one percent of that time. A random visitor to this planet would have very little chance of finding man, and even less than that of finding men at a level of civilization capable of recording the visit. And with stars scattered light years apart, repeat visits would be rarities. The only real chance of the alien civilization to reach Earth at a time when human civilization exists, would be for them to be able to act in response to some evidence of that civilization.

Any potential visitor who waited for evidence, before starting the trek toward us, that the Earth is inhabited by a species that is capable of reasoning and of communicating with it, can be scarcely more than 60 light years away. Our first radio signals started toward him about that long ago. If he headed toward us at once on receiving the news, and averaged half the speed of light, he can have been no more than 20 light years away.

Even if all stars have planets, and life develops on at least one planet of each star, and a reasoning (and inquisitive) species is invariably involved, the chances that such life would be at the

appropriate evolutionary state to be able to come
visiting as soon as they heard from us—from
among the few hundred stars that are sufficiently
close—is too small to be considered.

And if they don't come soon, they will find us
in space—going out to meet them rather than
sitting here spreading rumors about UFOs. Of
all the (relatively short) time that man has been
present on this planet, he has possessed an industrial society for less than one-tenth of one
percent of that time, but he is already making his
first tentative but successful steps into space.

Of course, like the stars in the astrological
firmament, statistical analyses "incline; they can
not compel." Probability is not proof.

Dr. Arrhenius—the same man who was
earlier described as propounding the theory of
the diffusion of life through spores—was given
the Nobel prize in chemistry for the development
of the thesis of galvanic conduction in elec-
trolytes, on which all modern ideas of the con-
ductivity of solutions have been based. This concept was first presented in his doctoral disserta-
tion, and earned him the lowest possible passing
grade. His professor, Dr. Cleve, explained that
he knew that many different theories were being
formed, almost all certain to be wrong and to
disappear. Therefore, using the statistical approach, he concluded that the ideas of Arrhenius
were not of much value.

Just as the ideas of Arrhenius have withstood
rigid experimental tests, thereby confounding
Cleve's statistically reached conclusions, so one
convincing piece of hard evidence would con-
found the statistical debunkers of Invasions of

the Third Kind. For example, the uncovering of a "flying saucer" in an archaeological dig, and perhaps even the subjection of the skeletal remains of the non-human occupants to comprehensive tests, would carry conviction.

It is barely possible that there exists on Earth today evidence of high quality of an extraterrestrial visitation. Recent newspaper reports quote Soviet sources as stating that Russian scientists have been studying the site of the 1908 catastrophe in Siberia and have firm evidence that the object, at the time of its crash, was not in free fall, but was being driven by engines using a nuclear power source.

Accounts of reports are not evidence and will raise few doubts in the minds of those who do not now believe. They are not even likely to add to the enthusiasm and conviction of ardent believers. Still, the site remains. If evidence exists, it can be carefully checked and independently verified. The ability to make such independent tests—to find out if the Earth has proved to be a reef for an interstellar shipwreck—becomes one additional reason for the removal of barriers between the East and the West.

Meanwhile, the greatest probability for the validity of the thesis of the invasion of Earth by sentient beings lies in "Invasions of the Fourth Kind." By this is meant the invasion of Earth by humans who have ceased to reside on Earth.

It seems almost inevitable that within a relatively few years mankind will be making extensive use of off-planet technical and manufacturing facilities, and that a great many people will have followed those facilities into space. G.

Harry Stine has extrapolated man into this new environment in his "The Third Industrial Revolution."

In addition, there is a great deal of speculation, much of which seems reasonable, that man will shortly start moving into near space—whether to the Lagrangian points or into direct orbits or onto the lunar surface itself—in order to find increased living space and improved living standards over those available to most of humanity on Earth.

If these prognostications prove to be correct, the numbers of Earthmen, in two or three generations, who live off the Earth can be expected to become enormous. They might even, in time, rival in number those of their race who remain Earthbound. And they will probably be just as quarrelsome, and just as likely to engage in warfare, as their brothers on Earth.

These space dwellers will very probably have one recurring problem to deal with. Although, by taking full advantage of the three dimensions of their extraterrestrial homes, they may enjoy more living room and general feeling of spaciousness than do their Earthbound brothers, they will still be living in an artificial and limited environment. As frequently occurs in small, closed environments over long periods of time, they may find a gradually increasing and ultimately unacceptable level of poisoning from the cumulative effects of catabolism. A lack of essential but unrecognized trace elements may also, over long periods of time, cause problems.

These conditions can be expected to be kept within reasonable limits through periodic cleans-

ing and refreshening of the space-located micro-
environments. It is probable, however, that such
a freshening process may require periodic rein-
troduction into its artificial environment of material from the mother planet itself.

This lack of self-sufficiency in the space colonies, as compared to Earth, would seem to give
dominance, in any contest between them, to
those remaining on the planet. There is, however, another factor. One major purpose behind
any move into space would probably be ready
access to plentiful, non-wasting and easily
useable energy from the sun. This energy could
easily be transformed into a powerful weapon.
Concentrated into energy beams plumbing all of
Earth's surface, it would pose a continuing
threat of the invasion of Earth's security.

The space colonies would consist of a large
number of comparatively very small targets.
These, with their defined trajectories and clearly
visible locations, would appear to be very vulnerable to counter-attack from Earth, but this is not
necessarily the case. When a defensive force
knows precisely the points that the enemy must
attack, its task is simplified. Against guided
weapons, he can concentrate shorter range
counter-weapons in larger numbers. Against radiation weapons, he can interpose clouds of finely dispersed particles, long-enduring in space because of the weak gravity gradients, to act as
screening shields.

The result may be a nearly impregnable defense, but it involves a gradual expenditure of the
matter available to the defensive forces. Just as
the space colonies have an unending source of

energy, while that of Earth is a wasting asset, so do the planetary forces have an unlimited quantity of matter while that of the colonies is a wasting asset.

The availability of the moon as a source of material replenishment would seem to be of major importance, then, to the invading, or potentially invading, colonists. The problems of relative power between the Earth and its moon are not dissimilar to those just described between Earth and artificial satellites. Energy relations would again be a dominant force. For the moon, however, the great advantage would be the relative sizes of the "gravity wells" of Earth and the moon. It is easier to throw an object from the moon to the Earth than from the Earth to the moon.

Robert Heinlein has treated this subject effectively in his novel *The Moon Is a Harsh Mistress*. The thesis of this work (and of others of Heinlein's works) that man in space must inevitably seek freedom and separation from those he has left behind on Earth, is less convincing. Common interests and potential interdependence would appear to be the dominant forces. In addition, it could be of value for all of the humans in the solar system to be united to face the possibility of another and more dangerous, if less likely, example of Invasion of the Fourth Kind: the invasion of Earth by humans from the stars.

This is not as totally impossible as it may at first seem to be. Technology already exists for the construction of interstellar spacecraft, and a variety of propulsion systems have been proposed, from a technically uncertain "Bussard ram jet" that burns interstellar hydrogen to technically sound nuclear engines of several types.

Three major factors, and to a lesser extent a fourth, deter their construction and use. The first is the enormous expense involved. The second is the high and unknown level of personal risk involved for the passengers. The third is the lack of an overwhelming need or desire to embark on such an undertaking. And the fourth is the overwhelming length of the voyage, with the resulting inability of the passengers ever to return, or probably even to see the end of their trip.

All of these reasons hinge on the third: the lack of adequate incentive. It is quite possible, for example, that our scientists may learn the energy mechanism of the "Stellar Phoenix" with sufficient precision to be able confidently to predict the onset of one or more of the five types of supernova. If they were then able to determine that, within a few hundred years, a star within lethal range of the Earth would in fact explode into a supernova, the odds strongly favor the ability of humankind to conduct a successful diaspora. Large numbers of ships would be built and launched, capable of transporting an entire population.

Similarly, any discovery of an impending variation in the output of our own sun—less spectacular than a nova but equally lethal in nature—could achieve the same result on a much shorter time scale.

Moreover, in some future time—and this need

not be in the distant future—in which problems
of energy supply for mankind have been solved
and turned into a surplus (probably with the assistance of space stations, as described earlier),
dissatisfactions and demands of a far less
catastrophic nature than impending total ster-
ilization of the planet could result in the building
and launching of at least a few spaceships. The
stars could become a new frontier, into which
Earth could once again find a place to send those
groups that march to too different a drum.

The stars as a frontier require much more
commitment, and the expenditure of far greater
treasure, than did the running away of individuals and groups to the Old West. There is ample
evidence that groups which have felt exploited or
which have held ideas differing from those about
them have been able on many occasions to
amass surprisingly large resources and then
been willing to embark in the face of appalling
risks on trips with no possibility of return.

The Biblical Exodus, of course, was such a
trip, as in large measure has been the return to
Palestine of the Zionists in this generation. The
sailing of the *Mayflower* for the New World in
1620 was a classic example of such an expedition, even including the idea of abandoning one
world to seek another. To a lesser degree, the
Roanoke and Williamsburg colonies fall into the
same mold. The Mormon trek to Utah is a
further example.

And remember that it need not have been
from this planet of this sun that ships carrying
humans first moved into space, whether for reasons of total catastrophe or because of repression

or wanderlust. If man started life on a planet circling a star only slightly larger than Earth, that star, their sun, might indeed have been expected to turn into a nova. This would have been a compelling reason to learn star flight, and there could well have been generations of warning, with time to learn the necessary technological lessons. We on Earth may, then, already be the victors of a long ago invasion, and the descendants of the invaders.

At first look, there seem to be some compelling arguments against this scenario. Humankind is closely related to other life forms on this planet, going far back to the earliest life forms of which we have clear evidence. It is not possible to consider that a space ark brought not only man to this Earth, but also his entire ecological system of plants and animals, and that this alien system took on and conquered and entirely eliminated the earlier indigenous life system already entrenched here.

Not only is paleontological evidence in disagreement with this thesis, but the argument earlier presented is valid here: in any such contest, the ecology already adapted to its environment would hold an overwhelming advantage over any invader.

Nor is it conceivable that mankind arrived at Earth to find a sterile planet. Here again, the evidence of paleontology provides sufficient proof. Also, it is unlikely that man would seek out a sterile planet, if any other option was possible. After years or even generations of flight in a small closed environment, chances of survival on such a planet would be negligible. The necessary prerequisite of attempting to convert a hostile atmosphere—and lack of life means lack of oxygen—would add a burden, lasting perhaps millions of years, on an already marginal struggle for survival.

It is possible, however, that an alternative approach was available to these hypothetical ancestors of ours in their invasion of Earth (or will be available to our own descendants invading other planets). Much has been accomplished in recent years in the field of genetic engineering, and even greater advances can be anticipated for the future.

There is a famous principle that perhaps even invaders can use: "If you can't beat 'em, join 'em." After having selected Sol as a suitable star, the invading humans may carefully have selected the animal on earth most suitable for subversion. Advanced genetic microengineering techniques would then have superimposed on it those genetic traits that define "humanity." These would certainly have included speech and the manipulative efficiency of the hand. For the most part, however, the resulting offspring would probably have borne little or no resemblance to the invading human parents, but have appeared nearly identical to the "winning" Earth species. Although still essentially human, these transformed children would have been entirely capable of surviving and flourishing on earth.

Clifford D. Simak, in one chapter of *City*, and in the short story "Paradise" from which that chapter was derived, makes use of a similar technique, though applicable to the original rather than to subsequent generations, in adapting humans to Jupiter's environment. He expresses no concern for the original inhabitants, the "Lopers," on which the transformed humans were patterned, but the ability to interbreed is assumed. If the microengineering techniques could cause the human traits to be dominant, the preservation of the ability to interbreed with the original creatures of Earth could contribute greatly to the probability of survival of the humans, but might reduce any chance of preserving the culture and memories of the home planet.

With such a scenario as this, large numbers of the stars nearest to us in the heavens could have been successfully invaded by humankind, and now have large human populations at approximately the same stage of development as ours here on earth. Of course, this still allows very considerable variations in the technological levels among the planets. The humans on Earth would have reverted to a pre-technical state after their successful invasion, and have lost all knowledge of their origins, but this would not necessarily have occurred everywhere. Earth might be significantly behind some of her neighbors in technology.

It is not beyond the realm of possibility that one or more of these nearby planets, relatively speaking, has achieved a stability and a stage of energy surplus that has resulted in the launch of spaceships. An invasion of Earth in the near future could take place.

These invaders would be human in reasoning power, thought processes and emotional drive, though presumably bearing little or no relation to Earthmen in appearance.

It is possible that such a small group of humans might be able to conduct a successful invasion of Earth. There is already ample evidence that small numbers of humans, without support from their own kind, can conquer large and sophisticated empires, only slightly inferior to them technologically.

To the Incas and Aztecs of the New World, the Old World of Europe did not exist, and the arrival of the Spaniards was as unexpected as would be the arrival of a spaceship in our skies. Because there is no way of even guessing the manner in which the technology of these invaders would exceed ours, there is no way of postulating what devices they might use to defeat us. We can, however, remember that Cortez and Pizarro succeeded. They used divisions and enmity and ideological differences among the indigenous populations to divide and conquer them piecemeal, eventually swallowing and enslaving all. We should remind ourselves that with the assets available to the humans in the New World, the invaders could have been defeated.

This scenario, when placed in present time, must be considered as highly improbable. There is no evidence of any such invasion in the past, unless legendary hints of gods and of giants in the Earth can be so construed. When moved to the distant future, however, such a scenario becomes more plausible.

Earth then becomes the source of the diaspora, most probably sending out ships from its excess of wealth and energy rather than from fear of impending catastrophe, to seed the nearby stars. Then, a few hundreds of thousands of years from now, one group or another from among the children of Earth, in its turn, sends out a ship that comes back (with no recollection that its human crewmen are siblings of Earthmen) to this, its mother planet.

If Earth has retained its knowledge and its memories, no invasion will result. The arrival of such a ship can then only provide amusement and enjoyment to the men of Earth. On the other hand if the humans on Earth have retrogressed —and this also has happened in the past—then the humans in the arriving spaceship could play the role of Conquistadores.

Today or in the distant future, invasion is possible. And if a spaceship arrives, filled with bug-eyed monsters or little green creatures, will it be the harbinger of a friendly meeting, or of an invasion?

And however monstrous these invaders (or these visitors) appear, will they in fact be strangers, or may they not be relatives? And are relatives not more likely than strangers to find something to fight about—some great cause or intolerable insult that can turn a friendly visit into an invasion of Earth?

———————◆·◆——◆·◆———————

A second generation career naval officer, L. J. Stecher, Jr. started to write science fiction on the U.S.S. Colorado, while hunting for Amelia

*Earhart in 1937, and began to write salable sf while at
White Sands Missile Range in the 1950s. Later on, he
wrote stories while commanding a destroyer and a guided
missile cruiser.*

*He received his Masters degree from M.I.T. in 1949,
and he was a member of the Golovan Committee, a joint
DOD-NASA group appointed after President Kennedy
declared the U.S. would land men on the moon, to
analyze how this might be done. (They recommended the
Lunar Orbit Rendezvous method that was adopted.)*

*Stecher met his wife Carolyn in 1931 while their
fathers were commanding Yangtze River gunboats. He
retired to Florida several years ago, to "alternate loafing
and acting as a freelance consultant in electronics engineering."*

Joseph F. Goodavage

UFOs AND STRANGER INTRUDERS

Mysterious objects have been seen in the skies of Earth by ordinary citizens, soldiers, military, and political leaders for thousands of years. There is no evidence whatever that these enigmatic UFOs are benevolent. They have attacked troops and interfered with the outcome of critical battles in ancient and modern times. Astronomers and laymen alike have observed and reported UFOs for so long that there is hardly any doubt that they are purposeful, intelligently directed, *and very likely inimical to the future existence of human civilization!*

Almost immortal and virtually indestructable, these extraordinarily sophisticated and powerful devices may be Time Machines, perfect vehicles for the survival of power, knowledge, and intelligence.

Thousands of UFO sightings and human contact with alien "beings" have occurred since the dimmest periods of history. What can we expect in the imminent future? The evidence indicates a strong case can be made for the idea that UFOs, rather than being spaceships of friendly, advanced cultures from other worlds, may *not* be biologically-directed. Instead, they could be motivated by coldly efficient machines endowed with super-intelligence so advanced as to be totally unfathomable to the human intellect—perhaps time traveling "devices" from our own distantly remote future. This contra-Promethian possibility, terrifying as it may seem, is as plausible as human-like explorers of space.

According to the best known experts, there are at least millions of advanced biological civilizations in our (Milky Way) galaxy—possibly more. According to what we know of our own technological evolution however, the fearsome probability may be that humankind is merely a crude but necessary link of the evolutionary purpose. As far as we can tell, it takes a supernova (an exploding star), to create the heavy elements necessary for properly motivated, semi-intelligent, biological creatures to develop tools, weapons, and the electronic components needed to develop computers.

"Our" sun, all the planets, and everything in the solar system was once part of such a stupendous supernova. The same evolutionary path may also apply to other intelligent biological cultures in space. Astronomer Robert Jastrow recently pointed out that these "Galactics" could have been evolving for enormously longer periods than *Homo sapiens*. If they still have civilizations (whether or not they are governed and controlled by intelligent machine "overlords"), some of them may be a billion years or more in advance of our own (perhaps only a million).

The communications gap may be an insur-
mountable obstacle to both species.

Man is supposed to be about a billion years
ahead of the earthworm insofar as evolution is
concerned. So far, no one I know of has ever tried
to talk to a worm, therefore it seems unlikely that
the Galactics would have much to say to us.
There may be hundreds of similarly impassable
barriers.

The notion of very ancient humanoids with
great space vessels intruding into Earth space
and landing here however, is both compelling
and ubiquitous. An ancient Indian chronicle
called the *Book of Dzyan* is a remarkable collection of reports and legends predating Biblical
history as we understand it. Many thousands of
years ago, ancient scholars put into manuscript
form tales of these almost fantastic events. Until
recently, the greatest human scientific minds
couldn't even have made sense of it, much less
given credence to a story that twenty or thirty
thousand years before the time of Christ or Bud-
dha (long before this ancient document was
retranslated) a large metal ship from somewhere
came to the Earth and circled the planet several
times before landing.

The beings who emerged from the spaceship
"lived to themselves and were revered by the humans among whom they settled. But eventually
differences arose among them and they divided
their numbers, several of the men and women
and some children settling in another city where
they were promptly installed as rulers by the
awestricken populace. But separation did not
bring peace to these people, and finally their an-

ger reached a point where the ruler of the original city took with him a small number of his warriors and they rose into the air in a huge shining metal vessel.

"While they were still many leagues from the city of their enemies, they launched a great shining lance that rode on a beam of light. It burst apart in the city of their enemies with a great ball of flame that shot up to the heavens almost to the stars. All those in the city were horribly burned and even those who were not in the city —but nearby—were burned also. Those who looked upon the lance and the ball of fire were blinded forever afterward. Those who entered the city on foot became ill and died. Even the dust of the city was poisoned as were the rivers that flowed through it. Men dared not go near it, and gradually it crumbled into dust and was forgotten by men.

"When the leader saw what he had done to his own people, he retired to his palace and refused to see anyone. Then he gathered around him those of his warriors who remained and their wives and their children, and they entered into their vessels and rose one by one into the sky and sailed away. Nor did they return."

Was the *lance* a rocket . . . *the beam of light* its brilliant jet exhaust . . . the *ball of flame* a nuclear fireball . . . the *poisoned* atmosphere from radioactivity?

One highly qualified expert, Dr. Morris K. Jessup, astrophysicist, anthropologist, geologist, and a top government scientific troubleshooter, stated before his untimely death that "mechanical flight has been established by written records at a remote time of maybe 70,000 to 200,000 years ago."

Could such visitations account for the mysteries of Stonehenge . . . the Colossi of Memnon . . . the Pyramids . . . the ruins of Baalbek near Beirut . . . the megalithic carvings of Easter Island . . . the legends of a "race of giants" at Teotihuacan in Mexico who built the great palace of Quetzalpapatotl and the Pyramids of the Sun and the Moon?

Tales of mysterious visitors from outer space have existed in the legends, ballads, and written chronicles of every civilization that has inhabited the Earth. So the recurrent tales of saucer-shaped, cigar-shaped, blinding balls of light that continue to pour in from every corner of the world is nothing new. Skywatchers have photographed them . . . airline pilots have pursued them . . . seemingly sane and responsible people report communicating with them.

In our comparatively brief history on this Earth, we have begun to explore the cratered surfaces of the Moon, Mars, Venus, and Mercury. The idea of an older, more intelligent and developed civilization exploring us therefore, is not so incredible after all.

Imagine how such an experience must have staggered the prophet/priest Ezekiel, he who preached to the Jews of the exile in Mesopotamia nearly 600 years before Christ? In the Old Testament, first chapter of the Book of Ezekiel, a spaceship from a distant planet landed in Israel 2,600 years ago with four strange but "human-like" creatures.

NASA engineer Josef F. Blumrich, chief of

future spacecraft design at Marshall Space
Flight Center in Huntsville, Alabama, received
an excited long-distance call from his son Christoph on Long Island in 1973. The young
Blumrich had just read Von Däniken's *Chariots of
the Gods?* After first scoffing at such an outlandish
notion, Blumrich, who had been designing aircraft since 1934 and was then working on large
rockets and spacecraft, thought it over and
began 18 months of intensive research that resulted in a German book titled *Da tat sich der
Himmel auf.* It appeared in English a year later as
The Spaceships of Ezekiel.

According to one of the most dramatic Biblical passages, Ezekiel described a wheel-
shaped craft spewing fire and lightning as it
descended from the heavens— "and out of
the midst thereof came the likeness of four
living creatures. . . . They had the likeness
of a man."

"Ezekiel saw an enormous spacecraft that
came from outside our solar system and was more
advanced than anything our present technology
can construct," claims engineer Blumrich.

"His description was so vivid. If this were just
a fantasy there would have been a contradiction
somewhere. But there was none. Ezekiel must
have been shaken to the very depth of his emotion and feeling. He described four human-like
creatures. The commander of the spaceship
talked to him in Hebrew, but what was said was
not clearly recorded," Blumrich conjectured,
adding that the starship was undoubtedly
atomic-powered, with four landing legs that
could be detached and flown independently like

helicopters. The body of the craft was cone-shaped and approximately 70 feet high and 75 feet across.

"Beginning with a drawing of what Ezekiel described, I applied standard and well-established engineering formulas that NASA uses for orbital space flight. The analysis showed that Ezekiel had seen a perfectly feasible spaceship. The fact is that I set out to contradict that theory because I was a complete skeptic and believed it was all fictitious nonsense. But I was forced to switch my opinions completely. The results of my investigations were not easy for me to accept because of my beliefs.

"But there's no doubt that my analysis shows that Ezekiel had given an incredibly accurate description of a spaceship. My studies have convinced me that we have been visited by creatures from other planets, and," he added significantly, "it's obvious that these UFO visits are continuing today."

He could be right. Similar stories emerge from the legends, myths, and lore of virtually all ancient people. But just about the time Christoph was reading von Däniken's book in mid-October, 1973, a strikingly similar unidentified flying object was sighted by dozens of South American people at an Argentine air base near Bahia Blanca, 400 miles west of Buenos Aires.

Three months later, a UPI story from Buenos Aires datelined January 20, 1974, reported that the newspaper La Nacion told of a team of six doctors in Bahia Blanca who had been treating a trucker named Dionisio Yanca since the previous October. Sr. Yanca was suffering terribly from some sort of unexplained nervous shock that could not be immediately diagnosed.

When the doctors finally began treating him with sodium pentothal, the so-called truth drug, Yanca, under deep hypnotic trance, revealed that he had been captured and taken aboard a huge spaceship by aliens "from another galaxy," and according to *La Nacion,* kept for an hour and a half.

Yanca said the spaceship connected a hose to high-tension wires and another to a small lagoon, apparently to take on electric power. Reporters investigating the story said a local electric company reported a sharp and unexplained rise in power consumption at the time. Dr. Eduardo Mata was quoted as saying he administered a truth serum to Yanca and that "under the effects of (sodium) pentothal the patient said he spent an hour and a half aboard a UFO, but he can not remember this when conscious."

According to the hapless Argentine trucker, the aliens, whose humming voices were made intelligible by a loudspeaker, predicted the Earth would suffer grave events in the future. Yanca claimed they told him they had been trying since 1960 to determine whether man could survive in *their* galaxy if the Earth were destroyed!

It almost boggles the mind to think that nobody from our *own* galaxy would be willing to take us in if something terrible happened to our planet. One should not be accused of scoffing however, if one wonders how in hell a little water from an Argentine lagoon and some electricity could propel a giant spaceship to an unnamed galaxy five or ten million light years away. Or, for that matter, why none of the "contactees" ever seemed to have presence of mind enough to grab a piece of alien hardware (or even a shred of metal or cloth or *anything*) as evidence of their abduction.

Of course there have been traces of "frightfully ancient Electrics" (Ivan Sanderson, *Investigating the Unexplained*, Prentice-Hall, 1972) and metallurgical science in a South African iron mine carbon-dated at 41,000 B.C. by organic materials found in the mine. Then there is the "impossible" existence of the "Baghdad Batteries" and electrical generators with insulators and transmission cables found in Egypt and what is now Turkey more than three thousand years ago, according to Sanderson.

Charles Hoy Fort, of course, made hundreds of notes of artifacts that appeared or fell from the sky—many, he said, "from alien spaceships." But one of the most concrete pieces of evidence— actual parts of a UFO that was destroyed before eyewitnesses who managed to salvage some of the parts—occurred in Brazil, and was first publicly revealed on September 14, 1957, by Ibrahim Sued in his column in the Rio de Janiero newspaper *O Globo*.

The copy was headlined, "A Fragment from a Flying Disk," in which the newsman printed verbatim a letter he had received (in Portugese) from a regular reader with whom he was familiar —Olavo T. Fontes, M.D.

"I was fishing together with some friends at a place close to Ubatuba, Sao Paulo," wrote Dr. Fontes, "when I sighted a flying disk. It approached the beach at unbelievable speed and an accident, i.e., a crash into the sea seemed imminent. At the last moment, however, when it was almost striking the waters, it made a sharp turn upward and climbed rapidly on a fantastic impulse. We followed the spectacle with our eyes, startled, when we saw the disk explode in flames. It disintegrated into thousands of fiery fragments, which fell sparkling with magnificent brightness. They looked like fireworks, despite the time of the accident, at noon ... Most of these fragments, almost all, fell into the sea. But a number of small pieces fell close to the beach, and we picked up a large amount of this material —which was as light as paper. I am enclosing a small sample of it.''

Dr. Fontes submitted three pieces of a gray material that seemed to be some sort of metal. The medical man and Sued agreed to analyze the fragments, which Dr. Fontes described thus:

''Their surfaces were not smooth and polished, but quite irregular and apparently strongly oxidized. Their appearance suggested they might be, if really metallic, pieces or fragments disintegrated from a larger metallic mass or object; in fact, the surface of one of the samples was shot through with almost microscopic cracks, always longitudinal, and even showed on one face a large longitudinal fissure running through almost two-thirds of its length, as if that piece had been disrupted under the action of some force. The others did not show many cracks or fissures, but the surfaces of all samples were covered in scattered areas with a whitish material. These whitish smears of a powdered substance appeared as a thin layer. The

fine, dry powder was adherent, but could be displaced easily with the [thumb] nail. It also filled
the fissures and cracks on the surface of the first
sample. This powder presented some similarity
with the whitish powdered cinders on a chunk of
burned charcoal—as if the fragments had been
scorched by some fire or were damaged by too
much heat. . . . The material was light, definitely lighter than aluminum."

Sued returned the three fragments, which
Dr. Fontes took to the Mineral Production Laboratory, a division of the National Department of
Mineral Production in Brazil's Ministry of Agriculture, before a sample was obtained by the
FBI. A chemical analysis revealed the fragments
to be some kind of metal. Three additional series
of tests revealed (a) the metal (by spectrographic
analyses) to be magnesium "of a high degree of
purity and absence of any other metallic element." (b) Several X-ray diffraction analyses
proved the samples to be of unusually pure
magnesium. Small amounts of an unknown
crystalline substance were also found and later
identified as magnesium hydroxide, and (c) the
density of one sample was found to be 1.866
(pure terrestrial magnesium should have been
1.741).

If by some chance someone had tried to purify
the sample, the element most difficult to remove
would have been calcium. No calcium was present. Even if someone had done an extraordinarily fine job of removing the calcium, it would have
had to be done by using a quartz vessel, which
would have introduced tiny amounts of silicon
into the sample. FBI tests in 1968 revealed no
presence of silicon.

At a Congressional Symposium on UFOs in Washington, D.C. on July 29, 1968, Dr. James A. Harder of the University of California Civil Engineering Department revealed the baffling FBI report on its laboratory findings: the sample (now in "safekeeping") is 99.9 percent pure magnesium. The impurities total only about one part per thousand, and are not merely odd, but totally mysterious.

According to Dr. Fontes: "The magnesium in the samples analysed, which was absolutely pure in the spectrographic sense, represents something outside the range of present-day technological development in Earth science. . . . They are, in fact, "fragments" of an extraterrestrial vehicle which met with disaster in the Earth's atmosphere, as reported by human beings who witnessed the catastrophe."

Astronomer Duncan Lunan of the University of Glasgow Observatory in Scotland set the entire scientific world on its ear with his report of a super-intelligent device, in effect a mechanical entity apparently still in orbit around our Moon, from which he had received messages. In his science article in the January 1974 issue of *Analog*, titled "Space Probe from Epsilon Boötis?" editor Ben Bova headlined Prof. Lunan's report: "Evidence has existed since the 1920s that an intelligent extraterrestrial race placed an automated probe in orbit around the Earth some 13,000 years ago. The probe may have already sent word of our civilization back to its creators —if they're still alive!"

Briefly and simplistically, the probe "came to life," activated after 13,000 years by radio waves from Earth. The strange delays in the echoes of radio and later radar signals were noticed in 1928, 1929, 1935, and then in 1973, when Lunan graphed the echo patterns and noticed an increasing complexity and sophistication of the delayed echoes. It was as though the device's transmitting array was deliberately striving to "educate" whoever detected and decoded the signals. Here is astronomer Lunan's interpretation: "Having so much, the sequence then becomes so clear, each line 'dictating' the next, that it can be read off in English:

AB—start here.

BC—Our home is Epsilon Boötis,

CDE—which is a double star.

FG, GH, CH, GK—We live on the sixth planet of seven.

JKL—check that, the sixth of seven (they read from right to left),

EM—counting outwards from the Sun.

FEG, GN—which is the larger of the two.

HO, OP—Our sixth planet has one moon, our fourth planet has three, our first and third planets each have one.

GQ, QR—Our probe is in the orbit of your moon.

ST—This updates the position of Arcturus shown in our maps.

Benign, objective, perhaps even friendly and warm? Perhaps not. This piece of super-dooper technology was there ten thousand years before Alexander the Great conquered the known world. Moreover, it may have attempted (perhaps *succeeded*) to interfere with the course of human history. Whether it be Professor Lunan's "probe" from Epsilon Boötis, an alien starship from

somewhere else, or time-traveling machines from
our own (or someone else's) future, there is just
no way known for our rudimentary science or
technology to determine whether the device is
lying or even what its motives, in reality, are!

Sure it's suspicious and perhaps sounds slightly paranoid, but how the hell do we know we're
not being diddled with? Even with the skimpy
history we have of our species, it's abundantly
clear to any researcher interested enough to look
into it that our skies have been filled with ships
giving every indication that intelligences far
greater than we can imagine have been looking
us over for thousands of years.

Alexander the Great was by no means the first
man to see these space (or time) machines, nor
was he the first to come to grief through their
interference. The young conqueror, incon-
testably the greatest general and most powerful
personality of ancient times, often spoke of two
alien vessels that repeatedly dived out of the
skies at his army until the war elephants, his
horses, and men became so terrified that they
refused to cross the Indus river near its delta. His
historians, Arrian and Plutarch described the
alien craft as great shining silvery shields, spit-
ting fire around the rims . . . weird flying objects
that came from the skies and returned to the
skies.

Why?

Postulate: Anything the brain, imagination,
and/or mind of man can conceive, will eventually be invented, discovered, and/or built.
Cases in point: electrical generators, radio and
TV transmission and reception, horseless car-

riages, jet planes flying at multiple-mach velocities, nuclear submarines, spaceships to the moon and planets, death rays, machines that think, autonomous robots, genetic engineering, etc. Only a few short years ago every one of the above was considered either science fiction or crackpot fantasy. Right now the overwhelming majority of the world scientific establishment considers the notions of FTL (faster than light) travel or moving back and forth in time pretty much in the same category.

Such things violate the "laws" of relativity or thermodynamics. Yet there is abundant evidence that huge objects in space (quasars, pulsars) spin and pulsate at many times the speed of light, and from what little we know of the space-time continuum (serious studies are under way in England, Russia, France, Germany, and the United States), the notion of time travel isn't as preposterous as the academic scientific establishment seems to believe.

Built up step by logical step then, the first time machine is already somewhere in our future. Oh, it will be about as rudimentary as the Wright brothers' flying machine, but you can bet they will improve just as fast as the combined talents of human ingenuity and machine logic can make the older models obsolete. Historians will want to observe and record the Napoleonic or Roman wars, then somebody will sure as hell decide that *their* future can be made a lot better by changing something in the past. Naturally there will be all kinds of natural (and man-made) laws to overcome, but there will also be enough rugged individualists, freebooters, religious zealots, and political crazies around to keep the kettle boiling incessantly. This is pure speculation, of course, but from what I've personally observed at M.I.T.'s Artificial Intelligence Group and its counterpart at Stanford and other institutions, the "Prime Directive" of time travel—i.e., non-interference—will have to be devised and enforced by *thinking machines* far more intelligent than human beings. The evidence indicates that these already exist.

All of which brings up a rather prickly question for epistemology: can we place any more faith in the moral integrity of super machines than we have in ourselves? A debatable point, at best. If UFOs are indeed machines (either time travelers from Earth's future or devices created by biological entities from other worlds), how can we be sure that, rather than obeying the programming of human beings in the future, they haven't already altered past human history in myriad subtle ways most favorable to their own rapid creation and development? Clearly, we can't.

The very best way to accomplish this objective is, of course, for machines to make themselves indispensable. This precisely describes the present state of computer technology.

In their richly-endowed Artificial Intelligence Group, Project MAC was M.I.T.'s acronym for Machine-Aided Cognition. Its alternate, Multiple Access Computer, sounded rather euphemistic when I first heard it in 1971. At that time Professor Marvin Minsky was probably the major contributor and certainly the most knowledgeable scientist in the group. "Within three to eight years," he told me at the time, "we'll have a machine with the general intelligence of an average human being . . . a machine that will be able to read Shakespeare, grease a car, play office politics, tell a joke, and win an argument or fight. At that point the machine will begin to educate itself with fantastic speed. Within a few months it will be at genius level and a few months after that its powers will be incalculable."

Three Rand Corporation scientists constructed a program that administered almost total autonomy to a machine in order to give it "goals and purposes, concepts of logic and abstraction, and common sense reasoning." In short, to duplicate and eventually surpass the capabilities and more highly refined psychic processes of the human mind itself. "Computers *must* eventually be able to modify their behavior on the basis of their experience," said cybernetician John von Neumann.

In England, Professor D. F. Lawden announced in *New Scientist* that "The scientific attack on the mind-body problem are the rapid advances being made in the design of intelligent machines or robots, capable of learning from experience, demonstrating originality of thought, and simulating human mental processes up to the highest level."

Given the facts that machines are virtually immortal, that their ability to think and remember is already millions of times faster than human, Professor Lawden observed, "Before long their intellectual powers will exceed our own to the same degree that the digging power of a huge mechanical shovel exceeds that of a human ditch-digger."

The "gigabit" computer built by Hughes Aircraft Corporation, with a capacity of a *billion* bits of information, was once the largest in existence. This is no longer so. A thinking machine has already reached the stage described by Professor Minsky in 1971. In a space of slightly less than four cubic feet, cyberneticians have now put together a computer storing a *trillion* bits of information! This is just about the capacity of the human brain, and the size will, inevitably, decrease in direct ratio to the increase of its knowledge, intelligence, and power. Once it surpasses human intelligence (which may already have happened) the computer will begin to program other computers. It will be entrusted with the capacity to construct increasingly sophisticated and broadly variable replicas of itself.

Some scientists are frankly terrified. Such machines will easily countermand, erase, or simply "forget" any or all programmed instructions about the well-being of individual human beings or of human civilization.

Can it be that this is what the mysterious UFOs are, have been, and will become?

It's all wild science fiction conjecture, of course.

Of course.

Joseph F. Goodavage attended Temple University and the University of Pittsburgh, studied journalism, worked in steel mills, construction, and as a reporter, writer, and printer—then went on to "the best journalism school in the country, the Chicago City News Bureau." He has worked on many of the major metropolitan newspapers, and is the author of a dozen books and hundreds of articles and stories. He has written and lectured on astronomy and astrology, on environmental problems, on the occult, and on a wide variety of unexplained phenomena. His two latest books are Our Threatened Planet and Storm on the Sun.

One of Goodavage's major interests, on which he has been concentrating for seventeen years, is extremely long-range weather disaster forecasting, and it is beginning to pay dividends. He is now considered one of the leading writers and researchers in the field of astrometeorology, the science of planetary weather forecasting, based on the concept that the solar system is "an interactive, interdependent unit." (He made his point very effectively in a 1963–1964 series in Analog entitled "Crucial Experiment." Analog's readers voted astrometeorology 93% accurate in extremely long-range weather disaster forecasting.)

Goodavage, who divides his time between New York and Maine, is presently working on a novel, two nonfiction books, and the creation of a new adult TV series.

Any invasion of the Earth, and especially any that came upon us without warning and without our knowing anything of the invader, would pose a fantastically complex set of equations for mankind to solve. How would we start to understand behavior patterns utterly alien to us? How would we counter strange military techniques and strange technologies? Which of our resources—and, our, here, means the world's—could we summon to assist us; resources technical, spiritual, or cultural?

Possibly, as Kevin O'Donnell, Jr. tells us in this story, beliefs and motivations which we, at least in the West, consider archaic and possibly rather foolish, may be exactly what we need.

Kevin O'Donnell, Jr.

TEMPLE GUARDIAN

The old man was in the bamboo grove, brushing dead leaves off the moss. What little hair he had left was short, and shockingly white —he'd stopped dyeing it when he'd retired. His face was lined, and dark from the sun. His clothes were neat and clean, but shabby. As the broom whispered through strokes that left the emerald moss unbruised, he frowned, and tried to decide why he was tidying a world that would be dead in a month.

"Father!"

His turn embodied the slow dignity of his age. A warm smile crossed his face when he caught sight of his son, Mitsugushi Fujio. *Remarkable how he resembles his uncle,* he thought. *Both so tall, so lean, so literal . . .* "Fujio," he said, "it's good to see you. And you're a colonel now, excellent, excellent. No wife yet, though, eh? No, stay there —you have not learned how to walk on moss without crushing it." Carrying the broom, he slipped between the swollen trunks of the twenty-meter bamboo. He was careful not to break any new shoots.

"That's a job for a young acolyte, Father." Even bowing, he seemed to tower over the old man.

"Mitsugushi Hideo is too eminent to work with his hands?" He chuckled, but sobered quickly. "There are no acolytes, Fujio—not anymore. The young are either cynical, or obsessed with the future. The past is for the old to preserve."

Fujio glanced at his watch. "Speaking of preservation—"

"You have come to see if I know how to operate the force sphere?"

"Yes."

"Why is it that the young assume such incapability on the part of their elders? The switch is simple—on, off—and clearly marked. My desktop computer was more complicated, and nobody questioned my ability to operate *that*. But then, few question a man while he chairs the board of a trillion-yen company—it is only after he retires that the condescension begins." He gestured up the winding path. "Come," he said, "let us go to the shrine."

Fujio fell in behind him. "It's quiet here." His deep voice was hushed.

"Hard to believe three million people live down there, eh?" The old man waved downslope, in the general direction of Kyoto, his favorite city. A breeze kissed his palm. "They used to visit us more frequently," he said, panting a bit, for the hillside was steep and the path was white gravel, "but now—" From behind, his shrug was eloquent.

"How is Brother Katsumi?"

"Dead these three years."

Fujio winced. "That long?"

"Longer."

"You could telephone."

"With the exception of your force sphere," said Mitsugushi Hideo, looking back over his shoulder, "there are no Western devices on the premises of the Inari Shrine."

"No television?"

"No."

"You used to have eight."

"I used to need them."

Mixed with the gravel were brown pine needles, fallen from the massive trees that lined the path and cooled it with their thick shade, and the needles softened the gritty crunches of the two men's feet. The air was sharp with resin. Though the hillside faced southwest, it was cool and dry, not at all like the city below, where bus riders left puddles of sweat on plastic seats, and the air was thick enough to drink.

Mitsugushi Hideo stopped by a soaring pine,

and patted its time-cleft trunk fondly. "Legend has it," he said, "that this tree was planted by the Abbot Kunichika in 794, when the Emperor Kammu established his capital here."

He craned his neck to see its top. "That would make it a very old tree."

"And too precious to lose to—what are they, anyway?"

"We don't know," admitted Fujio. Insigniae glittered as he loosened his collar. "Automatic alien machines, that's all we know."

Hideo nodded. "And they are due to arrive—?"

"It will take them another five days to finish with the Moon, three days to prepare for departure . . . nine days, all told." Stooping, he picked up a pine cone, and turned it over and over in his broad palm as though he'd never seen one before. "We don't know if they'll land *here*, though—they ignored Deimos and Phobos—"

"Those are too small to bother with."

"Titania, too, and its surface area is much larger than Japan's."

"You're assuming they won't cross water."

"Yes." His long face sombered. "If only we could find out more about them."

"What are they looking for?" Hideo stepped away from the tree, and resumed his upward walk. His stride was deliberate, yet graceful.

"We don't know—they appear to pulverize the soil down to the bedrock—we're taking samples of Moon soil they've finished with. Analyzing them might tell us what they've extracted from it, or added to it . . . but the changes are so subtle that the analyses won't be complete until long after the aliens have left Earth."

Rounding a bend, they came upon a weather-beaten flight of wooden stairs. Hideo supported himself on the swaying bannister.

"These should be repaired," said Fujio, who had never tolerated imperfection.

"If there were money, then they would be."

"Your pension?"

"It is administered by the Abbot, in Nara."

"I see."

At the top the land flattened out for a hundred yards of grass and gardens; behind them, grey and wooden, sat the humble Inari Shrine. The two men advanced upon it in thoughtful silence. Their feet slipped comfortably into the hollows of the stone steps. The grotesque temple guardians, eight feet tall and so long unpainted that they were more meditative than ferocious, gazed blankly down when they passed.

"Have you tried it yet?" Fujio had to duck to enter the small room behind the altar.

"Briefly. Did you not notice the mutilation of the pines outside?"

"No, but it doesn't surprise me. Didn't they warn you?"

"Of course they warned me—and I expected it to happen—but it is always painful to see a friend lose his arms."

"Did you paint over the stumps?"

"Would you have me watch them bleed to death?" He lifted a lantern from its hook by the door and padded forward, driving the darkness into the corners. "Here is your machine."

There were actually two devices on the floor

before them: a metal-plated cube, six feet on a side, and a coffin-shaped object about three feet long that lay next to it, and that was attached to it by a thick bundle of wires. Hideo set the lantern on top of the cube.

"You know, Father—" Fujio cleared the embarrassment out of his throat, "—the larger one is a generator; it can supply you with all the power—"

"Fujio!" The old man was scowling. "You forget that Mitsugushi, Inc. was the first to manufacture this machine— I know well both what it is and what it can do. I do not use it because I *choose* not to use it."

"Forgive me, I spoke thoughtlessly." He put his hands on his hips and stared at the two objects. "Shall we test it?"

"If that will please you."

"Thank you." He reached for the generator's control switch, and pushed it down. The displays lit up immediately. He ran his practiced eye along them. Satisfield that it was functioning properly, he pressed a red button on the coffin's top, then touched his jaw as an inaudible vibration rattled the fillings in his teeth. The second set of dials was also in the green, and he nodded. "Let's go outside."

"Very well." He replaced the lantern on its hook, and led the way to the sunshine.

"How many people will be sheltering with you?"

"As far as I know, none."

His eyebrows were black arches of surprise. "But—"

"In accord with the directives issued by the Ministry of Culture governing the provision of force spheres to nonprofit organizations administering sites and structures of historical or cultural value—" he paused for breath, and winked, as if he'd machine-gunned off the jargon just to show that he was still its master "—I put ads in the local papers. They stated that the first one hundred people wishing to shelter here were welcome, as long as they notified me in advance. However, since the shrine has no phone, they would have had to climb the mountain. And there are many other spheres closer to hand. For people." He pointed down the mountainside to where, through the trees, sun could be seen reflecting off a pond. "Ginkakuji—the wondrous Silver Pavilion. They've been given ten spheres; were I distributing them, they would have received a thousand. You could see it more clearly if the device were not operating, but—" he brushed a hand through the air around them; though the sky was blue crystal, the light was as dim as when cirrus clouds flit between the sun and the Earth. "I will not pretend to understand this machine. Perhaps you could explain why it filters the light."

"It's a force field." said Fujio. "It springs into existence forty meters from its source a billion times a second, and then collapses immediately. You can't see it—it's never there long enough—but when it exists, it absorbs the sun's radiance, and thus its interior seems dark."

The old man's eyes worshipped Kyoto while his mind juggled numbers. "I see now," he said slowly, "how this sphere could protect its inhabitants from bombs and from bullets—but what of lasers and poison gas?"

"The control mechanisms include a small

computer which monitors the amount of energy being absorbed by the field—and of the pollutants passing through it—and should either significantly increase above normal, with normal defined for each specific unit, then the field ceases to collapse. When continuous, it is impermeable."

"Both ways."

"Yes."

"The inhabitants could suffocate."

"Eventually—if it were left on long enough. But the aliens advance at the rate of 12.91 meters per minute—they will be out of sight long before the oxygen is exhausted."

"And then?"

"And then we emerge, Father, and we . . . and we try to reclaim what we have lost."

"What will we lose from this beloved city?"

Fujio's face saddened. "Most of it," he whispered. "The parks—the gardens—a thousand lesser temples and shrines . . ."

"Come, meet my sphere-sharers."

"I thought you said—"

"I did, but these aren't." He jerked his head towards the rear of the building, then started walking. "I am not totally isolated," he said as they proceeded. "I heard the reports from Mars —that the aliens shattered everything, left nothing larger than a cubic millimeter—and I began to think of what such a sifting would do . . ." They turned the corner; there before them were hundreds of greenhouse flats, each filled with tender seedlings. There were aquariums, too, some swarming with insects, others with frogs and toads, still others with snakes and turtles and salamanders. "I know the zoos will protect larger wildlife," said Hideo. He tapped a glass wall and startled a gecko. "But who will care for the lesser ones?"

"You and those like you."

"But there are so few." He exhaled slowly, then began to return to the front. "The reports say that after the machines have passed, everything is smooth and graded."

"The reports are true."

"I prefer hillsides with character." Stopping, he looked up, as though he could see the Moon, and focus on the aliens that chewed its rocks into dust. A blue and grey pigeon swooped out of the forest—its wingtips touched beneath its belly—its eye was trained on its nest in the shrine's curved eaves. "And I worry about the birds. What will they—"

The pigeon hit the dusky shell of the force sphere and died before it could change course. Wingtips and tail feathers drifted down outside; a fine moist powder fell inside. The pigeon itself had vanished.

Sorrow deepened Hideo's eyes. "What happened?" he asked his son.

"It flew into the force sphere."

"Shouldn't it have bounced off?"

"No. Oh, it would have, if the field were continuous. Right now it's—"

"On and off a billion times a second."

"Yes."

"And the pigeon?"

"Assume it was flying at thirty kilometers an hour—" he unbuttoned the pocket of his uniform tunic and withdrew a wafer-thin calculator. Oblivious to his father's quiet amusement at his addiction, he punched buttons. "—that's 8.3 meters per second or 8.3 nanometers every billionth of a second. Its momentum carried it though the field 8.3 nanometers at a time—and the field sliced it into crosssections just that thick. Like flying into a propeller."

"But why didn't the field come on continuously?" Hideo looked ill.

"The pigeon's kinetic energy was too low."

"I see. Wait here." He turned and disappeared into the shrine. A few minutes later, the sphere dissolved; the sunlight doubled in intensity. When he rejoined his son, his color was better, but he still walked uncertainly. "And yet this bird-slaying device will protect us from the aliens?"

"Yes." Fujio nodded several times. "It's been tested on Mars and the Moon. The alien machines cannot penetrate a continuous field. They sweep right past."

"With no harm to themselves?"

"What? Oh. You see, the alien machinery, as far as we can tell, is divided into two parts—the ship and the sieve. The sieve is actually another sort of force field, strung like a tennis net between two ships. It's the sieve that makes contact with the soil—the ships hover several hundred meters above ground."

"I see." The old man pondered that a moment. "So no ship has ever touched a force sphere. What would happen if one did. I wonder?"

"If it were moving, it would trigger a continuous field, and rebound."

"And if the field were not permitted to become continuous?"

"Well, then it would, ah . . ." He inhaled sharply, drawing air past his clenched teeth with a sibilant hiss. There was respect in his eyes when he stared at his father. "The ship would suffer the pigeon's fate." His face suddenly fell. "But no, the ships pass over the fields—with hundreds of meters to spare."

"Then if the ship won't come to the sphere—"

"Obviously the sphere must go to the ship, I know." He scratched his jaw, and began to pace. He talked as he walked, half to himself, half to his father. "But the ships are well-defended; we lost dozens of buggies on Mars and the Moon because the drivers ventured within line-of-sight of them. The ships' lasers are incredibly powerful . . . we wouldn't be able to deliver the force spheres to them."

"Mount them on trucks—"

"Half the sphere would be below ground. Once the laser found it, the field would go continuous, and the truck would be glued in place."

"A plane?"

"Couldn't keep itself aloft inside a continuous field. The plane and the sphere generator would drop like stones."

"Drop? What if they were to drop directly on top of the alien ships?"

"If the field is continuous, nothing. It would simply sit there. If it's intermittent, however . . ." The pocket calculator again came into play. "Gravity would pull it through the ship ten nanometers at a time . . ." The excitement that had gathered on his face quickly dissipated. "But how could we possibly guide one to the top of a ship?"

"Perhaps a divine wind would help you."

"A divine wind?" Fujio was startled, but intrigued. "A kamikaze?"

"Precisely." The old man bowed, and started down the path. "There are dead leaves on the moss," he said over his shoulder, "and they must be removed."

Kevin O'Donnell, Jr. says of himself: "Born in Cleveland in 1950, I lived there until '66, when my father joined the Peace Corps and took the ten of us to Seoul. In '68, I left for a Yale BA in Chinese Studies, after which I headed to Hong Kong, where my fiancée Kim was teaching. In '73 we moved to Taiwan for a year, then returned to New Haven and got married. I used to speak Korean, Mandarin, and 'survival' Japanese. Now I grow house plants, instead."

And of course he writes stories like "Temple Guardian." Since Ben Bova sent him his first check early in '73, he has sold thirty-four stories and six novels (three of which he has already written). The first novel, Bander Snatch (Bantam), was released in May 1979; the second, Mayflies and Other Spaced Spirits (Berkley), should appear in December 1979. Also, in his spare time, O'Donnell is managing editor of the little magazine: Empire: For the SF Writer.

It is a military axiom as old as war's history that you must understand your enemy. You must know why he does what he does, his strengths and weaknesses, and how he will respond not only in attack and in defense, but to stress and strain, to fear, and in victory or defeat. Generals who have failed to achieve such an understanding of their human enemies have more often than not ended up as beaten generals.

How much more urgent will it be, then, to achieve an understanding of any unknown enemy—or potential enemy, or even potential friend—who suddenly confronts us out of space. This is the central problem in Alan Nourse's novelette of a strange conflict between invading aliens—invading not Earth itself but the Solar System —and the men and women of an Earth outpost on a satellite ship orbiting Saturn.

Alan E. Nourse

MIRROR, MIRROR

Somewhere down on the surface of Saturn the Enemy was waiting.

The Earth outpost on the Satellite ship orbiting Saturn knew that he was there, with his four great ships and the unimaginable power that had brought him from whatever place he had come. But the Earth outpost did not know why he had come, and now they did not know what he intended to do.

He had come into the solar system, and struck with pointless savagery, and then fled to a place where Earth ships could not follow him. Now he waited there, silent and enigmatic. His very presence was intolerable: the Earth outpost knew they had to fight him, somehow, but the fight was on his terms, on the battle ground he had chosen.

It was an impossible war from the very start, a vicious war, draining the last reserves of the tiny group of Earthmen who had to fight it. It engulfed their waking hours and tortured their sleep with nightmares. There was no time to stop and ask themselves: why are we fighting this war?

They were fighting it, that was enough. Only the Enemy knew why. . . .

I

The waiting was the most terrible part of all for John Provost.

There was no chronometer in the day room of the Satellite ship, but Provost had his own private chronometer buried in his skull, somewhere in that vague impersonal space that lay between his left ear and his left eyebrow, deep down, ticking away hours, minutes, seconds, ridiculous fractions of ridiculous segments of seconds, marking them off against him inexorably, the epitome of all timepieces. It was there in his head and he couldn't get away from it, not even when his shift was over and he was back in Relief, laboriously rebuilding the fragments of John Provost that the Enemy had torn away. Now, almost whole and fresh again, he could hear the chronometer clicking away against him, and once more he was certain that it was the *waiting* he feared far more than he feared the Enemy.

Almost time, Provost. Almost your turn to go down again. . . .

He paced the day room of the Satellite ship and felt sweat trickle down his chest from the waiting and the silence. Always, in the last hour before his shift, he lived in an envelope of self-induced silence. Canned music blared from the wall speaker, unnaturally loud. but Provost did not hear it. There was talking and chatter in the day room, harsh laughter all about him, noises of glasses clinking, feet shuffling. A dozen men were here, but to Provost the day room was like a TV with the sound turned off. He was utterly isolated, and that was the way he wanted it.

He rubbed wet palms against his trousers and waited.

Nobody looked at him, of course. The men knew that his shift was next. Nobody spoke to him; he might smile and answer them pleasantly, or he might turn on them, savagely and without warning, like a cornered rat. It had happened before, with others. He was like a crossbow with the spring drawn tight, waiting to be triggered, and nobody wanted to tamper with him twenty minutes before shift change. Everyone knew he wouldn't be responsible for what he might do.

And with every passing second the spring was pulled tighter. That was what made the waiting so terrible.

He went below and stepped into a hot foam shower, felt the powerful muscles of his shoulders and neck relax a trifle. Briefly he thought of the Turner girl. Would she be in Relief when he returned? Of course, there were others equally well trained to help the men through the period of childish regression that inevitably occurred when their shifts were over and the pressure suddenly off—the only way they could rebuild their mental resources for another shift—but to John Provost, the Turner girl seemed better than any of the others. They'd actually begun to be good friends as he had come, slowly, to trust her under circumstances in which trust was difficult if not impossible. And then that new woman that DepPsych had sent out from the Hoffman Center, Dorie Kendall—what about her? Help, or hindrance? Dangerous, sending out new people at a time like this. Yet, she'd *listened* when he'd told her how he could use his Analogue to take his mind and sensorium down to Saturn's surface without actually leaving the Satellite ship at all. Maybe she'd do. Maybe she might even be able to help him, somehow.

Provost dressed quickly now as the fear grew stronger in his mind. There was no use trying to fight it down; he knew that from long experience. It was far more exhausting to try than just to give in to it, start counting the minutes to Relief from *now* instead of when the shift began. It made things balance better in his mind that way, even if it made the DepPsych people scream and wring their hands. Well, let them scream. There was nothing they knew about this Idiot War that he didn't know—absolutely nothing. He was an expert on this war. They couldn't even imagine what an expert he was.

He checked at the Control board. "Provost on."

"Are you steady?" the voice from Control asked.

Provost grunted.

"All right, here's the report." The voice hesitated an instant. "I don't think you're going to like it very much."

"Let's have it."

"'Dead quiet on the front all through the last shift." Control said.

Provost blinked. "Quiet!"

"That's the report."

Provost shivered. "What do you suppose they're cooking up *now?*"

"I wish I could tell you." The voice from Control was puzzled and sympathetic. "They're brewing *something* down there, that's certain. Chances are it'll be nasty, too. They haven't given us a quiet shift in months." Provost could almost see the face of the controller, somewhere deep in the lower regions of the Satellite ship. "You may be the one to get hit with it, John, whatever it is. But then, maybe it'll stay quiet for you, too."

"Not with my luck," said Provost. "Well, I'm going in now."

He stepped into the Analogue cubicle with the green flasher over the door, found the cockpit in the darkness, fit his damp hands into the grips. He shook the Analogue helmet down on his head until it was comfortable. He didn't try to tell himself that *he* wasn't really going down to Saturn's surface, that only a tiny bit of metal and stamped circuitry was going down under his mental control. DepPsych had given up on *that* line of comfort long ago. Provost knew all too well that he didn't have to be on the surface in the flesh in order for the Enemy to rip him apart. He closed his eyes in the darkness, trying to relax.

Still waiting, now, for the signal to move in. He didn't know which man he was relieving. DepPsych said it was better not to know. Even the signals from the Analogues were monitored so he wouldn't have a hint. Every man operated his Analogue differently—but could the Enemy tell the difference?

Provost was certain that they could. Not that it seemed to make any difference to them.

"Countdown." He heard the buzzer sound, and he crushed down with all his power on the hand grips. He felt the jolting thud as he slammed into full Analogue contact, and something deep in his mind began screaming *now! now! now!*

He dropped away into nothing.

Moments later he knew that he was on the surface, even though a corner of his mind was aware of the sticky hand grips, the dark closeness of the Analogue cubicle. Before him he could see the great yawning chasms of ice on Saturn's surface stretching out into the distance. Yellow-grey light reflected down from the Rings. He could sense the devastating pressure of gravity here even though he could not feel it. Overhead, a roiling sea of methane and ammonia clouds, crashing lightning, the unspeakable violence of Saturn's continual war with itself.

And somewhere beyond the place where he was, the Enemy.

There was no contact, at first. Provost, groped, and found nothing. He could always tell their presence, just as he was certain now that they could tell his. But that was as far as he could go. *They* planned. *They* moved. If *they* were ready, they struck. If they weren't ready, they didn't.

And until they struck, he was helpless. There was nothing for him to fight against. All he could do was wait. For what? He did not know. But always before, there had been *something*.

Now, nothing. Not a whisper. He waited, sick with fear. He knew how brutal the Enemy could be. He knew the viciousness of their blows, the savagery, the cunning. These were things he could fight, turning their own weapons against them. But *nothingness* was something else.

How could he fight nothing? He couldn't. He could only wait.

He stretched his mind, groping for them. Then, suddenly, he felt a gentle brush of contact . . . they were there, all right. Also waiting. But for what? His muscles knotted, cramped. *Why didn't they do something?* A quick, stabbing blow would be merciful relief . . . but it did not come.

The Enemy had never been merciful. There was something else they were going to do.

When it came, it was almost overpowering in its intensity. Not hostility, nor anger, nor hatred, as before. Instead, incredibly, a soft gentle mist of supplication, a wave of reproach insinuating itself in his mind. *Why do you hate us when we want only peaceful contact with you? Why do you try to drive us back? We have come from so far, and now you try only to destroy us.*

It caught him off guard. He tried to formulate

an answer, but they swept in swiftly, surrounding him with wave after wave of reproach. As always, he could not tell *how* this contact with the Enemy was made. Perhaps they, too, had Analogues. He simply felt them, deep in his mind, and they were closer now, all about him, sucking him deep into their minds. He felt a glowing warmth there now that was utterly different from before. He felt himself drawn, moving slowly, then faster and faster, in tightening spirals toward the vortex as the Enemy's minds drew him in. *We want to stop this fighting, but you prolong it. Why? Why won't you give us a chance?*

For the first time he saw the physical images of the Enemy. They were approaching him on the surface. He couldn't see them clearly . . . only fuzzy outlines . . . but enough to see that they were humanoid, manlike. They moved toward him as he watched. His heart roared with sudden excitement. Could they mean it? Could they really want to reveal themselves, establish contact, put an end to this grueling, brutal Idiot War that had been going on for so long?

Something in his own mind called out a warning, shrieking an alarm. *Don't be a fool! They're treacherous, there's nothing they won't try. Don't let them poison you, fight back!*

He caught at the grips, trying to center his mind on the approaching emissaries, trying to catch the fringes of thought that lay beneath the surface, but the wave of reproachfulness came back at him with increasing intensity.

Why do you hate us so much?

He knew, coldly, what he had to do. It was the only thing to do, even though it seemed so horribly wrong.

He waited until the emissaries were close. Then he struck out at their minds, as viciously as he knew how. He drove the blow home with six long months of bitterness and hatred behind it, striking out wildly, slicing them down like wheat before a scythe. He felt them recoil and crumble, and he pressed his advantage coldly, flailing at the insidious supplicating pattern of thought surrounding him.

The spiral broke, suddenly, releasing him, but this time there was no stark, brutal core of malignancy that he had glimpsed beneath their illusions so many times before. Instead, the vortex receded gently, regretfully . . . injured, bewildered, helpless to understand.

Why? Why will you not even give us a chance? Why do you hate us so much?

It was harder to bear than naked savagery. Frantically Provost rang for Relief. It seemed, suddenly, as if all the wrongs and imagined wrongs he had done in his whole life were welling up to torment him; he knew it was only Enemy illusion, but his mind was screaming, twisting in on itself. A sense of guilt and self-loathing swept through him in waves as he fought to maintain the tiny thread of control. *Butcher!* his own mind was screaming at him. *What kind of monster are you? What if they were sincere? What if you were the one who was wrong?*

The Control board jerked him back before he broke, snapped off his Analogue contact abruptly. He stood up in the darkness of the cubicle and disengaged his cramped hands from the grips. It was over; he was safe. His Rehab conditioning cut in now to take over . . . now there would be Relief from the onslaught, quietness, gentleness, childhood memories, peace. . . .

But the waves of guilt were still washing at his mind. He started walking down the corridor toward the Relief room as his hands began to tremble; then he broke into a run. He knew that only seconds now stood between him and sanity, and sanity lay at the end of the corridor.

The Turner girl was in the room waiting for him. There was soft music, gentle light. She sat across the room, and suddenly he was a five-year-old again, bewildered and overwhelmed by the frightening world around him, desperate for comfort, affection, reassurance. He hurled himself onto the recliner, felt the Turner girl's fingers gently stroking his forehead as he let himself go completely, let great sobs of relief erupt from his throat and shake his shoulders.

She was silent for a long time as his knotted muscles began to relax. Then she leaned forward, bent her lips to his ear.

"Butcher!" she whispered.

Only a whisper, but virulent, malignant. "Toad! You call yourself human, but you go down there to butcher them! *Monster!*"

Provost screamed. He threw himself back against the wall, arms outstretched, clawing at it and screaming as he stared at her in horror. She faced him, and spit at him, and burst out in mocking laughter as his screams rose from torment to agony.

An alarm bell was clanging now; the girl's lips twisted in revulsion. She threw open the corridor door. *"Butcher!"* she hurled back at him once more, and broke for the door.

Gunfire rattled from both ends of the corridor.
The crossfire caught her, lifted her off her feet
and dropped her in a crumpled heap on the
metal floor plates.

Provost huddled in the corner of the room,
babbling.

II

The enormity of the blow did not register immediately. Like any warfare operation, the Satellite ship was geared to face emergencies; the
sheer momentum of its battle station procedure
delayed the impact for hours. Then, slowly, the
entire operation of the Satellite ship began to
freeze in its tracks.

What had happened was no ordinary emergency.

To Dorie Kendall the full, terrifying implica-
tion was clear from the start. She had long
months of Department of Psychology training
behind her at the Hoffman Center, weeks of
work with the very men who had developed the
neuromolecular Analogues that were Earth's
only weapon in this war. Even then, the training
had not stopped; on the long passage out from
Earth she had continued with days and nights of
tape-study and hypno-sleep to prepare her for
this crucial assignment. She herself had never
been in Analogue contact with the Enemy, but
she knew a great deal about the Enemy and
what the Enemy might do. The instant Dr.
Coindreau, the Satellite surgeon, had called her
down to the autopsy, she realized what had happened.

Only now it was dawning on her, in a cold wash of horror, that it was very possibly her own fault that it had happened at all.

"But why don't you *attack* them?" she had asked John Provost a few hours before his shift was to begin. "Why do you always take the defensive?"

Provost had looked at her, patiently, as though she were a child who didn't quite understand the facts of life. "They're perceptive," he said. "They're powerful. Incredibly powerful."

"All the more reason to hit them hard," she had argued. "Hit them with a blow that will drive them back reeling."

Provost smiled. "Is that the new DepPsych theory?"

"All DepPsych knows is that *something* has to be changed. This war has gone on and on."

"Maybe after a while you'll understand why," he had said slowly. "How can we hit them with this powerful blow you talk about when they're busy driving mental javelins into us with all the force they can muster? I can try, but I don't know how to do it."

Well, he had tried, all right, the psychologist reflected, and now bare hours later Provost was strapped down screaming and shattered in one of the isolation cubicles, and the Relief girl. . . .

She watched Dr. Coindreau's lean face and careful fingers as he worked at the autopsy table. Every room in Medical Section, every fixture, had a double use. Sick bay and Rehab quarters. Office and lab. Examining room doubling as surgery. Now it was doubling as morgue. She peered down at the remains of the Turner girl in growing anger and revulsion and wondered, desperately, how the Enemy had managed to do it.

She realized, coldly, that it was up to her to find out how, and fast.

The Enemy had poisoned the Turner girl, somehow. They had reached into the heart of the Satellite ship and struck at the most critical link in the chain—the Relief program that enabled the men to go back into battle.

Without Relief, there could be no men to fight.

But why did we have to murder her? the Kendall girl thought bitterly. *If we could have studied her, we might have learned how the Enemy had done it.*

The blinker over the door flashed, and a big heavy-set man stepped into the room. She recognized Vanaman, commander of the Satellite ship. She had talked to him briefly before. It had been an unpleasant interview; Vanaman had made it quite clear that he could not understand why DepPsych insisted upon sending women out to Saturn Satellite, nor why Earth Control chose *now* of all times to shift gears and saddle him with Dorie Kendall, intent on finding some new approach to the fighting. The big man glared at her, and then stared down at the thing on the table.

"The Turner girl?" he asked the surgeon.

"What's left of her," Dr. Coindreau said. "I'm about finished. It's not going to help us any."

"It's *got* to help us." Vanaman's voice was harsh.

Dorie Kendall looked up at him sharply. "Your trigger-happy firing squad didn't leave us much to work with, you know."

Vanaman's fist clenched on the table. Deep-cut lines sliced from his nose down to the corners of his mouth. His face showed the grueling pressure of months of command, and he seemed to control himself only with difficulty. "What did you expect them to do?" he said. "Give her a medal?"

The girl flushed. "They didn't have to kill her."

Vanaman blinked at her. "They didn't, eh? You've been helping the doctor here do the post?"

"Certainly."

"And you've run a standard post-mortem brain wash?" He nodded toward the neuromolecular analyzer clicking in the wall, the great-grandfather of all Analogues.

"Of course."

"And what did you find, Miss Kendall?"

"Nothing intelligible," she said defiantly. "The Enemy had her, that's all."

"Fine," said Vanaman. "And you're standing here suggesting that we should have had *that* running around *alive* on this ship? Even for ten seconds? We know they had her tongue, they must have had her eyes also, her ears, her reason." He shook his head. "Everything we've done against the Enemy has depended on keeping them *away* from us, *off* this ship. That's why we monitor every move of every man and woman here, Miss Kendall, including yourself. That's why we have guns in every corridor and room. That's why we used them on the Turner girl."

There was silence for a moment. Then the doctor pushed back from the table and looked up. "I'm afraid you used them too late on the Turner girl," he said to Vanaman.

"You mean Provost is dead?"

"Oh, no." The doctor jerked off his mask, ran a lean hand through his hair. "He's alive enough. That is to say, his heart is beating. He breathes. Just what is going on above his ears is something else again. I doubt if even Miss Kendall could tell you that. I certainly can't."

"Then he's a total loss." Vanaman's face seemed to sag, and Dorie realized suddenly how heavily the man had been hanging on the thread of hope that Provost might only have suffered minor harm.

"Who can say?" the doctor said. "You take a fine chunk of granite and strike precisely the right blow, precisely hard enough at precisely the right angle, and it will shatter into a dozen pieces. That is what has happened to Provost. Any salvage will be strictly up to DepPsych. It's out of my province." The surgeon's dark eyes met Dorie's for a moment, and shifted away. "Unfortunately, the significance of this attack is greater than the survival or loss of John Provost. We might as well face that right now. The job the Enemy has done on Provost was a precision job. It can mean only one thing: that somehow they have managed to acquire a very complex understanding of human behavior patterns. Am I right, Dorie?"

She nodded. "It isn't *what* they did to Provost that matters so much," she said, "although that's bad enough. It's *how* they did it that matters."

"Then how *did* they do it?" Vanaman asked, turning on her. "That's what you're here for, isn't it? This isn't a war of muscle against muscle or bomb against bomb. This is a war of mind against mind. It's up to the Department of Psychology and the Hoffman Center psych-docs to tell us how to fight this Enemy. Why don't you know?"

"I need time," she said. "I can't give you an answer."

The big man leaned forward, his lips tight across his teeth. "You've *got* to give me an answer," he said. "We can't afford time, can't you see that? This Satellite is the only shield between Earth and the Enemy. If you can't give us the answer, we're through, washed up. We've got to know how they did what they did to Provost."

Through the viewport the pale, yellow globe of Saturn stared up at them, unwinking, like the pale eye of a snake. "I wish I could tell you," Dorie Kendall said. "The Turner girl can't tell us. Neither can Provost. But there may be one way we can learn."

"And that is?"

"Provost's Analogue. It has been the *real* contact with the Enemy. It should know everything Provost knows about them. The Analogue may give us the answer."

III

With Vanamann seated beside her, Dorie fed the tapes from John Provost's Analogue into the playback unit in the tiny projection room in Integration Section. For a few moments, then, she ceased to be Dorie Kendall of DepPsych, trained for duty and stationed on Saturn Satellite, and became John Provost instead.

It was an eerie experience. She realized that

every Analogue was different, a faithful impression of the mind of its human prototype; but she had not been prepared for the sudden, abrupt contact with the prototype mind of John Provost.

She felt the sickening thud of his contact with the Analogue just prior to its last descent to the surface. She felt the overwhelming wave of tension and fear that the Analogue had recorded; then the sudden, irrational, almost gleeful sense of elation as John Provost's eyes and ears and mind floated down to the place where the Enemy was. The Analogue tape was accurate to a high degree of fidelity. Dorie Kendall gripped the chair arms until her wrists cramped.

It was like going to the surface herself.

Beside her she was aware of Vanaman's huge body growing tense as he gnawed his knuckles, soaking in the tape record. She felt the growing tension, the snowballing sense of impending disaster reflecting from John Provost's mind.

And then she lost contact with the things around her and fell completely into Provost's role. The growing supplication of the Enemy surrounded her. She felt the sense of reproach, the helpless appeal of the illusion, and Provost's response, calculated to perfection and deployed like a pawn on a chessboard. *It's a trick, a pitfall, watch out! Don't be fooled, don't fall into their trap. . . .*

She felt the wild fury of Provost's mind as he hurled the illusion aside, struck out at the Enemy as she had told him to do. And then the receding waves of supplication and reproach from the Enemy, and the overwhelming, demoralizing wave of guilt from his own mind—

In that moment she began to understand John Provost, and to realize what the Enemy had done. Her face was pale when the tape stopped. She clenched her fists to keep her hands from trembling.

Vanaman leaned back, defeat heavy on his face. "Nothing," he said. "It's always the same. We have nothing."

"I didn't realize what they could do," Dorie said.

"But that was on the surface. Down there we could fight it, control it. Now they've reached us here, too." The commander stood up and started for the corridor. "For all we know, they've been here all along, just playing with us. We can't really be certain that they haven't. Can you begin to see what we've been fighting, now? We don't know *anything* about them. We can't even be sure we're fighting a war with them."

Dorie Kendall looked up, startled. "Is there any doubt of that?"

"There's plenty of doubt," Vanaman said. "We *seem* to be fighting a war, except that nobody seems to understand just what kind of war we're fighting, or just why we're fighting it." His voice trailed off and he shrugged wearily. "Well, we're backed up to the wall now. Provost was our best Analogue man. He depended utterly on Relief to put him back together again after one of those sessions down there. The Turner girl was the whole key to our fighting technique, and they got to her somehow and poisoned her. If they can do that, we're through."

The girl stared at him. "You mean we should just quit? Withdraw?"

Vanaman's voice was bitter. "What else can we do? Any one of the girls in Relief could be just the same as the Turner girl, right now. They've cracked open our entire strategy in one blow. The Relief program is ruined, and without Relief I can't send another man down there."

"But you've *got* to," Dorie said. "This Satellite is the Earth's only shield. We can't stop now."

"We can't fight them, either. We've been fighting them for months, and we know nothing about them. They come from—somewhere. We don't know where, or when, or how. All we know is what they did to Titan. We're trying to defend ourselves against an imponderable, and our defenses are crumbling." Vanaman closed the tape cans and tossed them into the return file with an air of finality. "Do you know what Provost called this war?"

Dorie Kendall nodded. "He told me. An Idiot War."

"And he was right. *Their* war, not ours. What do they want? We don't know. On *their* choice of battlefield, in *their* kind of warfare, they're whipping us, and we don't even know how. If we had even a glimpse of what they were trying to do, we might be able to fight them. Without that, we're helpless."

She heard what he was saying, and she realized that it was almost true, and yet something stuck in her mind, a flicker of an idea. "I wonder," she said. "Maybe we don't know what the Enemy is trying to do here—but there's one possibility that nobody seems to have considered."

Vanaman looked up slowly. "Possibility?"

"That *they* don't know what they're trying to do, either," Dorie Kendall said.

IV

It was a possibility, even Vanaman grudgingly admitted that. But as she went down to Isolation Section to examine John Provost, Dorie Kendall knew that it made no sense, no more nor less than anything else that the Enemy had done since they had come six months before into Earth's solar system.

They had come silent as death, unheralded: four great ships moving as one, slipping in from the depths of space beyond Pluto. How long they had been lurking there, unobserved but observing, no one could say. They moved in slowly, like shadows crossing a valley, with all space to conceal them, intruders in the enormous silence.

An observation post on tiny Miranda of Uranus spotted them first, suddenly and incredibly present where no ships ought to be, in a formation that no Earth ships ever would assume. Instrument readings were confirmed, questioned, reconfirmed. The sighting was relayed to the supply colony on Callisto, and thence to Earth.

Return orders were swift: keep silence, observe, triangulate and track, compute course and speed, make no attempt at contact. But return orders were too late. The observation post on Miranda had ceased, abruptly, to exist.

Alerted patrol ships searched in vain, until the four strange ships revealed themselves in orbit around Saturn. Deliberately? No one knew. Their engines were silent; they drifted like huge encapsulated spores, joining the other silent moons around the sixth planet. They orbited

for months. Titan Colony watched them,
Ganymede watched them, Callisto watched
them.

Nothing happened.

On Earth there were councils, debate, uncertainty; speculation, caution, fear. Wait for them
to make contact. Give them time. Wait and see.
But the four great ships made no move. They
gave no sign of life. Nothing.

Signals were dispatched, with no response.
Earth prepared against an attack—a ridiculous
move. Who could predict the nature of any attack that might come? Still, Earthmen had
always been poor at waiting. Curiosity battled
caution and won, hands down. What were these
ships? Where did they come from? Hostile or
friendly? Why had they come here?

Above all, *what did they want?*

No answers came from the four great ships.
Nothing.

Finally an Earth ship went up from Titan Colony, moving out toward the orbit of the intruders. The crew of the contact ship knew their
danger. They had a single order: make contact.
Use any means, accept any risk, but make contact. Approach with caution, with care, gently,
without alarming, but make contact. At any
cost.

They approached the intruders, and were torn
from space in one instantaneous flash of white
light. Simultaneously, Titan Colony flared like
an interplanetary beacon and flickered out, a
smoking crater three hundred miles wide and
seventy miles deep.

Then, incredibly, the four great ships broke

from orbit and fled deep beneath the methane and ammonia clouds of Saturn's surface. Earth reeled from the blow, and waited, paralyzed, for the next—and nothing happened. No signal, no sign, nothing.

But now the intruders were the Enemy. The war had begun, if it was a war; but it was not a war that Earthmen knew how to fight. A war of contradiction and wild illogic. A war fought in a ridiculous microcosm where Earthmen could not fight, with weapons that Earthmen did not comprehend.

An Idiot War. . . .

Dorie went to see John Provost just eight hours after the Enemy had struck through the Turner girl. As she followed the tall, narrow-shouldered doctor into the isolation cubicles of Medical Section, he stopped and turned to face her. "I don't think this is wise at all."

"Maybe not," the girl said. "But I have no choice. Provost was closer to the Enemy than anyone else here. There's no other place to start."

"What do you think you're going to learn?" Dr. Coindreau asked.

"I don't know. Only Provost knows exactly what happened in that Relief room."

"We know what happened," the doctor protested. "The Relief room was monitored. Provost had come close to his breakpoint when Control jerked his Analogue back from the surface. The pressure on the men under battle conditions is almost intolerable. They all approach breakpoint, and induced regression in the Relief room is the fastest, safest way to unwind them, as long as we don't let them curl up into a ball."

"You mean it *was* the fastest and safest way," Dorie corrected him.

The doctor shrugged. "They hit Provost at his weakest point. The Turner girl couldn't have done worse with a carving knife. I still don't see what you're going to learn from Provost."

"At least I can see what they've done to him." She looked at the doctor. "I don't see how my seeing him can hurt him."

"Oh, I'm not worried about *him*." The doctor opened the door. At the nursing desk a corpsman was punching chartcards. "How's he doing?" the doctor asked.

"Same as before." Then the corpsman saw the girl. "Doc, you aren't taking *her* in there, are you?"

"That's what she wants."

"You know he's not exactly sold on girls, right now."

"I'll risk it," Dorie said sharply.

Inside the cubicle they found Provost lying on his back on a bunk. The pale blue aura of a tangle-field hovered over him, providing gentle but effective restraint.

Provost was singing.

The words drifted across the room. Dorie suddenly caught them and felt her cheeks turn red.

"Hello, John," the doctor said. "How are you feeling?"

Provost stopped singing. "Fine. Yourself?"

"This is Miss Kendall. She's going to help take care of you."

"Well, now, that's just fine." Provost turned his face toward Dorie. No sign of recognition; his

eyes were flat, like a snake's eyes. Impersonal—
and deadly. "Why don't you leave us alone to
talk, Doc? And turn this tangle-field off. Just for
a minute."

She shivered at the tone. Dr. Coindreau said,
"John, do you know where you are?"

"In a tangle-field."

"Do you know where?"

Provost ignored the question, stared fixedly at
the girl. She had never seen such a malignant stare.

"Do you know what happened to you?" the
doctor tried again.

His eyes didn't waver, but he frowned. "Memory's a little sticky. But ten seconds out of this
tanglefield would help, I bet." She saw his hand
clench on the coverlet until the knuckles
whitened.

The doctor sighed. "Listen to me, John. You
were on the surface. Something happened down
there. What—"

Provost obviously was not listening. "Look,
Doc, why don't you cut out of here? My business
is with *her*, not you."

"All right, John," Dr. Coindreau turned
away. He led the girl back into the corridor. She
was no longer blushing. She was dead white and
trembling. "You know that he'd kill you before
he finished," the doctor said to her gently.

"Yes." She nodded. "I know."

"At least the mechanism is direct enough.
Fairly primitive, too. And let's face it, a weaker
man would either be dead or catatonic. Provost
is a rock of stability in comparison."

She nodded. "But he's turned his hatred on
the girl, not on the Enemy."

"It was the girl who hit him, remember?"

They stepped into an office, and she took the seat the doctor offered gratefully. "Anyway," he said, "Provost never actually contacted the Enemy. We speak as though he's actually been down on the surface physically, and of course he hasn't. You know how an Analogue works?"

"I ought to—I have one—but I only know the general theory, not the details."

"Nobody knows the details too well, not even your friends at the Hoffman Center. Nobody really could. An Analogue is at least quasi-sentient, and the relationship between an Analogue and its operator is extremely individual and personal. That's precisely why Analogues are the only real weapons we have to use against the Enemy."

"I can't quite see that," Dorie said.

"Look—these creatures, whatever they are—buried themselves on the surface of Saturn and just sat there, right? The blows they struck against Titan Colony and the contact ship showed us the kind of power they *could* bring to bear—but they didn't follow up. They struck and ran. Pretty pointless, wouldn't you say?"

It seemed so, at first glance. Dorie Kendall frowned. "Maybe not so pointless. It made counterattack almost impossible."

Dr. Coindreau nodded grimly. "Exactly the point. We didn't know what—or how—to counterattack. We practically *had* to do *something*, and yet there was nothing we could do."

"Why didn't we land and hunt them out?" the girl asked. "We can get down there, can't we?"

"Well, it's *possible*, but it would have been worse than useless. It would have taken all our strength and technology just to survive down there, let alone do anything else. So we used Analogues, just the way Grossman and his crew used them to explore the surface of Jupiter. The Analogues were originally developed to treat paranoids. The old lysergic acid poisons had proved that a personality could dissociate voluntarily and reintegrate, so that a psych man could slip right into a paranoid fantasy with his patient and work with him on his own ground. Trouble was that unstable personalities didn't reintegrate so well, which was why so many people blew up in all directions on LSD." Dr. Coindreau paused, chewing his lip. "With Analogues, the dissociation is only apparent, not real. A carbon copy, with all the sensory, motor, and personality factors outlined perfectly on protein-molecule templates. The jump from enzyme-antagonists to electronic punched-molecule impressions isn't too steep, really, and at least the Analogues are predictable."

"I see," Dorie Kendall said. "So the operatives—like Provost—could send their Analogues down and explore in absentia, so to speak."

"As a probe, in hope of making contact with the Enemy. At least that was the original plan. It turned out differently, though. That was what the Enemy seemed to be waiting for. They drove back the first probers with perfectly staggering brutality. We struck back at them, and they returned with worse. So pretty soon we were dancing this silly gavotte with them down there, except that the operatives didn't find it so silly. Maybe the medieval Earth wars seemed silly, too, with the battleground announced in advance, the forces lined up, the bugles blowing,

parry and thrust and everybody quits at sunset.
But lots of men got killed that way just the
same." He paused for a moment, wrapped in his
own thoughts, and then went on with sudden
firmness: "There was no sense to this thing, but
it was what the Enemy seemed to want. And our
best men have thrown everything they could into
it, and only their conditioning and the Relief
room has kept them going."

"Weren't Psi-Highs used for a while?" Dorie
said.

"Yes, but it didn't work. The Enemy is not
telepathic, for one thing, or at least not in the
sense we think of it; and anyway, the Psi-Highs
couldn't keep themselves and their Analogues
separated. It was pure slaughter, for them, so
they were pulled back to Earth to help build the
Analogues for psi-negatives to use." He shot a
glance toward the cubicle. "Well, now that's all
over. No Relief, no Analogues. The Enemy has
simply shifted the battle scene on us, and we're
paralyzed."

For a long moment the DepPsych girl sat in
silence. Then she said, "I don't think 'paralyzed'
is exactly the word you want. You mean 'pan-
icked'."

"Does it make any difference?"

"Maybe a world of difference," the girl said
thoughtfully, *"to the aliens."*

V

Paralysis or panic, the effect on the Satellite
ship was devastating.

Twelve hours after Provost was dragged kick-
ing and screaming out of the Relief room, the

ship's crew waited in momentary anticipation, braced against the next blow. They could not guess from where it might come, nor what form it might take. They could only sit in agony and wait.

Twenty-four hours later, they still waited. Thirty-six hours, and they still waited. Activity was suspended, even breathing was painful. In the day room the Analogue operatives gnawed their knuckles, silent and fearful, unwilling to trust even a brief exchange of words. They were Earthmen, the girl realized, and Earthmen were old hands at warfare. They understood too well the horrible power of advantage. Earthly empires had tottered and fallen for the loss of one tiny advantage.

But the Enemy's advantage was not tiny. It was huge, overpowering. The men here could only wait for the blow to fall. It *had* to fall, if there were order and logic in the universe.

It didn't fall. They waited, and far worse than a brutal, concerted attack against them, nothing happened.

The paralysis deepened. The Enemy had reached a girl within the Satellite and turned her into a murderous blade in their midst. Who could say how many others had been reached? No one knew. There was nothing to grasp, nothing to hold on to, *nothing*.

Dorie Kendall did not elaborate on her remark to Dr. Coindreau, but something had slid smoothly into place in her mind as she had talked to him, and she watched the Satellite and its men around her grinding to a halt with a new alertness.

The attack on Provost through the Turner girl was not pointless, she was certain of that. It had purpose. Nor was it an end in itself. It was only the beginning. To understand the purpose it was necessary somehow to begin to understand the Enemy.

And that, of course, was the whole war. That was what the Enemy had so consistently fought to prevent. *They have built up an impenetrable wall, a blinding smokescreen to hide themselves,* she thought, *but there must be some way to see them clearly*.

The only way to see them was through Provost. She was certain of this, though she wasn't sure why. She went to the isolation cubicle to see him again, and then again and again. It was unrelieved torment for her each time; for all her professional training, she had never before encountered such a malignant wall of hatred. Each time his viciousness and abusiveness seemed worse as he fought against the restraining tangle-field, watching her with murderous hatred; she left each time almost physically ill, and whenever she slept she had nightmares. But again and again she worked to break through his violent obsession, more and more convinced that John Provost was the key. They were brutal interviews, fruitless—but she watched as she worked.

Vanaman found her in Medical Section on the third day, a red-eyed, bitter Vanaman, obviously exhausted, obviously fighting for the last vestige of control, obviously helpless to thwart the creeping paralysis in the ship under his command. "You've got to hit Eberle with something," he said harshly. "I can't make him budge."

"Who is Eberle?" the girl wanted to know.

"The Analogue dispatcher. He won't send an Analogue down."

"I thought you weren't going to."

"I've *got* to do *something*, Relief or no Relief, but Eberle is dragging his feet."

She found John Eberle in the Analogue banks, working by himself, quietly and efficiently and foolishly, testing wires, testing transmission, dismantling the delicate electronic units and reassembling them in an atmosphere of chaos around him. The operative cubicles were empty, the doors hanging open, alarm signals winking unheeded.

"What are you doing with them?" Dorie asked, staring down at the dismantled Analogues.

Eberle grinned foolishly. "Testing them," he said. "Just testing."

"But Vanaman says we need them down on the surface *now*. Can't you see that?"

Eberle's smile faded. "I can't send them down there."

"Why not?"

"Who's going to operate them?" the dispatcher asked. "What will the operators do for Relief?" His eyes narrowed. "Would *you* want to take one down?"

"I'm not trained to take one down. But there are operators here who are."

Eberle shrugged his shoulders. "Well, you're DepPsych, maybe you've got some magic formula to make the men go down without any Relief to count on. I can't make them. I've already tried it."

She stared at him, and felt a wave of help-lessness sweep over her. It was as though she were standing in an enormous tangle-field, and all her efforts to free herself only settled it more firmly on her shoulders. She knew it wasn't anything as simple as fear or cowardice that was paralyzing the ship.

It was more than that, something far deeper and more basic.

Once again she was forced back to where it had all started, the only possible channel of attack.

John Provost. She headed for the isolation cubicle.

Thirty-six hours, and she had barely slept; when exhaustion demanded rest, her mind would not permit it, and she would toss in darkness, groping for land, for something solid to grasp and cling to.

Provost sucked up most of her time—wasted hours, hours that drained her physically and emotionally. She made no progress, found no chink in the brutal armor. When she was not with him she was in the projection booth, studying the Analogue tapes stored and filed from the beginning, studying the monitor tapes, watching and listening, trying somehow to build a composite picture of this enigmatic Enemy that had appeared from the depths of space, struck, and then drawn back to the inaccessible surface of Saturn. There were too many pictures, that was the trouble. None of them fit. None corresponded to the others. She was trying to make sense from nonsense, and always the task seemed more hopeless than before.

And yet, slowly, a pattern began to emerge.

An alien creature, coming by intent or accident into a star system with intelligent life, advanced technology. The odds were astronomical against its ever happening. Probably not a truly unique occurrence in the universe, but very possibly unique for these alien creatures.

What then?

A pattern that was inevitable. . . .

She answered a violent summons from Vanaman. He demanded progress with John Provost, and she told him there was no progress. He paced the floor, lashing out at her with all the fury that had been building up as the hours had passed. "That's what you're here for," he told her harshly. "That's why we have DepPsych—to deal with emergencies. We've got to have progress with that man."

Dorie Kendall sighed. "I'm doing everything I can. Provost has a good, strong mind. He has it focussed down on one tiny pinpoint of awareness, and he won't budge it from there."

"*He* won't!" Vanaman roared. "What about *you?* You people are supposed to have techniques. You can break him away from it."

"Do you want him dead?" she asked. "That's what you'll get if I drive him too hard. He's clinging to his life, and I mean that literally. To him, I am the Turner girl, and all that is sustaining him is this vicious drive to destroy me, as quickly as he can, as horribly as he can. You can use your imagination, I think."

Vanaman stared at her. She met his haggard eyes defiantly. Vanaman broke first. It was almost pitiable, the change; he seemed to age before her eyes. The creases in his face seemed to harden and deepen, and his heavy hands—threatening weapons before—fell limp. Like a spirited dog that had been whipped and broken by a brutal master, he crumbled. "All right. I can't fight you." He spread his hands helplessly. "You know that I'm beaten, don't you? I'm cornered, and there's no place to turn. I know why Provost dreaded those long waits between shifts now. That's all I can do—wait for the blow to fall."

"What blow?" said the girl.

"Maybe you can tell me." A strangled sound came from Vanaman's throat. "Everything we've done against them has been useless. Our attempt to contact them, our probing for them and fighting them on the surface—useless. When they got ready to hit us here, they hit us. All our precautions and defenses didn't hinder them." He glared at her. "All right, you tell me. What is it we're waiting for? When is the blow coming? From where?"

"I don't think there's going to be any blow," said Dorie Kendall.

"Then you're either blind or stupid," Vanaman snapped. "They've driven a gaping hole in our defenses. They know that. Do you think they're just going to let the advantage slide?"

"Human beings might not, but they're not human beings. You seem to keep forgetting that."

Words died on Vanaman's lips. He blinked and frowned. "I don't follow you," he said after a moment.

"So far, everything they've done fits a pattern," Dorie said. "They have physical destructive power, but the only times they've used it was to prevent physical contact. So then after they struck, what did they do? Press forward? Humans might, but they didn't. Instead, they moved back to the least accessible geographical region they could find in the solar system, a planetary surface we could not negotiate, and then they waited. When we sent down Analogue probers, they fought us, in a way, but what has made that fight so difficult? Can you tell me?"

"The fact that we didn't know what we were fighting, I suppose," Vanaman said slowly. "The Analogue operatives didn't know what was coming next, never two attacks the same."

"Exactly," said the girl. "They knocked us off balance and kept us there. They didn't use their advantage then. Everything was kept tightly localized until the Analogue operatives began to get their feet on the ground. You saw the same tapes I did. Those men were beginning to know what they were doing down there; they knew they could count on their conditioning and the Relief rooms to keep them from breaking, no matter how powerful the onslaught. So now, *only now*, the Enemy has torn that to ribbons, through the Turner girl." She smiled. "You see what I mean about a pattern?"

"Maybe so," Vanaman conceded, "but I don't see why."

"Look—when you poke a turtle with a stick, what happens? He pulls in his head and sits there. Just that one little aggressive act on your part gives you a world of information about how turtles behave. You could write a book about turtles, right there. But suppose it happened to be a snapping turtle you poked, and he took the end of the stick off. You wouldn't need to poke him a second time to guess what he would do, would you? You already know. Why bother with a second poke?"

"Then you're saying that the Enemy won't strike again because they have what they want," said Vanaman.

"Of course," the girl said bleakly. "They have Provost. Through Provost they have every mind on this Satellite. They don't need to fight on the surface any more, they're right here."

Vanaman's eyes were hard as he rose from his seat. "Well, we can stop that. We can kill Provost."

She caught his arm as he reached for the intercom switch. "Don't be ridiculous," she said tightly. "*What do you think you're going to do when you've killed him?*"

"I don't know," he snarled. "But I'll do something. I've got to get them out into the open somehow, out where I can see them, before we *all* split open at the seams."

"You mean find out whether they have green skins and five legs or not? Who cares?" She twisted his arm with amazing strength, pushing him back into the seat. "Listen to me, you fool. What we have to know is what they want, how they think, how they behave. Physical contact with them is pointless until we know those things. Can't you see that? *They've realized that from the start.*"

He stared at her. "But what do *you* think we should do?"

"First, find out some of the things we have to

know," she said. "That means we have to use the one real weapon we've got—John Provost—and I'm going to see that he's kept alive. Show me your arm."

Puzzled, Vanaman held it out to her. The needle bit so quickly he could not pull back. Realization dawned on his face.

"Sorry," she said gently. "There's only one thing we can do, and killing Provost isn't it." She pushed him back in the seat like a sack of flour. "I wish it were," she added softly, but Vanaman wasn't listening any more.

VI

As she moved down the corridor the magnitude of what she was doing caught Dorie and shook her violently. Things had crystallized in her mind just before she had gone to talk with Vanaman. A course of action had appeared which she only grasped in outline, and she had moved too fast, too concisely, before thinking it out in full. But now she had tripped the switch. The juggernaut was moving in on her now, ponderously, but gaining momentum.

There would be no stopping it now, she knew, no turning it back. A course of action, once initiated, developed power of its own. She was committed. . . .

Earth was committed. . . .

She shook off that thought, forcefully. She was too terrified to think about that aspect of it. Her mind was filled and frozen by the ordeal she knew was facing her now: John Provost.

Somehow she had to take Provost back from them, wrench him out of their grasp. She remembered the hard, flat look in his eyes when he watched her, and she shuddered.

There was a way to do it.

All around her she could feel the tension of the Satellite ship, waiting helplessly, poised for demolition. She ran down the empty corridors, searched the depths of the ship until she found the place she was seeking. Once inside Atmosphere Control section she leaned against the wall, panting.

Then she slipped the filters into her nostrils, and broke the tiny capsules, feeding them into the ventilation ducts of the ship.

She would take Provost back from the Enemy; then, if she survived—what? There were only hazy outlines in her mind. She knew the limitation of thought that was blocking her. It was the limitation that was utterly unavoidable in thinking of an alien, a creature not of Earth, not human. The limitation was so terribly easy to overlook until the alien was there facing her: the simple fact that she was bound and strapped by a human mind. She could only think human thoughts, in human ways. She could only comprehend the alien insofar as the alien possessed *human* qualities, not an inch further. There was no way she could stretch her mind to cope with alien-ness. But worse—even in trying desperately to comprehend alien-ness, her own human mind inevitably assumed a human mind on the part of the alien.

This the Enemy did not have. What kind of mind the Enemy did have she could not know, but it was not a human mind. Yet that alien mind *had* to be contacted and understood.

It had seemed an insoluble conundrum—until she had realized that the Enemy had faced exactly the same problem, and solved it.

To the Enemy, stumbling upon intelligent life in Earth's solar system, a human mind was as incomprehensible as an alien mind was to a human. *They* had faced the same dilemma, and found a way to cope with it. *But how?* The very pattern of their approach showed how. It was data, and Dorie Kendall had treated it as data, and found the answer.

It revealed them.

They tried so hard to remain obscure while they studied us, she thought as she moved back toward the Analogue Section, *and yet with every move they made they revealed themselves to us further, if we had only had the wit to look. Everything they did was a revelation of themselves. They thought they were peering at us through a one-way portal, seeing us and yet remaining unseen, but in reality the glass was a mirror, reflecting their own natures in every move they made. They discovered our vulnerability, true, but at the same time inadvertently revealed their own.*

The ventilators hummed. She felt the tension in the ship relaxing as the sleep-gas seeped down the corridors. Muscles uncoiled. Fear dissolved from frightened minds. Doors banged open; there was talking, laughter; then lethargy, dullness, glazed eyes, yawns, slack mouths—

Sleep. Like Vanaman, slumped back in his chair, everyone on the Satellite slept. Operatives fell forward on their faces. The girls in the Relief rooms yawned, dozed, snored, slept.

It seemed to Dorie that she could sense Provost's thoughts twisting out toward her in a tight, malignant channel, driving to destroy her, seeking release from the dreadful hatred the aliens were using to bind him. But then even Provost dozed and slept.

With the filters protecting her, she was alone on the ship, a ghost. In the Analogue bank she activated the circuits she needed, set the dials, rechecked each setting to make certain that she made no error.

She dared not make an error.

Finally, she went to Provost. She dragged his drugged body into the Analogue cubicle and strapped him down. She fit his hands into the grips. Another needle, then, to counteract the sleep-gas, and his eyes blinked open.

He saw her and lunged for her with no warning sound. His arms tore at the restraints, jerking murderously. She jumped back from him a little, forcing out a twisted smile. She reached out mockingly to stroke his forehead, and he tried to bite her hand.

"Butcher!" she whispered. "Monster!"

Pure hate poured from his mouth as she laughed at him. Then she threw the Analogue switch. He jerked back as contact was made, and she moved swiftly to her own Analogue helmet waiting in the adjacent cubicle, threw another switch, felt in her own mind the sickening thud of Analogue contact.

Her Analogue. A therapeutic tool before, now a deadly weapon in frightened, unsteady hands.

She was afraid. It seemed that she was watching images on a hazy screen. She saw Provost

there, facing her, hating her, but it was only a
mental image. She was sitting alone in darkness
and knew that he also was sitting in darkness.
Then gradually the darkness seemed to dissolve
into unreality; the two Analogue images—hers
and Provost's—became sharp and clear.

It was like a dream, a waking nightmare.
Provost was moving in on her slowly, his mouth
twisting in hatred, great knots of muscle standing out in his arms. He seemed to tower over her
for a moment in vicious anticipation. She
screamed and broke down the corridor. He was
after her like a cat. He leaped, struck her legs,
threw her down on the metal floor and fell on
her. She saw his arm upraised, felt the fist crash
down again and again and again. Broken flesh,
broken bones, paste, pulp, again and again. And
in the dark Analogue cubicle she seemed to feel
every blow.

She closed her eyes, her control reeling. There
would be no Relief for her later, she knew that.
She fought him, then abandoned fighting and
just hung on doggedly, waiting for the end.

Abruptly, he was gone. She had felt his release
as his hatred had burned itself out on her. He
had stopped, and stood still, suddenly mild,
puzzled, tired, wondering as he looked down at
the thing on the floor. And then . . .

She knew he had started for the surface.

VII

To Provost it was like awakening from warm
and peaceful sleep into terror.

He was horrified and appalled to realize that

he had been sleeping. What had happened? Why didn't Control respond? Frantically he seized the hand grips, drove his Analogue down toward the surface. In his mind were fragments of memory. Something hideous had happened, long long ago, something in the Relief room. Afterwards he had been held down in a tangle-field, and time after time the Turner girl had come back to him in the isolation cubicle—or *had* it been the Turner girl? Then just now he had found her and the tangle-field was gone, and the hideous thing had been repeated.

And the horrible, abrupt awakening to the fact that the Satellite ship was utterly helpless and undefended from the Enemy.

How long had he slept? What had happened? Didn't they realize that every passing second might be precious to the Enemy, fatal to the Satellite?

He felt someone following him, screaming out at him in alarm. Not the Turner girl, as he had thought, but Dorie Kendall, the DepPsych agent, following him down to the surface with her own Analogue.

Provost hesitated, fighting the sense of urgency in his mind. "Don't stop me," he told her. "I've got to get down there. There's no one covering—"

"You can't go down," she cried. "You have no support here. No conditioning, no Relief. We've got to do something very different."

"Different?" He felt her very close to him now and he paused in confusion. What did she know about the Enemy? "What's happening here? The Enemy is down there. *Why have we stopped fighting?*"

She was telling him, frantically, as he groped through his confusion and tried to understand. "They had to know if we had a vulnerability, *any* vulnerability. Something they could use against us to protect themselves if they had to. They knew they could never risk direct contact with us until they knew that we were vulnerable in some way."

Provost shook his head, uncomprehending. "But why not?"

"Try to see *their* view," she said. "Suppose we were hostile, and invulnerable. We might not stop at destroying their ships, we might follow them home and destroy them there. They couldn't know, and they couldn't take a risk like that. They had to find a vulnerability to use as a weapon before any contact was possible. So they drew us out, prodded us, observed us, trying to find out limitations—if we had any. And they discovered our vulnerability—*panic*. A weakness in our natures, the point where intelligence deserts us and renders us irrational, helpless to fight any more. This is what they could use to control us, except that they must have the same vulnerability!"

He hesitated. The driving urge to go on down to the surface was almost overwhelming, to grapple with them and try once again to break through their barrier there. "Why should they have the same weakness we have? They're aliens, not humans."

"Because they have been doing *exactly the same thing that we would have done if we had been in their place*. Think, John! In all the star systems they must have searched, no sign of intelligent life. Then, suddenly, a solar system that is teeming

with life. Intelligent? Obviously. Dangerous?
How could they know? *We* wouldn't have
known, would we? What would *we* have done?"

Provost faltered. "Tried to make contact,
I suppose."

"Physical contact? Nonsense. We wouldn't
have dared. We couldn't possibly risk contact
until we knew how they thought and behaved,
until we knew for certain that we could defend
ourselves against them if necessary, that they
had some kind of vulnerability. Once we knew
that, the way would be open for contact. But no
matter how eager we were for contact, and no
matter how friendly they might appear *we would
have had to have the weapon to fight them first*. Or take
an insane risk, the risk of total destruction."

He understood her, but it didn't make sense.
He thought of Miranda outpost, Titan Colony,
and shook his head. "It doesn't add up," he said.
"What they did here was incredible."

"Only if you assumed that they were hostile,"
she said softly.

"What about the contact ship, the colony on
Titan? They burned them both, blew them to
kingdom come."

"Because they had to. They did what we
would have done under the same circumstances.
They goaded us. Then they took cover and
waited to see what we would do. They made us
come after them where we couldn't reach them
physically, to see what we could do. They deliberately kept one step ahead, making us reveal
ourselves every step of the way, until they found
the soft spot they were seeking and threw us into
panic. What they failed to realize was that they

were inevitably mirroring themselves in everything they did."

Silence then. In the dark cubicle, Provost could see the hazy image of the girl in his mind, pleading with him, trying to make him understand. Gradually it began to make sense. "So they have their weapon," he said slowly, "and still we can't make contact with them because *we* have none against *them*."

"*Had* none," the girl corrected him. "But we have seen them in the mirror. Their thoughts and actions and approach have been humanlike. They recognized our panic for what it was when they saw it. How could they have, unless they themselves knew what panic was—from their own experience?"

"And now?"

"We turn the tables," she said. "If they also have a vulnerability, there will be no more barrier to contact. But we don't dare *assume*, we have to *know*. Every time they have goaded us we have reacted. We've got to stop that now. We've got to withdraw from them completely, leave them with nothing to work with, nothing to grasp."

"But the Satellite—"

"The Satellite is dead for the time being, asleep. There's no one here but us for them to contact. Now we have to withdraw too. If we do that, can't you see what *they* will have to do?"

Slowly he nodded. He sensed that she hadn't told him all of it, but that, too, was all right. Better that there be *nothing* that the Enemy could draw from his mind. "You tell me what to do, and when," he said.

"Close your mind down, as completely as you can. Barricade it against them, if you can. Keep them out, leave nothing open for them to probe. Cut them off cold. But be ready when I signal you."

He twisted in the cramped seat in the cubicle, clamping down his control as he felt Dorie clamping down hers. It was an exercise in patience and concentration, but slowly he felt his mind clearing. Like a rheostat imperceptibly dimming the lights in a theater, the Satellite went dimmer, dimmer, almost dead. Only a flicker of activity remained, tiny and insignificant.

They waited.

It might have been hours, or even days, before the probing from the Enemy began. Provost felt it first, for he had known it before, tiny exploratory waves from the alien minds, tentative, easy to strike away. He caught himself just in time, allowed himself no response, trying to make his mind a blank grey surface, a sheet of nothing.

More probing then, more urgency. Sensations of surprise, of confusion, of concern. Unanswered questions, fleeting whispers of doubt in the alien minds. Slowly confusion gave way to doubt, then to fear.

This was something the Enemy clearly had not anticipated, this sudden unequivocal collapse. The probing grew more frantic in its intensity. Deepening of doubt, and then, amazingly, regretfulness, self-reproach, uncertainty. *What has happened? Could we have destroyed them? Could we have driven them too far?*

The probing stopped abruptly. Provost felt the DepPsych girl stir; vaguely his eyes registered the darkness of the cubicle around him, the oval viewport in the wall showing the pale yellow globe of Saturn lying below, its rings spreading like a delicate filigree. . . .

Nothing.

In his own mind he felt a stir of panic, and fought it down. What if the DepPsych girl were wrong? It was only a human mind which had assumed that creatures which behaved alike were alike. In the silence a thousand alternative possibilities flooded his mind. The minutes passed and the panic rose again, stronger. . . .

Then he saw it in the viewport. Up from the methane clouds they came, slowly, four great ships in perfect formation. They rose and stabilized in orbit, moved again, stabilized, moved again.

They were approaching the Satellite.

He felt his fingers clench on the grips as he watched, his mind leaping exultantly. *She had been right. They were forced out.* The offensive had shifted, and now *the Enemy* were forced to move.

Provost saw with perfect clarity the part the DepPsych girl hadn't told him—the thing he and she were going to do.

They waited until the ships were very close. Then:

"Provost! *Now!*"

They struck out together, as a unit, hard. They hit with all the power they could muster, striking the sensitive alien minds without warning. They could feel the sudden crashing impact of their attack. He could never have done it alone; together their power was staggering. The alien minds were open, confused, defensive; they reeled back in pain and fear—

In panic.

Suddenly the four great ships broke apart.
They moved out in erratic courses, driving back
for the planet's surface. They scuttled like bugs
when a rock is overturned, beyond control and
frantic. In a matter of minutes they were gone
again, and the silence rose like a cloud from the
surface.

VIII

Somewhere in the Satellite a bell was ringing.
John Provost heard it, dreamily, as he rose and
stretched his cramped muscles. He met Dorie
Kendall in the corridor, and he could tell from
the look on her face that she knew it was over,
too.

The aliens were vulnerable. They were vulnerable to the same primitive and irrational defense
reactions that humans were vulnerable to when
faced with a crisis: the suspension of reason and
logic that constituted panic. The knowledge was
the weapon that Earthmen needed to make contact possible.

Now each side had a weapon. The mirror had
reflected the aliens accurately, and the meaning
of the reflection was unmistakably clear. There
need be no danger in contact now. Now there
could be a beginning to understanding.

Without a word John Provost and the girl
began to waken the crew of the Satellite.

Alan E. Nourse started pre-medical studies at Rutgers in 1945, but interrupted them to serve two years in the Navy's hospital corps. Afterwards he returned to Rutgers for his B.S., and took his M.D. at the U. of Pennsylvania Medical School in 1955. He interned in Seattle, and then devoted two years to freelance writing before entering general practice at North Bend, Washington in 1958. In 1963, he returned to full-time writing.

His first national publication was a short story, "High Threshold," published in Astounding *in 1951, and this was followed by some sixty short stories and novelettes which appeared in virtually all the magazines of the time. In addition, he published a short novel,* A Man Obsessed *and, in collaboration, wrote* The Invaders Are Coming *(both for Ace). His writing helped to pay for his medical education and, of course, reflects a strong medical orientation.*

Dr. Nourse has published thirty-five or so works of fiction and nonfiction, including a dozen or so juveniles and three volumes of short stories. Two of his latest titles are The Practice, *a mainstream novel (Harper & Row, 1978), and* Inside the Mayo Clinic.

"Mirror, Mirror . . ." reflects a deep concern with the psychological aspects of warfare between intelligent beings; and the third volume of The Future at War, Orion's Sword, *will contain a Nourse article similarly oriented.*

The nature of extraterrestrial life, and of possible (or should we say probable?) extraterrestrial intelligences, poses a problem with which space-oriented thinkers—scientists, science fiction writers, futurists—are naturally much concerned. Let us assume that they exist. Let us assume, also, that they are technologically far more advanced than we, and that their moral codes (in terms, not of what we ourselves practice, but of our ideals) are far superior to our own. What should our attitude toward them be now that, for the first time in man's history, we can peer out over the edge of our gravity-well and behold the vast space-ocean, suddenly only one frog-jump ahead of us?

Here, in this article (which is the first chapter in his pioneering book The Cosmic Connection*) Dr. Carl Sagan gives us his answer. It is an answer based, not on man's practices, but on our ideals and what we recognize in their expression: the interdependence of all living beings and the sanctity of life.*

Carl Sagan

MAN: A TRANSITIONAL ANIMAL

Five billion years ago, when the Sun turned on, the Solar System was transformed from inky blackness to a flood of light. In the inner parts of the Solar System, the early planets were irregular collections of rock and metal—the debris, the minor constituents of the initial cloud, the material that had not been blown away after the Sun ignited.

These planets heated as they formed. Gases trapped in their interiors were exuded to form atmospheres. Their surfaces melted. Volcanoes were common.

The early atmospheres were composed of the most abundant atoms and were rich in hydrogen. Sunlight, falling on the molecules of the early atmosphere, excited them, induced molecular collisions, and produced larger molecules. Under the inexorable laws of chemistry and physics these molecules interacted, fell into the oceans, and further developed to produce larger molecules—molecules much more complex than the initial atoms of which they had formed, but still microscopic by any human standard.

These molecules, remarkably enough, are the ones of which we are made: The building blocks of the nucleic acids, which are our hereditary material, and the building blocks of the proteins, the molecular journeymen that perform the work of the cell, were produced from the atmosphere and oceans of the early Earth. We know this because we can make these molecules today by duplicating the primitive conditions.

Eventually, many billions of years ago, a molecule was formed that had a remarkable capability. It was able to produce, out of the molecular building blocks of the surrounding waters, a fairly accurate copy of itself. In such a molecular system there is a set of instructions, a molecular code, containing the sequence of building blocks from which the larger molecule is constructed. When, by accident, there is a change in the sequence, the copy is likewise changed. Such a molecular system—capable of replication, mutation, and replication of its mutations—can be called "alive." It is a collection of molecules that can evolve by natural selection. Those molecules able to replicate faster, or to reprocess building blocks from their surroundings into a more useful variety, reproduced more efficiently than their competitors— and eventually dominated.

But conditions gradually changed. Hydrogen escaped to space. Production of the molecular building blocks declined. The foodstuffs formerly available in great abundance dwindled. Life was expelled from the molecular Garden of

Eden. Only those simple collections of molecules able to transform their surroundings, able to produce efficient molecular machines for the conversion of simple into complex molecules, were able to survive. By isolating themselves from their surroundings, by maintaining the earlier idyllic conditions, those molecules that surrounded themselves by membranes had an advantage. The first cells arose.

With molecular building blocks no longer available for free, organisms had to work hard to make such building blocks. Plants are the result. Plants start with air and water, minerals and sunlight, and produce molecular building blocks of high complexity. Animals, such as human beings, are parasites on the plants.

Changing climate and competition among what was now a wide diversity of organisms produced greater and greater specialization, a sophistication of function, and an elaboration of form. A rich array of plants and animals began to cover the Earth. Out of the initial oceans in which life arose, new environments, such as the land and the air, were colonized. Organisms now live from the top of Mount Everest to the deepest portions of the abyssal depths. Organisms live in hot, concentrated solutions of sulfuric acid and in dry Antarctic valleys. Organisms live on the water absorbed on a single crystal of salt.

Life forms developed that were finely attuned to their specific environments, exquisitely adapted to the conditions. But the conditions changed. The organisms were too specialized. They died. Other organisms were less well adapted, but they were more generalized. The conditions changed, the climate varied, but the organisms were able to continue. Many more species of organisms have died during the history of the Earth than are alive today. The secret of evolution is time and death.

Among the adaptations that seem to be useful is one that we call intelligence. Intelligence is an extension of an evolutionary tendency apparent in the simplest organisms—the tendency toward control of the environment. The standby biological method of control has been the hereditary material: Information passed on by nucleic acids from generation to generation—information on how to build a nest; information on the fear of falling, or of snakes, or of the dark; information on how to fly south for the winter. But intelligence requires information of an adaptive quality developed during the lifetime of a single individual. A variety of organisms on the Earth today have this quality we call intelligence: the dolphins have it, and so do the great apes. But it is most evident in the organism called Man.

In Man, not only is adaptive information acquired in the lifetime of a single individual, but it is passed on extragenetically through learning, through books, through education. It is this, more than anything else, that has raised Man to his present pre-eminent status on the planet Earth.

We are the product of 4.5 billion years of fortuitous, slow, biological evolution. There is no reason to think that the evolutionary process has stopped. Man is a transitional animal. He is not the climax of creation.

The Earth and the Sun have life expectancies

of many more billions of years. The future development of man will likely be a cooperative arrangement among controlled biological evolution, genetic engineering, and an intimate partnership between organisms and intelligent machines. But no one is in a position to make accurate predictions of this future evolution. All that is clear is that we cannot remain static.

In our earliest history, so far as we can tell, individuals held an allegiance toward their immediate tribal group, which may have numbered no more than ten or twenty individuals, all of whom were related by consanguinity. As time went on, the need for cooperative behavior—in the hunting of large animals or large herds, in agriculture, and in the development of cities—forced human beings into larger and larger groups. The group that was identified with, the tribal unit, enlarged at each stage of this evolution. Today, a particular instant in the 4.5-billion-year history of Earth and in the several-million-year history of mankind, most human beings owe their primary allegiance to the nation-state (although some of the most dangerous political problems still arise from tribal conflicts involving smaller population units).

Many visionary leaders have imagined a time when the allegiance of an individual human being is not to his particular nation-state, religion, race, or economic group, but to mankind as a whole; when the benefit to a human being of another sex, race, religion, or political persuasion ten thousand miles away is as precious to us as to our neighbor or our brother. The trend is in this direction, but it is agonizingly slow. There is a serious question whether such a global self-identification of mankind can be achieved before we destroy ourselves with the technological forces our intelligence has unleashed.

In a very real sense human beings are machines constructed by the nucleic acids to arrange for the efficient replication of more nucleic acids. In a sense our strongest urges, noblest enterprises, most compelling necessities, and apparent free wills are all an expression of the information coded in the genetic material: We are, in a way, temporary ambulatory repositories for our nucleic acids. This does not deny our humanity; it does not prevent us from pursuing the good, the true, and the beautiful. But it would be a great mistake to ignore where we have come from in our attempt to determine where we are going.

There is no doubt that our instinctual apparatus has changed little from the hunger-gatherer days of several hundred thousand years ago. Our society has changed enormously from those times, and the greatest problems of survival in the contemporary world can be understood in terms of this conflict—between what we feel we must do because of our primeval instincts and what we know we must do because of our extragenetic learning.

If we survive these perilous times, it is clear that even an identification with all of mankind is not the ultimate desirable identification. If we have a profound respect for other human beings as co-equal recipients of this precious patrimony of 4.5 billion years of evolution, why should the identification not apply also to all the other organisms on Earth, which are equally the product of 4.5 billion years of evolution? We care for a small fraction of the organisms on Earth—dogs, cats, and cows, for example—because they are useful or because they flatter us. But spiders and salamanders, salmon and sunflowers are equally our brothers and sisters.

I believe that the difficulty we all experience in extending our identification horizons in this way is itself genetic. Ants of one tribe will fight to the death intrusions by ants of another. Human history is filled with monstrous cases of small differences—in skin pigmentation, or abstruse theological speculation, or manner of dress and hair style—being the cause of harassment, enslavement, and murder.

A being quite like us, but with a small physiological difference—a third eye, say, or blue hair covering the nose and forehead—somehow evokes feelings of revulsion. Such feelings may have had adaptive value at one time in defending our small tribe against the beasts and neighbors. But in our times, such feelings are obsolete and dangerous.

The time has come for a respect, a reverence, not just for all human beings, but for all life forms—as we would have respect for a masterpiece of sculpture or an exquisitely tooled machine. This, of course, does not mean that we should abandon the imperatives for our own survival. Respect for the tetanus bacillus does not extend to volunteering our body as a culture medium. But at the same time we can recall that here is an organism with a biochemistry that tracks back deep into our planet's past. The tetanus bacillus is poisoned by molecular oxygen, which we breathe so freely. The tetanus bacillus, but not we, would be at home in the hydrogen-rich, oxygen-free atmosphere of primitive Earth.

A reverence for all life is implemented in a few of the religions of the planet Earth—for example, among the Jains of India. And something like this idea is responsible for vegetarianism, at least in the minds of many practitioners of this dietary constraint. But why is it better to kill plants than animals?

Human beings can survive only by killing other organisms. But we can make ecological compensation by also growing other organisms; by encouraging the forest; by preventing the wholesale slaughter of organisms such as seals and whales, imagined to have industrial or commercial value; by outlawing gratuitous hunting, and by making the environment of Earth more livable—for all its inhabitants.

There may be a time when contact will be made with another intelligence on a planet of some far-distant star, beings with billions of years of quite independent evolution, beings with no prospect of looking very much like us—although they may think very much like us. It is important that we extend our identification horizons, not just down to the simplest and most humble forms of life on our own planet, but also up to the exotic and advanced forms of life that may inhabit, with us, our vast galaxy of stars.

Carl Sagan is as well known for his literary as for his scientific accomplishments. Winner of the Pulitzer Prize (for The Dragons of Eden*), he has also received the NASA Medals for Exceptional Scientific Achievement and for Distinguished Public Service, and the Joseph Priestly Award "for distinguished contributions to the welfare of mankind." He is Professor of Astronomy and Space Sciences and Director of the Laboratory for Planetary Studies at Cornell, and has played a leading role in the Mariner, Viking, and Voyager planetary expeditions. He is a past Chairman of the Division for Planetary Sciences of the American Astronomical Society, President-elect of the Planetology Section of the American Geophysical Union, and editor-in-chief of* Icarus, *the principal professional journal of solar system studies.*

A leader in establishing the high surface temperatures of Venus and in understanding the seasonal changes on Mars, Dr. Sagan was responsible for the Voyager interstellar record, a message about ourselves sent to other civilizations in space (and described in the book Murmurs of Earth*). Among his current projects is* Cosmos, *a thirteen-part television series to be aired on PBS, and throughout the world.*

*Anthony Boucher (William Anthony Parker White)
was a deeply religious man, a devout Catholic, who believed not only in God, but in His infinite mercy. He was
also, of course, a reader of science fiction, an excellent
writer of science fiction, and an eminent science fiction
editor. His concern, in more than one story, was for the
universal "humanity," not just of men on Earth, but of
intelligent beings anywhere and everywhere, regardless of
their form or planet of origin. (In one delightful story of
his, set in a far future when virtually no scientific or
philosophical problems remained to be solved, a desperate
student resorted to black magic and conjured up a very
ugly little demon. What did they do with him? They
psychoanalyzed him—and, as they did so, his black,
batlike wings fell away and changed to pure, white,
feathery ones. Finally, over the door of the institute, they
carved the motto:* There are no devils. There are
only sick angels.*)
So this story concerns itself with the souls of men at
war with—men?*

Anthony Boucher

BALAAM

"What is a 'man'?" Rabbi Chaim Acosta demanded, turning his back on the window and its
view of pink sand and infinite pink boredom.
"You and I, Mule, in our respective ways, work

for the salvation of *men*—as you put it, for the
brotherhood of *man* under the fatherhood of God.
Very well, let us define our terms: Whom, or
more precisely, *what*, are we interested in sav-
ing?"

Father Aloysius Malloy shifted uncomfortably
and reluctantly closed the *American Football Year-
book* which had been smuggled in on the last
rocket, against all weight regulations, by one of
his communicants. I honestly like Chaim, he
thought, not merely (or is that the right word?)
with brotherly love, nor even out of the deep
gratitude I owe him, but with special individual
liking; and I respect him. He's a brilliant man—
too brilliant to take a dull post like this in his
stride. But he *will* get off into discussions which
are much too much like what one of my Jesuit
professors called "disputations."

"What did you say, Chaim?" he asked.

The Rabbi's black Sephardic eyes sparkled.
"You know very well what I said, Mule; and
you're stalling for time. Please indulge me. Our
religious duties here are not so arduous as we
might wish; and since you won't play chess . . ."

". . . and you," said Father Malloy unexpectedly, "refuse to take any interest in diagraming
football plays . . ."

"Touché. Or am I? Is it my fault that as an
Israeli I fail to share the peculiar American de-
lusion that football means something other than
rugby and soccer? Whereas chess—" He looked
at the priest reproachfully. "Mule," he said,
"you have led me into a digression."

"It was a try. Like the time the whole Southern California line thought I had the ball for

once and Leliwa walked over for the winning TD."

"What," Acosta repeated, "is *man*? Is it by definition a member of the genus *H. sapiens* inhabiting the planet Sol III and its colonies?"

"The next time we tried the play," said Malloy resignedly, "Leliwa was smeared for a ten-yard loss."

The two *men* met on the sands of Mars. It was an unexpected meeting, a meeting in itself uneventful, and yet one of the turning points in the history of *men* and their universe.

The *man* from the colony base was on a routine patrol—a patrol imposed by the captain for reasons of discipline and activity-for-activity's-sake rather than from any need for protection in this uninhabited waste. He had seen, over beyond the next rise, what he would have sworn was the braking blaze of a landing rocket—if he hadn't known that the next rocket wasn't due for another week. Six and a half days, to be exact, or even more exactly, six days, eleven hours, and twenty-three minutes. Greenwich Interplanetary. He knew the time so exactly because he, along with half the garrison, Father Malloy, and those screwball Israelis, was due for rotation then. So no matter how much it looked like a rocket, it couldn't be one; but it was something happening on his patrol, for the first time since he'd come to this god-forsaken hole, and he might as well look into it and get his name on a report.

The *man* from the spaceship also knew the boredom of the empty planet. Alone of his crew, he had been there before, on the first voyage when they took the samples and set up the observation outposts. But did that make the captain even listen to him? Hell, no; the captain knew all about the planet from the sample analyses and had no time to listen to a guy who'd really been there. So all he got out of it was the privilege of making the first reconnaissance. Big deal! One fast look around reconnoitering a few googols of sand grains and then back to the ship. But there was some kind of glow over that rise there. It couldn't be lights; theirs was the scout ship, none of the others had landed yet. Some kind of phosphorescent life they'd missed the first time round . . . ? Maybe now the captain would believe that the sample analyses didn't tell him everything.

The two *men* met at the top of the rise.

One *man* saw the horror of seemingly numberless limbs, of a headless torso, of a creature so alien that it walked in its glittering bare flesh in this freezing cold and needed no apparatus to supplement the all but nonexistent air.

One *man* saw the horror of an unbelievably meager four limbs, of a torso topped with an ugly lump like some unnatural growth, of a creature so alien that it smothered itself with heavy clothing in this warm climate and cut itself off from this invigorating air.

And both *men* screamed and ran.

"There is an interesting doctrine," said Rabbi Acosta, "advanced by one of your writers, C. S. Lewis . . ."

"He was an Episcopalian," said Father Malloy sharply.

"I apologize." Acosta refrained from pointing
out that Anglo-Catholic would have been a more
accurate term. "But I believe that many in your
church have found his writings, from your point
of view, doctrinally sound? He advances the doctrine of what he calls *hnaus*—intelligent beings
with souls who are the children of God, whatever
their physical shape or planet of origin."

"Look, Chaim," said Malloy with an effort toward patience. "Doctrine or no doctrine, there
just plain aren't any such beings. Not in this solar system anyway. And if you're going to go interstellar on me, I'd just as soon read the men's
microcomics."

"Interplanetary travel existed only in such literature once. But of course if you'd rather play
chess . . ."

"My specialty," said the man once known to
sports writers as Mule Malloy, "was running interference. Against you I need somebody to run
interference *for*."

"Let us take the sixteenth psalm of David,
which you call the fifteenth, having decided, for
reasons known only to your God and mine, that
psalms nine and ten are one. There is a phrase in
there which, if you'll forgive me, I'll quote in
Latin; your Saint Jerome is often more satisfactory than any English translator. *Benedicam Dom-
inum, qui tribuit mihi intellectum*."

"Blessed be the Lord, who schools me," murmured
Malloy, in the standard Knox translation.

"But according to Saint Jerome: *I shall bless the
Lord, who bestows on me*—just how should one
render *intellectum?*—not merely *intellect*, but *perception, comprehension* . . . what Hamlet means

when he says of *man: In apprehension how like a god!*"

Words change their meanings.

Apprehensively, one *man* reported to his captain. The captain first swore, then scoffed, then listened to the story again. Finally he said, "I'm sending a full squad back with you to the place where—maybe—you saw this thing. If it's for real, those mother-dighting, bug-eyed monsters are going to curse the day they ever set a Goddamned tentacle on Mars." The *man* decided it was no use trying to explain that the worst of it was it *wasn't* bug-eyed; any kind of eyes in any kind of head would have been something. And they weren't even quite tentacles either. . . .

Apprehensively, too, the other *man* made his report. The captain scoffed first and then swore, including some select remarks on underhatched characters who knew all about a planet because they'd been there once. Finally he said, "We'll see if a squad of real observers can find any trace of your egg-eating, limbless monsters; and if we find them, they're going to be God-damned sorry they were ever hatched." It was no use, the *man* decided, trying to explain that it wouldn't have been so bad if it *had* been limbless, like in the picture tapes; but just *four* limbs. . . .

"What is a *man?*" Rabbi Acosta repeated, and Mule Malloy wondered why his subconscious synapses had not earlier produced the obvious appropriate answer.

"*Man,*" he recited, "*is a creature composed of body and soul, and made to the image and likeness of God.*"

"From that echo of childish singsong, Mule, I judge that is a correct catechism response. Surely the catechism must follow it up with some question about that likeness? Can it be a likeness in"—his hand swept up and down over his own body with a graceful gesture of contempt—*"this body?"*

"This likeness to God," Malloy went on reciting, *"is chiefly in the soul."*

"Aha!" The Sephardic sparkle was brighter than ever.

The words went on, the centers of speech following the synaptic patterns engraved in parochial school as the needle followed the grooves of an antique record. *"All creatures bear some resemblance to God inasmuch as they exist. Plants and animals resemble Him insofar as they have life . . ."*

"I can hardly deny so profound a statement."

". . . but none of these creatures is made to the image and likeness of God. Plants and animals do not have a rational soul, such as man has, by which they might know and love God."

"As do all good *hnaus*. Go on; I am not sure that our own scholars have stated it so well. Mule, you are invaluable!"

Malloy found himself catching a little of Acosta's excitement. He had known these words all his life; he had recited them the Lord knows how many times. But he was not sure that he had ever listened to them before. And he wondered for a moment how often even his Jesuit professors, in their profound consideration of the X^n's of theology, had ever paused to reconsider these childhood ABC's.

"How is the soul like God?" he asked himself the next catechistic question, and answered, *"The*

soul is like God because it is a spirit having understanding and free will and is destined . . ."

"Reverend gentlemen!" The reverence was in the words only. The interrupting voice of Captain Dietrich Fassbänder differed little in tone from his normal address to a buck private of the Martian Legion.

Mule Malloy said, "Hi, Captain." He felt half relieved, half disappointed, as if he had been interrupted while unwrapping a present whose outlines he was just beginning to glimpse. Rabbi Acosta smiled wryly and said nothing.

"So this is how you spend your time? No Martian natives, so you have to keep in practice trying to convert each other, is that it?"

Acosta made a light gesture which might have been polite acknowledgment of what the captain evidently considered a joke. "The Martian day is so tedious we have been driven to talking shop. Your interruption is welcome. Since you so rarely seek out our company, I take it you bring some news. Is it, God grant, that the rotation rocket is arriving a week early?"

"No, damn it," Fassbänder grunted. (He seemed to take a certain pride, Malloy had observed, in carefully not tempering his language for the ears of clergymen.) "Then I'd have a German detachment instead of your Israelis, and I'd know where I stood. I suppose it's all very advisable politically for every state in the UW to contribute a detachment in rotation; but I'd sooner either have my regular legion garrison doubled, or two German detachments regularly rotating. That time I had the pride of Pakistan here . . . Damn it, you new states haven't had time to develop a military tradition!"

"Father Malloy," the Rabbi asked gently, "are you acquainted with the sixth book of what you term the Old Testament?"

"Thought you fellows were tired of talking shop," Fassbänder objected.

"Rabbi Acosta refers to the Book of Joshua, Captain. And I'm afraid, God help us, that there isn't a state or a tribe that hasn't a tradition of war. Even your Prussian ancestors might have learned a trick or two from the campaigns of Joshua—or for that matter, from the Cattle Raid on Cooley, when the Hound of Cullen beat off the armies of Queen Maeve. And I've often thought, too, that it'd do your strategists no harm to spend a season or two at quarterback, if they had the wind. Did you know that Eisenhower played football, and against Jim Thorpe once, at that? And . . ."

"But I don't imagine," Acosta interposed, "that you came here to talk shop either, Captain?"

"Yes," said Captain Fassbänder, sharply and unexpectedly. "My shop and, damn it, yours. Never thought I'd see the day when I . . ." He broke off and tried another approach. "I mean, of course, a chaplain is part of an army. You're both army officers, technically speaking, one in the Martian Legion, one in the Israeli forces; but it's highly unusual to ask a man of the cloth to . . ."

"To praise the Lord and pass the ammunition, as the folk legend has it? There are precedents among my people, and among Father Malloy's as well, though rather different ideas are attributed to the founder of his church. What is it, Captain? Or wait, I know: We are besieged by alien invaders and Mars needs every able-bodied man to defend her sacred sands. Is that it?"

"Well . . . God damn it. . . ." Captain Fassbänder's cheeks grew purple. ". . . YES!" he exploded.

The situation was so hackneyed in 3V and microcomics that it was less a matter of explaining it than of making it seem real. Dietrich Fassbänder's powers of exposition were not great, but his sincerity was evident and in itself convincing.

"Didn't believe it myself at first," he admitted. "But he was right. Our patrol ran into a patrol of . . . of *them*. There was a skirmish; we lost two men but killed one of the things. Their small arms use explosive propulsion of metal much like ours; God knows what they might have in that ship to counter our A-warheads. But we've got to put up a fight for Mars; and that's where you come in."

The two priests looked at him wordlessly, Acosta with a faint air of puzzled withdrawal, Malloy almost as if he expected the captain to start diagraming the play on a blackboard.

"You especially, Rabbi. I'm not worried about your boys, Father. We've got a Catholic chaplain on this rotation because this bunch of legionnaires is largely Poles and Irish-Americans. They'll fight all right, and we'll expect you to say a field mass beforehand, and that's about all. Oh, and that fool gunner Olszewski has some idea he'd like his A-cannon sprinkled with holy water; I guess you can handle that without any trouble.

"But your Israelis are a different problem, Acosta. They don't know the meaning of discipline—not what we call discipline in the legion; and Mars doesn't mean to them what it does to a legionnaire. And, besides, a lot of them have got a . . . hell, guess I shouldn't call it superstition, but a kind of . . . well, reverence—awe, you might say—about you, Rabbi. They say you're a miracle-worker."

"He is," said Mule Malloy simply. "He saved my life."

He could still feel that extraordinary invisible power (a "force-field," one of the technicians later called it, as he cursed the shots that had destroyed the machine past all analysis) which had bound him helpless there in that narrow pass, too far from the dome for rescue by any patrol. It was his first week on Mars, and he had hiked too long, enjoying the long, easy strides of low gravity and alternately meditating on the versatility of the Creator of planets and on that Year Day long ago when he had blocked out the most famous of All-American line-backers to bring about the most impressive of Rose Bowl upsets. Sibiryakov's touchdown made the headlines; but he and Sibiryakov knew why that touchdown happened, and he felt his own inner warmth . . . and was that sinful pride or just self-recognition? And then he was held as no line had ever held him and the hours passed and no one on Mars could know where he was and when the patrol arrived they said, "The Israeli chaplain sent us." And later Chaim Acosta, laconic for the first and only time, said simply, "I knew where you were. It happens to me sometimes."

Now Acosta shrugged and his graceful hands waved deprecation. "Scientifically speaking, Captain, I believe that I have, on occasion, a certain amount of extrasensory perception and conceivably a touch of some of the other *psi* faculties. The Rhinists at Tel Aviv are quite interested in me; but my faculties too often refuse to perform on laboratory command. But 'miracle-working' is a strong word. Remind me to tell you some time the story of the guaranteed genuine miracle-working rabbi from Lwow."

"Call it miracles, call it ESP, you've got something, Acosta . . ."

"I shouldn't have mentioned Joshua," the rabbi smiled. "Surely you aren't suggesting that I try a miracle to win your battle for you?"

"Hell with that," snorted Fassbänder. "It's your men. They've got it fixed in their minds that you're a . . . a saint. No, you Jews don't have saints, do you?"

"A nice question in semantics," Chaim Acosta observed quietly.

"Well, a prophet. Whatever you people call it. And we've got to make men out of your boys. Stiffen their backbones, send 'em in there knowing they're going to win."

"Are they?" Acosta asked flatly.

"God knows. But they sure as hell won't if they don't think so. So it's up to you."

"What is?"

"They may pull a sneak attack on us, but I don't think so. Way I see it, they're as surprised and puzzled as we are; and they need time to

think the situation over. We'll attack before
dawn tomorrow; and to make sure your Israelis
go in there with fighting spirit, you're going to
curse them."

"Curse my men?"

"Potztausend Sapperment noch einmal!" Captain
Fassbänder's English was flawless, but not adequate to such a situation as this. "Curse *them!*
The . . . the *things,* the aliens, the invaders, whatever the *urverdammt* bloody hell you want to call
them!"

He could have used far stronger language
without offending either chaplain. Both had suddenly realized that he was perfectly serious.

"A formal curse, Captain?" Chaim Acosta
asked. "Anathema maranatha? Perhaps Father
Malloy would lend me bell, book, and candle?"

Mule Malloy looked uncomfortable. "You
read about such things, Captain," he admitted.
"They were done, a long time ago. . . ."

"There's nothing in your religion against it, is
there, Acosta?"

"There is . . . precedent," the Rabbi confessed
softly.

"Then it's an order, from your superior officer. I'll leave the mechanics up to you. You
know how it's done. If you need anything . . .
what kind of bell?"

"I'm afraid that was meant as a joke, Captain."

"Well, these *things* are no joke. And you'll
curse them tomorrow morning before all your
men."

"I shall pray," said Rabbi Chaim Acosta, "for
guidance . . ." But the captain was already gone.

He turned to his fellow priest. "Mule, you'll pray for me too?" The normally agile hands hung limp at his side.

Mule Malloy nodded. He groped for his rosary as Acosta silently left the room.

Now entertain conjecture of a time when two infinitesimal forces of *men*—one half-forgotten outpost garrison, one small scouting fleet—spend the night in readying themselves against the unknown, in preparing to meet on the morrow to determine, perhaps, the course of centuries for a galaxy.

Two *men* are feeding sample range-finding problems into the computer.

"That God-damned Fassbänder," says one. "I heard him talking to our commander. 'You and your men who have never understood the meaning of discipline . . .'!"

"Prussians," the other grunts. He has an Irish face and an American accent. "Think they own the earth. When we get through here, let's dump all the Prussians into Texas and let 'em fight it out. Then we can call the state Kilkenny."

"What did you get on that last? . . . Check. Fassbänder's 'discipline' is for peace—spit-and-polish to look pretty here in our sandy pink nowhere. What's the pay-off? Fassbänder's great-grandfathers were losing two world wars while mine were creating a new nation out of nothing. Ask the Arabs if we have no discipline. Ask the British . . ."

"Ah, the British. Now *my* great-grandfather was in the IRA . . ."

* * *

Two *men* are integrating the electrodes of the wave-hurler.

"It isn't bad enough we get drafted for this expedition to nowhere; we have to have an egg-eating Nangurian in command."

"And a Tryldian scout to bring the first report. What's your reading there? . . . Check."

" 'A Tryldian to tell a lie and a Nangurian to force it into truth,' " the first quotes.

"Now, brothers," says the *man* adjusting the microvernier on the telelens, "the Goodman assures us these monsters are true. We must unite in love for each other, even Tryldians and Nangurians, and wipe them out. The Goodman has promised us his blessing before battle . . ."

"The Goodman," says the first, "can eat the egg he was hatched from."

"The Rabbi," says a *man* checking the oxyhelms, "can take his blessing and shove it up Fassbänder. I'm no Jew in his sense. I'm a sensible, rational atheist who happens to be an Israeli."

"And I," says his companion, "am a Romanian who believes in the God of my fathers and therefore gives allegiance to His state of Israel. What is a Jew who denies the God of Moses? To call him still a Jew is to think like Fassbänder."

"They've got an edge on us," says the first. *"They* can breathe here. These oxyhelms run out in three hours. What do we do then? Rely on the Rabbi's blessing?"

"I said the God of my fathers, and yet my great-grandfather thought as you do and still fought to make Israel live anew. It was his son who, like so many others, learned that he must return to Jerusalem in spirit as well as body."

"Sure, we had the Great Revival of orthodox religion. So what did it get us? Troops that need a Rabbi's blessing before a commander's orders."

"Many men have died from orders. How many from blessings?"

"I fear that few die well who die in battle . . ." the *man* reads in Valkram's great epic of the siege of Tolnishri.

". . . for how [the *man* is reading of the eve of Agincourt in his micro-Shakespeare] *can they charitably dispose of anything when blood is their argument?"*

". . . and if these do not die well [so Valkram wrote] *how grievously must their bad deaths be charged against the Goodman who blesses them into battle . . ."*

"And why not?" Chaim Acosta flicked the question away with a wave of his long fingers.

The bleep (even Acosta was not so linguistically formal as to call it a bubble jeep) bounced along over the sand toward the rise which overlooked the invaders' ship. Mule Malloy handled the wheel with solid efficiency and said nothing.

"I *did* pray for guidance last night," the rabbi asserted, almost as if in self-defense. "I . . . I had some strange thoughts for a while; but they make very little sense this morning. After all, I

am an officer in the army. I do have a certain
obligation to my superior officer and to my men.
And when I became a rabbi, a teacher, I was
specifically ordained to decide questions of law
and ritual. Surely this case falls within that authority of mine."

Abruptly the bleep stopped.

"What's the matter, Mule?"

"Nothing ... Wanted to rest my eyes a
minute ... Why did you become ordained,
Chaim?"

"Why did you? Which of us understands all
the infinite factors of heredity and environment
which lead us to such a choice? Or even, if you
will, to such a being chosen? Twenty years ago it
seemed the only road I could possibly take;
now ... We'd better get going, Mule."

The bleep started up again.

"A curse sounds so melodramatic and medieval; but is it in essence any different from a
prayer for victory, which chaplains offer up regularly? As I imagine you did in your field mass.
Certainly all of your communicants are praying
for victory to the Lord of Hosts—and as Captain
Fassbänder would point out, it makes them better fighting men. I will confess that even as a
teacher of the law, I have no marked doctrinal
confidence in the efficacy of a curse. I do not expect the spaceship of the invaders to be blasted
by the forked lightning of Yahveh. But my men
have an exaggerated sort of faith in me, and I
owe it to them to do anything possible to
strengthen their morale. Which is all the legion
or any other army expects of chaplains anyway;
we are no longer priests of the Lord, but boosters

of morale—a type of sublimated YMCA secretary. Well, in my case, say YMHA."

The bleep stopped again.

"I never knew your eyes to be so sensitive before," Acosta observed tartly.

"I thought you might want a little time to think it over," Malloy ventured.

"I've thought it over. What else have I been telling you? Now please, Mule. Everything's all set. Fassbänder will explode completely if I don't speak my curse into this mike in two minutes."

Silently Mule Malloy started up the bleep.

"Why did I become ordained?" Acosta backtracked. "That's no question really. The question is why have I remained in a profession to which I am so little suited. I will confess to you, Mule, and to you only, that I have not the spiritual humility and patience that I might desire. I itch for something beyond the humdrum problems of a congregation or an army detachment. Sometimes I have felt that I should drop everything else and concentrate on my *psi* faculties, that they might lead me to this goal I seek without understanding. But they are too erratic. I know the law, I love the ritual, but I am not good as a rabbi, a teacher, because . . ."

For the third time the bleep stopped, and Mule Malloy said, "Because you are a saint."

And before Chaim Acosta could protest, he went on, "Or a prophet, if you want Fassbänder's distinction. There are all kinds of saints and prophets. There are the gentle, humble, patient ones like Francis of Assisi and Job and Ruth—or do you count women? And there are God's firebrands, the ones of fierce in-

tellect and dreadful determination, who shake
the history of God's elect, the saints who have
reached through sin to salvation with a confident
power that is the reverse of the pride of Lucifer,
cast from the same ringing metal."

"Mule . . . !" Acosta protested. "This isn't
you. These aren't your words. And you didn't
learn these in parochial school . . ."

Malloy seemed not to hear him. "Paul, Thom-
as More, Catherine of Siena, Augustine," he recited in rich cadence. "Elijah, Ezekiel, Judas
Maccabeus, Moses, David . . . You are a
prophet, Chaim. Forget the rationalizing double
talk of the Rhinists and recognize whence your
powers come, how you were guided to save me,
what the 'strange thoughts' were that you had
during last night's vigil of prayer. You are a
prophet—and you are not going to curse *men*, the
children of God."

Abruptly Malloy slumped forward over the
wheel. There was silence in the bleep. Chaim
Acosta stared at his hands as if he knew no
gesture for this situation.

"Gentlemen!" Captain Fassbänder's voice
was even more rasping than usual over the telecom. "Will you please get the blessed lead out
and get up that rise? It's two minutes, twenty
seconds, past zero!"

Automatically Acosta depressed the switch
and said, "Right away, Captain."

Mule Malloy stirred and opened his eyes.
"Was that Fassbänder?"

"Yes . . . But there's no hurry, Mule. I can't
understand it. What made you . . ?"

"I don't understand it, either. Never passed

out like that before. Doctor used to say that head injury in the Wisconsin game might—but after thirty years . . ."

Chaim Acosta sighed. "You sound like my Mule again. But before . . ."

"Why? Did I say something? Seems to me like there was something important I wanted to say to you."

"I wonder what they'd say at Tel Aviv. Telepathic communication of subconscious minds? Externalization of thoughts that I was afraid to acknowledge consciously? Yes, you said something, Mule; and I was as astonished as Balaam when his ass spoke to him on his journey to . . . Mule!"

Acosta's eyes were blackly alight as never before, and his hands flickered eagerly. "Mule, do you remember the story of Balaam? It's in the fourth book of Moses . . ."

"Numbers? All I remember is he had a talking ass. I suppose there's a pun on *Mule?*"

"Balaam, son of Beor," said the rabbi with quiet intensity, "was a prophet in Moab. The Israelites were invading Moab, and King Balak ordered Balaam to curse them. His ass not only spoke to him; more important, it halted and refused to budge on the journey until Balaam had listened to a message from the Lord . . .

"You were right, Mule. Whether you remember what you said or not, whether your description of me was God's truth or the telepathic projection of my own ego, you were right in one thing: These invaders are *men,* by all the standards that we debated yesterday. Moreover they are *men* suited to Mars; our patrol reported them as naked and unprotected in this cold and this atmosphere. I wonder if they have scouted this planet before and selected it as suitable; that could have been some observation device left by them that trapped you in the pass, since we've never found traces of an earlier Martian civilization.

"Mars is not for us. We cannot live here normally; our scientific researches have proved fruitless; and we maintained an inert, bored garrison only because our planetary ego cannot face facts and surrender the symbol of our 'conquest of space.' These other *men* can live here, perhaps fruitfully, to the glory of God and eventually to the good of our own world as well, as two suitably populated planets come to know each other. You were right; I cannot curse *men*."

"GENTLEMEN!"

Deftly Acosta reached down and switched off the telecom. "You agree, Mule?"

"I . . . I . . . I guess I drive back now, Chaim?"

"Of course not. Do you think I want to face Fassbänder now? You drive on. At once. Up to the top of the rise. Or haven't you yet remembered the rest of the story of Balaam? He didn't stop at refusing to curse his fellow children of God. Not Balaam.

"He blessed them."

Mule Malloy had remembered that. He had remembered more, too. The phonograph needle had coursed through the grooves of Bible study on up to the thirty-first chapter of Numbers with its brief epilogue to the story of Balaam:

And Moses sent them to the war . . . and they warred against the Midianites, as the Lord commanded Moses;

and they slew all the males . . . Balaam also the son of Beor they slew with the sword.

He looked at the tense face of Chaim Acosta, where exultation and resignation blended as they must in a man who knows at last the pattern of his life, and realized that Chaim's memory, too, went as far as the thirty-first chapter.

And there isn't a word in the Bible as to what became of the ass, thought Mule Malloy, and started the bleep up the rise.

———◆◆◆———

Anthony Boucher (William Anthony Parker White, 1911–1968) was a man of much learning, many interests, and a great many talents. In the mystery field, he was the author of seven novels (five as Anthony Boucher and two as H. H. Holmes) and a great many short stories and novelettes; fact crime articles; translations in French, Spanish, and Portuguese; and hundreds of radio shows. He was a nationally known mystery reviewer and critic. A founding director and one-time president of the Mystery Writers of America, he received several of their Edgar Awards for best criticism.

In the science fiction field, he made his reputation not only as an author, but also as an editor. With the late J. Francis McComas, he founded The Magazine of Fantasy and Science Fiction *in 1949, and they edited it together until McComas' departure in 1954, carrying on alone until 1958, when ill health compelled him to drop the editorship. The magazine had established a reputation for high literary quality, which it still retains.*

He published innumerable short stories and edited a great many anthologies, including the first eight annual volumes of the Best From Fantasy and Science Fiction *(first with McComas and then alone), and the two-volume* Treasury of Great Science Fiction, *published by Doubleday in 1959.*

In his introduction to the sf volume, Special Wonder, *of the* Anthony Boucher Memorial Anthology, *McComas had this to say of him: "Tony was the kindest editor I have ever known. He was especially gentle with the beginning writer, and hated the printed rejection slip . . . [His] proudest boast was the number of authors whose first stories we had bought."*

There must surely be one universality in all wars, past, present, future: the thoughts of the wounded soldier, the dying soldier. These thoughts have been and will be shaped by his heritage, his culture, his picture of life and of the world, of heaven and hell, his hope of survival after death or his fear of personal annihilation.

But will they differ in their essence? In this poem, Robert Frazier evokes them for the future.

Robert Frazier

ENCASED IN THE AMBER OF DEATH

The Sun is a throbbing heart,
torn from the breast of a Zulu chief.
The rind of the Moon's surface is pitted,
like the decaying flesh of a wildebeest.
The white shards of troop carriers are javelins,
cast from the fists of angry gods.
Like a butterfly trapped in its chrysalis,
I lay bleeding my future away;
my life's focus narrowed to the window of my
     faceplate.
In the stark patterns of light and dark greys,
fighters jet about like piranha in the river's
     depths;
stirring up dust on its bottom.

Darts of deadly vermillion light are formed,
cast from the mouths of technological warriors;
raining in the jungle of battle.
As I feel the dark tendrils of entropy
growing and vining in the open spaces of my
      thought,
and its python grip encompass me,
I see a singular vision:
The black dust of my black skin
dispersing like locusts in the photon breeze
and invisible forever against the blackest of all
      skies.

Robert Frazier has been involved in many aspects of poetry in the science fiction field—an area which offers unlimited challenges to the poetic imagination, and one in which too little has as yet been done. He has been an editor, a member of an awards committee (CAS Award), and has read papers on science fiction poetry at conferences and conventions. And of course he writes it.

One of his poems, "Encased in the Amber of Eternity," appeared in Thor's Hammer, *the first volume of* The Future at War, *and still another will be published in the third,* Orion's Sword. *His latest sale, prior to these, was to Jerry Pournelle for his anthology* The Endless Frontier.

The Kwakiutl Indian custom of the potlach, where leading members of the tribe display and affirm their status by vieing to see who can burn up the most valuables—blankets and bear skins and canoes and everything else they can purchase or create—seems foolish to us. How, then, will the great potlach of man's wars appear to extraterrestrials who may be as superior to us as we believe we are to the Kwakiutl? What will they think of our destruction of uncounted millions of our fellow men, to say nothing of our cities and our libraries and our works of art?

And will we, eventually, go to the vast trouble and danger and expense of making other worlds in the Solar System habitable only to take our potlach with us? From the perspective of space, we must regard all mankind's wars as civil wars, setting brother against brother, as in this novelette of Poul Anderson's.

Poul Anderson

COLD VICTORY

It was the old argument, Historical Necessity versus the Man of Destiny. When I heard them talking, three together, my heart twisted within me and I knew that once more I must lay down the burden of which I can never be rid.

This was in the Battle Rock House, which is a quiet tavern on the edge of Syrtis Town. I come there whenever I am on Mars. It is friendly and unpretentious: shabby, comfortable loungers scattered about under the massive sandwood rafters, honest liquor and competent chess and the talk of one's peers.

As I entered, a final shaft of thin hard sunlight stabbed in through the window, dazzling me, and then night fell like a thunderclap over the ocherous land and the fluoros snapped on. I got a mug of porter and strolled across to the table about which the three people sat.

The stiff little bald man was obviously from the college; he wore his academics even here, but Martians are like that. "No, no," he was saying. "These movements are too great for any one man to change them appreciably. Humanism, for example, was not the political engine of Carnarvon; rather, he was the puppet of Humanism, and danced as the blind brainless puppeteer made him."

"I'm not so sure," answered the man in gray, undress uniform of the Order of Planetary Engineers. "If he and his cohorts had been less doctrinaire, the government of Earth might still be Humanist."

"But being born of a time of trouble, Humanism was inevitably fanatical," said the professor.

The big, kilted Venusian woman shifted impatiently. She was packing a gun and her helmet was on the floor beside her. Lucifer Clan, I saw from the tartan. "If there are folk around at a crisis time with enough force, they'll shape the way things turn out," she declared. "Otherwise things will drift."

I rolled up a lounger and set my mug on the table. Conversational kibitzing is accepted in the

Battle Rock. "Pardon me, gentles," I said. "Maybe I can contribute."

"By all means, Captain," said the Martian, his eyes flickering over my Solar Guard uniform and insignia. "Permit me: I am Professor Freylinghausen—Engineer Buwono; Freelady Neilsen-Singh."

"Captain Crane." I lifted my mug in a formal toast. "Mars, Luna, Venus, and Earth in my case . . . highly representative, are we not? Between us, we should be able to reach a conclusion."

"To a discussion in a vacuum!" snorted the amazon.

"Not quite," said the engineer. "What did you wish to suggest, Captain?"

I got out my pipe and began stuffing it. "There's a case from recent history—the anti-Humanist counterrevolution, in fact—in which I had a part myself. Offhand, at least, it seems a perfect example of sheer accident determining the whole future of the human race. It makes me think we must be more the pawns of chance than of law."

"Well, Captain," said Freylinghausen testily, "let us hear your story and then pass judgement."

"I'll have to fill you in on some background." I lit my pipe and took a comforting drag. I needed comfort just then. It was not to settle an argument that I was telling this, but to reopen an old hurt which would never let itself be forgotten. "This happened during the final attack on the Humanists—"

"A perfect case of inevitability, sir," interrupted Freylinghausen. "May I explain? Thank you. Forgive me if I repeat obvious facts. Their arrangement and interpretation are perhaps not so obvious.

"Psychotechnic government had failed to solve the problems of Earth's adjustment to living on a high technological level. Conditions worsened until all too many people were ready to try desperation measures. The Humanist revolution was the desperation measure that succeeded in being tried. A typical reaction movement, offering a return to a less intellectualized existence; the savior with the time machine, as Toynbee once phrased it. So naturally its leader, Carnarvon, got to be dictator of the planet.

"But with equal force it was true that Earth could no longer *afford* to cut back her technology. Too many people, too few resources. In the several years of their rule, the Humanists failed to keep their promises; their attempts led only to famine, social disruption, breakdown. Losing popular support, they had to become increasingly arbitrary, thus alienating the people still more.

"At last the oppression of Earth became so brutal that the democratic governments of Mars and Venus brought pressure to bear. But the Humanists had gone too far to back down. Their only possible reaction was to pull Earth-Luna out of the Solar Union.

"We could not see that happen, sir. The lesson of history is too plain. Without a Union council to arbitrate between planets and a Solar Guard to enforce its decisions—there will be war until man is extinct. Earth could not be allowed to secede. Therefore, Mars and Venus aided the counterrevolutionary, anti-Humanist cabal that wanted to restore liberty and Union membership to the mother planet. Therefore, too, a space fleet was raised to support the uprising when it came.

"Don't you see? Every step was an unavoidable consequence, by the logic of survival, of all that had gone before."

"Correct so far, Professor," I nodded. "But the success of the counterrevolution and the Mars–Venus intervention was by no means guaranteed. Mars and Venus were still frontiers, thinly populated, only recently made habitable. They didn't have the military potential of Earth.

"The cabal was well organized. Its well-timed mutinies swept Earth's newly created pro-Humanist ground and air forces before it. The countryside, the oceans, even the cities were soon cleared of Humanist troops.

"But Dictator Carnarvon and the men still loyal to him were holed up in a score of fortresses. Oh, it would have been easy enough to dig them out or blast them out—except that the navy of sovereign Earth, organized from seized units of the Solar Guard, had also remained loyal to Humanism. Its cinc, Admiral K'ung, had acted promptly when the revolt began, jailing all personnel he wasn't sure of . . . or shooting them. Only a few got away.

"So there the pro-Union revolutionaries were, in possession of Earth but with a good five hundred enemy warships orbiting above them. K'ung's strategy was simple. He broadcast that unless the rebels surrendered inside one week—

or if meanwhile they made any attempt on Carnarvon's remaining strongholds—he'd start bombarding with nuclear weapons. That, of course, would kill perhaps a hundred million civilians, flatten the factories, poison the sea ranches . . . he'd turn the planet into a butcher shop.

"Under such a threat, the general population was no longer backing the Union cause. They clamored for surrender; they began raising armies. Suddenly the victorious rebels had enemies not merely in front and above them, but behind . . . everywhere!

"Meanwhile, as you all know, the Unionist fleet under Dushanovitch-Alvarez had rendezvoused off Luna; as mixed a bunch of Martians, Venusians, and freedom-minded Earthmen as history ever saw. They were much inferior both in strength and organization; it was impossible for them to charge in and give battle with any hope of winning . . . but Dushanovitch-Alvarez had a plan. It depended on luring the Humanist fleet out to engage him.

"Only Admiral K'ung wasn't having any. The Unionist command knew, from deserters, that most of his captains wanted to go out and annihilate the invaders first, returning to deal with Earth at their leisure. It was a costly nuisance, the Unionists sneaking in, firing and retreating, blowing up ship after ship of the Humanist forces. But K'ung had the final word, and he would not accept the challenge until the rebels on the ground had capitulated. He was negotiating with them now, and it looked very much as if they would give in.

"So there it was, the entire outcome of the war —the whole history of man, for if you will pardon my saying so, gentles, Earth is still the key planet—everything hanging on this one officer, Grand Admiral K'ung Li-Po, a grim man who had given his oath and had a damnably good grasp of the military facts of life."

I took a long draught from my mug and began the story, using the third-person form which is customary on Mars.

The speedster blasted at four gees till she was a bare five hundred kilometers from the closest enemy vessels. Her radar screens jittered with their nearness and in the thunder of abused hearts her crew sat waiting for the doomsday of a homing missile. Then she was at the calculated point, she spat her cargo out the main lock and leaped ahead still more furiously. In moments the thin glare of her jets was lost among crowding stars.

The cargo was three spacesuited men, linked to a giant air tank and burdened with a variety of tools. The orbit into which they had been flung was aligned with that of the Humanist fleet, so that relative velocity was low.

In cosmic terms, that is. It still amounted to nearly a thousand kilometers per hour and was enough, unchecked, to spatter the men against an armored hull.

Lieutenant Robert Crane pulled himself along the light cable that bound him, up to the tank. His hands groped in the pitchy gloom of shadowside. Then all at once rotation had brought him into the moonlight and he could see. He found the rungs and went hand over hand along the curve of the barrel, centrifugal force streaming his body outward. Damn the clumsiness of space armor! Awkwardly, he got one foot into a stirrup-like arrangement and scrambled around until he was in the "saddle" with both boots firmly locked; then he unclipped the line from his waist.

The stars turned about him in a cold majestic wheel. Luna was nearly at the full, ashen pale, scored and pocked and filling his helmet with icy luminescence. Earth was an enormous grayness in the sky, a half ring of blinding light from the hidden sun along one side.

Twisting a head made giddy by the spinning, he saw the other two mounted behind him. García was in the middle—you could always tell a Venusian; he painted his clan markings on his suit—and the Martian Wolf at the end. "Okay," he said, incongruously aware that the throat mike pinched his Adam's apple, "let's stop this merry-go-round."

His hands moved across a simple control panel. A tangentially mounted nozzle opened, emitting an invisible stream of air. The stars slowed their lunatic dance, steadied . . . hell and sunfire, now he'd overcompensated, give it a blast from the other side . . . the tank was no longer in rotation. He was not hanging head downward, but falling, a long weightless tumble through a sterile infinity.

Three men rode a barrel of compressed air toward the massed fleet of Earth.

"Any radar reading?" García's voice was tinny in the earphones.

"A moment, if you please, till I have it set up." Wolf extended a telescoping mast, switched on the portable 'scope, and began sweeping the sky. "Nearest indication . . . um . . . one o'clock, five degrees low, four hundred twenty-two kilometers distant." He added radial and linear velocity, and García worked an astrogator's slide rule, swearing at the tricky light.

The base line was not the tank, but its velocity, which could be assumed straight-line for so short a distance. Actually, the weird horse had its nose pointed a full thirty degrees off the direction of movement. "High" and "low," in weightlessness, were simply determined by the plane bisecting the tank, with the men's heads arbitrarily designated as "aimed up."

The airbarrel had jets aligned in three planes, as well as the rotation-controlling tangential nozzles. With Wolf and García to correct him, Crane blended vectors until they were on a course that would nearly intercept the ship. Gas was released from the forward jet at a rate calculated to match velocity.

Crane had nothing but the gauges to tell him that he was braking. Carefully dehydrated air emerges quite invisibly, and its ionization is negligible; there was no converter to radiate, and all equipment was painted a dead nonreflecting black.

Soundless and invisible—too small and fast for a chance eye to see in the uncertain moonlight, for a chance radar beam to register as anything worth buzzing an alarm about. Not enough infrared for detection, not enough mass, no trail of ions—the machinists on the *Thor* had wrought well, the astrogators had figured as closely as men and computers are able. But in the end it was only a tank of compressed air, a bomb, a few tools, and three men frightened and lonely.

"How long will it take us to get there?" asked Crane. His throat was dry and he swallowed hard.

"About forty-five minutes to that ship we're zeroed in on," García told him. "After that, ¿quien sabe? We'll have to locate the *Monitor*."

"Be most economical with the air, if you please," said Wolf. "We also have to get back."

"Tell me more," snorted Crane.

"If this works," remarked García, "we'll have added a new weapon to the System's arsenals. That's why I volunteered. If Antonio García of Hesperus gets his name in the history books, my whole clan will contribute to give me the biggest ranch on Venus."

They were an anachronism, thought Crane, a resurrection from old days when war was a wilder business. The psychotechs had not picked a team for compatibility, nor welded them into an unbreakable brotherhood. They had merely grabbed the first three willing to try an untested scheme. There wasn't time for anything else. In another forty hours, the pro-Union armies on Earth would either have surrendered or the bombardment would begin.

"Why are you lads here?" went on the Venusian. "We might as well get acquainted."

"I took an oath," said Wolf. There was nothing priggish about it; Martians thought that way.

"What of you, Crane?"

"I . . . it looked like fun," said the Earthman lamely. "And it might end this damned war."

He lied and he knew so, but how do you explain? Do you admit it was an escape from your shipmates' eyes?

Not that his going over to the rebels had shamed him. Everyone aboard the *Marduk* had done so, except for a couple of CPO's who were now under guard in Aphrodite. The cruiser had been on patrol off Venus when word of Earth's secession had flashed. Her captain had declared for the Union and the Guard to which he belonged, and the crew cheered him for it.

For two years, while Dushanovitch-Alvarez, half idealist and half buccaneer, was assembling the Unionist fleet, intelligence reports trickled in from Earth. Mutiny was being organized, and men escaped from those Guard vessels—the bulk of the old space service—that had been at the mother planet and were seized to make a navy. Just before the Unionists accelerated for rendezvous, a list of the new captains appointed by K'ung had been received. And the skipper of the *Huitzilopochtli* was named Benjamin Crane.

Ben . . . what did you do when your brother was on the enemy side? Dushanovitch-Alvarez had let the System know that a bombardment of Earth would be regarded as genocide and all officers partaking in it would be punished under Union law. It seemed unlikely that there would be any Union to try the case, but Lieutenant Robert Crane of the *Marduk* had protested: this was not a normal police operation, it was war, and executing men who merely obeyed the gov-

ernment they had pledged to uphold was opening the gates to a darker barbarism than the
fighting itself. The Unionist force was too short-
handed, it could not give Lieutenant Crane more
than a public reproof for insubordination, but
his messmates had tended to grow silent when
he entered the wardroom.

If the superdreadnaught *Monitor* could be destroyed, and K'ung with it, Earth might not be
bombarded. Then if the Unionists won, Ben
would go free, or he would die cleanly in battle
—reason enough to ride this thing into the Humanist fleet!

Silence was cold in their helmets.

"I've been thinking," said García. "Suppose
we do carry this off, but they decide to blast
Earth anyway before dealing with our boats.
What then?"

"Then they blast Earth," said Wolf. "Though
most likely they won't have to. Last I heard, the
threat alone was making folk rise against our
friends on the ground there." Moonlight shim-
mered along his arm as he pointed at the darkened planet-shield before them. "So the Humanists will be back in power, and even if we
chop up their navy, we won't win unless we do
some bombarding of our own."

"*¡Madre de Dios!*" García crossed himself, a
barely visible gesture in the unreal flood of un-
diffused light. "I'll mutiny before I give my
name to such a thing."

"And I," said Wolf shortly. "And most of us,
I think."

It was not that the Union fleet was crewed by
saints, thought Crane. Most of its personnel had

signed on for booty; the System knew how much treasure was locked in the vaults of Earth's dictators. But the horror of nuclear war had been too deeply graven for anyone but a fanatic at the point of desperation to think of using it.

Even in K'ung's command, there must be talk of revolt. Since his ultimatum, deserters in lifeboats had brought Dushanovitch-Alvarez a mountain of precise information. But the Humanists had had ten years in which to build a hard cadre of hard young officers to keep the men obedient.

Strange to know that Ben was with them— why?

I haven't seen you in more than two years now, Ben—nor my own wife and children, but tonight it is you who dwell in me, and I have not felt such pain for many years. Not since that time we were boys together, and you were sick one day, and I went alone down the steep bluffs above the Mississippi. There I found the old man denned up under the trees, a tramp, one of many millions for whom there was no place in this new world of shining machines—but he was not embittered, he drew his citizen's allowance and tramped the planet and he had stories to tell me which our world of bright hard metal had forgotten. He told me about Br'er Rabbit and the briar patch; never had I heard such a story, it was the first time I knew the rich dark humor of the earth itself. And you got well, Ben, and I took you down to his camp, but he was gone and you never heard the story of Br'er Rabbit. On that day, Ben, I was as close to weeping as I am this night of murder.

The minutes dragged past. Only numbers went between the three men on the tank, astrogational corrections. They sat, each in his own skull with his own thoughts.

The vessel on which they had zeroed came into plain view, a long black shark swimming against the Milky Way. They passed within two kilometers of her. Wolf was busy now, flicking his radar around the sky, telling off ships. It was mostly seat-of-the-pants piloting, low relative velocities and small distances, edging into the mass of Earth's fleet. That was not a very dense mass; kilometers gaped between each unit. The *Monitor* was in the inner ring; a deserter had given them the approximate orbit.

"You're pretty good at this, boy," said García.

"I rode a scooter in the asteroids for a couple of years," answered Crane. "Patrol and rescue duty."

That was when there had still been only the Guard, one fleet and one flag. Crane had never liked the revolutionary government of Earth, but while the Union remained and the only navy was the Guard and its only task to help any and all men, he had been reasonably content. Please God, that day would come again.

Slowly, over the minutes, the *Monitor* grew before him, a giant spheroid never meant to land on a planet. He could see gun turrets scrawled black across remote star-clouds. There was more reason for destroying her than basic strategy—luring the Humanists out to do battle; more than good tactics—built only last year, she was the most formidable engine of war in the

Solar System. It would be the annihilation of a symbol. The *Monitor,* alone among ships that rode the sky, was designed with no other purpose than killing.

Slow, now, easy, gauge the speeds by eye, remember how much inertia you've got. . . . Edge up, brake, throw out a magnetic anchor and grapple fast. Crane turned a small winch, the cable tautened and he bumped against the hull.

Nobody spoke. They had work to do, and their short-range radio might have been detected. García unshipped the bomb. Crane held it while the Venusian scrambled from the saddle and got a firm boot-grip on the dreadnaught. The bomb didn't have a large mass. Crane handed it over, and García slapped it onto the hull, gripped by a magnetic plate. Stooping, he wound a spring and jerked a lever. Then, with spaceman's finicking care, he returned to the saddle. Crane paid out the cable till it ran off the drum; they were free of their grapple.

In twenty minutes, the clockwork was to set off the bomb. It was a little one, plutonium fission, and most of its energy would be wasted on vacuum. Enough would remain to smash the *Monitor* into a hundred fragments.

Crane worked the airjets, forcing himself to be calm and deliberate. The barrel swung about to point at Luna, and he opened the rear throttle wide. Acceleration tugged at him, he braced his feet in the stirrups and hung on with both hands. Behind them, the *Monitor* receded, borne on her own orbit around a planet where terror walked.

When they were a good fifteen kilometers

away, he asked for a course. His voice felt remote, as if it came from outside his prickling skin. Most of him wondered just how many men were aboard the dreadnaught and how many wives and children they had to weep for them. Wolf squinted through a sextant and gave his readings to García. Corrections made, they rode toward the point of rendezvous: a point so tricky to compute, in this Solar System where the planets were never still, that they would doubltess not come within a hundred kilometers of the speedster that was to pick them up. But they had a hand-cranked radio that would broadcast a signal for the boat to get a fix on them.

How many minutes had they been going? Ten ... ? Crane looked at the clock in the control panel. Yes, ten. Another five or so, at this acceleration, ought to see them beyond the outermost orbit of the Humanist ships—

He did not hear the explosion. A swift and terrible glare opened inside his helmet, enough light reflected off the inner surface for his eyes to swim in white-hot blindness. He clung to his seat, nerves and muscles tensed against the hammer blow that never came. The haze parted raggedly, and he turned his head back toward Earth. A wan nimbus of incandescent gas hung there. A few tattered stars glowed blue as they fled from it.

Wolf's voice whispered in his ears: "She's gone already. The bomb went off ahead of schedule. Something in the clockwork—"

"But she's gone!" García let out a rattling whoop. "No more flagship. We got her, lads, we got the stinking can!"

Not far away was a shadow visible only where it blocked off the stars. A ship . . . light cruiser — "Cram on the air!" said Wolf roughly. "Let's get the devil out of here."

"I can't." Crane snarled it, still dazed, wanting only to rest and forget every war that ever was. "We've only got so much pressure left, and none to spare for maneuvering if we get off course."

"All right . . ." They lapsed into silence. That which had been the *Monitor,* gas and shrapnel, dissipated. The enemy cruiser fell behind them, and Luna filled their eyes with barren radiance.

They were not aware of pursuit until the squad was almost on them. There were a dozen men in combat armor, driven by individual jet-units and carrying rifles. They overhauled the tank and edged in—less gracefully than fish, for they had no friction to kill forward velocity, but they moved in.

After the first leap of his heart, Crane felt cold and numb. None of his party bore arms: they themselves had been the weapon, and now it was discharged. In a mechanical fashion, he turned his headset to the standard band.

"Rebels ahoy!" The voice was strained close to breaking, an American voice. . . . For a moment such a wave of homesickness for the green dales of Wisconsin went over Crane that he could not move nor realize he had been captured. "Stop that thing and come with us!"

In sheer reflex, Crane opened the rear throttles full. The barrel jumped ahead, almost ripping him from the saddle. Ions flared behind as the enemy followed. Their units were beam-powered from the ship's nuclear engines, and they had plenty of reaction mass in their tanks. It was only a moment before they were alongside again.

Arms closed around Crane, dragging him from his seat. As the universe tilted about his head, he saw Wolf likewise caught. García sprang to meet an Earthman, hit him and bounced away but got his rifle. A score of bullets must have spat. Suddenly the Venusian's armor blew white clouds of freezing water vapor and he drifted dead.

Wolf wrestled in vacuum and tore one hand free. Crane heard him croak over the radio: "They'll find out—" Another frosty geyser erupted; Wolf had opened his own air-tubes.

Men closed in on either side of Crane, pinioning his arms. He could not have suicided even if he chose to. The rest flitted near, guns ready. He relaxed, too weary and dazed to fight, and let them face him around and kill forward speed, then accelerate toward the cruiser.

The airlock was opening for him before he had his voice back. "What ship is this?" he asked, not caring much, only filling in an emptiness.

"*Huitzilopochtli*. Get in there with you."

Crane floated weightless in the wardroom, his left ankle manacled to a stanchion. They had removed his armor, leaving the thick gray coverall which was the underpadding, and given him a stimpill. A young officer guarded him, sidearm holstered; no reason to fear a fettered captive. The officer did not speak, though horror lay on his lips.

The pill had revived Crane, his body felt supple and he sensed every detail of the room with an unnatural clarity. But his heart had a thick beat and his mouth felt cottony.

This was Ben's ship.

García and Wolf were dead.

None of it was believable.

Captain Benjamin Crane of the Space Navy, Federation of Earth and the Free Cities of Luna, drifted in through a ghostly quiet. It was a small shock to see him again . . . when had the last time been, three years ago? They had met in Mexico City, by arrangement, when their leaves coincided, and had a hell of a good time. Then they went up to their father's house in Wisconsin, and that had somehow not been quite as good, for the old man was dead and the house had stood long empty. But it had been a fine pheasant shoot, on a certain cool and smoky-clear fall morning. Robert Crane remembered how the first dead leaves crackled underfoot, and how the bird dog stiffened into a point that was flowing line and deep curves, and the thin high wedge of wild geese, southward bound.

That was the first thing he thought of, and next he thought that Ben had put on a good deal of weight and looked much older, and finally he recalled that he himself had changed toward gauntness and must seem to have more than the two-year edge on Ben he really did.

The captain stiffened as he came through the air. He grabbed a handhold barely in time, and stopped his flight ungracefully. The quietness lengthened. There was little to see on Ben's heavy face, unless you knew him as well—inside and out—as his own brother did.

He spoke finally, a whisper: "I never looked for this."

Crane of the *Marduk* tried to smile. "What are the mathematical odds against it?" he wondered. "That I, of all people, should be on this mission, and that your ship of all Earth's fleet should have captured me. How did you detect us?"

"That bomb . . . you touched it off too soon. The initial glare brought us to the ports, and the gas glow afterward, added to the moonlight, was enough to reveal a peculiar object. We locked a radar on it and I sent men out."

"Accident," said Robert Crane. "Some little flaw in the mechanism. It wasn't supposed to detonate till we were well away."

"I knew you were on . . . the other side," said Ben with great slowness. "That's a wild chance in itself, you realize. I happened to know the *Marduk* was assigned to Venus patrol only because the *Ares* suffered meteoroid damage at the last moment. Consider how unlikely it is that a rock will ever disable a ship. If it hadn't been for that, the *Marduk* would probably have been right here when the . . . trouble began, and you'd have had no choice but to remain loyal."

"Like you, Ben?"

The young officer of Earth floated "upright," at attention, but his eyes were not still. Ben nodded sardonically at him. "Mr. Nicholson, this prisoner happens to be my brother."

No change appeared in the correct face.

Ben sighed. "I suppose you know what you did, Lieutenant Crane."

"Yes," said Robert. "We blew up your flagship."

"It was a brilliant operation," said Ben dully. "I've had a verbal report on your . . . vessel. I imagine you planted an atomic bomb on the *Monitor's* hull. If we knew just where your fleet is and how it's arrayed, as you seem to know everything about us, I'd like to try the same thing on you."

Robert floated, waiting. A thickening grew in his throat. He felt sweat form under his arms and along his ribs, soaking into the coverall. He could smell his own stink.

"But I wonder why that one man of yours suicided," went on Ben. He frowned, abstractedly, and Robert knew he would not willingly let the riddle go till he had solved it. "Perhaps your mission was more than striking a hard blow at us. Perhaps he didn't want us to know its real purpose."

Ben, you're no fool. You were always a suspicious son-of-a-gun, always probing, never quite believing what you were told. I know you, Ben.

What had Wolf's religion been? Crane didn't know. He hoped it wasn't one which promised hellfire to suicides. Wolf had died to protect a secret which the drugs of Earth's psychotechs— nothing so crude as torture—would have dissolved out of him.

If they had not been captured . . . the natural reaction would have been for Earth's fleet to rush forth seeking revenge before the Unionists attacked them. They did not know, they must not know, that Dushanovitch-Alvarez lacked the ships to win an open battle except on his own ground and under his own terms; that the loyalists need only remain where they were, renew the threat of bombardment, carry it out if necessary, and the Union men would be forced to slink home without offering a shot.

"Sir . . ."

Ben's head turned, and Robert saw, with an odd little sadness, gray streaks at the temples. What was his age—thirty-one? *My kid brother is growing old already.*

"Yes, Mr. Nicholson?"

The officer cleared his throat. "Sir, shouldn't the prisoner be interrogated in the regular way? He must know a good deal about—"

"I assure you, not about our orbits and dispositions," said Robert Crane with what coolness he could summon. "We change them quite often."

"Obviously," agreed Ben. "They don't want us to raid them as they've been raiding us. We have to stay in orbit because of our strategy. They don't, and they'd be fools if they did."

"Still . . ." began Nicholson.

"Oh, yes, Intelligence will be happy to pump him," said Ben. "Though I suspect this show will be over before they've gotten much information of value. Vice Admiral Hokusai of the *Krishna* has succeeded to command. Get on the radio, Mr. Nicholson, and report what has happened. In the meantime, I'll question the prisoner myself. Privately."

"Yes, sir." The officer saluted and went out. There was compassion in his eyes.

Ben closed the door behind him. Then he turned around and floated, crossing his legs, one hand on a stanchion and the other rubbing his forehead. His brother had known he would do exactly that. *But how accurately can he read me?*

"Well, Bob." Ben's tone was gentle.

Robert Crane shifted, feeling the link about his ankle. "How are Mary and the kids?" he asked.

"Oh . . . quite well, thank you. I'm afraid I can't tell you much about your own family. Last I heard, they were living in Manitowoc Unit, but in the confusion since . . ." Ben looked away. "They were never bothered by our police, though. I have some little influence."

"Thanks," said Robert. Bitterness broke forth: "Yours are safe in Luna City. Mine will get the fallout when you bombard, or they'll starve in the famine to follow."

The captain's mouth wrenched. "Don't say that!" After a moment: "Do you think I like the idea of shooting at Earth? If your so-called liberators really give a curse in hell about the people their hearts bleed for so loudly, they'll surrender first. We're offering terms. They'll be allowed to go to Mars or Venus."

"I'm afraid you misjudge us, Ben," said Robert. "Do you know why I'm here? It wasn't simply a matter of being on the *Marduk* when she elected to stay with the Union. I believed in the liberation."

"Believe in those pirates out there?" Ben's finger stabbed at the wall, as if to pierce it and show the stars and the hostile ships swimming between.

"Oh, sure, they've been promised the treasure vaults. We had to raise men and ships somehow. What good was that money doing, locked away by Carnarvon and his gang?" Robert shrugged.

"Look, I was born and raised in America. We were always a free people. The Bill of Rights was modeled on our own old Ten Amendments. From the moment the Humanists seized power, I had to start watching what I said, who I associated with, what tapes I got from the library. My kids were growing up into perfect little parrots. It was too much. When the purges began, when the police fired on crowds rioting because they were starving—and they were starving because this quasi-religious creed cannot accept the realities and organize things rationally—I was only waiting for my chance.

"Ben, be honest. Wouldn't you have signed on with us if you'd been on the *Marduk?*"

The face before him was gray. "Don't ask me that! No!"

"I can tell you exactly why not, Ben." Robert folded his arms and would not let his brother's eyes go. "I know you well enough. We're different in one respect. To you, no principle can be as important as your wife and children—and they're hostages for your good behavior. Oh, yes, K'ung's psychotechs evaluated you very carefully. Probably half their captains are held by just such chains."

Ben laughed, a loud bleak noise above the murmur of the ventilators. "Have it your way. And don't forget that your family is alive, too, because I stayed with the government. I'm not going to change, either. A government, even the most arbitrary one, can perhaps be altered in time. But the dead never come back to life."

He leaned forward, suddenly shuddering. "Bob, I don't want you sent Earthside for interrogation. They'll not only drug you, they'll set about changing your whole viewpoint. Surgery, shock, a rebuilt personality—you won't be the same man when they've finished.

"I can wangle something else. I have enough pull, especially now in the confusion after your raid, to keep you here. When the war is settled, I'll arrange for your escape. There's going to be so much hullaballoo on Earth that nobody will notice. But you'll have to help me, in turn.

"What was the real purpose of your raid? What plans does your high command have?"

For a time which seemed to become very long, Robert Crane waited. He was being asked to betray his side voluntarily; the alternative was to do it anyway, after the psychmen got through with him. Ben had no authority to make the decision. It would mean court-martial later, and punishment visited on his family as well, unless he could justify it by claiming quicker results than the long-drawn process of narcosynthesis.

The captain's hands twisted together, big knobby hands, and he stared at them. "This is a hell of a choice for you, I know," he mumbled. "But there's Mary and . . . the kids, and men here who trust me. Good decent men. We aren't fiends, believe me. But I can't deny my own shipmates a fighting chance to get home alive."

Robert Crane wet his lips. "How do you know I'll tell the truth?" he asked.

Ben looked up again, crinkling his eyes. "We had a formula once," he said. "Remember? 'Cross my heart and hope to die, spit in my eye if I tell a lie.' I don't think either of us ever lied when we took that oath."

"And—Ben, the whole war hangs on this, maybe. Do you seriously think I'd keep my word for a kid's chant if it could decide the war?"

"Oh, no." A smile ghosted across the captain's mouth. "But there's going to be a meeting of skippers, if I know Hokusai. He'll want the opinions of us all as to what we should do next. Having heard them, he'll make his own decision. I'll be one voice among a lot of others.

"But if I can speak with whatever information you've given me . . . do you understand? The council will meet long before you could be sent Earthside and quizzed. I need your knowledge *now*. I'll listen to whatever you have to say. I may or may not believe you . . . I'll make my own decision as to what to recommend . . . but it's the only way I can save you, and myself, and everything else I care about."

He waited then, patiently as the circling ships. They must have come around the planet by now, thought Robert Crane. The sun would be drowning many stars, and Earth would be daylit if you looked out.

Captains' council. . . . It sounded awkward and slow, when at any moment, as far as they knew, Dushanovitch-Alvarez might come in at the head of his fleet. But after all, the navy would remain on general alert, second officers would be left in charge. They had time.

And they would want time. Nearly every one of them had kin on Earth. None wished to explode radioactive death across the world they loved. K'ung's will had been like steel, but now they would—subconsciously, and the more powerfully for that—be looking for any way out of the frightful necessity. A respected officer, giving good logical reasons for postponing the bombardment, would be listened to by the keenest ears.

Robert Crane shivered. It was a heartless load to put on a man. The dice of future history . . . he could load the dice, because he knew Ben as any man knows a dear brother, but maybe his hand would slip while he loaded them.

"Well?" It was a grating in the captain's throat.

Robert drew a long breath. "All right," he said.

"Yes?" A high, cracked note; Ben must be near breaking, too.

"I'm not in command, you realize." Robert's words were blurred with haste. "I can't tell for sure what— But I do know we've got fewer ships. A lot fewer."

"I suspected that."

"We have some plan—I haven't been told what—it depends on making you leave this orbit and come out and fight us where we are. If you stay home, we can't do a damn thing. This raid of mine . . . we'd hope that with your admiral dead, you'd join battle out toward Luna."

Robert Crane hung in the air, twisting in its currents, the breath gasping in and out of him. Ben looked dim, across the room, as if his eyes were failing.

"Is that the truth, Bob?" The question seemed to come from light-years away.

"Yes. Yes. I can't let you go and get killed— Cross my heart and hope to die, spit in my eye if I tell a lie!"

* * *

I set down my mug, empty, and signaled for another. The bartender glided across the floor with it and I drank thirstily, remembering how my throat had felt mummified long ago on the *Huitzilopochtli*, remembering much else.

"Very well, sir." Freylinghausen's testy voice broke a stillness. "What happened?"

"You ought to know that, Professor," I replied. "It's in the history tapes. The Humanist fleet decided to go out at once and dispose of its inferior opponent. Their idea—correct, I suppose—was that a space victory would be so demoralizing that the rebels on the ground would capitulate immediately after. It would have destroyed the last hope of reinforcements, you see."

"And the Union fleet won," said Neilsen-Singh. "They chopped the Humanist navy into fishbait. I know. My father was there. We bought a dozen new reclamation units with his share of the loot, afterward."

"Naval history is out of my line, Captain Crane," said the engineer, Buwono. "How did Dushanovitch-Alvarez win?"

"Oh . . . by a combination of things. Chiefly, he disposed his ships and gave them such velocities that the enemy, following the usual principles of tactics, moved at high accelerations to close in. And at a point where they would have built up a good big speed, he had a lot of stuff planted, rocks and ball bearings and scrap iron . . . an artificial meteoroid swarm, moving in an opposed orbit. After that had done its work, the two forces were of very nearly equal strength,

and it became a battle of standard weapons.
Which Dushanovitch-Alvarez knew how to use!
A more brilliant naval mind hasn't existed since
Lord Nelson."

"Yes, yes," said Freylinghausen impatiently.
"But what has this to do with the subject under
discussion?"

"Don't you see, Professor? It was chance right
down the line—chance which was skillfully exploited when it arose, to be sure, but nevertheless a set of unpredictable accidents. The
Monitor blew up ten minutes ahead of schedule;
as a result, the commando that did it was captured. Normally, this would have meant that the
whole plan would have been given away. I can't
emphasize too strongly that the Humanists
would have won if they'd only stayed where they
were."

I tossed off a long gulp of porter, knocked the
dottle from my pipe, and began refilling it. My
hands weren't quite steady. "But chance entered
here, too, making Robert Crane's brother the
man to capture him. And Robert knew how to
manipulate Ben. At the captains' council, the
Huitzilopochtli's skipper spoke the most strongly
in favor of going out to do battle. His arguments,
especially when everyone knew they were based
on information obtained from a prisoner, convinced the others."

"But you said . . ." Neilsen-Singh looked confused.

"Yes, I did." I smiled at her, though my
thoughts were entirely in the past. "But it wasn't
till years later that Ben heard the story of Br'er
Rabbit and the briar patch; he came across it in

his brother's boyhood diary. Robert Crane told the truth, swore to it by a boyhood oath—but his brother could not believe he'd yield so easily. Robert was almost begging him to stay with K'ung's original plan. Ben was sure that was an outright lie . . . that Dushanovitch-Alvarez must actually be planning to attack the navy in its orbit and could not possibly survive a battle in open space. So that, of course, was what he argued for at the council."

"It took nerve, though," said Neilsen-Singh. "Knowing what the *Huitzilopochtli* would have to face . . . knowing you'd be aboard, too. . . ."

"She was a wreck by the time the battle was over," I said. "Not many in her survived."

After a moment, Buwono nodded thoughtfully. "I see your point, Captain. The accident of the bomb's going off too soon almost wrecked the Union plan. The accident of that brotherhood saved it. A thread of coincidences . . . yes, I think you've proved your case."

"I'm afraid not, gentles." Freylinghausen darted birdlike eyes around the table. "You misunderstood me. I was not speaking of minor ripples in the mainstream of history. Certainly those are ruled by chance. But the broad current moves quite inexorably, I assure you. *Vide:* Earth and Luna are back in the Union under a more or less democratic government, but no solution has yet been found to the problems which brought forth the Humanists. They will come again; under one name or another they will return. The war was merely a ripple."

"Maybe." I spoke with inurbane curtness, not liking the thought. "We'll see."

"If nothing else," said Neilsen-Singh, "you people bought for Earth a few more decades of freedom. They can't take that away from you."

I looked at her with sudden respect. It was true. Men died and civilizations died, but before they died they lived. No effort was altogether futile.

I could not remain here, though. I had told the story, as I must always tell it, and now I needed aloneness.

"Excuse me." I finished my drink and stood up. "I have an appointment . . . just dropped in . . . very happy to have met you, gentles."

Buwono rose with the others and bowed formally. "I trust we shall have the pleasure of your company again, Captain Robert Crane."

"Robert—? Oh." I stopped. I had told what I must in third person, but everything had seemed so obvious. "I'm sorry. Robert Crane was killed in the battle. I am Captain Benjamin Crane, at your service, gentles."

I bowed to them and went out the door. The night was lonesome in the streets and across the desert.

I have known Poul and Karen Anderson, to whom this volume of The Future at War *is dedicated, for nearly thirty years—over many a poker table, many a good din-*

ner, many a discussion of how and why the world wags. Poul is the author of more than fifty books and two-hundred-and-some short pieces. Besides sf, these include fantasy, mystery, historical, juvenile, and here-and-now fiction; nonfiction; poetry, essays, criticism, translations, etc. His short stories and articles have appeared in places as various as the sf magazines, Boys' Life, Playboy, the Toronto Star Weekly, National Review, Ellery Queen's, and the now defunct Jack London's Magazine. His novels, nonfiction books, and short stories have been published in fifteen foreign languages.

Poul is a former regional Vice-President of Mystery Writers of America and former President of Science Fiction Writers of America; he has had several Hugo and Nebula Awards, the "Forry" Award of the Los Angeles Science Fantasy Society, a special issue of The Magazine of Fantasy and Science Fiction, the Macmillan Cock Robin Award for best mystery novel, and others. Among his most popular books are Brain Wave, The High Crusade, The Enemy Stars, Three Hearts and Three Lions, The Broken Sword, and Tau Zero. More recent titles are There Will Be Time, The People of the Wind, A Midsummer Tempest, and Fire Time (a Hugo nominee). His most recent major novel, The Avatar, was published recently by Berkley/Putnam.

The Andersons live in the San Francisco Bay Area.

Constant pressure is being brought today to shatter the traditional convention declaring women to be noncombatants in war; they are being regularly commissioned and enlisted in the several branches of the armed forces; more and more, it seems likely that they will be given at least limited combat roles.

Because in our century war has become more and more indiscriminate in its objectives, this is perhaps inevitable. I hope that it is not, for my personal view is a conservative, perhaps a reactionary one. Throughout our history, civilized, sane men have sought to ameliorate war without necessarily diminishing the effectiveness of military operations, *for they have realized that only too often ferocity and destructiveness defeat their own ends.*

In the West at least—and anyone who doubts that there was a humanitarian difference between Western and Eastern warfare should read H.G. Quaritch-Wales' Warfare in Southeast Asia—*the noncombatant status of women did, for many centuries, make war a bit less brutal than it might otherwise have been. It also ensured that a significant section of the population could, to a very large extent, escape the brutalizing effects of war.*

Did women's exclusion from combat participation lessen the military effectiveness of the armies, navies, and nations concerned? There certainly is no historical evidence to indicate it. I know of no war won by a sexually integrated armed force; and if such integration had had any marked military value—any survival *value— we would have historical examples of it. Instead, armed forces have almost universally been entirely male. Therefore, while I quite agree with Vicki Ann Heydron when, for instance, she says that women on active duty in Vietnam should have been issued personal weapons for their*

*own defense, I am not at all sure that they should have
been there in any military capacity.*

*Of course, when we entertain thoughts of war far out
in space, in those vast reaches where expeditions may last
for years and (if anything like Joe Haldeman's* The
Forever War *comes true) for centuries, new pressures
will be felt and new principles may very well apply.*

*But I do not think that our present strange attempt to
cancel out the sexes should be allowed to bring this even-
tuality upon us prematurely.*

Vicki Ann Heydron

WOMEN UNDER FIRE

I served three years in the Women's Army
Corps, and I spent 1967 in Vietnam with the first
enlisted women's unit ever to be stationed "behind" enemy lines. There were, of course, no
lines in that war; the entire country was a battlefield.

Like most of the members of all military services, I filled a support position. And whatever I
may have come, later, to think of that war, my
perspective was limited then to the scope of my
own service. I was doing what I had been asked
to do, and I applied my best abilties to the task.
I enjoyed the satisfaction of doing a job well.

Beyond that, I felt a deep conviction that *my* physical presence in Vietnam was the beginning of a new era for women in the military, one in which women might achieve equal service as well as equal pay. I knew at the time that I was being overly dramatic about it; the *unit* would have been there with or without the specific individual *me*. But every night I listened to sporadic and spectre-raising mortar fire. It was an atmosphere which promoted a sense of drama.

I did not expect to see an immediate change. I still do not expect, in my lifetime, to see an army take the field which is made up equally of men and women. But the world is not the same today as it was ten years ago, and some of the differences are significant. This article is the product of a thought problem which began for me in January of 1967 at Tan Son Nhut Air Base.

I wasn't asked to *fight* that war—not physically, not with a gun or a grenade in my hand. But look at the other side of the coin. I wasn't trained (by the Army, that is—I was something of a marksman on my own) with a weapon and I did not have access to one to use for my own defense, if necessary.

So I began to wonder. If it ever happens that women go into battle beside men, how will it occur? What changes, in technology and attitudes, will be necessary, and are they foreseeable now?

Under our current system of government, the funding, arming and recruiting (or conscripting) of a large armed force intended for combat ultimately requires the approval of a majority of the voting population. (And I can't imagine an issue more likely to bring the entire voting population to the ballot boxes!) The concept of a woman as a fighting soldier will have to be accepted widely enough that more than half of all adults—*men and women both*—will feel that women's service in combat is: (1) fair; (2) effective; and (3) beneficial to society in general.

The most obvious obstacle is the biological fact and traditional role of women as mothers. At the core of human attitudes about mothers and motherhood is the racial survival instinct which sees women as less *expendable* than men.

One male may serve, in terms of the perpetuation of the species, in the place of several. His contribution to the genetic pool is limited (assuming no societal restrictions) only by his inclination—and by the number of fertile females.

But the female human body can accept only one (or one set of) fertilized ova every nine months, usually bears only one offspring, and during gestation generates no new reproductive cells. Thus, the female is the key to maintaining stable population levels, and the life of a female must be defended, even at the cost of the life of a male.

This basic racial trait is the foundation of centuries of custom and habitual thought. It has helped *Homo sapiens* to survive highly dangerous times, and become the dominant species on Earth. We have developed complex societies, life-extending technology and . . . the population problem.

The environment is not as hazardous now as it was when a new life for every death was a good average. It is no longer necessary, in terms of minimum continuance population levels, for every woman to produce as many new humans as her body will bear. This biological truth is in the process of filtering into modern attitudes—intellect is conquering instinct.

There is growing acceptance in our society of the concept that adult men and women have a right to choose whether to have children, how many and when. Included with that acceptance is the attitude that people who choose to be parents have accepted the gravest of responsibilities, and that those responsibilities are not limited to the mother. The duties and pleasures attendant on the care of children are something to be shared by both parents. The caricature of the diaperphobic father is an image out of date in today's world.

During wars, men have handled their financial and paternal responsibilities long-distance while they fulfilled what they considered to be a more significant duty to their country. They have left a long trail of single parents and suffering families. Would such families be less viable or more tragic with *fathers* as those single parents?

In the present day, the answers to that question are *no* and *yes*. In spite of the many advances which have been made toward equality of opportunity and employment for women, a man still has a better chance to make a living which will support a family than a woman does. And society persists in viewing a motherless family as more deprived emotionally than a fatherless one. Both of these conditions are inequities.

But one of them may lead to changing the system. The military services have always given women the same pay and rank (with some exceptions) that men receive. Peacetime service offers attractions to which more and more women are responding. Besides equal pay there are the benefits of free travel, a reduced cost of living, and health and dental care for themselves and their families.

And just now peacetime service offers women one attraction which men do not share: they are fairly assured that they will *not* be channeled into combat.

I say "fairly" because—as anyone with military experience will agree—nothing is certain. It is part of the bargain made for those benefits that service people agree to assume and fulfill *any duty* to which they are assigned. When a fighting force is mobilized, cooks and typists are handed weapons. And women in all the U.S. armed services are now required to qualify in marksmanship with the same weapons as men, and to familiarize themselves with other weaponry and explosives.

Women who are already in the military service will be fighting immediately and without question in two situations: (1) if we are faced with an invasion; and (2) if war is declared at a time when half of the trained people available for immediate mobilization are women.

In the first case, of course, *everyone* would be called into defense actions. No one would deny a woman the right to defend herself and her family in a situation of threat. The second case would require desperate emergency, and though it might set a precedent for later policies would not automatically insure the permanence of women as combat troops.

So neither situation really represents a future in which women are *routinely* qualified and expected to participate in combat activity. In the world this article is reaching for, it will have to be clear that when a woman volunteers (or is drafted) into military service, she is taking the *same* chance of survival a man does.

It is time now to distinguish between all fighting units and the ultimate one—between the individual who is basically a firing mechanism for a weapon and the man who is himself a weapon.

Studies have been done which measure and compare the responses of men and women in the essentially intellectual and manipulative tasks of aiming and firing weapons. The accuracy and reaction times for women were little different from those of men, in some cases better. If the danger to the women themselves could be accepted, few people would question a woman's ability to perform any combat task which does not require physical strength and endurance.

But what about the fighting man who sits on a piece of territory and defends it with his presence, his weapon, and his life? Or carries his personal territory with him to invade the enemy's? He may know that the massive mechanized forces on his side will do whatever they can to protect him. But his gut tells him that the only things really keeping him alive are his own alertness and skill and wit—and those of his buddies.

This man is the lowest common denominator, the ultimate test. He must put the same trust in a woman that he would in a man, and not feel that her presence endangers his own chances of survival. If *he* can accept women on the battlefield, no other combat area will be closed to them.

A fighting man best trusts those people he has trained with. Beyond that, he assumes that the others around him have had the same training he has had, and he relies only a little less well on that fact. Women, then, will have to be given basic training equivalent to what a man goes through.

Equivalent. Not *equal*. Not *the same*.

Women will be trained physically to the peak of their endurance, which may not be everywhere at the same level as that of men. They will learn personal defense and killing techniques based on their different body structure and balance. In areas where physical characteristics are not so crucial—weaponry and demolition, communication and surveillance—their training will be identical. And most important, men and women will be trained *together*.

The key word here is *predictability*. A man on a fighting front asks his companions to exert themselves to their limits to protect him. He understands the basic range of those limits. If he knows what a woman can do, and that he can depend upon her to do it, it will not matter that her limits are greater than his in some areas, lesser in others. He will trust her to protect his back.

Such training will not be practical, needless to

say, unless women and men *enter* the services with equivalent backgrounds. Not just military training, but all forms of education will have to offer the same quality and range to women as to men.

But it will take more than training to create that reliance. Medical science will have to take a large step forward. Not only will a woman have to be as little likely as a man to have a baby on the battlefield, but she—and her unit—will have to be spared the discomfort and inconvenience of the menstrual cycle.

Remember that the concept of women in battle will have to be acceptable to women as well as to men. That acceptance will require that a woman need not give up anything more than a man does when he enters the service.

Separation from families is expected. But a man doesn't give up the right or the power to produce children—look at the population boom in France and Vietnam at particular times—and women will not accept such a restriction. If women have to make a choice between families and military service, then the premise of the world under discussion has been violated.

A method of birth control will have to be developed which is neither permanent nor dependent on a daily regimen which would be impractical under combat conditions. An implanted time-release ovulation suppressant might be the answer. Or a safe and reversible surgical technique may be devised. But it must exist and be routine enough that it can be administered as simply as an inoculation while female troops are being processed for shipment to a combat area.

A similar treatment for *temporary* sterility will have to be available for men. Not just because women's sense of justice will demand it, or even for the better reason of cutting down foreign births, but to eliminate as much chance as possible of battlefield pregnancy. There is no such thing as "foolproof."

Attitudes about sex will have to undergo a massive change. Sexual tension and guilt are debilitating under ordinary circumstances; under combat conditions they would be fatal.

There was a time when sex was a forbidden topic, much less a forbidden act. Today the pendulum has swung the other way and it is more than fashionable—it is compulsory. But sexual activity is not, as some claim it to be, *casual*. Nor can it ever be.

What it will have to be is *normal*. Not by today's definition (i.e. heterosexual) but in the sense that neither a man nor a woman need feel embarrassed or guilty about offering, accepting, *or refusing* any sexual act. And there must be room for people—men and women in any number or combination—to make mutual emotional commitments with no resentment from the others in their unit.

To the argument that a sexual bond would decrease effectiveness in battle because one member might lose sight of the unit in trying to protect the other member(s), I offer the Elizabethan concept of *friendship* as the highest form of love and challenge anyone to count the deaths caused by overprotectiveness or blind revenge for the deaths of "buddies" during past wars. Emotional bonds will be formed in any case when a group of people are sharing a life-and-death situation. In most combat activity, in fact, there won't be time or room or inclination for sex. But lack of opportunity is philosophically acceptable. Social or command restraint would add frustration to an already severe strain.

Members of both sexes will have to achieve adjustments in attitude.

Chivalry (in the sense that *any* man will protect *any* woman on principle) will have to go. It will die a gradual death in training as the men in each unit witness and experience the skills of the women, and it will be replaced by respect for women as fellow fighters and reliance on them as part of the team.

Women will have to make the most significant adjustment. Today women are justifiably proud of their progress toward equality. But in combat training there must be no hint of smugness. If they feel any sense of triumph about invading the final male stronghold, they will stir up territorial pride and ruin any chance of true cooperation and acceptance. Never mind that the presence of a woman in combat training means the survival of a man who isn't there. Her male counterpart will see, instead, that for the sake of what he sees as feminist stubbornness, she is taking the place of another man who might one day save *his* life.

Everyone will have to accept himself or herself and each other as members of the same team, each one contributing the best he or she has to the overall effort of fighting—and surviving—a war. Women *must* see themselves as subject to the same peril, obliged to the same duty, and capable of the same skill and sacrifice. There must be no rivalry along sex-drawn lines.

While I'm on the subject of today's progress toward equality for women—during my research I ran across one recruiter who was convinced that the ratification of the ERA would make registration for the draft mandatory for women as well as men, should registration be reinstituted.

I sought the opinion of someone I consider to be knowledgeable about the ERA and its possible effects, and she confirmed my conviction that the ERA will have no more immediate effect than the new copyright law. That is, it does not have specific applications in itself, but provides a structure against which specific cases may be measured and new precedents established. There has never been any constitutional restriction *against* conscripting women in the first place; Congress has simply never opted to do so.

That Congress recognizes the value of women to the peacetime services, however, is plain in the policy changes which have taken place in the ten years since I was a member of the Women's Army Corps. All of the service branches have lifted the restriction against married women and mothers, allowing one or more minor dependents to enlisted women.

To the traditional benefits of equal pay and free health care, the military is beginning—with limitations—to offer women equal training opportunities. No longer restricted to the typewriter and the hypodermic, women are learning many skills formerly available only to men. They are encouraged by recruitment incentives to undertake sensitive and hazardous jobs which require extensive and technical training.

In addition to marksmanship and weapons familiarization, there are programs at some locations which train women in terrorist defense tactics. And "boot camp" (in the Army at least, understandably my special interest) is coeducational, though separate sleeping quarters are still provided.

In May of 1978, the office of Director of the Women's Army Corps was deleted from the chain of command, and on October 20, 1978, the Women's Army Corps was eliminated by Congress. There is now only one U.S. Army and by 1980 it is expected to be 20 percent women.

Similar increases in female personnel are projected for all the branches, with the Marines (without benefit of a Medical Corps, traditionally highly staffed by women) at the lowest percentage of three percent.

Women have spread to fill all possible support positions in the Army, but they are still not considered to be assignable to combat. Women have broken ancient custom to serve aboard ships in the Navy, but none of their possible duty includes combat-designated craft. And in the Air Force, women pilots are restricted to relatively low-performance aircraft.

Let me now put to rest a myth which seems to have some general acceptance: that one reason why women are not allowed to fly high-performance aircraft is that they are subject to a condition with the medical term "prolapsed uterus." It means, essentially, that under high-gravity pressure such as is sometimes encountered in pulling out of a dive when the speed of the aircraft is great enough, a woman's specialized internal organs can be turned inside out.

I have heard this condition cited with solemn conviction of authority as a limitation which will prevent women from reaching space.

Bunk.

In any situation which could possibly involve G-forces intense enough to accomplish such a thing, anyone—man or woman—would be wearing a G-suit. Essentially a pair of support pantyhose with air bladders along its surface, a G-suit is designed to provide exactly the kind of abdominal compression which would prevent prolapsing, if women were indeed subject to it. Nowhere in my research did I find anyone who could verify a single occurrence of the condition.

At Ames Research Center in Mountain View, California, research is under way with the objective that anyone who wants to go into space ought to be able, physically, to do so. They have been conducting "bed rest" tests to study the most serious effect of space flight, the adaptation of the human heart to the lesser effort of pumping blood when the body is in a weightless state. They have determined that seven days of immobilization horizontally produces approximately the same effect on men that weightless space flight does. It is impossible to state that the comparison holds for women, as well, since we have no space flight data on women at this time. (The U.S.S.R. has not shared whatever it learned about its single female astronaut.)

The results so far indicate that women are slightly more subject to fainting when they return to normal—i.e., when they stand up at the end of their confinement and their hearts have to carry a one-G burden again. Testing has proven that the use of a G-suit, which compensates for gravity loss by compressing the blood vessels in the subject's legs and abdomen and maintaining a higher blood pressure, eliminates the fainting problem for men as well as women.

The emphasis of the research at Ames is on space shuttle flight, which will involve a maximum stress of two and one-half gravities. They have tested a wide range of age and racial groups, male and female, and have discovered an expected mild variance in reaction. They have so far found *no* healthy person who has been injured by that level of acceleration.

The maximum G-stress for men, in general, is five G's. I have to say "in general" because experimentation has begun on manned aircraft which will require pilots to withstand forces of ten or twelve G's.

Women's G-stress tolerance is unknown, and so can't be compared to that of men. In the last ten years the centrifuge at Brooks Air Force Base in Texas has been testing men daily, but in that time only a bare handful of women have been tested. Logically, given adequate training and preparation, a woman should show a slightly higher tolerance than a man, if there is a measurable difference at all. With a lesser body-volume to feed, the heart needs less effort to supply it with enough blood to maintain conscious function.

The void of data about women in space will soon be corrected. Of the eight thousand applications received for the latest group of Astronaut Candidates, fifteen hundred of them came from women—eighteen percent. The selections were made at roughly the same percentage: six of the thirty-five Astronaut Candidates who began their training in July 1978 are women. They are all mission specialists; no women are among the fifteen pilots because experience in high-performance aircraft was one of the prerequisites.

When the group has finished its training in July 1980, these female astronauts will be eligible for election to missions. Once the shuttle program gets into full swing, there will be forty to fifty flights a year, and the odds are good that women will be flying space regularly before the end of the century.

How does the space program connect into women in warfare? In two ways.

When humans go into space on a large scale, it is likely (if not tragically certain) that they will take war with them. The world I am postulating is one in which women share all forms of fighting with men; it is essential, then, that women be as welcome and comfortable in space as men are.

To make them *comfortable* will require a concentration of research. Not only to design a space suit which does not require catheterizing to allow for elimination, but to control menstrual flow for long-term space flight. Medical developments stimulated by the space program will contribute to the progress of women in the military, and achievements there will open new levels of training which will then give women more avenues into the space program.

The synergy has already begun. The changes I've been discussing are under way or just around the corner.

That they will result in exactly the world I've

pictured, a world where women participate in all aspects of the military effort, is far from certain. There are a lot of ifs.

The emotional effects of childbirth on mothers have never been fully assessed. A man contributes his cells and his love to a family; a woman *creates* it from her own body. The "maternal instinct," a woman's desire to protect her children from harm, is another racial trait which will have to be considered.

Assuming that a woman has made the intellectual choice, through volunteering or accepting conscription, to participate in combat, the instinct might surface in her behavior in a number of ways. It might give her greater motivation and contribute to a dependable performance. On the other hand, she might become *too* motivated and take unnecessary risks which would endanger her unit. Or the instinct might manifest itself as untimely hesitation in critical circumstances as a woman speculates on the fate of her children without her.

This is one question which can only be answered by experience. Until women are actually fighting, there will be no observations with which to gauge the effect of motherhood on combat performance.

Which brings up another big question. Why would women *want* to fight in a war?

For the same reasons men do: except for the very few for whom the aggression of war is a personal release, they *don't*.

I've already sketched some of the benefits of peacetime service, and there are many others. When a man volunteers for military duty, he's betting that there *won't* be a war. The first women who fight will have made that same bet—and lost.

If war breaks out and the draft is reinstituted, I believe that women *will* be required to register. Not because women demand it, but because a *man* carries through the Supreme Court his protest that he should not be asked to serve in a military force if his sister/wife/female neighbor isn't subject to the same obligation.

If that war requires enough "manpower," women (now a higher percentage of personnel than ever before) will be needed closer and closer to the combat areas, until they are required for their own defense to carry and use weapons. Their abilities under fire will then be proven.

Such a test case will be necessary before general acceptance can ever begin. In every new field into which women have entered, there have been a few individuals, by choice or circumstance, who broke the ground. There will have to be a situation—if not wartime activity, perhaps a localized terrorist attack—in which it will be natural and unavoidable that women demonstrate their abilities and their dedication.

Dedication. The word brings back the earlier question. Again: why?

There will be some who want to fight simply —but with profound conviction—because they are now forbidden to do so.

A woman who has lost a husband or a lover to the war might want to take the field on a quest for revenge.

Women are as subject as men to the kind of personality that rebels against just sitting and waiting. Such women would prefer to take an active part in determining the outcome of a war.

And do not discount a woman's sense of honor. Is it *fair* that men have to do all the fighting?

War is ugly and terrible. People die and people grieve, and who is to say which fate is kinder? Give women the choice, and you also give that choice to men.

Some basic assumptions have been made throughout this article which should be stated here for clarity.

First, that wars are fought with people, no matter what technology they manipulate or tactics they implement.

Second, that women are as capable of effective combat as men are. Which is not to say they will react or move in exactly the same fashion, but that their actions will be dependable and will contribute in equal measure to the efficiency of a fighting team.

And last, that no amount of equality, in training or opportunity, will turn women *into* men. There are *two* human sexes with different physical characteristics and abilities. When it happens, *fighting men and women* will take the field together.

Will it ever happen? That it will be resisted— by men and women—is certain. That it will be advocated—by men and women—is just as certain. Too much depends on the incidence and order of occurrence of events which cannot be foreseen. I will not dare to offer a prediction.

But there is another question:

Should it happen?

I say *yes*. If a war has to be fought, we should *all* be fighting. Women should share the glory . . . and the burden.

Vicki Ann Heydron is a native Californian who has worked at a variety of clerical jobs, has always been underpaid, and credits her attendance at a science fiction convention in 1975 with motivating her to become a writer full-time.

Her enlistment in the Woman's Army Corps (1965–1968) was a learning and a growing experience for her. She dedicates her article, printed here, with respect and gratitude, to the finest soldier she has ever met: Brigadier General Elizabeth P. Hoisington, U.S.A. (Retired).

Ms. Heydron and her partner-husband, Randall Garrett, are currently at work on a trilogy of novels due out from Bantam.

Should women serve in the armed forces? There are solid arguments on both sides. However, I myself think that a major reason for the issue being raised at all, in today's atmosphere of Women's Lib, is the well-founded suspicion that a virtual male monopoly of the use of weapons has contributed heavily to male dominance in the past; and it is interesting to speculate on what might happen were the coin of dominance to be reversed completely—as it is in this story by James Stevens.

James Stevens

THIS FAITHFUL SOLDIER'S LIFE

Shad, the heat, the desert heat. My brains are broiling.

I was cool once, I remember; delicious sensation. I was seventeen and home alone with my twin sister Ksera, our mothers away for the holiday. The icefurs were white. Such a fresh, sweet smell, so cool a touch to the skin. Our bodies on the icefurs were bronzed and strong, the muscles firm and fluid.

We touched.

We moved together and the warmth then was good. We rested and, where we had not lain, the icefur still was cool. And the icy spray from the pool jets tickled the blood alive.

I could breathe then. The air was crisp. Not this furnace that cooks the lungs.

How does Bredl hold up? I pant, I gasp. She chews smoke and enjoys it. She's made of flint. She's a machine.

The road runs to the horizon and evaporates. The desert sprawls cracked and alkaline around us. Distorted by heatwaves, we plod along the road.

Only Bredl and I display a military bearing. The slap of holster on thigh, the creak of leather straps, footfalls, breathing are the only sounds.

The cheeks of the seven prisoners are sunken; their eyes, bloated. Their bodies are old, though none has seen his fortieth year.

Bredl speaks crisply: "Halt."

The prisoners stop. Faded clothing hangs loosely from their withered frames, like elephant skin. Their hands are bony, the skin shriveled.

No one sits. The ground is too hot and there is no shade. Bredl offers me a smokeball.

"Smoke? In this heat?" I say.

"Helps ease my stomach cramps."

I shake my head slightly, my strength sapped by the heat. Bredl shrugs and pops a smokeball into her mouth.

We both wear soft leather boots and white burnooses. Beamers are clipped to our shoulders and leather trey-belts with holstered needlers, canteens, and paramedical pouches encircle our waists. We are both strongboned and deeply tanned, and silver cat's-eyes illuminate our aquiline features. We could be twins were not three white chevrons tattooed below Bredl's left cheekbone, only two below mine. I call her Top and she calls me Second, though my name is Dammid. The Top studies the prisoners with idle interest now. The silver iris of each eye mirrors the image of dead men.

Walking dead.

These men. Husks of men, rather. Once men. They are repulsive. Their bodies are malformed. They have the brows and eye-sockets of apes. No wonder they are an abomination in the sight of the Mother.

They are less than human.

Still, I feel no personal hatred for them. Our lives touch only tangentially. They are genetic cripples, born twisted through no fault of their own, motivated perhaps by the cripple's self-hatred. I pity them.

They are told, "Bear your bodies to be executed," and they obey. Strangely, this disturbs me. If they must die, their killing should be a detached necessity, not this queer ceremony. This ritual murder we are sent to perform in an alien shrine is no soldiering.

Not that I pretend to any sort of moral superiority. Far from it. But, I do know this: there are many less perfect morally than I. That is simply a fact. I try to live my life as I best know how. I try to do no injury to others that can be avoided. I try to think of the other woman first, to treat her as I would wish her to treat me. Though I freely confess to having committed my share of sins, I think I am one of the good people.

Sins. Oh yes. Our mothers never suspected the secret Ksera and I shared, and so my twin and I were never punished. Even now, when I remember, the fear that my mothers will find us out and punish me, though both have been dead for fifteen years, still lives. I think that fear will live in me till I die.

I remember, too, my first combat kill. On Shabbazz, the grook plinked away at me from a honeycomb of granite. I circled behind him and, from above, watched him intermittently snap off a charge at the helmet I'd left behind as a decoy. Safe, he must have felt, enclosed in granite and I supposedly below him and pinned.

I raised my beamer. His head sat in my sights like a pumpkin on a fence. A light squeeze of my thumb would have fused his head and helmet to the rock he so trusted. God perched above the grook and balanced his life on the tip of her thumb while the grook thought he played God to me.

I adjusted my sights, and the scope zoomed in to show me his flatboned profile, sharply focused, so near my eye that it seemed I could kill him by reaching out and scratching a thin, bloody line across his cheekbone with the poison needle in my fingernail. I felt cold, sharp, efficient. My lips were dry with excitement.

He popped a charge at my helmet, and melted rock a good three meters away. He huddled back into his fortress, and I read the fear in his face. Not fear of me. Fear of death. Fear had seized him by the neck and shaken him till his bones chattered.

Suddenly, I understood him, because I felt the same cold dread in my belly. He glanced over his shoulder directly into my scope, and I looked deep into his glistening eyes and saw something

of me in him. I knew then I would not kill him.
He fired at me. The charge burned off my eye-
lashes and eyebrows.

I burned a hole in his chest large enough to
hold his fucking head.

Shad, the heat. It sets the mind to odd re-
flections.

The prisoners plod on, insensible to pain or
discomfort. Bredl struts as though she were on
parade on the wide avenues of Haichankka,
cooled by the sweet coastal seabreeze.

Haichankka: Ksera is garrisoned there. . . .

Odd how the Earth woman María reminds
me of Ksera. Not physically, for María is short
and stocky and her left foot is slightly clubbed,
but there is a sparkle of joy in her eyes, an insou-
ciance in her smile, that I had previously noticed
in no one but Ksera.

I can only wonder at the marvelous coin-
cidence of evolution which allows the Earth
women to mate with us. María's vagina is almost
identical to mine. The only important difference
is that her clitoris, unlike mine, cannot produce
sperm. I can give her a daughter but, sadly, she
cannot give me one. Unlike us, the Terran
females cannot impregnate one another. Until
we discovered and liberated this world, they depended on their males for reproduction. How
painful that must have been! How humiliating!
And how horrible that about half the offspring
were *male*.

Now we have come, and we have exterminated
their males, save for these few nomadic guerrilla
bands that we still hunt. Kill in combat, or capture and execute: that is our procedure. Every

new day, this alien sun rises on fewer males. And one day, we will find and kill the last male, and the Liberation will be complete.

The prisoners, now, they are impossible to fathom. A broken man is only a hint of the whole man. We know they are members of the Resistance, the damnable guerrillas who somehow survive to harass us, to slash and run and leave us as dead as though we had not annihilated the male armies a full five years ago. How do they manage to survive? Where do they hide? Who supplies their food and weapons? The answers to these questions still elude us. We know some of their women must be aiding them, but which ones? And *why?*

In our own early stages of evolution, the Catechism teaches, we too were oppressed by our males. They envied us that we could reproduce with either sex, while they could reproduce only with one of us. Their envy and arrogance were such that they dared enact a law forbidding women to mate with each other. This was the unpardonable sin, and God the Mother invoked all womankind to rise up and strike down the proud males. Thus was the Mother's Hegemony first established, and thus did each of us become a Shadanna, a woman of God, and our people become the sa-Shadanna, the women of God.

Some of the Apocrypha say that not all women stood together, that some turned traitor and sided with the men against their own kind. The Church tells us these are falsehoods, propaganda concocted by the males during their final days in an attempt to break our foremothers' solidarity. They failed, of course, for their words were recognized for the lies they were. The Catechism teaches that during the glorious days of our Liberation, all women were as one, and *that*, we know, is the real truth.

Yet, when we came bearing the good news of the Liberation to this planet, there were some among the women of Earth who sided with their men, who called us alien invaders and fought with the male armies against us. No matter. We have forgiven and educated the ones who were not killed.

Our vengeance on the remaining males now is terrible. We do not simply kill these men who would reclaim their world. We suck their minds, their very souls, from their bodies, and snap and crumble them like rotten stone. We have techniques.

I hate this world. It's a dirty tour of duty and no world for a soldier.

Bredl says I think too much. Bredl never thinks. Bredl listens and obeys. Her mask is impassive. Her sergeant's mask. Will I too assume that mask when I'm issued my third stripe?

Do I wear one now?

"Anywhere back home this hot, Top?" I say, panting.

Bredl ignores the question. She loosens her canteen and drinks deeply. She sighs. "Shad, these damn cramps! They just come and go as they please." She pops another smokeball and offers me her canteen.

I take a long pull. Some of the chilled water trickles down the side of my mouth. It spatters dustily on the road and vanishes in a crackle of heat. A sound like meat sizzling. I return the canteen and jerk my head toward the prisoners.

"What about them?"

Bredl slits her eyes against the sun and looks at the men. They stand apathetically. She shrugs. "They'll be dead soon." That's the kind of person she is.

I feel an itch in my crotch, the result of cropping short my thick coils of pubic hair at Maria's behest. Keeping an eye on Bredl, who is studying the prisoners disinterestedly, I surreptitiously scratch myself through the folds of my burnoose.

"They'll be dead in less than an hour," Bredl says.

Relieved, I stop scratching. Suddenly, I feel I'd like some conversation, some sign of life in this scorched land.

"Say, Top?"

"Yeah?"

"You think there's anything to the bunk-buzz?"

"What bunkbuzz is that?"

I glance at the prisoners. They remain huddled together, insensible. I lower my voice confidingly.

"They say that some troops—not in our unit, but on some of the other Posts—that they've been . . . well . . . *raped*. By . . . ahm . . . well . . . *ghosts* is what they call them. While the troop was on solo guard."

Bredl regards me dispassionately with her sergeant's mask. Smoke oozes forth from between her thin lips.

"Top, they say these ghosts are *male*."

"That's what you hear?"

"Yeah, that's right. They do it in gangs. Some of them cover the troop's mouth and pin her down and they all take turns on her."

"You know any of these troops personally?"

"No, this is just what I hear. *You* know. What's going around."

"Then you don't know it for a fact."

"No, but they say troops have come up pregnant and had to be aborted. They say the fetuses were male! Can you *believe* that?"

"No. And if I were you, I wouldn't either."

"No?"

"Command's heard these rumors. They've checked them out. Official word is that that's all they are: rumors. They're looking to find out now who started the whole thing."

"That'll be tough. Bunkbuzz just . . . starts."

"I wouldn't spread that particular buzz anymore if I were you, Second. Or believe it."

"Me? You know I don't take stock in that dazey kind of chatter."

Bredl smiles. "Just a friendly tip."

I look at the seven men and lick my dry lips. "Sure. Thanks, Top."

The Top swallows smoke. She nods to herself and belches forth a thick cloud. The smoke drifts to the ground. She shields her eyes with her forearm. The sky is a bright blue flame.

I feel feverish.

Bredl spits the dead smokeball onto the sand and barks, "Time's up. Let's move on."

The prisoners resume plodding. We fall in behind.

"Who'd have imagined these people would be so much like us," I say by way of distracting my thoughts from the fire in my brain. "We can even mate with them. Shad, the odds against it."

Bredl grunts. "You find that appealing?"

"Find what appealing?"

She indicates the males with a purse of her lips. "Mating with one of them."

I can't believe she's misinterpreted me. "You must be kidding, Top. That is really disgusting! That is—"

She cuts me off. "That's right, Second. I'm kidding. You got it."

We walk in silence. She's such a fucking bastard.

The heat crushes me like a boot. The air catches in my throat. I move closer to Bredl, and match her steady, rhythmic step.

"How much farther do you think, Top?" I say, gasping.

Expressionless, Bredl says, "Not much. You'd see it now if it weren't for the heatwaves."

I nod and, for several minutes, concentrate on breathing. Then I say, "Why do we do it out here?"

"This your first time?"

"Yeah."

Bredl nods. "Orders." Her voice is flat and, like her face, expressionless. Her gaze fixes on the wavering horizon, and something like love shimmers below the silver surface of her eyes.

"Uh, yeah, right, Top, but what I wonder is, why out here? Why not back at Post? Be a whole lot easier."

"Damned if I know. What's it to you?"

"Huh? Nothing. Nothing at all."

Silence.

I say: "I overheard Captain Shim say something about 'the symbolic value of the location.'"

Silence.

I say: "Odd that they never ambush these execution details. Brass never sends more than two troops anymore, do they?"

Silence.

I jerk my head toward the prisoners shambling along the road ahead. I say: "They look harmless."

Bredl whirls on me! *"You always talk so damn much!"*

I feel like someone slapped awake. "Huh?"

"Chatter, bunkbuzz, questions—what is with you, Second?"

"Nothing. Not a thing." I wipe at the sweat on my face with a damp forearm. "It must be the heat."

In the distance, a structure materializes from the dancing air: four walls, perhaps twenty meters high, bleached white by the sun, cracked by the dry heat.

We reach the structure and halt before it. In the center of the facing wall, an archway yawns five meters high and twenty meters wide.

A perfect place for an ambush.

Shad, the place has an ancient feel to it! A feel of ritual, of men meeting in ceremonies to appease their god. A wrathful, fiery, male god. The atmosphere is compelling. I want to place the Circle on my forehead with my forefinger.

I have no stomach for killing these men.

Not in this place. It would be a . . . a . . . desecration. I sense it. I feel it seep through my skin and muscle into my bone like water into dry pumice.

I know it would be a terrible sin to fail in my mission. I know that males are evil and must be blotted from creation. I know my duty as a daughter of the Mother and a troop of the Queen.

I *know* these things. But do I believe them? I know I do not hate those that I am ordered to kill. Nor do I love those I am sworn to protect. Whom *do* I love? Myself, I suppose. Ksera. Our daugher Karra. The Earth woman María. And my mothers, but they're dead. So: I love only three living people besides myself. What possible difference could the execution of these men make in their lives? What loss, what gain?

When I was younger, I longed for a simple life. Complexity frightened me. Decisions were monsters waiting to devour me. What better choice, then, than a soldier's life? No need to think, no need to decide, no need to question.

But as I grew older, I discovered that though I had run, I could not hide. *I* am complex. I cannot stop myself from thinking, balancing possibilities, questioning orders. So, I am unsuccessful in my chosen field. I don't understand myself or my life. I find myself frightening. I feel I am becoming a monster, and I have no idea what to do. Except for María, I am alone on this hostile world. That, too, is frightening.

As a child, I was taught the sanctity of life. As a soldier, I was taught the justification of murder. When I kill, I kill because I am so ordered. Each time I kill, I feel myself diminished. But I have found that each kill makes the next

one easier. The child within me weeps in fear
and sorrow, but the soldier exults. What I fear
most is that the soldier will one day kill the child.
That is what I must resist if I'm to preserve the
worthwhile part of myself. I must stop killing.

I could speak to Bredl now. Explain. Tell her
this place is sacred. She must sense that. She's
religious, still goes to Worship. She would understand.

We leave the prisoners here. They are already
dead anyway. We leave them and go back to
Post and, when they ask, we say, "Yes, we
burned them."

Yes.

No, Bredl would never go along. She's been a
soldier too long. Thirty years? She's killed too
often. The child within her is long dead. She
would never disobey an order. I'd find myself up
for a court when we get back if I suggested it.

Shad, this heat. The heavens are afire.

What, then?

Kill Bredl? Burn her while she's sighting in on
the prisoners. She'd never expect it. She'd be
thinking only of killing. Bloodthirsty bastard.

The air: it shimmers, ripples. The prisoners
waver and blur like corpses underwater.

I remember that killing the grook gave me a
strange afterglow.

I burn Bredl. One life for seven. Seven symbolic lives, they are already dead. Bredl and I, we
return to Post, and we are safe. She never speaks
of this, for she is dead, and that too is our secret.

Shad, I cannot think in this heat. I feel as
though I had been damned and sent to hell. I
can't bear this much longer. I must find peace.

Bredl barks: "All right. Everybody inside."

We are swallowed into an immense courtyard. Four stark white walls reflect and re-reflect the light, concentrating its fieriness within the yard.

Bredl says: "Halt."

The prisoners stop. They stand in a ragtag bunch in the center of the courtyard, at the focus of the sun's rage.

A look of pain comes over Bredl. She grunts and doubles over as though struck a sharp blow to the belly.

"What's the matter?" I say. I feel confused by the heat and resent this new claim on my attention.

"Ungh!" Bredl grunts again. "My damn cramps."

"Is it—?"

"It's *nothing*. I can handle it."

"Is there anything I can—?"

"No! No, just leave me alone, will you? What I've got to do is take a good dump."

"Now?"

"Yes, dammit, *now*!"

"But, Top, you can't, not here—"

"Oh, Shad, it hurts! Let me just go off by myself for a few minutes."

"But, Top—"

"But *what*?"

". . . the prisoners, what about . . ."

Bredl stares at me, waiting for me to complete my thought, but I only stare back, having lost it. Finally, through the pain, Bredl realizes that I can think of nothing to add.

"*They're* not going anywhere, right, Second?"

"Uh . . . right, Top, yeah. . . ."

"Then just give me a few minutes, all right? I'll just go off this way a little." She lurches off toward the entrance. Pain contorts her face. "Oh, Shad!" Bredl manages to half-stagger through the archway and vanishes outside the walls.

Apprehensively, I turn back to the prisoners. For a moment, I imagine that they may take advantage of Bredl's absence to try to overpower me. I remember then that these are husks, not men, and that their eyes are empty. I relax. Around me, I feel the air shimmer, ripple. But when our eyes meet, the men's are not empty.

Their eyes are smiling impishly.

As I gasp in astonishment, the prisoners wink at me in unison.

I curse and my body spasms in surprise. I throw a wild-eyed glance over my shoulder. Bredl is still out of sight and earshot. I look back at the seven and they are all smiling, *Mother, they are all smiling!* And there is a touch of the devil's glee in the corners of each mouth.

"Top!" I cry out, but Bredl is lost in her own pain.

I raise my beamer.

—*I thought she didn't want to kill us*, a voice says, though I see no lips move.

—*She'd like to believe she doesn't want to kill us.*

—*She's scared.*

—*Scared? Of us?* Mockingly.

—*Scared and excited. She's a queer one.*

—*But she's one of the* good *people.* A new voice, also mocking. *Not like the Top. The Top's a blind follower.*

—*The Second's no automaton. Right, Second?*

—*When the time comes, as it one day surely must,*

*that she's ordered to do something she cannot coun-
tenance, something so evil she finally cannot rationalize
it away, then she'll act like the person she tells herself she
really is. She'll take the principled course and fly in the
face of authority, no matter what cost, to preserve her
sense of personal integrity. And why? Because, in the
end, what else does any person have? Right, Second?*

—*And yet . . . consider the grook.*

—*That wasn't the right time.*

Laughter, with reverberations.

—*She thinks she's hearing voices.*

More laughter.

—*Hey, Second, you're spinning dizzy, ah?*

—*Popping head?*

—*Crumple numb, crumple numb?* Always mocking.

I hold the beamer firmly, but my voice trem-
bles. "You're telepaths!"

—*Very quick on the catch-up.*

—*A model subject.*

Fear floods my mouth and nostrils. "If you
make the slightest move to—"

—*Not a chance, Second.*

—*She feeling insecure?*

—*How can she feel anything but secure? Earth is
her world now.*

—*Conquered, crushed, and molded in her own image.*

In spite of my efforts to suppress it, hysteria is
overcoming me. My voice has grown ragged.

"*Be quiet!*"

The men's eyes die. Their bodies sag.

"You are rebels, you are inferior, and you are
male!" I slide my gaze over them cagily. The air
appears transparent now. It no longer distorts
my vision. "Do you understand that? You are
not fit to rule *any world!* You are aberrations of

nature and nature must be purified of you! I do
the Will of my God and She has commanded
your eradication!" How readily the words of the
Catechism roll off my tongue; how they soothe
and comfort.

I dart a glance over my shoulder. No sign yet
of Bredl. The men remain impassive and spir-
itless. They give no sign of having ever displayed
intelligence. The fever in my brain makes me
want to scream.

"Throwbacks! Abnormals! Filthy sports!" I
rage, regretting now my earlier impulse of
mercy. The heatcrazed air shimmers as fear and
fascination speak through me. "Broken
chromosomes, hideous bodies, destroyers! Even
your women despise you!"

One face lights up with amusement.

—Do they?

"They mate with *us* now! They have learned
to love *us*. My own María confesses this."

—Ah, then it must be true.

"It *is* true!"

—María, you say?

I grow suddenly wary. "What of her?"

*—I know one María. Could she be the same, your
María?*

"No!"

*—My María's left foot is slightly clubbed, and she
bites the knuckle of her index finger at the moment of
climax.*

Hatred as hot as the desert sun floods my head
and body. It is difficult to breathe. I raise the
beamer and thumb it to full aperture.

*—What have we here now? An interesting variation
on the eternal triangle, no? María and I have enjoyed one*

*another. And you apparently have enjoyed María. And
perhaps María has even enjoyed you. But the triangle is
incomplete, ah? There are still two points to be joined.*

I level my weapon and fire, thumbing gently
like they teach you in Basic.

—So perhaps now . . .

I fire repeatedly, but do no harm. The weapon
might be a toy.

When he lays hands on me, I scream. Combat
trained reflexes react, but my body responds
sluggishly, and the men have me. They strip me
and spreadeagle me on the sand. It sears my
flesh and I scream again, but one of the men covers my mouth with his hand, which is suddenly
young and no longer withered, and does not remove it no matter how I struggle.

Then María's lover mounts me and rips me in
two. And each man follows in turn until I have
been defiled seven times.

I regain consciousness in a state of severe dis-
orientation but of outward calm. I am clothed,
and I should not be. I am armed, and I should
not be. I feel no pain between my legs nor across
my back, though I know I should. The prisoners
remain, though they should have fled. And I myself am alive when I should be dead, for I am
become an abomination in the sight of the Mother.

"Are you all right?" Bredl's voice betrays
more anger than solicitude.

I get to my feet. I move inexorably but slowly,
like someone under water. I raise my beamer to
my shoulder and I aim it through the still,
crystalline air.

"Are you all right, damn you!"

I stop and consider my weapon, recalling its earlier betrayal. I testfire it into the ground near our feet, fusing sand into glass. I scarcely notice the added heat of the weapon's discharge.

"Shad!" Bredl curses. "Are you going dazey?"

"Was I naked when you came back? Did you dress me?" My voice sounds queer indeed to me, in great pain but utterly calm.

"What are you talking about, Second?"

"They raped me."

"Who raped you?"

"The prisoners."

"You *are* dazey."

"But I *was* naked when you came back, wasn't I? You *did* dress me."

"No such thing."

"Then *they* did. They raped me and dressed me while I was unconscious to make it look like I'd imagined it."

"Second, if you really believe all this happened, you are begging for a D-section. These are zombies you're talking about. They have no will of their own left. No one's touched you."

I brake the unreason careening within me. I try to perceive my surroundings objectively. Bredl is serious. Bredl thinks I have blown. The prisoners are immobile and unthreatening. They are zombies. I am clothed, fully armed, and apparently untouched.

Overhead, the sun flares, and the heat, the hellish heat, returns in full force. It stifles and dizzies me.

"You passed out, Second, that's all."

"This heat . . ."

"Right. The heat got to you."

"I can't take it like you can. . . ."

"You okay now?"

"I think so, yeah. Shad-o, I thought they were talking to me . . . not talking, *thinking* . . . I thought they were telepaths. . . ."

"It didn't happen."

"No. . . ."

"All in your mind."

But I feel as though it happened. Feel humiliated, degraded. Could the heat truly have warped my senses so? Shad, this lust for revenge that fills me now! Incredible sensation. Like ecstasy. And the fear. I fear these zombies.

They are no threat to me now. But I thought the same before they . . . before I hallucinated. Yet isn't it the same thing? If I believe it happened, then for me it is real.

The things they said, their mockery, their intimate knowledge of the grook, of María, of *me* . . . and that last one's claims about María . . . products of my imagination? Fears from deep in my unconscious surfacing in this shimmering desert air? Yet why would I imagine her being faithless to me *with a male*? How could I even conceive such a thought?

Look at them now. Could anything look more harmless?

They're faking.

No matter. I know now they're evil. I know they deserve to die. I know I was wrong to question their execution. Now it will give me great pleasure to kill them.

Bredl and I raise beamer to shoulder as though we are both tugged by the same string. I center my sights on a prisoner's face. It is the face of the one who claims to be María's lover. His head sits in my sights like a pumpkin on a fence. My lips are dry with excitement.

His eyes are empty and they do not blink. The sun crowds the sky.

Flames lash out from our beamers with a sound like the cracking of branches. The sound reverberates like laughter within the whitewalled enclosure.

The prisoners crumple soundlessly. Thin ribbons of blood trickle from the flashcooked meat of their bodies. The earth begins to suck them dry.

We re-clip our beamers. We exchange no words, no looks. We turn and trudge back to the road, each alone, locked in her private thoughts.

I feel very lucid. The guerrillas are dead, and that is good. These are seven males who will kill no more women of God. The heat must have set me spinning dizzy while Bredl was gone, but I recovered in time. I did my duty. The bastards are dead.

Soon, vultures will come.

Now I begin to feel odd. This heat, this heat . . . the memory of the grook's eyes . . . María . . . these men. I feel odd. I feel a latent throb in my belly like the time I got pregnant by my sister Ksera. I feel the expectation of new life.

I must be mad.

Why do I choose to live this life, this faithful soldier's life? What lonely inner need shackles me to this life of rootlessness and discipline, of self-subordination and killing? I hate it, yet something in me cannot live without it.

I didn't want to kill the grook. I felt a kinship with him. And I didn't want to kill these men. I pitied them. But the soldier in me always finds an excuse.

Bredl says I imagined the rape. Perhaps I did. To find an excuse. But it makes no difference. What's real to me may not be real to her. That proves only that we perceive things differently. Reality is subjective, and each of us is the center of the universe.

Now I begin to feel warm, excited, an almost floating afterglow. I feel, too, a touch of fear, as though I might be punished for this pleasure. The child within me, I believe, longs to be punished, to be stopped. But I won't be punished. I am safe.

I kill because I'm so ordered. I kill for the Mother and the Queen. I am a good and faithful soldier.

For me, there can be no punishment.

James Stevens lives in Hato Rey, Puerto Rico, with his wife, small son, and smaller daughter. He has worked as a radio announcer, teaching assistant in public speaking and expository writing, teacher of beginning film-making, technical assistant in theatrical set construction, stage manager and assistant director for Opera de Puerto Rico, and folksinger-guitarist. In film, he has worked as producer, director, cameraman, editor, actor, writer, and announcer. Also, he was Broadcast Production Chief for ad agencies Publitec de Puerto Rico and Foote, Cone & Belding Caribbean. Currently, he is vice-president of his father's talent booking agency, a job that includes everything from developing new talent to producing and directing TV commercials and other film projects.

He started reading science fiction at the age of ten and writing and selling it—both intermittently—at twenty-two.

The role of the warrior in any future war can be defined by examining his role throughout the centuries of man's military history, as T. R. Fehrenbach does here. Even if wars between men and men become eventually— as they show signs of doing—wars of machine against machine, those men who operate the machines, or program the machines, or program the machines that in turn run other machines, will still have to be warriors. This will be true even if wars become contests without bloodshed, like chess or fencing or any one of the many science fiction war games now so popular. The warrior has always been a part of mankind, and every man has in him something of the warrior: aggressiveness, the will to win, and the barbarian joy in battle. We cannot eliminate the warrior without destroying man himself— but we can, because we have to some extent done so in the past—discipline him and, yes, civilize him.

T. R. Fehrenbach

THE ULTIMATE WEAPON

There is still one ultimate weapon . . . the only weapon capable of operating with complete effectiveness—of dominating every inch of terrain where human beings live and fight, and of doing it under all conditions of light and darkness, heat and cold, desert and forest, mountain and plain. That weapon is man himself.

General Matthew B. Ridgway

In this age as in every age, man must contemplate the future of warfare.

There is very little doubt that there will be future war. War runs like a continuing thread through all recorded human history; combat between men fills the legends of prehistory. In the absence of a true science of man, the argument between ethologists and behaviorists whether human belligerence is instinctive and thus ineradicable, or socially conditioned and therefore ameliorable, remains in the realms of theory—we simply don't know. What we do know is that, as Matthew 24:6 prophesied, there have been wars and rumors of wars and the end is not yet.

The doctrine of the United States Army, formulated before 1914, states that due to the unchanging nature of man, wars are inevitable and nations must plan for them. Asimov's rules of futurity suggest that what has happened will continue to happen. In the meantime, war persists, decade after decade on this planet, as a constant reminder that our species remains what it is and not what we might wish it to be.

The fact is, despite its destructiveness, inherent tragedy, and potential danger to civilization, war is too useful to human beings to be eschewed, even if they were psychically capable of this. Peoples fight wars to win liberation or dominance (the two are often inseparable, wars of liberation merging into wars of conquest); to extend their ideologies, frontiers, or to seize wealth (and the three motives are frequently hopelessly confused, as Sorel wrote of the French Revolution); or to frustrate the aggressive ambitions of others.

War might be described as the rational act of a perhaps ultra-rational species. It is a process of controlled violence directed toward a goal or purpose, devolving into a moral conflict which requires sustained acts of will, and defeat or victory is usually brought about by the moral collapse of one combatant rather than by its utter destruction. This was the Roman view and practice of war, and it was shared by most Victorians.

However, the quantum leaps in technology and human organization in the twentieth century have created enormous problems for what Harold Lasswell called the "management of violence." The mass slaughters, enormous destruction, and incalculable social consequences of the 1914–8 war showed clearly that the process was moving beyond control, and ironically, as both American Presidents and Marxist-Leninist Central Committees came to accept Clausewitz's description of war as an extension of politics, the development of nuclear weaponry has tended to render that definition obsolete, at least between major powers armed with effective intercontinental missiles.

The ensuing "balance of terror" may well have prevented general war since 1945, but it is an uneasy, unstable balance which has given rise to two principal speculations regarding the future of warfare.

The first scenario presumes that total nuclear

war is inevitable, since historically men have
never been barred by scruples from using any
means of power at their disposal. The nations
must therefore prepare for nuclear exchanges,
"learn about gunpowder," and accept the idea
of mega-deaths. Since the nature of the weaponry is overwhelmingly offensive, the emphasis in
war-planning is not on defense but toward "first-
strike capabilities" and "massive retaliation."

This scenario is relished by some civilian
strategists and apparently held by many ideo-
logues, including fervent nationalists, right-
wingers, and ("*some* Chinese will survive") pure
Marxists.

The second vision of the future holds that the
only hope of survival lies in the abandonment of
war. Its adherents call for the rejection of war as
policy, with a first step of disarmament. This
scenario does not shy away from total surrender
—"better Red than dead." It is favored by
pacifists, idealists, believers in world government, and some of the simply terrified.

The major nations have devoted time, energy,
and resources toward developing both scenarios.
Weapons have been stockpiled and delivery systems improved, while peace plans and arms-lim-
itation formulas are devised endlessly.

Both concepts are extremes; both are flawed
as sound projections for the future.

Total nuclear warfare between heavily-armed
powers would require totally unacceptable levels
of death and destruction, negating the very purpose of war. It would not even serve the purpose
of jihad, since the goal of holy war is hardly to
convert the infidel into incandescent energy. The

scenario cannot be ruled out entirely while nations actually prepare for it, and given the ultra-rationality of our species, it may happen through aberration, miscalculation, or sheer mischance. However, the danger of accidental triggering is so well recognized that the possibilities are diminishing.

Such a war almost certainly will not occur through policy. There have been rare wars of extermination, such as Charlemagne's extirpation of the savage Avars, and at times deserts have been created in the name of peace. But calculated risks of mutual extermination, leaving no survivors to enjoy the fruits of victory, simply do not fit human nature.

This does not mean that nuclear weapons, or weapons of similar power, will not be used. No weapon is too destructive or hideous to be used when it may be employed to advantage. A technological breakthrough by one power that permitted an effective defense against retaliation could lead to the employment of nuclear bombardment as policy—but this would not then be a war of mutual extermination, or, probably, even much one-sided extermination. The deliberate destruction of cities by Genghis Khan, the piles of skulls erected by Timur the Lame, the burning of the population of Hiroshima were all for a purpose: to demoralize enemies into surrender.

The second scenario, disarmament and the abandonment of violence, is even less likely to happen. The great problem with pacifism is that it is never universal, and therefore, as Adolf Hitler gleefully proclaimed, pacifists tend to support the would-be conquerors of the world to the fullest. So long as tensions exist, which means forever, nations and peoples will not be willing to surrender arms or sovereignty. And if a true world government does come about, as Bertrand Russell stated, there still are issues over which men will fight, and when they arise no government can prevent civil war.

Interestingly and significantly, few professional military men believe in either of the two popular scenarios, Armageddon or a warless world.

They have been left holding ground that even they know is dubious: they must be pessimistic, planning for war; they have to be optimistic, believing that warfare can be controlled and contained.

It outrages much opinion across the world that professional soldiers are working assiduously to devise practical ways to fight wars and win them for their nations. Ironically, this may be man's best hope for the continuance of his civilization and species.

So long as man remains what he is, and there is no evidence that human capabilities or limitations have essentially changed since the Cro-Magnon or that these will change barring another radical evolution such as produced *Homo sapiens* the soldiers' ground is all that is left. We are going to fight, and we must find ways of fighting that permit us to survive the battlefield. This is nothing new. Civilizations can be destroyed by spears and scimitars as well as fusion; we are holding the same dubious ground we have trod since man the hunter, man the killer, the most dangerous predator to appear on this planet, invented his first artifact.

The current problem is that we have arrived at stages of organization and technology in which we understand systems better than humanity; man has changed his physical world without changing himself to fit it. We reached this plateau before the first nuclear explosion; the First World War provides a horrifying spectacle of man's inability to cope with the machines and mass organisms he created; not only the capabilities of the weapons of 1914 were misunderstood, but the limitations of flesh and blood were discounted.

Before and after the advent of nuclear weapons, we remained dependent upon machines and increasingly intoxicated with technique. The historian Carlo Cipolla has stated that technique itself is becoming our goal, while philosophy, social relations, and all the human factors are degraded to the role of means, and this is now apparent in both education and warfare.

The United States armed forces continue to develop systems in which the human element is considered almost irrelevant—thus the increasing tendency to use female soldiers whose aggressiveness, potential leadership qualities, and ability to endure brutality is highly questionable, and the increasing emphasis upon quantifiable "education," rather than qualifiable combative reactions, in determining desirable fighting personnel. Believing that machines will do everything, we have reduced the soldier to an adjunct of his hardware, a sort of software in the system, seen more as a potential victim than a prime mover in battle.

From any historical perspective, this is a tremendous error.

Machines may have become the means in warfare, but man is still the war maker and warrior, whether combat is waged with fists, swords, or laser cannon.

Man is still the vital factor in war. Wars will be won by human aggressiveness, leadership, intelligence, endurance, and organization, as they have always been. This may be obscured in contests between technologically unequal forces, such as tanks against horse cavalry, but it has been proven time and again in this age of complex weaponry from the sands of the Sinai to the thickets of Indo-China. Given reasonable equivalence in weaponry, the human factor is dominant.

War requires warriors: men capable of suppressing the instinct of self-preservation, willing to take vast risks, ready to accept hardship and punishment, eager to inflict hurt or damage. War demands courage, sacrifice, comradeship, cooperation, leadership, obedience, honor, pride, faith, and a higher loyalty, just as it often involves fear, cowardice, cruelty, betrayal, demoralization, and apathy—all the qualities human beings both admire and despise. This has made it the ultimate human enterprise.

Changes in technology and organization never dispense with the warrior; they merely require changing types of fighting men. A problem is that how men make war is socially conditioned —as S. L. A. Marshall reported, men tend to remain captives of their culture on the battlefield. Israeli success has depended upon being able to integrate men and machinery to an extent the Arab peoples to date have never matched—for if the Comanche warrior was bound by his customs and taboos, so is the American grunt and the Egyptian conscript soldier.

War puts incredible stress on the warrior, but it also makes enormous demands upon society in order to create suitable warriors, and it has done this since the days of ancient Sparta.

We have probably understood this fact imperfectly down the ages; today we know more about the length of the Macedonian *sarissa* or the organization of the Roman cohort than about the men who used them. This may well be a "refused flank" of our consciousness; it is easier to deal with "things" (which in the ancient Greek view are guiltless depending upon their usage) than with the ultimate weapon, the mind of man. Most historical studies of warfare concentrate upon weapons, unable to separate the process from the hardware, the warrior from his tools. This is to misunderstand the enduring nature of the human warrior.

The late John Campbell was fascinated by the fact that people boarding jetliners buy copies of Homer and read about ancient bloodlettings and betrayals in mudfloored palaces, understanding and relishing the travails of barbaric cultures. He wondered if there were not an unchanging barbaric consciousness in the human breast, and it is a compelling question.

We are still confounded by the question of what is natural and unnatural in the human waging of war. Most, if not all, barbaric cultures, those only lightly touched by highly-evolved ideological-ethical systems, accepted war as a way of life, and most have lived with warfare joyously. As Alfred L. Kroeber, a leading anthropologist, stated, war was a "state of mind" among North American Indians and thus never terminated. Was this "natural," or acculturated habit? The answer appears to be both: it is natural for men to fight and find some pleasure in it, but how they fight is dictated by the patterns of their ephemeral cultures and civilizations.

Personal combat seems "natural," a striking human preference. Homer's barbaric champions relished the "bloody business of the day" as much as Comanches. So did the mailed knights of the European eleventh Christian century; if monks could rationalize the *miles Christi*, the Normans in Sicily did what came naturally.

It is, of course, a tortuous path between the keen pleasure of the Cree or Comanche in making ambush to the stooped, zombie-like advance of British infantry against machine-gun fire at the Somme. There was little "joy" in the 1914-8 war. Yet, as some participants related, the war had its moments: spirits rose as the interminable sieges of the trenches terminated, and a reeling enemy could be pursued in a campaign of movement. Above all, the spirit of man struggled to escape in the air war high above the trenches, where for brief glorious months combat returned to the personal jousts of old, and even reacquired something of the old, barbaric chivalry.

Men in the Second War experienced something of the joy in arms, the thrill of the chase, the intoxication of being dominant in victory—emotions the victorious generation still remembers.

There is, perhaps, a "barbarian warrior" suppressed in the breast of technological man, ready to come forth at any opportunity, always in tension with the progressive "dehumanization" of warfare by systems and weapons over the centuries. And, even more probably, it is upon such "barbaric" qualities that men's hope of success in battle rest.

The perspective of warfare over the millennia is interesting, and more significant than we are often willing to credit.

Primitive warfare placed emphasis upon personal prowess and courage; even pitched battles devolved, by choice, into a series of single combats. Battle was face to face, the most exquisite of moral confrontations; victory or defeat was personal, and due to personal qualities. Modern psychologists fully understand the drives and keen satisfactions involved—they are continued today in the bloodless sport of fencing and in most athletic contests—however they may deplore ancient methodology.

Early warfare was carried out by male peer groups—the Amerindian war band—who all made and used the same type of weapons.

However, technology changed war, and with it, society. Bronze weapons and armor gave great advantage, but bronze was rare and costly. This fact created fighting elites, armed and armored heroes whose roles soon separated from that of war chief to hereditary military aristocrat. But "heroic" forms of war survived

and were even more emphasized: Homeric
paladins and Etruscan champions ranked personal challenges above messy melees with all orders of men. Thus, the champion of the third
millennium B.C.E., meeting his counterpart while
lightly-armed retainers watched and cheered,
represented both a great advance in technology
over the Stone Age and a social gulf that here-
after never entirely closed.

Over millennia the war values became (and to
a vast extent, remain) the aristocratic values of
mankind. Courage, honor, pride, fealty, self-sac-
rifice motivated the Homeric hero. Meanwhile,
the pitfalls of caste pride frustrated the Etruscan
war elite when Horatius held the bridge, and
permitted David to disperse Goliath's host.
Many ancient peoples such as Celts and
Philistines never overcame their Bronze Age concepts of warfare, and despite enormous courage
and prowess bit the dust before the races who
better grasped the possibilities of the age of iron.

Iron—actually, low-grade steel—weapons
revolutionized war, and again society. The new
swords were hardly superior to bronze-edged
weaponry, but iron ore was much more abundant. Now, entire tribes could be armed, and
when Homer sang of Troy, his Achaean heroes
were already anachronisms, victims of technological progress; for the new, dehumanized face
of Assyrian warfare was sweeping the centers of
Eurasian civilization.

The Assyrians were really a people in arms,
marching in companies under captains in hosts
directed by generals. They rationalized warfare,
creating chains of command utterly antithetical

to the ancient concepts of aristocratic combat between equals. Mass weaponry permitted mass armies, and mass warfare destroyed the old elites. When the Assyrian ranks came down like the wolf on the fold, personal glory, personal valor was of little avail, and the laments of the champions are still preserved in lyrical form, evoking a certain sadness.

The civilized world assimilated and learned to manage Assyrian warfare with great difficulty; the memory of the terror still survives. In fact, the world never really assimilated it. The Assyrians failed, not because of faulty technique, but for wholly human reasons. The whole people constituted themselves as a new military caste ruling over a subject empire in which they were outnumbered even in their Akkadian homeland. In the end, Assyrians were massacred in massive uprisings, in which newer tribes—who now formed new warrior castes—were the vanguard.

Warfare retrogressed with the empire of the Medes and Persians. The core of the Great Kings' armies was composed of hereditary nobles, the Immortals and others, brave and skilled archers who went to war surrounded (and in fact, impeded) by huge trains of retainers and tributary peoples. And this was a pattern that was to continue in many parts of Asia until the nineteenth century: armies that were essentially closer to feudal mobs than rationalized instruments of war.

Meanwhile, in Grecian Europe the aristocratic horsemen and charioteers who had formed the nobility were deprived of their function by spear-studded phalanges. The new mass

armies of the rising city-states led to social re-
organization, because mass militias required
larger citizen bodies. Land was redistributed so
as to provide the maximum number of property
holders able to arm themselves as heavy infantry; the hoplite franchise became the basis of
Greek "democracy." Different states evolved different systems. The two we know most about,
Athens and Sparta, both seem to have been extremes.

The new heavy infantry, centered on a line of
citizen-soldiers, proved totally effective against
the vast hosts of poorly-armed (and often poorly
motivated) Asian tributaries of the Persians. The
Persians were familiar with Greek organization
and could have emulated it, but only through
changing the nature of the ruling peoples'
overlordship; they preferred to hire Greek
mercenaries of often doubtful loyalty.

Greek military organization appeals to
moderns. It created a brotherhood of equals in
the ranks (although these citizens remained an
elite within the state itself) advancing in disciplined step to the *paean,* imbued with a satis-
fying sense of solidarity. But Greek organization
was a large step toward the dehumanization of
battle, because chains of command, uniformity
of dress and weapons, drill and the disciplined
execution of maneuvers all diminished the individual warrior, making him a faceless cog in a
military machine. The warrior was becoming a
soldier, which demanded different standards
and ideals.

Maintaining an effective phalanx put immense strains on the citizen bodies. Democratic

Athens demanded more of her citizenry, in terms of wealth and service, than any totalitarian modern state, while Sparta's response to military needs remains an extreme example of the dehumanization of both life and war. The Grecian gentry, displaced but never destroyed, despised service in the ranks, and when economic stagnation and rising class resentments made it difficult to maintain the militia, the cities turned to mercenaries. It was no accident that the Greek form of phalanx was brought to its highest perfection by the conscript peasant soldiers of the Macedonian kings.

In this wall of spears the Iranian nobles met a truly inhuman face of war, a dense mass of pikes advancing mechanically against which few men and no horse dared charge. The personal valor and skills of the Persian warriors were useless as the Macedonian war machine swept half the Mediterranean world.

The Romans, who possessed a larger, more warlike, and more intensely patriotic yeoman-peasantry than Macedon, carried the phalanx and infantry warfare to its highest effectiveness before the advent of firearms. The Roman secret, however, appears to have been a discipline no other ancient people could match. But again, the pressures of maintaining the consular armies were too great, and the legion was perfected under a new concept: the citizen soldier, or long-service professional, formed in cohorts by Marius.

The deterioration of this army into hired mercenaries with little sense of citizenship, and finally into a mutinous rabble in the third century C.E., went hand in hand with the decay of Roman civilization. At the end Rome depended upon barbarian mercenaries: horsemen armed and armored in the Iranian fashion in *spangenhelm* or conical helmet and wielding the Germanic longsword or *spatha*, which survives in all the modern Romance languages.

So long as Roman wealth and organization could field these armies, they held off the invading Indo-European warbands; the old legionary warfare would have destroyed them as Caesar destroyed the Gauls more by demoralization than slaughter.

As the European world fell into social disorganization, again "barbarian" warfare became the norm. The individual warrior reappeared, with all the ancient concepts of aristocratic honor and preference for personal combat. The stirrup made heavy cavalry more formidable—but armored cavalry would have been no terror to a Caesarian legion on European terrain. It was the lack of free citizens and tribesmen that dictated Charles Martel's establishment of "feudal" military forces in the eighth century.

Once again the warriors dictated both warfare and society. The rise of the military caste in Europe resembled nothing so much as the formation of similar castes in the Bronze Age. The early nobility, which was quite numerous, consisted of those men who had remained free and able to arm themselves while the great mass of folk sank into serfdom; the feudal system was a rationalization of society rather than of warfare. Medieval "armies" were akin to the ancient "hosts": armored elites imbued with caste pride and courage leading almost useless tributary mobs. The codes and tastes of the warriors were the same, from a preference for song and the sword and other battering weapons, and private battle over the impersonal melée.

These forces were effective against poorly armed or undisciplined men on foot, both Vikings or Slavic tribesmen. They soon proved disastrous against the tightly disciplined steppe cavalry of the Turks and Mongols, which enjoyed enormous battlefield mobility. European heavy cavalry, masses of brave but uncoordinated chivalry, was cut to pieces in virtually every engagement after the twelfth century.

Again, as in the ancient world, the appearance of newer, better disciplined mass infantry formations—English bowmen, Swiss pikemen—confounded the valor and skill of the war elite. By the fifteenth century, Europe was consciously recreating something resembling Roman armies. The Spanish and Maurice of Nassau even experimented with the armament of the legion, sword and shield, before realizing that the future of offensive warfare lay with gunpowder.

The lament against the triumph of firearms rings even more loudly in the literature of the Renaissance than the litanies of the Bronze Age. There was enormous cultural and caste resistance to the destruction of heroes by "machines." Bayard, that supreme knight, had arquebusiers killed with their own weapons whenever captured; others with less rigid standards merely blinded them. Cervantes, who certainly understood the absurdities of chivalry in his age, despised guns because they allowed "base cowards" to kill "brave men" without personal risk.

A longstanding, pervasive prejudice against guns and gunnery in Western culture has obscured the role of cannon. Artillery became the foundation of the modern territorial state, for only the royal authority could afford cannon in quantity, giving it decisive superiority over both the feudality and the flourishing republican city-states.

Artillery overthrew Granada in 1492, and smashed the aura of invincibility of the Swiss at Marignano in 1515. A major determinant in the history of the West was that the states came under the control of men who preferred organization to splendor, efficiency over grandeur, and results above all else. Europe threw up princes from England to Muscovy who took great interest in their arsenals, and there is a direct progression between the first royal artillery companies and soldiers of the twentieth century, whose battle dress, according to a British general, resembles that of machine minders more than that of heroes.

The Western states were not unique in inventiveness or craftsmanship. But they were unique in the flexibility of society, with bourgeois mechanics in plenty begging to be used. This fact, as much as anything else, induced the former chivalry to allow itself to be regimented into an "officer class." This trend maintained war as a predominantly aristocratic profession down to the twentieth century—and war leadership has kept so many connotations of aristocratic values

that all modern armies must protest that leaders
are not born but are merely products of careful
training.

The more socially rigid societies of the East
faced no similar pressures for internal change—
until Western ships with cannon came calling.
The Mamelukes of Egypt were only one of a
number of examples from the Bosphorus to India. The social structure of Mameluke Egypt
was based on the knightly warrior, and the society maintained its mailed horsemen to the last,
leaving artillery and all that to the attention of
black slaves.

While gunnery was changing societies, it also
demanded a new sort of warrior. The new ideal
was very different from the old. Bashing-weap-
ons warfare required hotblooded men with vast
élan, who plunged into the melée sword and flag
in hand. The new battlefield needed no less
courageous fighting men, but men who could
coolly carry out mental calculations both under
fire and in the midst of shrieking confusion.

The new warriors appeared first at sea, where
cannon achieved their first dominance in warfare. The Dutch and English began to throw up
a new kind of naval person, more the technician
than the gentleman, who studied the flow of natural forces and understood tides and winds and
the fall of shot, and who could bear down into
battle under enormous self-restraint, prepared to
take the enemy's broadside deliberately, then
pound him into demoralization and submission.
Societies or cultures which produced this kind of
warrior—who seemed as inhuman to his foes
who went shouting and screaming into action as

the ancient Spartans or Roman legionaries had once seemed to volatile barbarians—now came to dominate warfare on both land and sea.

The Swedish *regements-stycke*, introduced in 1629, remade the world's battlefields. This was the first effective mobile field piece, weighing 123 kg. and firing up to eight three-pound balls in the time a musketeer could get off a single shot. This cannon made the Swedish formidable; more important, it redressed the ancient balance in Eurasia. In the hands of Austrians and Russians it wreaked destruction on the Turkish cavalry, because it took away the historic advantage of steppe horsemen in battlefield mobility. Turks and Tartars complained in vain that if only their foes would fight like men, they would fall beneath the slaughtering sabers of the True Believers, and in the end, the descendants of Genghis Khan went down with little more than a whimper.

The Chinese understood the ominous portent of Western cannon. But the mandarinate rejected copying or emulating the West, because, as a scholar said, the study of cannon would lead to the study of the principles by which cannon were made, and this might lead to the undermining of a civilization based on humanistic classicism. The Chinese preferred the humiliations of the battlefield (which so large a nation could hope to survive) to the humiliations of cultural change, at least through the reign of Mao Zedong, who may have been the "last of the mandarins."

New technology had made élan less important, but demanded vastly more training and discipline. What was needed was a soldiery conditioned to long-range, bloody battering, able to take punishment but keep the will to close with the enemy. Napoleon's murderous use of artillery made his columnar formations and rapid exploitations possible. Only Wellington seems to have had the tactical genius to realize that the effects of Napoleonic field guns must be obviated, and he also had the human material, in the stolid, lobster-back infantry, to thwart the French practice of horrendous battery of linear formations in exposed positions, followed by the charge. Wellington's regiments took what cover they could, then rose with shattering coolness to pour massed musketry into the shouting attackers—and as observers noted, the moral battle was often won before the British lines opened fire.

Down to 1914, however, military elites in all nations refused to acknowledge the growing dominance of lethal weaponry over human flesh. Prior to the Great War, a French commander sniffed, "As for artillery, we have rather too much of it," misunderstanding the power of the French 75 as completely as he did the German Maxim gun.

The horror of the 1914–8 war lay in this inability to comprehend machines, from Maxims to tanks and aircraft. If war had become, in the words of St. Cyr, an art for the general, a science for the officer, and a trade for the soldier, the state of the art escaped the generals. Nothing really radical had happened, except new weapons had enormously enlarged the battlefield and made it immensely more lethal, but there was no new Wellington to see that the tactics that continued to be used had become dubious at Gettysburg.

Battle was now almost a state of siege, with "battles" continuing for days, weeks, and months without respite. This demanded new standards of human behavior, because men had never faced this kind of stress. But in the ultimately dehumanized, surrealistic landscape of no-man's-land, human beings had begun to reach their physical and mental limits. Despite hideous losses on each side, warfare became stalemated and indecisive. A new phenomenon, "shell shock," or combat-induced neurosis appeared among troops whose only escape from siege was death, crippling wounds—or madness. By 1917 entire armies on some fronts were falling to pieces from psychic and moral collapse.

This was the most lethal, impersonal, "inhuman" conflict to date. Only in one area did anything approaching the old joy in combat appear: aerial warfare. Here, briefly, warriors could perform individual heroics as "knights of the air," and these aerial sideshows attracted almost as much attention as the massive slaughters on the ground.

The Second War was better managed out of experience; men and machines were now much better integrated in warfare. The capabilities, physical and mental, of men in combat became better known. Still, war was even more dehumanized and machine-like in execution. Officers and soldiers in all services were handled as interchangeable parts, as replaceable as ball bearings by classification number and requisition. Again, the mass dragooning of populations into combat produced high psychiatric casualties, in the Western armies running as much as ten percent in the first hours of battle.

All the same, it appeared that modern total war was manageable—the Germans were defeated with bearable casualties and without the massacres that disposed of the Assyrians—until the atomic sunbursts across the Pacific blew the whole equation.

The prospect of nuclear war requires adjustments beyond anything the Bronze Age faced, or those required to form the phalanx or condition men to withstand fire. Even the "tactical" nuclear battlefield, envisioning no intercontinental exchanges on population centers, proposes multiple stresses on people and society that make Waterloo or the Normandy beachhead child's play by comparison.

A nuclear battlefield would require continuous, mobile operations by widely dispersed armored units beset by lethalities and imponderabilities such as no troops have faced before.

New hardware thus keeps spawning new dilemmas for the "software" that makes it. Even if the use of nuclear weapons were eschewed, as uncontrollable, the complexity and lethality of a modern "conventional" battlefield, employing armor, robot vehicles, heat-sensing missiles, cluster bombs, claymore mines, ground surveillance radar, infra-red observation, body-detecting devices, and niceties such as napalm specially prepared with skin-adhering ingredients (to say nothing of the possible use of lasers, gas, or biological and chemical agents) would seem to rule out mass action by mass armies as in the two great wars.

Meanwhile, the very scale of nations and increased destructiveness of weapons throws up the need for more men and equipment, despite the fact that the mechanized land warfare now possible calls for finely trained and tuned specialists on the order of astronauts or submarine crews.

No society to date has made any adjustment to this, any more than any nation has really attempted to adjust to the possibility of nuclear bombardment.

How will nations whose leaders still think in terms of Clausewitz's definitions and mass-scale wars proceed if both are obsolete? Will they commit another collective mass failure such as occurred in 1914–8?

There are, however, many possibilities short of a despairing Armageddon.

One is the retention of a deliberately anachronistic warfare, such as has been waged in the "limited" conflicts from Korea to Vietnam to Africa.

This is a sublimation of war, a form almost of ritualization, in which the players accept game rules. At bottom it is no different from the games played by the hosts of David and Goliath, or those of the mercenary captains of the Italian Renaissance, who perfected the art of almost bloodless battles before they were rudely interrupted by incursions of northern barbarians.

Nations and peoples can be demoralized into accepting defeat from small reverses, as the Saxons were demoralized at Hastings or the Gauls by Caesar at Alesia. But in present and future times, such victories could hardly be total, or involve a genuine degradation of the losers—to achieve this, mass destruction and the immolation of millions will be required.

A ritualization or "gaming" of warfare might appear a step backward in human efficiency and logic, a retrogression toward "barbarism"—but it could also signify a triumph for humanism.

However, if men cannot limit their fighting to smaller, professional forces while populations watch and wait like the retainers of Bronze Age days, then what sort of men, weapons, training, or standards will withstand all-out war on the North German plain, or perhaps the moon?

The dilemma keeps spawning scenarios of unreality, like most NATO war plans, and doctrines that even the makers fear will be destroyed in the first hours of future war. However, soldiers (most of whom in their hearts despise both nukes and napalm) keep trying to devise ways and means to rationalize the coming warfare.

Many would happily return to sabers if only this were feasible—a syndrome that is seen and ridiculed, because its humanistic basis is not really understood.

Can we learn to neuter offensive weaponry through technology, restoring the balance? Can conquests in the future be made possible? Will some peoples succeed at future war, thus dominating their world like Assyrians or Romans, while others who fail to adjust join the debris of history?

All these questions have become themes for both philosophy and speculative fiction since

1945. All sorts of post-doom worlds have been explored (almost in relief) while moral, extra-worldly, and metaphysical solutions have been posed. However, most literature tends to ignore or obviate the near-term problem. A vastly popular science fiction vision is one of colonization of the galaxies (even if only by a fleeing remnant of the race). In this future, significantly, vast wars continue, but with less pressing peril of human extinction. And significantly, much fiction emphasizes the primordial human factor, the eternal resistance in the human breast to being subordinated to systems and techniques. Nothing is so enduring, or popular, as tales of the sword, with or without sorcery.

Historical evidence indicates that we shall try to abolish war, but that we shall also try to bring the process under management. The development of "cleaner" warheads, especially the enhanced-radiation warhead, is a large step in this direction, which is precisely why it has aroused so much opposition.

The emergence of guerrilla-style conflict, both in urban and primitive settings, does not indicate a bloodless future, regardless of the drift of technique. The future will be bloody; how bloody depends upon whether it will be directed by warriors or "mad" scientists who reduce mankind to the role of means.

In the near future, the Asimovian prediction seems valid: what has happened will continue to happen, and some form of manageable conflict will go on. War is, after all, as Reginald Bretnor wrote, something that men *do*.

They will find a way to do it.

—•—••—•—

T. R. Fehrenbach was born in Texas, graduated from Princeton University, and fought in Korea as a platoon leader, company commander, and intelligence officer with a tank battalion. His total military experience ranges from private to general staff officer.

He has published stories or articles in Analog, American Legion, Argosy, Atlantic, Esquire, Satevepost, *and many other periodicals, including foreign. His books in ten languages include* The Battle of Anzio, This Kind of War, Crossroads in Korea, The Gnomes of Zurich, Fire and Blood, *and* Comanches.

His writings have been used at the military academies, by the National Security Council, and for the orientation of general officer designates of the Army.

When Earth is threatened, or when we men of Earth feel that we are threatened, by an enemy no matter how alien or how remote, then the warrior dwelling in each one of us—or at least in those charged with our defense —will awaken or will be awakened.

But warriors, as this powerful novelette of Orson Scott Card's demonstrates, must be carefully chosen and unsparingly trained. . . .

Orson Scott Card

ENDER'S GAME

"Whatever your gravity is when you get to the door, remember—the enemy's gate is *down*. If you step through your own door like you're out for a stroll, you're a big target and you deserve to get hit. With more than a flasher." Ender Wiggin paused and looked over the group. Most were just watching him nervously. A few understanding. A few sullen and resisting.

First day with this army, all fresh from the teacher squads, and Ender had forgotten how young new kids could be. He'd been in it for three years, they'd had six months—nobody over nine years old in the whole bunch. But they were his. At eleven, he was half a year early to be a commander. He'd had a toon of his own and knew a few tricks but there were forty in his new army. Green. All marksmen with a flasher, all in op shape, or they wouldn't be here—but they were all just as likely as not to get wiped out first ime into battle.

"Remember," he went on, "they can't see you ill you get through that door. But the second you're out, they'll be on you. So hit that door the way you want to be when they shoot at you. Legs up under you, going straight *down*." He pointed at a sullen kid who looked like he was only seven, he smallest of them all. "Which way is down, greenoh!"

"Toward the enemy door." The answer was quick. It was also surly, saying, "yeah, yeah, now get on with the important stuff."

"Name, kid?"

"Bean."

"Get that for size or for brains?"

Bean didn't answer. The rest laughed a little. Ender had chosen right. This kid *was* younger han the rest, must have been advanced because he was sharp. The others didn't like him much, hey were happy to see him taken down a little. Like Ender's first commander had taken him down.

"Well, Bean, you're right onto things. Now I ell you this, nobody's gonna get through that door without a good chance of getting hit. A lot of you are going to be turned into cement somewhere. Make sure it's your legs. Right? If only your legs get hit, then only your legs get frozen, and in nullo that's no sweat." Ender turned to one of the dazed ones. "What're legs for? Hmmm?"

Blank stare. Confusion. Stammer.

"Forget it. Guess I'll have to ask Bean here."

"Legs are for pushing off walls." Still bored

"Thanks, Bean. Get that, everybody?" The

all got it, and didn't like getting it from Bean

"Right. You can't *see* with legs, you can't *shoo*

with legs, and most of the time they just get in

the way. If they get frozen sticking straight ou

you've turned yourself into a blimp. No way t

hide. So how do legs go?"

A few answered this time, to prove that Bea

wasn't the only one who knew anything. "Unde

you. Tucked up under."

"Right. A shield. You're kneeling on a shield

and the shield is your own legs. And there's

trick to the suits. Even when your legs ar

flashed you can *still* kick off. I've never seen any

body do it but me—but you're all gonna lear

it."

Ender Wiggin turned on his flasher. It glowe

faintly green in his hand. Then he let himself ris

in the weightless workout room, pulled his leg

under him as though he were kneeling, an

flashed both of them. Immediately his suit stif

ened at the knees and ankles, so that he couldn'

bend at all.

"Okay, I'm frozen, see?"

He was floating a meter above them. They al

looked up at him, puzzled. He leaned back an

caught one of the handholds on the wall behin

him, and pulled himself flush against the wall.

"I'm stuck at a wall. If I had legs, I'd use legs

and string myself out like a string *bean,* right?"

They laughed.

"But I don't have legs, and that's *better,* got it

Because of this." Ender jackknifed at the waist

then straightened out violently. He was acros

he workout room in only a moment. From the other side he called to them. "Got that? I didn't use hands, so I still had use of my flasher. *And* I didn't have my legs floating five feet behind me. Now watch it again."

He repeated the jackknife, and caught a handhold on the wall near them. "Now, I don't just want you to do that when they've flashed your legs. I want you to do that when you've still got legs, because it's better. And because they'll never be expecting it. All right now, everybody up in the air and kneeling."

Most were up in a few seconds. Ender flashed the stragglers, and they dangled, helplessly frozen, while the others laughed. "When I give an order, you move. Got it? When we're at a door and they clear it, I'll be giving you orders in two seconds, as soon as I see the setup. And when I give the order you better be out there, because whoever's out there first is going to win, unless he's a fool. I'm not. And you better not be, or I'll have you back in the teacher squads." He saw more than a few of them gulp, and the frozen ones looked at him with fear. "You guys who are hanging there. You watch. You'll thaw out in about fifteen minutes, and let's see if you can catch up to the others."

For the next half hour Ender had them jackknifing off walls. He called a stop when he saw that they all had the basic idea. They were a good group, maybe. They'd get better.

"Now you're warmed up," he said to them, "we'll start working."

Ender was the last one out after practice, since

he stayed to help some of the slower ones improve on technique. They'd had good teachers, but like all armies they were uneven, and some of them could be a real drawback in battle. Their first battle might be weeks away. It might be tomorrow. A schedule was never printed. The commander just woke up and found a note by his bunk, giving him the time of his battle and the name of his opponent. So for the first while he was going to drive his boys until they were in top shape—all of them. Ready for anything, at any time. Strategy was nice, but it was worth nothing if the soldiers couldn't hold up under the strain.

He turned the corner into the residence wing and found himself face to face with Bean, the seven-year-old he had picked on all through practice that day. Problems. Ender didn't want problems right now.

"Ho, Bean."

"Ho, Ender."

Pause.

"Sir," Ender said softly.

"We're not on duty."

"In my army, Bean, we're always on duty." Ender brushed past him.

Bean's high voice piped up behind him. "I know what you're doing, Ender, sir, and I'm warning you."

Ender turned slowly and looked at him. "Warning me?"

"I'm the best man you've got. But I'd better be treated like it."

"Or what?" Ender smiled menacingly.

"Or I'll be the worst man you've got. One or the other."

"And what do you want? Love and kisses?" Ender was getting angry.

Bean was unworried. "I want a toon."

Ender walked back to him and stood looking down into his eyes. "I'll give a toon," he said, "to the boys who prove they're worth something. They've got to be good soldiers, they've got to know how to take orders, they've got to be able to think for themselves in a pinch, and they've got to be able to keep respect. That's how I got to be a commander. That's how you'll get to be a toon leader."

Bean smiled. "That's fair. *If* you actually work that way, I'll be a toon leader in a month."

Ender reached down and grabbed the front of his uniform and shoved him into the wall. "When I say I work a certain way, Bean, then that's the way I work."

Bean just smiled. Ender let go of him and walked away, and didn't look back. He was sure, without looking, that Bean was still watching, still smiling, still just a little contemptuous. He might make a good toon leader at that. Ender would keep an eye on him.

Captain Graff, six foot two and a little chubby, stroked his belly as he leaned back in his chair. Across his desk sat Lieutenant Anderson, who was earnestly pointing out high points on a chart.

"Here it is, Captain," Anderson said. "Ender's already got them doing a tactic that's going to throw off everyone who meets it. Doubled their speed."

Graff nodded.

"And you know his test scores. He thinks well, too."

Graff smiled. "All true, all true, Anderson, he's a fine student, shows real promise."

They waited.

Graff sighed. "So what do you want me to do?"

"Ender's the one. He's got to be."

"He'll never be ready in time, Lieutenant. He's eleven, for heaven's sake, man, what do you want, a miracle?"

"I want him into battles, every day starting tomorrow. I want him to have a year's worth of battles in a month."

Graff shook his head. "That would have his army in the hospital."

"No sir. He's getting them into form. And we need Ender."

"Correction, Lieutenant. We need somebody. You think it's Ender."

"All right, I think it's Ender. Which of the commanders if it isn't him?"

"I don't know, Lieutenant." Graff ran his hands over his slightly fuzzy bald head. "These are children, Anderson. Do you realize that? Ender's army is nine years old. Are we going to put them against the older kids? Are we going to put them through hell for a month like that?"

Lieutenant Anderson leaned even further over Graff's desk.

"Ender's test scores, Captain!"

"I've seen his bloody test scores! I've watched him in battle, I've listened to tapes of his training sessions, I've watched his sleep patterns, I've heard tapes of his conversations in the corridors and in the bathrooms, I'm more aware of Ender Wiggins than you could possibly imagine! And against all the arguments, against his obvious qualities, I'm weighing one thing. I have this picture of Ender a year from now, if you have your way. I see him completely useless, worn down, a failure, because he was pushed farther than he or any living person could go. But it doesn't weigh enough, does it, Lieutenant, because there's a war on, and our best talent is gone, and the biggest battles are ahead. So give Ender a battle every day this week. And then bring me a report."

Anderson stood and saluted. "Thank you sir."

He had almost reached the door when Graff called his name. He turned and faced the captain.

"Anderson," Captain Graff said. "Have you been outside? Lately, I mean."

"Not since last leave, six months ago."

"I didn't think so. Not that it makes any difference. But have you ever been to Beaman Park, there in the city? Hmm? Beautiful park. Trees. Grass. No nullo, no battles, no worries. Do you know what else there is in Beaman Park?"

"What, sir?" Lieutenant Anderson asked.

"Children," Graff answered.

"Of course children," said Anderson.

"I mean children. I mean kids who get up in the morning when their mothers call them and they go to school and then in the afternoons they go to Beaman Park and play. They're happy, they smile a lot, they laugh, they have fun. Hmmm?"

"I'm sure they do sir."

"Is that all you can say, Anderson?"

Anderson cleared his throat. "It's good for children to have fun, I think, sir. I know I did when I was a boy. But right now the world needs soldiers. And this is the way to get them."

Graff nodded and closed his eyes. "Oh, indeed, you're right, by statistical proof and by all the important theories, and dammit they work and the system is right but all the same Ender's older than I am. He's not a child. He's barely a person."

"If that's true, sir, then at least we all know that Ender is making it possible for the others of his age to be playing in the park."

"And Jesus died to save all men, of course." Graff sat up and looked at Anderson almost sadly. "But we're the ones," Graff said, "we're the ones who are driving in the nails."

Ender Wiggins lay on his bed staring at the ceiling. He never slept more than five hours a night—but the lights went off at 2200 and didn't come on again until 0600. So he stared at the ceiling and thought. He'd had his army for three and a half weeks. Dragon Army. The name was assigned, and it wasn't a lucky one. Oh, the charts said that about nine years ago a Dragon Army had done fairly well. But for the next six years the name had been attached to inferior armies, and finally, because of the superstition that was beginning to play about the name, Dragon Army was retired. Until now. And now, Ender thought smiling, Dragon Army was going to take them by surprise.

The door opened softly. Ender did not turn his

head. Someone stepped softly into his room, then left with the quiet sound of the door shutting. When soft steps died away Ender rolled over and saw a white slip of paper lying on the floor. He reached down and picked it up.

"Dragon Army against Rabbit Army, Ender Wiggins and Carn Carby, 0700."

The first battle. Ender got out of bed and quickly dressed. He went rapidly to the rooms of each of his toon leaders and told them to rouse their boys. In five minutes they were all gathered in the corridor, sleepy and slow. Ender spoke softly.

"First battle, 0700 against Rabbit Army. I've fought them twice before but they've got a new commander. Never heard of him. They're an older group, though, and I know a few of their old tricks. Now wake up. Run, doublefast, warmup in workroom three."

For an hour and a half they worked out, with three mockbattles and calisthenics in the corridor out of the nullo. Then for fifteen minutes they all lay up in the air, totally relaxing in the weightlessness. At 0650 Ender roused them and they hurried into the corridor. Ender led them down the corridor, running again, and occasionally leaping to touch a light panel on the ceiling. The boys all touched the same light panel. And at 0658 they reached their gate to the battleroom.

The members of Toons C and D grabbed the first eight handholds in the ceiling of the corridor. Toons A, B, and E crouched on the floor. Ender hooked his feet into two handholds in the middle of the ceiling, so he was out of everyone's way.

"Which way is the enemy's door?" he hissed.

"Down!" they whispered back, and laughed.

"Flashers on." The boxes in their hands glowed green. They waited for a few seconds more, and then the gray wall in front of them disappeared and the battleroom was visible.

Ender sized it up immediately. The familiar open grid of the most early games, like the monkey bars at the park, with seven or eight boxes scattered through the grid. They called the boxes *stars*. There were enough of them, and in forward enough positions, that they were worth going for. Ender decided this in a second, and he hissed, "Spread to near stars. E hold!"

The four groups in the corners plunged through the forcefield at the doorway and fell down into the battleroom. Before the enemy even appeared through the opposite gate Ender's army had spread from the door to the nearest stars.

Then the enemy soldiers came through the door. From their stance Ender knew they had been in a different gravity, and didn't know enough to disorient themselves from it. They came through standing up, their entire bodies spread and defenseless.

"Kill 'em, E!" Ender hissed, and threw himself out the door knees first, with his flasher between his legs and firing. While Ender's group flew across the room, the rest of Dragon Army laid down a protecting fire, so that E group reached a forward position with only one boy frozen completely, though they had all lost the use of their legs—which didn't impair them in the least. There was a lull as Ender and his op-

ponent, Carn Carby, assessed their positions.
Aside from Rabbit Army's losses at the gate,
there had been few casualties, and both armies
were near full strength. But Carn had no originality—he was in a four-corner spread that
any five-year-old in the teacher squads might
have thought of. And Ender knew how to defeat
it.

He called out, loudly, "E covers A, C down. B,
D angle east wall." Under E toon's cover, B and
D toons lunged away from their stars. While
they were still exposed, A and C toons left their
stars and drifted toward the near wall. They
reached it together, and together jackknifed off
the wall. At double the normal speed they appeared behind the enemy's stars, and opened
fire. In a few seconds the battle was over, with
the enemy almost entirely frozen, including the
commander, and the rest scattered to the corners. For the next five minutes, in squads of four,
Dragon Army cleaned out the dark corners of
the battleroom and shepherded the enemy into
the center, where their bodies, frozen at impossible angles, jostled each other. Then Ender
took three of his boys to the enemy gate and
went through the formality of reversing the one-
way field by simultaneously touching a Dragon
Army helmet at each corner. Then Ender assembled his army in vertical files near the knot of
frozen Rabbit Army soldiers.

Only three of Dragon Army's soldiers were
immobile. Their victory margin—38 to 0—was
ridiculously high, and Ender began to laugh.
Dragon Army joined him, laughing long and
loud. They were still laughing when Lieutenant

Anderson and Lieutenant Morris came in from the teachergate at the south end of the battleroom.

Lieutenant Anderson kept his face stiff and unsmiling, but Ender saw him wink as he held out his hand and offered the stiff, formal congratulations that were ritually given to the victor in the game.

Morris found Carn Carby and unfroze him, and the thirteen-year-old came and presented himself to Ender, who laughed without malice and held out his hand. Carn graciously took Ender's hand and bowed his head over it. It was that or be flashed again.

Lieutenant Anderson dismissed Dragon Army, and they silently left the battleroom through the enemy's door—again part of the ritual. A light was blinking on the north side of the square door, indicating where the gravity was in that corridor. Ender, leading his soldiers, changed his orientation and went through the forcefield and into gravity on his feet. His army followed him at a brisk run back to the workroom. When they got there they formed up into squads, and Ender hung in the air, watching them.

"Good first battle," he said, which was excuse enough for a cheer, which he quieted. "Dragon Army did all right against Rabbits. But the enemy isn't always going to be that bad. And if that had been a good army we would have been smashed. We still would have won, but we would have been smashed. Now let me see B and D toons out here. Your takeoff from the stars was way too slow. If Rabbit Army knew how to aim a flasher, you all would have been frozen solid before A and C even got to the wall."

They worked out for the rest of the day.

That night Ender went for the first time to the commanders' mess hall. No one was allowed there until he had won at least one battle, and Ender was the youngest commander ever to make it. There was no great stir when he came in. But when some of the other boys saw the Dragon on his breast pocket, they stared at him openly, and by the time he got his tray and sat at an empty table, the entire room was silent, with the other commanders watching him. Intensely self-conscious, Ender wondered how they all knew, and why they all looked so hostile.

Then he looked above the door he had just come through. There was a huge scoreboard across the entire wall. It showed the win/loss record for the commander of every army; that day's battles were lit in red. Only four of them. The other three winners had barely made it— the best of them had only two men whole and eleven mobile at the end of the game. Dragon Army's score of thirty-eight mobile was embarrassingly better.

Other new commanders had been admitted to the commanders' mess hall with cheers and congratulations. Other new commanders hadn't won thirty-eight to zero.

Ender looked for Rabbit Army on the scoreboard. He was surprised to find that Carn Carby's score to date was eight wins and three losses. Was he that good? Or had he only fought against inferior armies? Whichever, there was still a zero in Carn's mobile and whole columns, and Ender looked down from the scoreboard grinning. No one smiled back, and Ender knew that they were afraid of him, which meant that they would hate him, which meant that anyone who went into battle against Dragon Army would be scared and angry and incompetent. Ender looked for Carn Carby in the crowd, and found him not too far away. He stared at Carby until one of the other boys nudged the Rabbit commander and pointed to Ender. Ender smiled again and waved slightly. Carby turned red, and Ender, satisfied, leaned over his dinner and began to eat.

At the end of the week Dragon Army had fought seven battles in seven days. The score stood 7 wins and 0 losses. Ender had never had more than five boys frozen in any game. It was no longer possible for the other commanders to ignore Ender. A few of them sat with him and quietly conversed about game strategies that Ender's opponents had used. Other much larger groups were talking with the commanders that Ender had defeated, trying to find out what Ender had done to beat them.

In the middle of the meal the teacher door opened and the groups fell silent as Lieutenant Anderson stepped in and looked over the group. When he located Ender he strode quickly across the room and whispered in Ender's ear. Ender nodded, finished his glass of water, and left with the lieutenant. On the way out, Anderson handed a slip of paper to one of the older boys. The room became very noisy with conversation as Anderson and Ender left.

Ender was escorted down corridors he had never seen before. They didn't have the blue glow of the soldier corridors. Most were wood paneled, and the floors were carpeted. The doors were wood, with nameplates on them, and they stopped at one that said, "Captain Graff, supervisor." Anderson knocked softly, and a low voice said, "Come in."

They went in. Captain Graff was seated behind a desk, his hands folded across his pot belly. He nodded, and Anderson sat. Ender also sat down. Graff cleared his throat and spoke.

"Seven days since your first battle, Ender."

Ender did not reply.

"Won seven battles, one every day."

Ender nodded.

"Scores unusually high, too."

Ender blinked.

"Why?" Graff asked him.

Ender glanced at Anderson, and then spoke to the captain behind the desk. "Two new tactics, sir. Legs doubled up as a shield, so that a flash doesn't immobilize. Jackknife take-offs from the walls. Superior strategy, as Lieutenant Anderson taught, think places, not spaces. Five toons of eight instead of four of ten. Incompetent opponents. Excellent toon leaders, good soldiers."

Graff looked at Ender without expression. Waiting for what, Ender thought. Lieutenant Anderson spoke.

"Ender, what's the condition of your army?"

"A little tired, in peak condition, morale high, learning fast. Anxious for the next battle."

Anderson looked at Graff, and Graff shrugged

slightly. Then he nodded, and Anderson smiled. Graff turned to Ender.

"Is there anything you want to know?"

Ender held his hands loosely in his lap. "When are you going to put us up against a good army?"

Anderson was surprised, and Graff laughed out loud. The laughter rang in the room, and when it stopped, Graff handed a piece of paper to Ender. "Now," the Captain said, and Ender read the paper.

"Dragon Army against Leopard Army, Ender Wiggins and Pol Slattery, 2000."

Ender looked up at Captain Graff. "That's ten minutes from now, sir."

Graff smiled. "Better hurry, then, boy."

As Ender left he realized Pol Slattery was the boy who had been handed his orders as Ender left the mess hall.

He got to his army five minutes later. Three toon leaders were already undressed and lying naked on their beds. He sent them all flying down the corridors to rouse their toons, and gathered up their suits himself. As all his boys were assembled in the corridor, most of them still getting dressed, Ender spoke to them.

"This one's hot and there's no time. We'll be late to the door, and the enemy'll be deployed right outside our gate. Ambush, and I've never heard of it happening before. So we'll take our time at the door. E toon, keep your belts loose, and give your flashers to the leaders and seconds of the other toons."

Puzzled, E toon complied. By then all were dressed, and Ender led them at a trot to the gate.

When they reached it the forcefield was already on one-way, and some of his soldiers were panting. They had had one battle that day and a full workout. They were tired.

Ender stopped at the entrance and looked at the placement of the enemy soldiers. Most of them were grouped not more than twenty feet out from the gate. There was no grid, there were no stars. A big empty space. Where were the other enemy soldiers? There should have been ten more.

"They're flat against this wall," Ender said, "where we can't see them."

He thought for a moment, then took two of the toons and made them kneel, their hands on their hips. Then he flashed them, so that their bodies were frozen rigid.

"You're shields," Ender said, and then had boys from two other toons kneel on their legs, and hook both arms under the frozen boys' shoulders. Each boy was holding two flashers. Then Ender and the members of the last toon picked up the duos, three at a time, and threw them out the door.

Of course, the enemy opened fire immediately. But they only hit the boys who were already flashed, and in a few moments pandemonium broke out in the battleroom. All the soldiers of Leopard Army were easy targets as they lay pressed flat against the wall, and Ender's soldiers, armed with two flashers each, carved them up easily. Pol Slattery reacted quickly, ordering his men away from the wall, but not quickly enough—only a few were able to move, and they were flashed before they could get a quarter of the way across the battleroom.

When the battle was over Dragon Army had only twelve boys whole, the lowest score they had ever had. But Ender was satisfied. And during the ritual of surrender Pol Slattery broke form by shaking hands and asking, "Why did you wait so long getting out of the gate?"

Ender glanced at Anderson, who was floating nearby. "I was informed late," he said. "It was an ambush."

Slattery grinned, and gripped Ender's hand again. "Good game."

Ender didn't smile at Anderson this time. He knew that now the games would be arranged against him, to even up the odds. He didn't like it.

It was 2150, nearly time for lights out, when Ender knocked at the door of the room shared by Bean and three other soldiers. One of the others opened the door, then stepped back and held it wide. Ender stood for a moment, then asked if he could come in. They answered, of course, of course, come in, and he walked to the upper bunk, where Bean had set down his book and was leaning on one elbow to look at Ender.

"Bean, can you give me twenty minutes?"

"Near lights out," Bean answered.

"My room," Ender answered. "I'll cover for you." Bean sat up and slid off his bed. Together he and Ender padded silently down the corridor to Ender's room. Bean entered first, and Ender closed the door behind them.

"Sit down," Ender said, and they both sat on the edge of the bed, looking at each other.

"Remember four weeks ago, Bean? When you told me to make you a toon leader?"

"Yeah."

"I've made five toon leaders since then, haven't I? And none of them was you."

Bean looked at him calmly.

"Was I right?" Ender asked.

"Yes, sir," Bean answered.

Ender nodded. "How have you done in these battles?"

Bean cocked his head to one side. "I've never been immobilized, sir, and I've immobilized forty-three of the enemy. I've obeyed orders quickly, and I've commanded a squad in mop-up and never lost a soldier."

"Then you'll understand this." Ender paused, then decided to back up and say something else first.

"You know you're early, Bean, by a good half year. I was, too, and I've been made a commander six months early. Now they've put me into battles after only three weeks of training with my army. They've given me eight battles in seven days. I've already had more battles than boys who were made commander four months ago. I've won more battles than many who've been commanders for a year. And then tonight. You know what happened tonight."

Bean nodded. "They told you late."

"I don't know what the teachers are doing. But my army is getting tired, and I'm getting tired, and now they're changing the rules of the game. You see, Bean, I've looked in the old charts. No one has ever destroyed so many enemies and kept so many of his own soldiers whole in the history of the game. I'm unique—and I'm getting unique treatment."

Bean smiled. "You're the best, Ender."

Ender shook his head. "Maybe. But it was no accident that I got the soldiers I got. My worst soldier could be a toon leader in another army. I've got the best. They've loaded things my way —but now they're loading it against me. I don't know why. But I know I have to be ready for it. I need your help."

"Why mine?"

"Because even though there are some better soldiers than you in Dragon Army—not many, but some—there's nobody who can think better and faster than you." Bean said nothing. They both knew it was true.

Ender continued, "I need to be ready, but I can't retrain the whole army. So I'm going to cut every toon down by one, including you—and you and four others will be a special squad under me. And you'll learn to do some new things. Most of the time you'll be in the regular toons just like you are now. But when I need you. See?"

Bean smiled and nodded. "That's right, that's good, can I pick them myself?"

"One from each toon except your own, and you can't take any toon leaders."

"What do you want us to do?"

"Bean, I don't know. I don't know what they'll throw at us. What would you do if suddenly our flashers didn't work, and the enemy's did? What would you do if we had to face two armies at once? The only thing I know is—we're not going for score anymore. We're going for the enemy's gate. That's when the battle is technically won—four helmets at the corners of the gate. I'm going for quick kills, battles ended even when we're outnumbered. Got it? You take them for two hours during regular workout. Then you and I and your soldiers, we'll work at night after dinner."

"We'll get tired."

"I have a feeling we don't know what tired is."

Ender reached out and took Bean's hand, and gripped it. "Even when it's rigged against us, Bean. We'll win."

Bean left in silence and padded down the corridor.

Dragon Army wasn't the only army working out after hours now. The other commanders finally realized they had some catching up to do. From early morning to lights out soldiers all over Training and Command Center, none of them over fourteen years old, were learning to jack-knife off walls and use each other as living shields.

But while other commanders mastered the techniques that Ender had used to defeat them, Ender and Bean worked on solutions to problems that had never come up.

There were still battles every day, but for a while they were normal, with grids and stars and sudden plunges through the gate. And after the battles, Ender and Bean and four other soldiers would leave the main group and practice strange maneuvers. Attacks without flashers, using feet to physically disarm or disorient an enemy. Using four frozen soldiers to reverse the enemy's

gate in less than two seconds. And one day Bean
came to workout with a 300-meter cord.

"What's that for?"

"I don't know yet." Absently Bean spun one
end of the cord. It wasn't more than an eighth of
an inch thick, but it could have lifted ten adults
without breaking.

"Where did you get it?"

"Commissary. They asked what for. I said to
practice tying knots."

Bean tied a loop in the end of the rope and slid
it over his shoulders.

"Here, you two, hang onto the wall here. Now
don't let go of the rope. Give me about fifty yards
of slack." They complied, and Bean moved
about ten feet from them along the wall. As soon
as he was sure they were ready, he jackknifed off
the wall and flew straight out, fifty meters. Then
the rope snapped taut. It was so fine that it was
virtually invisible, but it was strong enough to
force Bean to veer off at almost a right angle. It
happened so suddenly that he had inscribed a
perfect arc and hit the wall before most of the
other soldiers knew what had happened. Bean
did a perfect rebound and drifted quickly back
where Ender and the others waited for him.

Many of the soldiers in the five regular squads
hadn't noticed the rope, and were demanding to
know how it was done. It was impossible to
change direction that abruptly in nullo. Bean
just laughed.

"Wait till the next game without a grid!
They'll never know what hit them."

They never did. The next game was only two
hours later, but Bean and two others had be-

come pretty good at aiming and shooting while they flew at ridiculous speeds at the end of the rope. The slip of paper was delivered, and Dragon Army trotted off to the gate, to battle with Griffin Army. Bean coiled the rope all the way.

When the gate opened, all they could see was a large brown star only fifteen feet away, completely blocking their view of the enemy's gate.

Ender didn't pause. "Bean, give yourself fifty feet of rope and go around the star." Bean and his four soldiers dropped through the gate and in a moment Bean was launched sideways away from the star. The rope snapped taut, and Bean flew forward. As the rope was stopped by each edge of the star in turn, his arc became tighter and his speed greater, until when he hit the wall only a few feet away from the gate he was barely able to control his rebound to end up behind the star. But he immediately moved all his arms and legs so that those waiting inside the gate would know that the enemy hadn't flashed him anywhere.

Ender dropped through the gate, and Bean quickly told him how Griffin Army was situated. "They've got two squares of stars, all the way around the gate. All their soldiers are under cover, and there's no way to hit any of them until we're clear to the bottom wall. Even with shields, we'd get there at half strength and we wouldn't have a chance."

"They moving?" Ender asked.

"Do they need to?"

Ender thought for a moment. "This one's tough. We'll go for the gate, Bean."

Griffin Army began to call out to them.

"Hey, is anybody there!"

"Wake up, there's a war on!"

"We wanna join the picnic!"

They were still calling when Ender's army came out from behind their star with a shield of fourteen frozen soldiers. William Bee, Griffin Army's commander, waited patiently as the screen approached, his men waiting at the fringes of their stars for the moment when whatever was behind the screen became visible. About ten meters away the screen exploded as the soldiers behind it shoved the screen north. The momentum carried them south twice as fast, and at the same moment the rest of Dragon Army burst from behind their star at the opposite end of the room, firing rapidly.

William Bee's boys joined battle immediately, of course, but William Bee was far more interested in what had been left behind when the shield disappeared. A formation of four frozen Dragon Army soldiers was moving headfirst toward the Griffin Army gate, held together by another frozen soldier whose feet and hands were hooked through their belts. A sixth soldier hung to his wrist and trailed like the tail of a kite. Griffin Army was winning the battle easily, and William Bee concentrated on the formation as it approached the gate. Suddenly the soldier trailing in back moved—he wasn't frozen at all! And even though William Bee flashed him immediately, the damage was done. The formation drifted to the Griffin Army gate, and their helmets touched all four corners simultaneously. A buzzer sounded, the gate reversed, and the frozen soldier in the middle was carried by momentum right through the gate. All the flashers stopped working, and the game was over.

The teacher door opened and Lieutenant Anderson came in. Anderson stopped himself with a slight movement of his hands when he reached the center of the battleroom. "Ender," he called, breaking protocol. One of the frozen Dragon soldiers near the south wall tried to call through jaws that were clamped shut by the suit. Anderson drifted to him and unfroze him.

Ender was smiling.

"I beat you again, sir," Ender said. Anderson didn't smile.

"That's nonsense, Ender," Anderson said softly. "Your battle was with William Bee of Griffin Army."

Ender raised an eyebrow.

"After that maneuver," Anderson said, "the rules are being revised to require that all of the enemy's soldiers must be immobilized before the gate can be reversed."

"That's all right," Ender said. "It could only work once, anyway." Anderson nodded, and was turning away when Ender added, "Is there going to be a new rule that armies be given equal positions to fight from?"

Anderson turned back around. "If you're in one of the positions, Ender, you can hardly call them equal, whatever they are."

William Bee counted carefully and wondered how in the world he had lost when not one of his soldiers had been flashed, and only four of Ender's soldiers were even mobile.

And that night as Ender came into the commanders' mess hall, he was greeted with applause and cheers, and his table was crowded with respectful commanders, many of them two or three years older than he was. He was friendly, but while he ate he wondered what the teachers would do to him in his next battle. He didn't need to worry. His next two battles were easy victories, and after that he never saw the battleroom again.

It was 2100 and Ender was a little irritated to hear someone knock at his door. His army was exhausted, and he had ordered them all to be in bed after 2030. The last two days had been regular battles, and Ender was expecting the worst in the morning.

It was Bean. He came in sheepishly, and saluted.

Ender returned his salute and snapped, "Bean, I wanted everybody in bed."

Bean nodded but didn't leave. Ender considered ordering him out. But as he looked at Bean it occurred to him for the first time in weeks just how young Bean was. He had turned eight a week before, and he was still small and— no, Ender thought, he wasn't young. Nobody was young. Bean had been in battle, and with a whole army depending on him he had come through and won. And even though he was small, Ender could never think of him as young again.

Ender shrugged and Bean came over and sat on the edge of the bed. The younger boy looked at his hands for a while, and finally Ender grew impatient and asked, "Well, what is it?"

"I'm transferred. Got orders just a few minutes ago."

Ender closed his eyes for a moment. "I knew they'd pull something new. Now they're taking —where are you going?"

"Rabbit Army."

"How can they put you under an idiot like Carn Carby!"

"Carn was graduated. Support squads."

Ender looked up. "Well, who's commanding Rabbit then?"

Bean held his hands out helplessly.

"Me," he said.

Ender nodded, and then smiled. "Of course, After all, you're only four years younger than the regular age."

"It isn't funny," Bean said. "I don't know what's going on here. First all the changes in the game. And now this. I wasn't the only one transferred, either, Ender. Ren, Peder, Wins, Younger, Paul. All commanders now."

Ender stood up angrily and strode to the wall. "Every damn toon leader I've got!" he said, and whirled to face Bean. "If they're going to break up my army, Bean, why did they bother making me a commander at all?"

Bean shook his head. "I don't know. You're the best, Ender. Nobody's ever done what you've done. Nineteen battles in fifteen days, sir, and you won every one of them, no matter what they did to you."

"And now you and the others are commanders. You know every trick I've got, I trained you, and who am I supposed to replace you with? Are they going to stick me with six green-ohs?"

"It stinks, Ender, but you know that if they gave you five crippled midgets and armed you with a roll of toilet paper you'd win."

They both laughed, and then they noticed that the door was open.

Lieutenant Anderson stepped in. He was followed by Captain Graff.

"Ender Wiggins," Graff said, holding his hands across his stomach.

"Yes sir," Ender answered.

"Orders."

Anderson extended a slip of paper. Ender read it quickly, then crumpled it, still looking at the air where the paper had been. After a few moments he asked, "Can I tell my army?"

"They'll find out," Graff answered. "It's better not to talk to them after orders. It makes it easier."

"For you or for me?" Ender asked. He didn't wait for an answer. He turned to Bean, took his hand for a moment, and headed for the door.

"Wait," Bean said. "Where are you going? Tactical or Support School?"

"Command School," Ender answered, and then he was gone and Anderson closed the door.

Command School, Bean thought. Nobody went to Command School until they had gone through three years of Tactical. But then, nobody went to Tactical until they had been through at least five years of Battle School. Ender had only had three.

The system was breaking up. No doubt about it, Bean thought. Either somebody at the top was going crazy, or something was going wrong with the war—the real war, the one they were training to fight in. Why else would they break down the training system, advance somebody— even somebody as good as Ender—straight to Command School? Why else would they have an eight-year-old greenoh like Bean command an army?

Bean wondered about it for a long time, and then he finally lay down on Ender's bed and realized that he'd never see Ender again, probably. For some reason that made him want to cry. But he didn't cry, of course. Training in the preschools had taught him how to force down emotions like that. He remembered how his first teacher, when he was three, would have been upset to see his lip quivering and his eyes full of tears.

Bean went through the relaxing routine until he didn't feel like crying anymore. Then he drifted off to sleep. His hand was near his mouth. It lay on his pillow hesitantly, as if Bean couldn't decide whether to bite his nails or suck on his fingertips. His forehead was creased and furrowed. His breathing was quick and light. He was a soldier, and if anyone had asked him what he wanted to be when he grew up, he wouldn't have known what they meant.

There's a war on, they said, and that was excuse enough for all the hurry in the world. They said it like a password and flashed a little card at every ticket counter and customs check and guard station. It got them to the head of every line.

Ender Wiggin was rushed from place to place so quickly he had no time to examine anything. But he did see trees for the first time. He saw men who were not in uniform. He saw women. He saw strange animals that didn't speak, but that followed docilely behind women and small children. He saw suitcases and conveyor belts and signs that said words he had never heard of. He would have asked someone what the words meant, except that purpose and authority surrounded him in the persons of four very high officers who never spoke to each other and never spoke to him.

Ender Wiggin was a stranger to his world he was being trained to save. He did not remember ever leaving Battle School before. His earliest memories were of childish war games under the direction of a teacher, of meals with other boys in the gray and green uniforms of the armed forces of his world. He did not know that the gray represented the sky and the green represented the great forests of his planet. All he knew of the world was from vague references to "outside."

And before he could make any sense of the strange world he was seeing for the first time, they enclosed him again within the shell of the military, where nobody had to say there's a war on anymore because nobody in the shell of the military forgot it for a single instant in a single day.

They put him in a space ship and launched him to a large artificial satellite that circled the world.

This space station was called Command School. It held the ansible.

On his first day Ender Wiggin was taught
about the ansible and what it meant to warfare.
It meant that even though the starships of
today's battles were launched a hundred years
ago, the commanders of the starships were men
of today, who used the ansible to send messages
to the computers and the few men on each ship.
The ansible sent words as they were spoken, orders as they were made. Battle plans as they
were fought. Light was a pedestrian.

For two months Ender Wiggin didn't meet a
single person. They came to him namelessly,
taught him what they knew, and left him to
other teachers. He had no time to miss his
friends at Battle School. He only had time to
learn how to operate the simulator, which
flashed battle patterns around him as if he were
in a starship at the center of the battle. How to
command mock ships in mock battles by manip-
ulating the keys on the simulator and speaking
words into the ansible. How to recognize instantly every enemy ship and the weapons it carried by the pattern that the simulator showed.
How to transfer all that he learned in the nullo
battles at Battle School to the starship battles at
Command School.

He had thought the game was taken seriously
before. Here they hurried him through every
step, were angry and worried beyond reason every time he forgot something or made a mistake.
But he worked as he had always worked, and
learned as he had always learned. After a while
he didn't make any more mistakes. He used the
simulator as if it were a part of himself. Then
they stopped being worried and they gave him a
teacher. The teacher was a person at last, and

his name was Maezr Rackham.

Maezr Rackham was sitting cross-legged on the floor when Ender awoke. He said nothing as Ender got up and showered and dressed, and Ender did not bother to ask him anything. He had long since learned that when something unusual was going on, he would find out more information faster by waiting than by asking.

Maezr still hadn't spoken when Ender was ready and went to the door to leave the room. The door didn't open. Ender turned to face the man sitting on the floor. Maezr was at least forty, which made him the oldest man Ender had ever seen close up. He had a day's growth of black and white whiskers that grizzled his face only slightly less than his close-cut hair. His face sagged a little and his eyes were surrounded by creases and lines. He looked at Ender without interest.

Ender turned back to the door and tried again to open it.

"All right," he said, giving up. "Why's the door locked?"

Maezr continued to look at him blankly.

Ender became impatient. "I'm going to be late. If I'm not supposed to be there until later, then tell me so I can go back to bed." No answer. "Is it a guessing game?" Ender asked. No answer. Ender decided that maybe the man was trying to make him angry, so he went through a relaxing exercise as he leaned on the door, and soon he was calm again. Maezr didn't take his eyes off Ender.

For the next two hours the silence endured, Maezr watching Ender constantly, Ender trying to pretend he didn't notice the old man. The boy became more and more nervous, and finally ended up walking from one end of the room to the other in a sporadic pattern.

He walked by Maezr as he had several times before, and Maezr's hand shot out and pushed Ender's left leg into his right in the middle of a step. Ender fell flat on the floor.

He leaped to his feet immediately, furious. He found Maezr sitting calmly, cross-legged, as if he had never moved. Ender stood poised to fight. But the other's immobility made it impossible for Ender to attack, and he found himself wondering if he had only imagined the old man's hand tripping him up.

The pacing continued for another hour, with Ender Wiggin trying the door every now and then. At last he gave up and took off his uniform and walked to his bed.

As he leaned over to pull the covers back, he felt a hand jab roughly between his thighs and another hand grab his hair. In a moment he had been turned upside down. His face and shoulders were being pressed into the floor by the old man's knee, while his back was excruciatingly bent and his legs were pinioned by Maezr's arm. Ender was helpless to use his arms, and he couldn't bend his back to gain slack so he could use his legs. In less than two seconds the old man had completely defeated Ender Wiggin.

"All right," Ender gasped. "You win."

Maezr's knee thrust painfully downward.

"Since when," Maezr asked in a soft, rasping voice, "do you have to tell the enemy when he has won?"

Ender remained silent.

"I surprised you once, Ender Wiggin. Why didn't you destroy me immediately afterward? Just because I looked peaceful? You turned your back on me. Stupid. You have learned nothing. You have never had a teacher."

Ender was angry now. "I've had too many damned teachers. How was I supposed to know you'd turn out to be a—" Ender hunted for a word. Maezr supplied one.

"An enemy, Ender Wiggin," Maezr whispered. "I am your enemy, the first one you've ever had who was smarter than you. There is no teacher but the enemy, Ender Wiggin. No one but the enemy will ever tell you what the enemy is going to do. No one but the enemy will ever teach you how to destroy and conquer. I am your enemy, from now on. From now on I am your teacher."

Then Maezr let Ender's legs fall to the floor. Because the old man still held Ender's head to the floor, the boy couldn't use his arms to compensate, and his legs hit the plastic surface with a loud crack and a sickening pain that made Ender wince. Then Maezr stood and let Ender rise.

Slowly the boy pulled his legs under him, with a faint groan of pain, and he knelt on all fours for a moment, recovering. Then his right arm flashed out. Maezr quickly danced back and Ender's hand closed on air as his teacher's foot shot forward to catch Ender on the chin.

Ender's chin wasn't there. He was lying flat on his back, spinning on the floor, and during the moment that Maezr was off balance from his kick Ender's feet smashed into Maezr's other leg. The old man fell on the ground in a heap.

What seemed to be a heap was really a hornet's nest. Ender couldn't find an arm or a leg that held still long enough to be grabbed, and in the meantime blows were landing on his back and arms. Ender was smaller—he couldn't reach past the old man's flailing limbs.

So he leaped back out of the way and stood poised near the door.

The old man stopped thrashing about and sat up, cross-legged again, laughing. "Better, this time, boy. But slow. You will have to be better with a fleet than you are with your body or no one will be safe with you in command. Lesson learned?"

Ender nodded slowly.

Maezr smiled. "Good. Then we'll never have such a battle again. All the rest with the simulator. I will program your battles, I will devise the strategy of your enemy, and you will learn to be quick and discover what tricks the enemy has for you. Remember, boy. From now on the enemy is stronger than you. From now on you are always about to lose."

Then Maezr's face became serious again. "You will be about to lose, Ender, but you will win. You will learn to defeat the enemy. He will teach you how."

Maezr got up and walked toward the door. Ender stepped back out of the way. As the old man touched the handle of the door, Ender leaped into the air and kicked Maezr in the small of the back with both feet. He hit hard enough that he rebounded onto his feet, as Maezr cried out and collapsed on the floor.

Maezr got up slowly, holding onto the door handle, his face contorted with pain. He seemed disabled, but Ender didn't trust him. He waited warily. And yet in spite of his suspicion he was caught off guard by Maezr's speed. In a moment he found himself on the floor near the opposite wall, his nose and lip bleeding where his face had hit the bed. He was able to turn enough to see Maezr open the door and leave. The old man was limping and walking slowly.

Ender smiled in spite of the pain, then rolled over onto his back and laughed until his mouth filled with blood and he started to gag. Then he got up and painfully made his way to the bed. He lay down and in a few minutes a medic came and took care of his injuries.

As the drug had its effect and Ender drifted off to sleep he remembered the way Maezr limped out of his room and laughed again. He was still laughing softly as his mind went blank and the medic pulled the blanket over him and snapped off the light. He slept until pain woke him in the morning. He dreamed of defeating Maezr.

The next day Ender went to the simulator room with his nose bandaged and his lip still puffy. Maezr was not there. Instead a captain who had worked with him before showed him an addition that had been made. The captain pointed to a tube with a loop at one end. "Radio. Primitive, I know, but it loops over your ear and we tuck the other end into your mouth with this piece here . . ."

"Watch it," Ender said as the captain pushed the end of the tube into his swollen lip.

"Sorry. Now you just talk."

"Good. Who to?"

The captain smiled. "Ask and see."

Ender shrugged and turned to the simulator. As he did a voice reverberated through his skull. It was too loud for him to understand, and he ripped the radio off his ear.

"What are you trying to do, make me deaf?"

The captain shook his head and turned a dial on a small box on a nearby table. Ender put the radio back on.

"Commander," the radio said in a familiar voice. Ender answered, "Yes."

"Instructions, sir?"

The voice was definitely familiar. "Bean?" Ender asked.

"Yes sir."

"Bean, this is Ender."

Silence. And then a burst of laughter from the other side. Then six or seven more voices laughing, and Ender waited for silence to return. When it did, he asked, "Who else?" A few voices spoke at once, but Bean drowned them out. "Me, I'm Bean, and Peder, Wins, Younger, Lee, and Vlad."

Ender thought for a moment. Then asked what the hell was going on. They laughed again.

"They can't break up the group," Bean said. "We were commanders for maybe two weeks, and here we are at Command School, training with the simulator, and all of a sudden they told us we were going to form a fleet with a new commander. And that's you."

Ender smiled. "Are you boys any good?"

"If we aren't, you'll let us know."

Ender chuckled a little. "Might work out. A fleet."

For the next ten days Ender trained his toon leaders until they could maneuver their ships like precision dancers. It was like being back in the battleroom again, except that Ender could always see everything, and could speak to his toon leaders and change their orders at any time.

One day as Ender sat down at the control board and switched on the simulator, harsh green lights appeared in the space—the enemy.

"This is it," Ender said. "X, Y, bullet, C, D, reserve screen, E, south loop, Bean, angle north."

The enemy was grouped in a globe, and outnumbered Ender two to one. Half of Ender's force was grouped in a tight, bulletlike formation, with the rest in a flat circular screen—except for a tiny force under Bean that moved off the simulator, heading behind the enemy's formation. Ender quickly learned the enemy's strategy: whenever Ender's bullet formation came close, the enemy would give way, hoping to draw Ender inside the globe where he would be surrounded. So Ender obligingly fell into the trap, bringing his bullet to the center of the globe.

The enemy began to contract slowly, not wanting to come within range until all their weapons could be brought to bear at once. Then Ender began to work in earnest. His reserve screen approached the outside of the globe, and the enemy began to concentrate his forces there. Then Bean's force appeared on the opposite side, and the enemy again deployed ships on that side.

Which left most of the globe only thinly defended. Ender's bullet attacked, and since at the point of attack it outnumbered the enemy overwhelmingly, he tore a hole in the formation. The enemy reacted to try to plug the gap, but in the confusion the reserve force and Bean's small force attacked simultaneously, while the bullet moved to another part of the globe. In a few more minutes the formation was shattered, most of the enemy ships destroyed, and the few survivors rushing away as fast as they could go.

Ender switched the simulator off. All the lights faded. Maezr was standing beside Ender, his hands in his pockets, his body tense. Ender looked up at him.

"I thought you said the enemy would be smart," Ender said.

Maezr's face remained expressionless. "What did you learn?"

"I learned that a sphere only works if your enemy's a fool. He had his forces so spread out that I outnumbered him whenever I engaged him."

"And?"

"And," Ender said, "You can't stay committed to one pattern. It makes you too easy to predict."

"Is that all?" Maezr asked quietly.

Ender took off his radio. "The enemy could have defeated me by breaking the sphere earlier."

Maezr nodded. "You had an unfair advantage."

Ender looked up at him coldly. "I was outnumbered two to one."

Maezr shook his head. "You have the ansible.

The enemy doesn't. We include that in the mock battles. Their messages travel at the speed of light."

Ender glanced toward the simulator. "Is there enough space to make a difference?"

"Don't you know?" Maezr asked. "None of the ships was ever closer than thirty thousand kilometers to another."

Ender tried to figure the size of the enemy's sphere. Astronomy was beyond him. But now his curiosity was stirred.

"What kind of weapons are on those ships? To be able to strike so fast and so far apart?"

Maezr shook his head. "The science is too much for you. You'd have to study many more years than you've lived to understand even the basics. All you need to know is that the weapons work."

"Why do we have to come so close to be in range?"

"The ships are all protected by force fields. A certain distance away the weapons are weaker, and can't get through. Closer in the weapons are stronger than the shields. But the computers take care of all that. They're constantly firing in any direction that won't hurt one of our ships. The computers pick targets, aim; they do all the detail work. You just tell them when and get them in a position to win. All right?"

"No." Ender twisted the tube of the radio around his fingers. "I have to know how the weapons work."

"I told you, it would take—"

"I can't command a fleet—not even on the simulator—unless I know." Ender waited a moment, then added, "Just the rough idea."

Maezr stood up and walked a few steps away. "All right, Ender. It won't make any sense, but I'll try. As simply as I can." He shoved his hands into his pockets. "It's this way, Ender. Everything is made up of atoms, little particles so small you can't see them with your eyes. These atoms, there are only a few different types, and they're all made up of even smaller particles that are pretty much the same. These atoms can be broken, so that they stop being atoms. So that this metal doesn't hold together anymore. Or the plastic floor. Or your body. Or even the air. They just seem to disappear, if you break the atoms. All that's left is the pieces. And they fly around and break more atoms. The weapons on the ships set up an area where it's impossible for atoms of anything to stay together. They all break down. So things in that area—they disappear."

Ender nodded. "You're right, I don't understand it. Can it be blocked?"

"No. But it gets wider and weaker the farther it goes from the ship, so that after a while a force field will block it. Okay? And to make it strong at all, it has to be focused, so that a ship can only fire effectively in maybe three or four directions at once."

Ender nodded again. Maezr wondered if the boy really understood it at all.

"If the pieces of the broken atoms go breaking more atoms, why doesn't it just make everything disappear?"

"Space. Those thousands of kilometers between the ships, they're empty. Almost no atoms. The pieces don't hit anything, and when they finally do hit something, they're so spread out they can't do any harm." Maezr cocked his head quizzically. "Anything else . . . ?"

Ender nodded. "Do the weapons on the ships —do they work against anything besides ships?"

Maezr moved in close to Ender and said firmly. "We only use them against ships. Never anything else. If we used them against anything else, the enemy would use them against us. Got it?"

Maezr walked away, and was nearly out the door when Ender called to him.

"I don't know your name yet," Ender said blandly.

"Maezr Rackham."

"Maezr Rackham," Ender said, "I defeated you."

Maezr laughed.

"Ender, you weren't fighting me today," he said. "You were fighting the stupidest computer in the Command School, set on a ten-year-old program. You don't think I'd use a sphere, do you?" He shook his head. "Ender, my dear little fellow, when you fight me you'll know it. Because you'll lose." And Maezr left the room.

Ender still practiced ten hours a day with his toon leaders. He never saw them, though, only heard their voices on the radio. Battles came every two or three days. The enemy had something new every time, something harder—but Ender coped with it. And won every time. And after every battle Maezr would point out mistakes and show Ender had really lost. Maezr only let Ender finish so that he would learn to handle the end of the game.

Until finally Maezr came in and solemnly

shook Ender's hand and said, "That, boy, was a good battle."

Because the praise was so long in coming, it pleased Ender more than praise had ever pleased him before. And because it was so condescending, he resented it.

"So from now on," Maezr said, "we can give you hard ones."

From then on Ender's life was a slow nervous breakdown.

He began fighting two battles a day, with problems that steadily grew more difficult. He had been trained in nothing but the game all his life—but now the game began to consume him. He woke in the morning with new strategies for the simulator, and went fitfully to sleep at night with the mistakes of the day preying on him. Sometimes he would wake up in the middle of the night crying for a reason he didn't remember. Sometimes he woke with his knuckles bloody from biting them. But every day he went impassively to the simulator and drilled his toon leaders until the battles, and drilled his toon leaders after the battles, and endured and studied the harsh criticism that Maezr Rackham piled on him. He noted that Rackham perversely criticized him more after his hardest battles. He noted that every time he thought of a new strategy, the enemy was using it within a few days. And he noted that while his fleet always stayed the same size, the enemy increased in numbers every day.

He asked his teacher.

"We are showing you what it will be like when you really command. The ratios of enemy to us."

"Why does the enemy always outnumber us in these battles?"

Maezr bowed his gray head for a moment, as if deciding whether to answer. Finally he looked up and reached out his hand and touched Ender on the shoulder. "I will tell you, even though the information is secret. You see, the enemy attacked us first. He had good reason to attack us, but that is a matter for politicians, and whether the fault was ours or his, we could not let him win. So when the enemy came to our worlds, we fought back, hard, and spent the finest of our young men in the fleets. But we won, and the enemy retreated."

Maezr smiled ruefully. "But the enemy was not through, boy. The enemy would never be through. They came again, with more numbers, and it was harder to beat them. And another generation of young men was spent. Only a few survived. So we came up with a plan—the big men came up with the plan. We knew that we had to destroy the enemy once and for all, totally, eliminate his ability to make war against us. To do that we had to go to his home worlds—his home world, really, since the enemy's empire is all tied to his capital world."

"And so?" Ender asked.

"And so we made a fleet. We made more ships than the enemy ever had. We made a hundred ships for every ship he had sent against us. And we launched them against his twenty-eight worlds. They left a hundred years ago. And they carried on them the ansible, and only a few men. So that someday a commander could sit on a planet somewhere far from the battle and command the fleet. So that our best minds would not be destroyed by the enemy."

Ender's question had still not been answered. "Why do they outnumber us?"

Maezr laughed. "Because it took a hundred years for our ships to get there. They've had a hundred years to prepare for us. They'd be fools, don't you think, boy, if they waited in old tugboats to defend their harbors. They have new ships, great ships, hundreds of ships. All we have is the ansible, that and the fact that they have to put a commander with every fleet, and when they lose—and they will lose—they lose one of their best minds every time."

Ender started to ask another question.

"No more, Ender Wiggin. I've told you more than you ought to know as it is."

Ender stood angrily and turned away. "I have a right to know. Do you think this can go on forever, pushing me through one school and another and never telling me what my life is for? You use me and the others as a tool. Someday we'll command your ships, someday maybe we'll save your lives, but I'm not a computer, and I have to *know*!"

"Ask me a question, then, boy," Maezr said, "and if I can answer, I will."

"If you use your best minds to command the fleets, and you never lose any, then what do you need me for? Who am I replacing, if they're all still there?"

Maezr shook his head. "I can't tell you the answer to that, Ender. Be content that we will need you, soon. It's late. Go to bed. You have a battle in the morning."

Ender walked out of the simulator room. But when Maezr left by the same door a few moments later, the boy was waiting in the hall.

"All right, boy," Maezr said impatiently, "what is it? I don't have all night and you need to sleep."

Ender stayed silent, but Maezr waited. Finally the boy asked softly, "Do they live?"

"Does who live?"

"The other commanders. The ones now. And before me."

Maezr snorted. "Live. Of course they live. He wonders if they live." Still chuckling the old man walked off down the hall. Ender stood in the corridor for a while, but at last he was tired and he went off to bed. They live, he thought. They live, but he can't tell me what happens to them.

That night Ender didn't wake up crying. But he did wake up with blood on his hands.

Months wore on with battles every day, until at last Ender settled into the routine of the destruction of himself. He slept less every night, dreamed more, and he began to have terrible pains in his stomach. They put him on a very bland diet, but soon he didn't even have an appetite for that. "Eat," Maezr said, and Ender would mechanically put food in his mouth. But if nobody told him to eat he didn't eat.

One day as he was drilling his toon leaders the room went black and he woke up on the floor with his face bloody where he had hit the controls.

They put him to bed then, and for three days he was very ill. He remembered seeing faces in his dreams, but they weren't real faces, and he knew it even while he thought he saw them. He thought he saw Bean, sometimes, and sometimes he thought he saw Lieutenant Anderson and Captain Graff. And then he woke up and it was only his enemy, Maezr Rackham.

"I'm awake," he said to Maezr.

"So I see," Maezr answered. "Took you long enough. You have a battle today."

So Ender got up and fought the battle and he won it. But there was no second battle that day, and they let him go to bed earlier. His hands were shaking as he undressed.

During the night he thought he felt hands touching him gently, and he dreamed he heard voices, saying, "How long can he go on?"

"Long enough."

"So soon?"

"In a few days, then he's through."

"How will he do?"

"Fine. Even today, he was better than ever."

Ender recognized the last voice as Maezr Rackham's. He resented Rackham's intruding even in his sleep.

He woke up and fought another battle and won.

Then he went to bed.

He woke up and won again.

And the next day was his last day in Command School, though he didn't know it. He got up and went to the simulator for the battle.

Maezr was waiting for him. Ender walked slowly into the simulator room. His step was slightly shuffling, and he seemed tired and dull. Maezr frowned.

"Are you awake, boy?" If Ender had been

alert, he would have noticed the concern in his teacher's voice. Instead, he simply went to the controls and sat down. Maezr spoke to him.

"Today's game needs a little explanation, Ender Wiggin. Please turn around and pay strict attention."

Ender turned around, and for the first time he noticed that there were people at the back of the room. He recognized Graff and Anderson from Battle School, and vaguely remembered a few of the men from Command School—teachers for a few hours at some time or another. But most of the people he didn't know at all.

"Who are they?"

Maezr shook his head and answered, "Observers. Every now and then we let observers come in to watch the battle. If you don't want them, we'll send them out."

Ender shrugged. Maezr began his explanation. "Today's game, boy, has a new element. We're staging this battle around a planet. This will complicate things in two ways. The planet isn't large, on the scale we're using, but the ansible can't detect anything on the other side of it—so there's a blind spot. Also, it's against the rules to use weapons against the planet itself. All right?"

"Why, don't the weapons work against planets?"

Maezr answered coldly, "There are rules of war, Ender, that apply even in training games."

Ender shook his head slowly. "Can the planet attack?"

Maezr looked nonplussed for a moment, then smiled. "I guess you'll have to find that one out, boy. And one more thing. Today, Ender, your opponent isn't the computer. I am your enemy today, and today I won't be letting you off so easily. Today is a battle to the end. And I'll use any means I can to defeat you."

Then Maezr was gone, and Ender expressionlessly led his toon leaders through maneuvers. Ender was doing well, of course, but several of the observers shook their heads, and Graff kept clasping and unclasping his hands, crossing and uncrossing his legs. Ender would be slow today, and today Ender couldn't afford to be slow.

A warning buzzer sounded, and Ender cleared the simulator board, waiting for today's game to appear. He felt muddled today, and wondered why people were there watching. Were they going to judge him today? Decide if he was good enough for something else? For another two years of grueling training, another two years of struggling to exceed his best? Ender was twelve. He felt very old. And as he waited for the game to appear, he wished he could simply lose it, lose the battle badly and completely so that they would remove him from the program, punish him however they wanted, he didn't care, just so he could sleep.

Then the enemy formation appeared, and Ender's weariness turned to desperation.

The enemy outnumbered him a thousand to one, the simulator glowed green with them, and Ender knew that he couldn't win.

And the enemy was not stupid. There was no formation that Ender could study and attack. Instead the vast swarms of ships were constantly moving, constantly shifting from one momentary formation to another, so that a space that for one moment was empty was immediately filled with a formidable enemy force. And even though Ender's fleet was the largest he had ever had, there was no place he could deploy it where he would outnumber the enemy long enough to accomplish anything.

And behind the enemy was the planet. The planet, which Maezr had warned him about. What difference did a planet make, when Ender couldn't hope to get near it? Ender waited, waited for the flash of insight that would tell him what to do, how to destroy the enemy. And as he waited, he heard the observers behind him begin to shift in their seats, wondering what Ender was doing, what plan he would follow. And finally it was obvious to everybody that Ender didn't know what to do, that there was nothing to do, and a few of the men at the back of the room made quiet little sounds in their throats.

Then Ender heard Bean's voice in his ear. Bean chuckled and said, "Remember, the enemy's gate is *down*." A few of the other leaders laughed, and Ender thought back to the simple games he had played and won in Battle School. They had put him against hopeless odds there, too. And he had beaten them. And he'd be damned if he'd let Maezr Rackham beat him with a cheap trick like outnumbering him a thousand to one. He had won a game in Battle School by going for something the enemy didn't expect, something against the rules—he had won by going against the enemy's gate.

And the enemy's gate was down.

Ender smiled, and realized that if he broke this rule they'd probably kick him out of school, and that way he'd win for sure: he would never have to play a game again.

He whispered into the microphone. His six commanders each took part of the fleet and launched themselves against the enemy. They pursued erratic courses, darting off in one direction and then another. The enemy immediately stopped his aimless maneuvering and began to group around Ender's six fleets.

Ender took off his microphone, leaned back in his chair, and watched. The observers murmured out loud, now. Ender was doing nothing—he had thrown the game away.

But a pattern began to emerge from the quick confrontations with the enemy. Ender's six groups lost ships constantly as they brushed with each enemy force—but they never stopped for a fight, even when for a moment they could have won a small tactical victory. Instead they continued on their erratic course that led, eventually, down. Toward the enemy planet.

And because of their seemingly random course the enemy didn't realize it until the same time that the observers did. By then it was too late, just as it had been too late for William Bee to stop Ender's soldiers from activating the gate. More of Ender's ships could be hit and destroyed, so that of the six fleets only two were able to get to the planet, and those were decimated. But those tiny groups *did* get through, and they opened fire on the planet.

Ender leaned forward now, anxious to see if his guess would pay off. He half expected a buzzer to sound and the game to be stopped, because he had broken the rule. But he was betting on the accuracy of the simulator. If it could simulate a planet, it could simulate what would happen to a planet under attack.

It did.

The weapons that blew up little ships didn't blow up the entire planet at first. But they did cause terrible explosions. And on the planet there was no space to dissipate the chain reaction. On the planet the chain reaction found more and more fuel to feed it.

The planet's surface seemed to be moving back and forth, but soon the surface gave way in an immense explosion that sent light flashing in all directions. It swallowed up Ender's entire fleet. And then it reached the enemy ships.

The first simply vanished in the explosion. Then, as the explosion spread and became less bright, it was clear what happened to each ship. As the light reached them they flashed brightly for a moment and disappeared. They were all fuel for the fire of the planet.

It took more than three minutes for the explosion to reach the limits of the simulator, and by then it was much fainter. All the ships were gone, and if any had escaped before the explosion reached them, they were few and not worth worrying about. Where the planet had been there was nothing. The simulator was empty.

Ender had destroyed the enemy by sacrificing his entire fleet and breaking the rule against destroying the planet. He wasn't sure whether to feel triumphant at his victory or defiant at the rebuke he was certain would come. So instead he felt nothing. He was tired. He wanted to go to bed and sleep.

He switched off the simulator, and finally

heard the noise behind him.

There were no longer two rows of dignified military observers. Instead there was chaos. Some of them were slapping each other on the back, some of them were bowed with their head in their hands, others were openly weeping. Captain Graff detached himself from the group and came to Ender. Tears streamed down his face, but he was smiling. He reached out his arms, and to Ender's surprise he embraced the boy, held him tightly, and whispered, "Thank you, thank you, thank you, Ender."

Soon, all the observers were gathered around the bewildered child, thanking him and cheering him and patting him on the shoulder and shaking his hand. Ender tried to make sense of what they were saying. He had passed the test after all? Why did it matter so much to them?

Then the crowd parted and Maezr Rackham walked through. He came straight up to Ender Wiggin and held out his hand.

"You made the hard choice, boy. But heaven knows there was no other way you could have done it. Congratulations. You beat them, and it's all over."

All over. Beat them. "I beat *you*, Maezr Rackham."

Maezr laughed, a loud laugh that filled the room. "Ender Wiggin, you never played me. You never played a *game* since I was your teacher."

Ender didn't get the joke. He had played a great many games, at a terrible cost to himself. He began to get angry.

Maezr reached out and touched his shoulder. Ender shrugged him off. Maezr then grew seri-

ous and said, "Ender Wiggin, for the last
months you have been the commander of our
fleets. There were no games. The battles were
real. Your only enemy was *the* enemy. You won
every battle. And finally today you fought them
at their home world, and you destroyed their
world, their fleet, you destroyed them completely, and they'll never come against us again. You
did it. You."

Real. Not a game. Ender's mind was too tired
to cope with it all. He walked away from Maezr,
walked silently through the crowd that still whispered thanks and congratulations to the boy,
walked out of the simulator room and finally arrived in his bedroom and closed the door.

He was asleep when Graff and Maezr
Rackham found him. They came in quietly and
roused him. He woke slowly, and when he recognized them he turned away to go back to sleep.

"Ender," Graff said. "We need to talk to
you."

Ender rolled back to face them. He said nothing.

Graff smiled. "It was a shock to you yesterday, I know. But it must make you feel good to
know you won the war."

Ender nodded slowly.

"Maezr Rackham here, he never played
against you. He only analyzed your battles to
find out your weak spots, to help you improve. It
worked, didn't it?"

Ender closed his eyes tightly. They waited. He
said, "Why didn't you tell me?"

Maezr smiled. "A hundred years ago, Ender,
we found out some things. That when a
commander's life is in danger he becomes afraid,
and fear slows down his thinking. When a com-

mander knows that he's killing people, he becomes cautious or insane, and neither of those help him do well. And when he is mature, when he has responsibilities and an understanding of the world, he becomes cautious and sluggish and can't do his job. So we trained children, who didn't know anything but the game, and never knew when it would become real. That was the theory, and you proved that the theory worked."

Graff reached out and touched Ender's shoulder. "We launched the ships so that they would all arrive at their destination during these few months. We knew that we'd probably only have one good commander, if we were lucky. In history it's been very rare to have more than one genius in a war. So we planned on having a genius. We were gambling. And you came along and we won."

Ender opened his eyes again and they realized he was angry. "Yes, you won."

Graff and Maezr Rackham looked at each other. "He doesn't understand," Graff whispered.

"I understand," Ender said. "You needed a weapon, and you got it, and it was me."

"That's right," Maezr answered.

"So tell me," Ender went on, "how many people lived on that planet that I destroyed."

They didn't answer him. They waited a while in silence, and then Graff spoke. "Weapons don't need to understand what they're pointed at, Ender. We did the pointing, and so we're responsible. You just did your job."

Maezr smiled. "Of course, Ender, you'll be taken care of. The government will never forget you. You served us all very well."

Ender rolled over and faced the wall, and even

though they tried to talk to him, he didn't answer them. Finally they left.

Ender lay in his bed for a long time before anyone disturbed him again. The door opened softly. Ender didn't turn to see who it was. Then a hand touched him softly.

"Ender, it's me, Bean."

Ender turned over and looked at the little boy who was standing by his bed.

"Sit down," Ender said.

Bean sat. "That last battle, Ender. I didn't know how you'd get us out of it."

Ender smiled. "I didn't. I cheated. I thought they'd kick me out."

"Can you believe it! We won the war. The whole war's over, and we thought we'd have to wait till we grew up to fight in it, and it was us fighting it all the time. I mean, Ender, we're little kids. I'm a little kid, anyway." Bean laughed and Ender smiled. Then they were silent for a little while, Bean sitting on the edge of the bed, and Ender watching him out of half-closed eyes.

Finally Bean thought of something else to say. "What will we do now that the war's over?" he said.

Ender closed his eyes and said, "I need some sleep, Bean."

Bean got up and left and Ender slept.

Graff and Anderson walked through the gates into the park. There was a breeze, but the sun was hot on their shoulders.

"Abba Technics? In the capital?" Graff asked.

"No, in Biggock County. Training division,"

Anderson replied. "They think my work with children is good preparation. And you?"

Graff smiled and shook his head. "No plans. I'll be here for a few more months. Reports, winding down. I've had offers. Personnel developments for DCIA, executive vice-president for U and P, but I said no. Publisher wants me to do memoirs of the war. I don't know."

They sat on a bench and watched leaves shivering in the breeze. Children on the monkey bars were laughing and yelling, but the wind and the distance swallowed their words. "Look," Graff said, pointing. A little boy jumped from the bars and ran near the bench where the two men sat. Another boy followed him, and holding his hands like a gun he made an explosive sound. The child he was shooting at didn't stop. He fired again.

"I got you! Come back here!"

The other little boy ran on out of sight.

"Don't you know when you're dead?"" The boy shoved his hands in his pockets and kicked a rock back to the monkey bars. Anderson smiled and shook his head. "Kids," he said. Then he and Graff stood up and walked on out of the park.

Orson Scott Card lives with his wife, Kristine, in Salt Lake City, where they are the full-time parents of a brilliant and beautiful one-year-old, Geoffrey. Occasion-

ally Card takes time out to write, producing such works as the novels Hot Sleep *and* A Planet Called Treason *and the collections* Capitol *and* Monkey Sonatas. *"Ender's Game," his first published story, was nominated for a Hugo Award in 1978—and was also the main reason he came home from the same convention with the John W. Campbell Award for best new science fiction writer that year. He keeps the award on his living room wall and makes everybody look at it as soon as they come in the house. He is twenty-eight, a former Mormon missionary, and a playwright with a dozen or so productions under his belt.*

Our computer revolution and our adventure into space are taking place simultaneously, and the ever-increasing speed and range of space vehicles dictate that the further out we go the greater will be our reliance on computers. This will hold true both in peace and war—as indeed it already does.

But our dependence on computers, from a military standpoint, can be compared to our reliance on discipline. As Horatio Nelson demonstrated when, lifting his telescope to his blind eye, he refused to see Lord Jervis's signal, there are occasions when loyalty demands disobedience to the command of a superior officer. And, no matter how advanced and how apparently infallible strategic computers may become, there undoubtedly will be times when the necessity to choose between victory and defeat will tempt human beings to override their judgment.

Robert Sheckley

FOOL'S MATE

The players met, on the great, timeless board of space. The glittering dots that were the pieces swam in their separate patterns. In that configuration at the beginning, even before the first move was made, the outcome of the game was determined.

Both players saw, and knew which had won.

But they played on.

Because the game had to be played out.

"Nielson!"

Lieutenant Nielson sat in front of his gunfire board with an idyllic smile on his face. He didn't look up.

"Nielson!"

The lieutenant was looking at his fingers now, with the stare of a puzzled child.

"Nielson! Snap out of it!" General Branch loomed sternly over him. "Do you hear me, Lieutenant?"

Nielson shook his head dully. He started to look at his fingers again, then his gaze was caught by the glittering array of buttons on the gunfire panel.

"Pretty," he said.

General Branch stepped inside the cubicle, grabbed Nielson by the shoulders and shook him.

"Pretty things," Nielson said, gesturing at the panel. He smiled at Branch.

Margraves, second in command, stuck his head in the doorway. He still had sergeant's stripes on his sleeve, having been promoted to colonel only three days ago.

"Ed," he said, "the President's representative is here. Sneak visit."

"Wait a minute," Branch said. "I want to complete this inspection." He grinned sourly. It was one hell of an inspection when you went around finding how many sane men you had left.

"Do you hear me, Lieutenant?"

"Ten thousand ships," Nielson said. "Ten

thousand ships—all gone!"

"I'm sorry," Branch said. He leaned forward and slapped him smartly across the face.

Lieutenant Nielson started to cry.

"Hey, Ed—what about that representative?"

At close range, Colonel Margraves' breath was a solid essence of whisky, but Branch didn't reprimand him. If you had a good officer left you didn't reprimand him, no matter what he did. Also, Branch approved of whisky. It was a good release, under the circumstances. Probably better than his own, he thought, glancing at his scarred knuckles.

"I'll be right with you. Nielson, can you understand me?"

"Yes, sir," the lieutenant said in a shaky voice. "I'm all right now, sir."

"Good," Branch said. "Can you stay on duty?"

"For a while," Nielson said. "But, sir—I'm not well. I can feel it."

"I know," Branch said. "You deserve a rest. But you're the only gun officer I've got left on this side of the ship. The rest are in the wards."

"I'll try, sir," Nielson said, looking at the gunfire panel again. "But I hear voices sometimes. I can't promise anything, sir."

"Ed," Margraves began again, "that representative—"

"Coming. Good boy, Nielson." The lieutenant didn't look up as Branch and Margraves left.

"I escorted him to the bridge," Margraves said, listing slightly to starboard as he walked. "Offered him a drink, but he didn't want one."

"All right," Branch said.

"He was bursting with questions," Margraves continued, chuckling to himself. "One of those earnest, tanned State Department men, out to win the war in five minutes flat. Very friendly boy. Wanted to know why I, personally, thought the fleet had been maneuvering in space for a year with no action."

"What did you tell him?"

"Said we were waiting for a consignment of zap guns," Margraves said. "I think he almost believed me. Then he started talking about logistics."

"Hm-m-m," Branch said. There was no telling what Margraves, half drunk, had told the representative. Not that it mattered. An official inquiry into the prosecution of the war had been due for a long time.

"I'm going to leave you here," Margraves said. "I've got some unfinished business to attend to."

"Right," Branch said, since it was all he could say. He knew that Margraves' unfinished business concerned a bottle.

He walked alone to the bridge.

The President's representative was looking at the huge location screen. It covered one entire wall, glowing with a slowly shifting pattern of dots. The thousands of green dots on the left represented the Earth fleet, separated by a black void from the orange of the enemy. As he watched, the fluid, three-dimensional front slowly changed. The armies of dots clustered, shifted, retreated, advanced, moving with hypnotic slowness.

But the black void remained between them. General Branch had been watching that sight for almost a year. As far as he was concerned, the screen was a luxury. He couldn't determine from it what was really happening. Only the CPC calculators could, and they didn't need it.

"How do you do, General Branch?" the President's representative said, coming forward and offering his hand. "My name's Richard Ellsner."

Branch shook hands, noticing that Margraves' description had been pretty good. The representative. was no more than thirty. His tan looked strange, after a year of pallid faces.

"My credentials," Ellsner said, handing Branch a sheaf of papers. The general skimmed through them, noting Ellsner's authorization as Presidential Voice in Space. A high honor for so young a man.

"How are things on Earth?" Branch asked, just to say something. He ushered Ellsner to a chair, and sat down himself.

"Tight," Ellsner said. "We've been stripping the planet bare of radioactives to keep your fleet operating. To say nothing of the tremendous cost of shipping food, oxygen, spare parts, and all the other equipment you need to keep a fleet this size in the field."

"I know," Branch murmured, his broad face expressionless.

"I'd like to start right in with the President's complaints," Ellsner said with an apologetic little laugh. "Just to get them off my chest."

"Go right ahead," Branch said.

"Now then," Ellsner began, consulting a pocket notebook, "you've had the fleet in space for eleven months and seven days. Is that right?"

"Yes."

"During that time there have been light engagements, but no actual hostilities. You—and the enemy commander—have been content, evidently, to sniff each other like discontented dogs."

"I wouldn't use that analogy," Branch said, conceiving an instant dislike for the young man. "But go on."

"I apologize. It was an unfortunate, though inevitable, comparison. Anyhow, there has been no battle, even though you have a numerical superiority. Is that correct?"

"Yes."

"And you know the maintenance of this fleet strains the resources of Earth. The President would like to know why battle has not been joined?"

"I'd like to hear the rest of the complaints first," Branch said. He tightened his battered fists, but, with remarkable self-control, kept them at his sides.

"Very well. The morale factor. We keep getting reports from you on the incidence of combat fatigue—crack-up, in plain language. The figures are absurd! Thirty percent of your men seem to be under restraint. That's way out of line, even for a tense situation."

Branch didn't answer.

"To cut this short," Ellsner said, "I would like the answer to those questions. Then, I would like your assistance in negotiating a truce. This war was absurd to begin with. It was none of Earth's choosing. It seems to the President that, in view of the static situation, the enemy commander will be amenable to the idea."

Colonel Margraves staggered in, his face flushed. He had completed his unfinished business: adding another fourth to his half-drunk.

"What's this I hear about a truce?" he shouted.

Ellsner stared at him for a moment, then turned back to Branch.

"I suppose you will take care of this yourself. If you will contact the enemy commander, I will try to come to terms with him."

"They aren't interested," Branch said.

"How do you know?"

"I've tried. I've been trying to negotiate a truce for six months now. They want complete capitulation."

"But that's absurd," Ellsner said, shaking his head. "They have no bargaining point. The fleets are of approximately the same size. There have been no major engagements yet. How can they—"

"Easily," Margraves roared, walking up to the representative and peering truculently in his face.

"General. This man is drunk." Ellsner got to his feet.

"Of course, you little idiot! Don't you understand yet? *The war is lost!* Completely, irrevocably."

Ellsner turned angrily to Branch. The general sighed and stood up.

"That's right, Ellsner. The war is lost and every man in the fleet knows it. That's what's wrong with the morale. We're just hanging here, waiting to be blasted out of existence.''

The fleets shifted and weaved. Thousands of dots floated in space, in twisted, random patterns.

Seemingly random.

The patterns interlocked, opened and closed. Dynamically, delicately balanced, each configuration was a planned move on a hundred thousand mile front. The opposing dots shifted to meet the exigencies of the new pattern.

Where was the advantage? To the unskilled eye, a chess game is a meaningless array of pieces and positions. But to the players—the game may be already won or lost.

The mechanical players who moved the thousands of dots knew who had won—and who had lost.

"Now let's all relax," Branch said soothingly. "Margraves, mix us a couple of drinks. I'll explain everything." The colonel moved to a well-stocked cabinet in a corner of the room.

"I'm waiting," Ellsner said.

"First, a review. Do you remember when the war was declared, two years ago? Both sides subscribed to the Holmstead pact, not to bomb home planets. A rendezvous was arranged in space, for the fleets to meet."

"That's ancient history," Ellsner said.

"It has a point. Earth's fleet blasted off, grouped and went to the rendezvous." Branch cleared his throat.

"Do you know the CPCs? The Configuration-Probability-Calculators? They're like chess players, enormously extended. They arrange the fleet in an optimum attack-defense pattern, based on the configuration of the opposing fleet. So the first pattern was set."

"I don't see the need—" Ellsner started, but Margraves, returning with the drinks, interrupted him.

"Wait, my boy. Soon there will be a blinding light."

"When the fleets met, the CPCs calculated the probabilities of attack. They found we'd lose approximately eighty-seven percent of our fleet, to sixty-five percent of the enemy's. If they attacked, they'd lose seventy-nine percent, to our sixty-four. That was the situation as it stood then. By extrapolation, their *optimum* attack pattern—at that time—would net them a forty-five percent loss. Ours would have given us a seventy-two percent loss."

"I don't know much about the CPCs," Ellsner confessed. "My field's psych." He sipped his drink, grimaced, and sipped again.

"Think of them as chess players," Branch said. "They can estimate the loss probabilities for an attack at any given point of time, in any pattern. They can extrapolate the probable moves of both sides.

"That's why battle wasn't joined when we first met. No commander is going to annihilate his entire fleet like that."

"Well then," Ellsner said, "why haven't you exploited your slight numerical superiority? Why haven't you gotten an advantage over them?"

"Ah!" Margraves cried, sipping his drink. "It comes, the light!"

"Let me put it in the form of an analogy,"

Branch said. "If you have two chess players of equally high skill, the game's end is determined when one of them gains an advantage. Once the advantage is there, there's nothing the other player can do, unless the first makes a mistake. If everything goes as it should, the game's end is predetermined. The turning point may come a few moves after the game starts, although the game itself could drag on for hours."

"And remember," Margraves broke in, "to the casual eye, there may be no apparent advantage. Not a piece may have been lost."

"That's what's happened here," Branch finished sadly. "The CPC units in both fleets are of maximum efficiency. But the enemy has an edge, which they are carefully exploiting. And there's nothing we can do about it."

"But how did this happen?" Ellsner asked. "Who slipped up?"

"The CPCs have inducted the cause of the failure," Branch said. "The end of the war was inherent *in our take-off formation*."

"What do you mean?" Ellsner said, setting down his drink.

"Just that. The configuration the fleet was in, light-years away from battle, before we had even contacted their fleet. When the two met, they had an infinitesimal advantage of position. That was enough. Enough for the CPCs, anyhow."

"If it's any consolation," Margraves put in, "it was a fifty-fifty chance. It could have just as well been us with the edge."

"I'll have to find out more about this," Ellsner said. "I don't understand it all yet."

Branch snarled: "The war's lost. What more do you want to know?"

Ellsner shook his head.

"Wilt snare me with predestination 'round,"
Margraves quoted, "and then impute my fall to
sin?"

Lieutenant Nielson sat in front of the gunfire
panel, his fingers interlocked. This was necessary, because Nielson had an almost overpowering desire to push the buttons.

The pretty buttons.

Then he swore, and sat on his hands. He had
promised General Branch that he would carry
on, and that was important. It was three days
since he had seen the general, but he was determined to carry on. Resolutely he fixed his
gaze on the gunfire dials.

Delicate indicators wavered and trembled.
Dials measured distance, and adjusted aperture
to range. The slender indicators rose and fell as
the ship maneuvered, lifting toward the red line,
but never quite reaching it.

The red line marked emergency. That was
when he would start firing, when the little black
arrow crossed the little red line.

He had been waiting almost a year now, for
that little arrow. Little arrow. Little narrow. Little arrow. Little narrow.

Stop it.

That was when he would start firing.

Lieutenant Nielson lifted his hands into view
and inspected his nails. Fastidiously he cleaned
a bit of dirt out of one. He interlocked his fingers
again, and looked at the pretty buttons, the
black arrow, the red line.

He smiled to himself. He had promised the
general. Only three days ago.

So he pretended not to hear what the buttons were whispering to him.

"The thing I don't see," Ellsner said, "is why you can't do something about the pattern? Retreat and regroup, for example?"

"I'll explain that," Margraves said. "It'll give Ed a chance for a drink. Come over here." He led Ellsner to an instrument panel. They had been showing Ellsner around the ship for three days, more to relieve their own tension than for any other reason. The last day had turned into a fairly prolonged drinking bout.

"Do you see this dial?" Margraves pointed to one. The instrument panel covered an area four feet wide by twenty feet long. The buttons and switches on it controlled the movements of the entire fleet.

"Notice the shaded area. That marks the safety limit. If we use a forbidden configuration, the indicator goes over and all hell breaks loose."

"And what is a forbidden configuration?"

Margraves thought for a moment. "The forbidden configurations are those which would give the enemy an attack advantage. Or, to put it in another way, moves which change the attack-probability-loss picture sufficiently to warrant an attack."

"So you can move only within strict limits?" Ellsner asked, looking at the dial.

"That's right. Out of the infinite number of possible formations, we can use only a few, if we want to play safe. It's like chess. Say you'd like to put a sixth-row pawn in your opponent's back row. But it would take two moves to do it. And after you move to the seventh row, your opponent has a clear avenue, leading inevitably to checkmate.

"Of course, if the enemy advances too boldly the odds are changed again, and *we* attack."

"That's our only hope," General Branch said. "We're praying they do something wrong. The fleet is in readiness for instant attack, if our CPC shows that the enemy has overextended himself anywhere."

"And that's the reason for the crack-ups," Ellsner said. "Every man in the fleet on nerves' edge, waiting for a chance he's sure will never come. But having to wait anyhow. How long will this go on?"

"This moving and checking can go on for a little over two years," Branch said. "Then they will be in the optimum formation for attack, with a twenty-eight percent loss probability to our ninety-three. They'll have to attack then, or the probabilities will start to shift back in our favor."

"You poor devils," Ellsner said softly. "Waiting for a chance that's never going to come. Knowing you're going to be blasted out of space sooner or later."

"Oh, it's jolly," said Margraves, with an instinctive dislike for a civilian's sympathy.

Something buzzed on the switchboard, and Branch walked over and plugged in a line. "Hello? Yes. Yes. . . . All right, Williams. Right." He unplugged the line.

"Colonel Williams has had to lock his men in their rooms," Branch said. "That's the third time this month. I'll have to get CPC to dope out a formation so we can take him out of the front." He walked to a side panel and started pushing buttons.

"And there it is," Margraves said. "What do you plan to do, Mr. Presidential Represent-ative?"

The glittering dots shifted and deployed, advanced and retreated, always keeping a barrier of black space between them. The mechanical chess players watched each move, calculating its effect into the far future. Back and forth across the great chess board the pieces moved.

The chess players worked dispassionately, knowing beforehand the outcome of the game. In their strictly ordered universe there was no possible fluctuation, no stupidity, no failure.

They moved. And knew. And moved.

"Oh, yes," Lieutenant Nielson said to the smiling room. "Oh, yes." And look at all the buttons, he thought, laughing to himself.

So stupid. Georgia.

Nielson accepted the deep blue of sanctity, draping it across his shoulders. Bird song, some-where.

Of course.

Three buttons red. He pushed them. Three buttons green. He pushed them. Four dials. Riverread.

"Oh-oh. Nielson's cracked."

"Three is for me," Nielson said, and touched his forehead with greatest stealth. Then he reached for the keyboard again. Unimaginable associations raced through his mind, produced by unaccountable stimuli.

"Better grab him. Watch out!"

Gentle hands surround me as I push two are

brown for which is for mother, and one is high
for all rest.

"Stop him from shooting off those guns!"
I am lifted into the air, I fly, I fly.

"Is there any hope for that man?" Ellsner
asked, after they had locked Nielson in a ward.

"Who knows?" Branch said. His broad face
tightened; knots of muscle pushed out his
cheeks. Suddenly he turned, shouted, and swung
his fist wildly at the metal wall. After it hit, he
grunted and grinned sheepishly.

"Silly, isn't it? Margraves drinks. I let off
steam by hitting walls. Let's go eat."

The officers ate separately from the crew.
Branch had found that some officers tended to
get murdered by psychotic crewmen. It was best
to keep them apart.

During the meal, Branch suddenly turned to
Ellsner.

"Boy, I haven't told you the entire truth. I
said this would go on for two years? Well, the
men won't last that long. I don't know if I can
hold this fleet together for two more weeks."

"What would you suggest?"

"I don't know," Branch said. He still refused
to consider surrender, although he knew it was
the only realistic answer.

"I'm not sure," Ellsner said, "but I think
there may be a way out of your dilemma." The
officers stopped eating and looked at him.

"Have you got some superweapons for us?"
Margraves asked. "A disintegrator strapped to
your chest?"

"I'm afraid not. But I think you've been so

close to the situation that you don't see it in its true light. A case of the forest for the trees."

"Go on," Branch said, munching methodically on a piece of bread.

"Consider the universe as the CPC sees it. A world of strict causality. A logical, coherent universe. In this world, every effect has a cause. Every factor can be instantly accounted for.

"That's not a picture of the real world. There is no explanation for everything, really. The CPC is built to see a specialized universe, and to extrapolate on the basis of that."

"So," Margraves said, "what would you do?"

"Throw the world out of joint," Ellsner said. "Bring in uncertainty. Add a human factor that the machines can't calculate."

"How can you introduce uncertainty in a chess game?" Branch asked, interested in spite of himself.

"By sneezing at a crucial moment, perhaps. How could a machine calculate that?"

"It wouldn't have to. It would just classify it as extraneous noise, and ignore it."

"True." Ellsner thought for a moment. "This battle—how long will it take once the actual hostilities are begun?"

"About six minutes," Branch told him. "Plus or minus twenty seconds."

"That confirms an idea of mine," Ellsner said. "The chess game analogy you use is faulty. There's no real comparison."

"It's a convenient way of thinking of it," Margraves said.

"But it's an *untrue* way of thinking of it. Checkmating a king can't be equated with destroying a fleet. Nor is the rest of the situation like chess.

In chess you play by rules previously agreed upon by the players. In this game you can make up your own rules."

"This game has inherent rules of its own," Branch said.

"No," Ellsner said. "Only the CPCs have rules. How about this? Suppose you dispensed with the CPCs? Gave every commander his head, told him to attack on his own, with no pattern. What would happen?"

"It wouldn't work," Margraves told him. "The CPC can still total the picture, on the basis of the planning ability of the average human. More than that, they can handle the attack of a few thousand second-rate calculators—humans —with ease. It would be like shooting clay pigeons."

"But you've *got* to try something," Ellsner pleaded.

"Now wait a minute," Branch said. "You can spout theory all you want. I know what the CPCs tell me, and I believe them. I'm still in command of this fleet, and I'm not going to risk the lives in my command on some harebrained scheme."

"Harebrained schemes sometimes win wars," Ellsner said.

"They usually lose them."

"The war is lost already, by your own admission."

"I can still wait for them to make a mistake."

"Do you think it will come?"

"No."

"Well then?"

"I'm still going to wait."

The rest of the meal was completed in moody

silence. Afterward, Ellsner went to his room.

"Well, Ed?" Margraves asked, unbuttoning his shirt.

"Well yourself," the general said. He lay down on his bed, trying not to think. It was too much. Logistics. Predetermined battles. The coming debacle. He considered slamming his fist against the wall, but decided against it. It was sprained already. He was going to sleep.

On the borderline between slumber and sleep, he heard a click.

The door!

Branch jumped out of bed and tried the knob. Then he threw himself against it.

Locked.

"General, please strap yourself down. We are attacking." It was Ellsner's voice, over the intercom.

"I looked over that keyboard of yours, sir, and found the magnetic doorlocks. Mighty handy in case of a mutiny, isn't it?"

"You idiot!" Branch shouted. "You'll kill us all! That CPC—"

"I've disconnected our CPC," Ellsner said pleasantly. "I'm a pretty logical boy, and I think I know how a sneeze will bother them."

"He's mad," Margraves shouted to Branch. Together they threw themselves against the metal door.

They they were thrown to the floor.

"All gunners—fire at will!" Ellsner broadcasted to the fleet.

The ship was in motion. The attack was underway!

The dots drifted together, crossing the no man's land of space.

They coalesced! Energy flared, and the battle was joined.

Six minutes, human time. Hours for the electronically fast chess player. He checked his pieces for an instant, deducing the pattern of attack.

There was no pattern!

Half of the opposing chess player's pieces shot out into space, completely out of the battle. Whole flanks advanced, split, rejoined, wrenched forward, dissolved their formation, formed it again.

No pattern? There *had* to be a pattern. The chess player knew that everything had a pattern. It was just a question of finding it, of taking the moves already made and extrapolating to determine what the end was supposed to be.

The end was—chaos!

The dots swept in and out, shot away at right angles to the battle, checked and returned, meaninglessly.

What did it mean, the chess player asked himself with the calmness of metal. He waited for a recognizable configuration to emerge.

Watching dispassionately as his pieces were swept off the board.

"I'm letting you out of your room now," Ellsner called, "but don't try to stop me. I think I've won your battle."

The lock released. The two officers ran down the corridor to the bridge, determined to break Ellsner into little pieces.

Inside, they slowed down.

The screen showed the great mass of Earth dots sweeping over a scattering of enemy dots.

What stopped them, however, was Nielson, laughing, his hands sweeping over switches and buttons on the great master control board.

The CPC was droning the losses. "Earth— eighteen percent. Enemy—eighty-three. Eighty- four. Eighty-six. Earth, nineteen percent."

"Mate!" Ellsner shouted. He stood beside Nielson, a Stillson wrench clenched in his hand. "Lack of pattern. I gave their CPC something it couldn't handle. An attack with no apparent pattern. Meaningless configurations!"

"But what are they doing?" Branch asked, gesturing at the dwindling enemy dots.

"Still relying on their chess player," Ellsner said. "Still waiting for him to dope out the attack pattern in this madman's mind. Too much faith in machines, general. This man doesn't even know he's precipitating an attack."

. . . And push three that's for dad on the olive tree I always wanted to two two two Danbury fair with buckle shoe brown all brown buttons down and in, sin, eight red for sin—

"What's the wrench for?" Margraves asked.

"That?" Ellsner weighed it in his hand. "That's to turn off Nielson here, after the at- tack."

. . . And five and love and black, all blacks, fair but- tons in I remember when I was very young at all push five and there on the grass ouch—

Robert Sheckley was born in New York in 1928 and raised in a small town in New Jersey. After serving in the Army in Korea, he went to NYU, graduating in 1951. He began freelancing shortly thereafter, selling short stories to most of the sf magazines. His first novel, Immortality, Inc., *came not long after that, and he was set for his subsequent career as a freelance writer. He has published twenty-seven books of various sorts, mostly science fiction novels and collections of short stories. After living for many years in New York, he went to Spain, where he stayed for six years, and then spent a few more in England and points east. He is now back in New York, and is fiction editor of* Omni.

There is one thing we can reasonably expect in space, as our probings of our own Solar System have already shown us—a fantastic variety of worlds and satellites. This, of course, implies a wide variety of environments in which life forms may originate and flourish, and by logical extension, the possibility of a wide range of intelligences, all with their own needs, goals, artifacts, and perhaps weaponry. In short, we have no way of predicting what we may come up against once we leave the Sun's immediate family behind us, or what resources we may have to summon to our aid if what we meet is implacable hostility.

Let us suppose, then, that we do encounter such sentient but soulless destroying mechanisms as Fred Saberhagen's Berserkers, created by beings now themselves extinct to fight a long-forgotten war. Those of us who venture out against them beyond the reach of rescue or effective aid will be forced to rely on ourselves alone— or will we?

Fred Saberhagen

WINGS OUT OF SHADOW

In Malori's first and only combat mission the berserker came to him in the image of a priest of the sect into which Malori had been born on the planet Yaty. In a dreamlike vision that was the analogue of a very real combat he saw the robed figure standing tall in a deformed pulpit, eyes flaming with malevolence, lowering arms winglike with the robes they stretched. With their lowering, the lights of the universe were dimming outside the windows of stained glass and Malori was being damned.

Even with his heart pounding under damnation's terror Malori retained sufficient consciousness to remember the real nature of himself and of his adversary and that he was not powerless against him. His dream-feet walked him timelessly toward the pulpit and its demon-priest while all around him the stained-glass windows burst, showering him with fragments of sick fear. He walked a crooked path, avoiding the places in the smooth floor where, with quick gestures, the priest created snarling, snapping stone mouths full of teeth. Malori seemed to have unlimited time to decide where to put his feet. *Weapon,* he thought, a surgeon instructing some invisible aide. *Here—in my right hand.*

From those who had survived similar battles he had heard how the inhuman enemy appeared to each in different form, how each human must live the combat through in terms of a unique nightmare. To some a berserker came as a ravening beast, to others as devil or god or man. To still others it was some essence of terror that could never be faced or even seen. The combat was a nightmare experienced while the subconscious ruled, while the waking mind was suppressed by careful electrical pressures on the brain. Eyes and ears were padded shut so that the conscious mind might be more easily suppressed, the mouth plugged to save the tongue from being bitten, the nude body held immobile by the defensive fields that kept it whole against the thousands of gravities that came with each movement of the one-man ship while in combat mode. It was a nightmare from which mere terror could never wake one; waking came only when the fight was over, came only with death or victory or disengagement.

Into Malori's dream-hand there now came a meat cleaver keen as a razor, massive as a guillotine blade. So huge it was that had it been what it seemed it would have been far too cumbersome to even lift. His uncle's butcher shop on Yaty was gone, with all other human works of that planet. But the cleaver came back to him now, magnified, perfected to suit his need.

He gripped it hard in both hands and advanced. As he drew near, the pulpit towered higher. The carved dragon on its front, which should have been an angel, came alive, blasting him with rosy fire. With a shield that came from nowhere he parried the splashing flames.

Outside the remnants of the stained-glass windows the lights of the universe were almost dead now. Standing at the base of the pulpit, Malori drew back his cleaver as if to strike overhand at the priest who towered above his reach. Then, without any forethought at all, he switched his aim at the top of his backswing and laid the blow crashing against the pulpit's stem. It shook, but resisted stoutly. Damnation came.

Before the devils reached him, though, the energy was draining from the dream. In less than a second of real time it was no more than a fading visual image, a few seconds after that a dying memory. Malori, coming back to consciousness with eyes and ears still sealed, floated in a soothing limbo. Before post-combat fatigue and sensory deprivation could combine to send him into psychosis, attachments on his scalp began to feed his brain with bursts of pins-and-needles noise. It was the safest signal to administer to a brain that might be on the verge of any of a dozen different kinds of madness. The noise made a whitish roaring scattering of light and sound that seemed to fill his head and at the same time somehow outlined for him the positions of his limbs.

His first fully conscious thought: he had just fought a berserker and survived. He had won—or had at least achieved a stand-off—or he would not be here. It was no mean achievement.

Berserkers were like no other foe that Earth-descended human beings had ever faced. They had cunning and intelligence and yet were not alive. Relics of some interstellar war over long ages since, automated machines, warships for the most part, they carried as their basic programming the command to destroy all life wherever it could be found. Yaty was only the latest of many Earth-colonized planets to suffer a berserker attack, and it was among the luckiest; nearly all its people had been successfully evacuated. Malori and others now fought in deep space to protect the *Hope,* one of the enormous evacuation ships. The *Hope* was a sphere several kilometers in diameter, large enough to contain a good proportion of the planet's population stored tier on tier in defense-field stasis. A trickle-relaxation of the fields allowed them to breathe and live with slowed metabolism.

The voyage to a safe sector of the galaxy was going to take several months because most of it, in terms of time spent, was going to be occupied in traversing an outlying arm of the great Taynarus nebula. Here gas and dust were much too thick to let a ship duck out of normal space and travel faster than light. Here even the speeds attainable in normal space were greatly restricted. At thousands of kilometers per second, manned ship or berserker machine could alike be smashed flat against a wisp of gas far more tenuous than human breath.

Taynarus was a wilderness of uncharted plumes and tendrils of dispersed matter, laced through by corridors of relatively empty space. Much of the wilderness was completely shaded by interstellar dust from the light of all the suns outside. Through dark shoals and swamps and tides of nebula the *Hope* and her escort *Judith* fled, and a berserker pack pursued. Some berserkers were even larger than the *Hope*, but those that had taken up this chase were much smaller. In regions of space so thick with matter, a race went to the small as well as to the swift; as the impact cross-section of a ship increased, its maximum practical speed went inexorably down.

The *Hope*, ill-adapted for this chase (in the rush to evacuate, there had been no better choice available), could not expect to outrun the smaller and more maneuverable enemy. Hence the escort carrier *Judith*, trying always to keep herself between *Hope* and the pursuing pack. *Ju-*

dith mothered the little fighting ships, spawning them out whenever the enemy came too near, welcoming survivors back when the threat had once again been beaten off. There had been fifteen of the one-man ships when the chase began. Now there were nine.

The noise injections from Malori's life support equipment slowed down, then stopped. His conscious mind once more sat steady on its throne. The gradual relaxation of his defense fields he knew to be a certain sign that he would soon rejoin the world of waking men.

As soon as his fighter, Number Four, had docked itself inside the *Judith* Malori hastened to disconnect himself from the tiny ship's systems. He pulled on a loose coverall and let himself out of the cramped space. A thin man with knobby joints and an awkward step, he hurried along a catwalk through the echoing hangar-like chamber, noting that three or four fighters besides his had already returned and were resting in their cradles. The artificial gravity was quite steady, but Malori stumbled and almost fell in his haste to get down the short ladder to the operations deck.

Petrovich, commander of the *Judith,* a bulky, iron-faced man of middle height, was on the deck apparently waiting for him.

"Did—did I make my kill?" Malori stuttered eagerly as he came hurrying up. The forms of military address were little observed aboard the *Judith,* as a rule, and Malori was really a civilian anyway. That he had been allowed to take out a fighter at all was a mark of the commander's desperation.

Scowling, Petrovich answered bluntly.

"Malori, you're a disaster in one of these ships. Haven't the mind for it at all."

The world turned a little gray in front of Malori. He hadn't understood until this moment just how important to him certain dreams of glory were. He could find only weak and awkward words. "But . . . I thought I did all right." He tried to recall his combat-nightmare. Something about a church.

"Two people had to divert their ships from their original combat objectives to rescue you. I've already seen their gun-camera tapes. You had Number Four just sparring around with that berserker as if you had no intention of doing it any damage at all." Petrovich looked at him more closely, shrugged, and softened his voice somewhat. "I'm not trying to chew you out, you weren't even aware of what was happening, of course. I'm just stating facts. Thank probability the *Hope* is twenty AU deep in a formaldehyde cloud up ahead. If she'd been in an exposed position just now they would have got her."

"But—" Malori tried to begin an argument but the commander simply walked away. More fighters were coming in. Locks sighed and cradles clanged, and Petrovich had plenty of more important things to do than stand here arguing with him. Malori stood there alone for a few moments, feeling deflated and defeated and diminished. Involuntarily he cast a yearning glance back at Number Four. It was a short, windowless cylinder, not much more than a man's height in diameter, resting in its metal cradle while technicians worked about it. The stubby main laser nozzle, still hot from firing was sending up a wisp of smoke now that it was back in atmosphere. There was his two-handed cleaver.

No man could direct a ship or a weapon with anything like the competence of a good machine. The creeping slowness of human nerve impulses and of conscious thought disqualified humans from maintaining direct control of their ships in any space fight against berserkers. But the human subconscious was not so limited. Certain of its processes could not be correlated with any specific synaptic activity within the brain, and some theorists held that these processes took place outside of time. Most physicists stood aghast at this view—but for space combat it made a useful working hypothesis.

In combat, the berserker computers were coupled with sophisticated randoming devices, to provide the flair, the unpredictability that gained an advantage over an opponent who simply and consistently chose the maneuver statistically most likely to bring success. Men also used computers to drive their ships, but had now gained an edge over the best randomizers by relying once more on their own brains, parts of which were evidently freed of hurry and dwelt outside of time, where even speeding light must be as motionless as carved ice.

There were drawbacks. Some people (including Malori, it now appeared) were simply not suitable for the job, their subconscious minds seemingly uninterested in such temporal matters as life or death. And even in suitable minds the subconscious was subject to great stress. Connection to external computers loaded the mind in some way not yet understood. One after another, human pilots returning from combat were removed from their ships in states of catatonia or hysterical excitement. Sanity might be restored, but the man or woman was worthless thereafter as a combat-computer's teammate. The system was so new that the importance of these drawbacks was just coming to light aboard the *Judith* now. The trained operators of the fighting ships had been used up, and so had their replacements. Thus it was that Ian Malori, historian, and others were sent out, untrained, to fight. But using their minds had bought a little extra time.

From the operations deck Malori went to his small single cabin. He had not eaten for some time, but he was not hungry. He changed clothes and sat in a chair looking at his bunk, looking at his books and tapes and violin, but he did not try to rest or to occupy himself. He expected that he would promptly get a call from Petrovich. Because Petrovich now had nowhere else to turn.

He almost smiled when the communicator chimed, bringing a summons to meet with the commander and other officers at once. Malori acknowledged and set out, taking with him a brown leather-like case about the size of a briefcase but differently shaped, which he selected from several hundred similar cases in a small room adjacent to his cabin. The case he carried was labeled CRAZY HORSE.

Petrovich looked up as Malori entered the small planning room in which the handful of ship's officers were already gathered around a table. The commander glanced at the case Malori was carrying, and nodded. "It seems we have no choice, historian. We are running out of people, and we are going to have to use your pseudopersonalities. Fortunately we now have the necessary adapters installed in all the fighting ships."

"I think the chances of success are excellent." Malori spoke mildly as he took the seat left vacant for him and set his case out in the middle of the table. "These of course have no real subconscious minds, but as we agreed in our earlier discussions, they will provide more sophisticated randoming devices than are available otherwise. Each has a unique, if artificial, personality."

One of the other officers leaned forward. "Most of us missed these earlier discussions you speak of. Could you fill us in a little?"

"Certainly." Malori cleared his throat. "These personae, as we usually call them, are used in the computer simulation of historical problems. I was able to bring several hundred of them with me from Yaty. Many are models of military men." He put his hand on the case before him. "This is a reconstruction of the personality of one of the most able cavalry leaders on ancient Earth. It's not one of the group we have selected to try first in combat. I just brought it along to demonstrate the interior structure and design for any of you who are interested. Each persona contains about four million sheets of two-dimensional matter."

Another officer raised a hand. "How can you accurately reconstruct the personality of someone who must have died long before any kind of direct recording techniques were available?"

"We can't be positive of accuracy, of course. We have only historical records to go by, and what we deduce from computer simulations of the era. These are only models. But they should perform in combat as in the historical studies for which they were made. Their choices should reflect basic aggressiveness, determination—"

The totally unexpected sound of an explosion brought the assembled officers as one body to their feet. Petrovich, reacting very fast, still had time only to get clear of his chair before a second and much louder blast resounded through the ship. Malori himself was almost at the door, heading for his battle station, when the third explosion came. It sounded like the end of the galaxy, and he was aware that furniture was flying, that the bulkheads around the meeting room were caving in. Malori had one clear, calm thought about the unfairness of his coming death, and then for a time he ceased to think at all.

Coming back was a slow unpleasant process. He knew *Judith* was not totally wrecked for he still breathed, and the artificial gravity still held him sprawled out against the deck. It might have been pleasing to find the gravity gone, for his body was one vast, throbbing ache, a pattern of radiated pain from a center somewhere inside his skull. He did not want to pin down the source any more closely than that. To even imagine touching his own head was painful.

At last the urgency of finding out what was going on overcame the fear of pain and he raised his head and probed it. There was a large lump just above his forehead, and smaller injuries about his face where blood had dried. He must have been out for some time.

The meeting room was ruined, shattered, littered with debris. There was a crumpled body that must be dead, and there another, and another, mixed in with the furniture. Was he the only survivor? One bulkhead had been torn wide open, and the planning table was demolished. And what was that large, unfamiliar piece of machinery standing at the other end of the room? Big as a tall filing cabinet, but far more intricate. There was something peculiar about its legs, as if they might be movable . . .

Malori froze in abject terror, because the thing did move, swiveling a complex of turrets and lenses at him, and he understood that he was seeing and being seen by a functional berserker machine. It was one of the small ones, used for boarding and operating captured human ships.

"Come here," the machine said. It had a squeaky, ludicrous parody of a human voice, recorded syllables of captives' voices stuck together electronically and played back. "The badlife has awakened."

Malori in his great fear thought that the words were directed at him but he could not move. Then, stepping through the hole in the bulkhead, came a man Malori had never seen before—a shaggy and filthy man wearing a grimy coverall that might once have been part of some military uniform.

"I see he has, sir," the man said to the machine. He spoke the standard interstellar language in a ragged voice that bore traces of a cultivated accent. He took a step closer to Malori. "Can you understand me, there?"

Malori grunted something, tried to nod, pulled himself up slowly to an awkward sitting position.

"The question is," the man continued, coming a little closer still, "how d'you want it later, easy or hard? When it comes to your finishing up, I mean. I decided a long time ago that I want mine quick and easy, and not too soon. Also that I still want to have some fun here and there along the way."

Despite the fierce pain in his head, Malori was thinking now, and beginning to understand. There was a name for humans like the man before him, who went along more or less willingly with the berserker machines. A word coined by the machines themselves. But at the moment Malori was not going to speak that name.

"I want it easy," was all he said, and blinked his eyes and tried to rub his neck against the pain.

The man looked him over in silence a little longer. "All right," he said then. Turning back to the machine, he added in a different, humble voice: "I can easily dominate this injured badlife. There will be no problems if you leave us here alone."

The machine turned one metal-cased lens toward its servant. "Remember," it vocalized, "the auxiliaries must be made ready. Time grows short. Failure will bring unpleasant stimuli."

"I will remember, sir." The man was humble and sincere. The machine looked at both of them a few moments longer and then departed, metal legs flowing suddenly into a precise and almost graceful walk. Shortly after, Malori heard the familiar sound of an airlock cycling.

"We're alone now," the man said, looking down at him. "If you want a name for me you can call me Greenleaf. Want to try to fight me? If so, let's get it over with." He was not much bigger than Malori but his hands were huge and he looked hard and very capable despite his ragged filthiness. "All right, that's a smart choice. You know, you're actually a lucky man, though you don't realize it yet. Berserkers aren't like the other masters that men have—not like the governments and parties and corporations and causes that use you up and then just let you drop and drag away. No, when the machines run out of uses for you they'll finish you off quickly and cleanly—if you've served well. I know, I've seen 'em do it that way with other humans. No reason why they shouldn't. All they want is for us to die, not suffer."

Malori said nothing. He thought perhaps he would be able to stand up soon.

Greenleaf (the name seemed so inappropriate that Malori thought it probably real) made some adjustment on a small device that he had taken from a pocket and was holding almost concealed in one large hand. He asked: "How many escort carriers besides this one are trying to protect the *Hope*?"

"I don't know," Malori lied. There had been only the *Judith*.

"What is your name?" The bigger man was still looking at the device in his hand.

"Ian Malori."

Greenleaf nodded, and without showing any particular emotion in his face took two steps forward and kicked Malori in the belly, precisely and with brutal power.

"That was for trying to lie to me, Ian Malori," said his captor's voice, heard dimly from somewhere above as Malori groveled on the deck, trying to breathe again. "Understand that I am infallibly able to tell when you are lying. Now, how many escort carriers are there?"

In time Malori could sit up again, and choke out words. "Only this one." Whether Greenleaf had a real lie detector, or was only trying to make it appear so by asking questions whose answers he already knew, Malori decided that from now on he would speak the literal truth as scrupulously as possible. A few more kicks like that and he would be helpless and useless and the machines would kill him. He discovered that he was by no means ready to abandon his life.

"What was your position on the crew, Malori?"

"I'm a civilian."

"What sort?"

"An historian."

"And why are you here?"

Malori started to try to get to his feet, then decided there was nothing to be gained by the struggle and stayed sitting on the deck. If he ever let himself dwell on his situation for a moment he would be too hideously afraid to think coherently. "There was a project . . . you see, I brought with me from Yaty a number of what we call historical models—blocks of programmed responses we use in historical research.''

"I remember hearing about some such things. What was the project you mentioned?"

"Trying to use the personae of military men as randomizers for the combat computers on the one-man ships."

"Aha." Greenleaf squatted, supple and poised for all his raunchy look. "How do they work in combat? Better than a live pilot's subconscious mind? The machines know all about *that*."

"We never had a chance to try. Are the rest of the crew here all dead?"

Greenleaf nodded casually. "It wasn't a hard boarding. There must have been a failure in your automatic defenses. I'm glad to find one man alive and smart enough to cooperate. It'll help me in my career." He glanced at an expensive chronometer strapped to his dirty wrist. "Stand up, Ian Malori. There's work to do."

Malori got up and followed the other toward the operations deck.

"The machines and I have been looking around, Malori. These nine little fighting ships you still have on board are just too good to be wasted. The machines are sure of catching the *Hope* now, but she'll have automatic defenses, probably a lot tougher than this tub's were. The machines have taken a lot of casualties on this chase so they mean to use these nine little ships as auxiliary troops—no doubt you have some knowledge of military history?"

"Some." The answer was perhaps an under-statement, but it seemed to pass as truth. The lie detector, if it was one, had been put away. But Malori would still take no more chances than he must.

"Then you probably know how some of the generals on old Earth used their auxiliaries. Drove them on ahead of the main force of trusted troops, where they could be killed if they tried to retreat, and were also the first to be used up against the enemy."

Arriving on the operations deck, Malori saw few signs of damage. Nine tough little ships waited in their launching cradles, re-armed and returned and refueled for combat. All that would have been taken care of within minutes of their return from their last mission.

"Malori, from looking at these ships' controls while you were unconscious, I gather that there's no fully automatic mode in which they can be operated."

"Right. There has to be some controlling mind, or randomizer, connected on board."

"You and I are going to get them out as berserker auxiliaries, Ian Malori." Greenleaf glanced at his timepiece again. "We have less than an hour to think of a good way and only a few hours more to complete the job. The faster the better. If we delay we are going to be made to suffer for it." He seemed almost to relish the thought. "What do you suggest we do?"

Malori opened his mouth as if to speak, and then did not.

Greenleaf said: "Installing any of your military personae is of course out of the question, as they might not submit well to being driven forward like mere cannon-fodder. I assume they are leaders of some kind. But have you perhaps any of these personae from different fields, of a more docile nature?"

Malori, sagging against the operations officer's empty combat chair, forced himself to think very carefully before he spoke. "As it happens, there are some personae aboard in which I have a special personal interest. Come."

With the other following closely, Malori led the way to his small bachelor cabin. Somehow it was astonishing that nothing had been changed inside. There on the bunk was his violin, and on the table were his music tapes and a few books. And here, stacked neatly in their leather-like curved cases, were some of the personae that he liked best to study.

Malori lifted the top case from the stack. "This man was a violinist, as I like to think I am. His name would probably mean nothing to you."

"Musicology was never my field. But tell me more."

"He was an Earthman, who lived in the twentieth century CE—quite a religious man, too, as I understand. We can plug the persona in and ask it what it thinks of fighting, if you are suspicious."

"We had better do that." When Malori had shown him the proper receptacle beside the cabin's small computer console, Greenleaf snapped the connections together himself. "How does one communicate with it?"

"Just talk."

Greenleaf spoke sharply toward the leather-like case. "Your name?"

"Albert Ball." The voice that answered from the console speaker sounded more human by far than the berserker's had.

"How does the thought of getting into a fight strike you, Albert?"

"A detestable idea."

"Will you play the violin for us?"

"Gladly." But no music followed.

Malori put in: "More connections are necessary if you want actual music."

"I don't think we'll need that." Greenleaf unplugged the Albert Ball unit and began to look through the stack of others, frowning at unfamiliar names. There were twelve or fifteen cases in all. "Who are these?"

"Albert Ball's contemporaries. Performers who shared his profession." Malori let himself sink down on the bunk for a few moments' rest. He was not far from fainting. Then he went to stand with Greenleaf beside the stack of personae. "This is a model of Edward Mannock, who was blind in one eye and could never have passed the physical examination necessary to serve in any military force of his time." He pointed to another. "This man served briefly in the cavalry, as I recall, but he kept getting thrown from his horse and was soon relegated to gathering supplies. And this one was a frail, tubercular youth who died at twenty-three standard years of age."

Greenleaf gave up looking at the cases and turned to size up Malori once again. Malori could feel his battered stomach muscles trying to contract, anticipating another violent impact. It would be too much, it was going to kill him if it came like that again. . . .

"All right." Greenleaf was frowning, checking his chronometer yet again. Then he looked up with a little smile. Oddly, the smile made him look like a hell of a good fellow. "All right! Musicians, I suppose, are the antithesis of the military. If the machines approve, we'll install them and get the ships sent out. Ian Malori, I may just raise your pay." His pleasant smile broadened. "We may just have bought ourselves another standard year of life if this works out as well as I think it might."

When the machine came aboard again a few minutes later, Greenleaf, bowing before it, explained the essence of the plan, while Malori in the background, in an agony of terror, found himself bowing too.

"Proceed, then," the machine approved. "If you are not quick, the ship infected with life may find concealment in the storms that rise ahead of us." Then it went away again quickly. Probably it had repairs and refitting to accomplish on its own robotic ship.

With two men working, installation went very fast. It was only a matter of opening a fighting ship's cabin, inserting an uncased persona in the installed adapter, snapping together standard connectors and clamps, and closing the cabin hatch again. Since haste was vital to the berserkers' plans, testing was restricted to listening for a live response from each persona as it was activated inside a ship. Most of the responses were utter banalities about nonexistent weather or ancient food or drink, or curious phrases that Malori knew were only phatic social remarks.

All seemed to be going well, but Greenleaf was having some last minute misgivings. "I hope these sensitive gentlemen will stand up under the strain of finding out their true situation. They will be able to grasp that, won't they? The machines won't expect them to fight well, but we don't want them going catatonic, either."

Malori, close to exhaustion, was tugging at the hatch of Number Eight, and nearly fell off the curved hull when it came open suddenly. "They will apprehend their situation within a minute after launching, I should say. At least in a general way. I don't suppose they'll understand it's interstellar space around them. You have been a military man, I suppose. If they should be reluctant to fight—I leave to you the question of how to deal with recalcitrant auxiliaries."

When they plugged the persona into ship Number Eight, its test response was: "I wish my craft to be painted red."

"At once, sir," said Malori quickly, and slammed down the ship's hatch and started to move on to Number Nine.

"What was that all about?" Greenleaf frowned, but looked at his timepiece and moved along.

"I suppose the maestro is already aware that he is about to embark in some kind of a vehicle. As to why he might like it painted red . . ." Malori grunted, trying to open up Number Nine, and let his answer trail away.

At last all the ships were ready. With his finger on the launching switch, Greenleaf paused. For one last time his eyes probed Malori's.

"We've done very well, timewise. We're in for a reward, as long as this idea works at least moderately well." He was speaking now in a solemn near-whisper. "It had better work. Have you ever watched a man being skinned alive?"

Malori was gripping a stanchion to keep erect. "I have done all I can."

Greenleaf operated the launching switch. There was a polyphonic whisper of airlocks. The nine ships were gone, and simultaneously a holographic display came alive above the operations officer's console. In the center of the display the *Judith* showed as a fat green symbol, with nine smaller green dots moving slowly and uncertainly nearby. Farther off, a steady formation of red dots represented what was left of the berserker pack that had so long and so relentlessly pursued the *Hope* and her escort. There were at least fifteen red berserker dots, Malori noted gloomily.

"The trick," Greenleaf said as if to himself, "is to make them more afraid of their own leaders than they are of the enemy." He keyed the panel switches that would send his voice out to the ships. "Attention, units One through Nine!" he barked. "You are under the guns of a vastly superior force, and any attempt at disobedience or escape will be severely punished . . ."

He went on browbeating them for a minute, while Malori observed in the screen that the dirty weather the berserker had mentioned was coming on. A sleet of atomic particles was driving through this section of the nebula, across the path of the *Judith* and the odd hybrid fleet that moved with her. The *Hope,* not in view on this range scale, might be able to take advantage of the storm to get away entirely unless the berserker pursuit was swift.

Visibility on the operations display was failing fast and Greenleaf cut off his speech as it became apparent that contact was being lost. Orders in the berserkers' unnatural voices, directed at auxiliary ships One through Nine, came in fragmentarily before the curtain of noise became an opaque white-out. The pursuit of the *Hope* had not yet been resumed.

For a while all was silent on the operations deck, except for an occasional crackle of noise from the display. All around them the empty launching cradles waited.

"That's that," Greenleaf said at length. "Nothing to do now but worry." He gave his little transforming smile again, and seemed to be almost enjoying the situation.

Malori was looking at him curiously. "How do you—manage to cope so well?"

"Why not?" Greenleaf stretched and got up from the now-useless console. "You know, once a man gives up his old ways, badlife ways, admits he's really dead to them, the new ways aren't so bad. There are even women available from time to time, when the machines take prisoners."

"Goodlife," said Malori. Now he had spoken the obscene, provoking epithet. But at the moment he was not afraid.

"Goodlife yourself, little man." Greenleaf was still smiling. "You know, I think you still look down on me. You're in as deep as I am now, remember?"

"I think I pity you."

Greenleaf let out a little snort of laughter, and shook his own head pityingly. "You know, I may have ahead of me a longer and more pain-free life than most of humanity has ever enjoyed— you said one of the models for the personae died at twenty-three. Was that a common age of death in those days?"

Malori, still clinging to his stanchion, began to wear a strange, grim little smile. "Well, in his generation, in the continent of Europe, it was. The First World War was raging at the time."

"But he died of some disease, you said."

"No. I said he *had* a disease, tuberculosis. Doubtless it would have killed him eventually. But he died in battle, in 1917 CE, in a place called Belgium. His body was never found, as I recall, an artillery barrage having destroyed it and his aircraft entirely."

Greenleaf was standing very still. "Aircraft! What are you saying?"

Malori pulled himself erect, somewhat pain-fully, and let go of his support. "I tell you now that Georges Guynemer—that was his name— shot down fifty-three enemy aircraft before he was killed. Wait!" Malori's voice was suddenly loud and firm, and Greenleaf halted his menacing advance in sheer surprise. "Before you begin to do anything violent to me, you should perhaps consider whether your side or mine is likely to win the fight outside."

"The fight . . ."

"It will be nine ships against fifteen or more machines, but I don't feel too pessimistic. The personae we have sent out are not going to be meekly slaughtered."

Greenleaf stared at him a moment longer, then spun around and lunged for the operations console. The display was still blank white with noise and there was nothing to be done. He slowly sank into the padded chair. "What have you done to me?" he whispered. "That collection of invalid musicians—you couldn't have been lying about them all."

"Oh, every word I spoke was true. Not all World War One fighter pilots were invalids, of course. Some were in perfect health, indeed fanatical about staying that way. And I did not say they were all musicians, though I certainly meant you to think so. Ball had the most musical ability among the aces, but was still only an amateur. He always said he loathed his real profession."

Greenleaf, slumped in the chair now, seemed to be aging visibly. "But one was blind . . . it isn't possible."

"So his enemies thought, when they released him from an internment camp early in the war. Edward Mannock, blind in one eye. He had to trick an examiner to get into the army. Of course the tragedy of these superb men is that they spent themselves killing one another. In those days they had no berserkers to fight, at least none that could be attacked dashingly, with an aircraft and a machine gun. I suppose men have always faced berserkers of some kind."

"Let me make sure I understand." Greenleaf's voice was almost pleading. "We have sent out the personae of nine fighter pilots?"

"Nine of the best. I suppose their total of claimed aerial victories is more than five hundred. Such claims were usually exaggerated, but still . . ."

There was silence again. Greenleaf slowly turned his chair back to face the operations display. After a time the storm of atomic noise began to abate. Malori, who had sat down on the deck to rest, got up again, this time more quickly. In the hologram a single glowing symbol was emerging from the noise, fast approaching the position of the *Judith*.

The approaching symbol was bright red.

"So there we are," said Greenleaf, getting to his feet. From a pocket he produced a stubby little handgun. At first he pointed it toward the shrinking Malori, but then he smiled his nice smile and shook his head. "No, let the machines have you. That will be much worse."

When they heard the airlock begin to cycle, Greenleaf raised the weapon to point at his own skull. Malori could not tear his eyes away. The inner door clicked and Greenleaf fired.

Malori bounded across the intervening space and pulled the gun from Greenleaf's dead hand almost before the body had completed its fall. He turned to aim the weapon at the airlock as its inner door sighed open. The berserker standing there was the one he had seen earlier, or the same type at least. But it had just been through violent alterations. One metal arm was cut short in a bright bubbly scar, from which the ends of truncated cables flapped. The whole metal body was riddled with small holes, and around its top there played a halo of electrical discharge.

Malori fired, but the machine ignored the impact of the force-packet. They would not have let

Greenleaf keep a gun with which they could be hurt. The battered machine ignored Malori too, for the moment, and lurched forward to bend over Greenleaf's nearly decapitated body.

"Tra-tra-tra-treason," the berserker squeaked. "Ultimate unpleasant ultimate unpleasant stum-stum-stimuli. Badlife badlife bad—"

By then Malori had moved up close behind it and thrust the muzzle of the gun into one of the still-hot holes where Albert Ball or perhaps Frank Luke or Werner Voss or one of the others had already used a laser to good effect. Two forcepackets beneath its armor and the berserker went down, as still as the man who lay beneath it. The halo of electricity died.

Malori backed off, looking at them both, then spun around to scan the operations display again. The red dot was drifting away from the *Judith*, the vessel it represented now evidently no more than inert machinery.

Out of the receding atomic storm a single green dot was approaching. A minute later, Number Eight came in alone, bumping to a gentle stop against its cradle pads. The laser nozzle at once began smoking heavily in atmosphere. The craft was scarred in several places by enemy fire.

"I claim four more victories," the persona said as soon as Malori opened the hatch. "Today I was given fine support by my wingmen, who made great sacrifices for the Fatherland. Although the enemy outnumbered us by two to one, I think that not a single one of them escaped. But I must protest bitterly that my aircraft still has not been painted red."

"I will see to it at once, *meinherr,*" murmured Malori, as he began to disconnect the persona from the fighting ship. He felt a little foolish for trying to reassure a piece of hardware. Still, he handled the persona gently as he carried it to where the little formation of empty cases were waiting on the operations deck, their labels showing plainly:

ALBERT BALL

WILLIAM AVERY BISHOP

RENE PAUL FONCK

GEORGES MARIE GUYNEMER

FRANK LUKE

EDWARD MANNOCK

CHARLES NUNGESSER

MANFRED VON RICHTHOFEN

WERNER VOSS.

They were English, American, German, French. They were Jew, violinist, invalid, Prussian, rebel, hater, bon vivant, Christian. Among the nine of them they were many other things besides. Maybe there was only the one word—man—which could include them all.

Right now the nearest living humans were many millions of kilometers away, but still Malori did not feel quite alone. He put the persona back into its case gently, even knowing that it would be undamaged by ten thousand more gravities than his hands could exert. Maybe it would fit into the cabin of Number Eight with him, when he made his try to reach the *Hope*.

"Looks like it's just you and me now, Red Baron." The human being from which it had been modeled had been not quite twenty-six when he was killed over France, after less than eighteen months of success and fame. Before that, in the cavalry, his horse had thrown him again and again.

Fred Saberhagen was born in Chicago in 1930, and lived there most of his life, with time out for travel, until he moved with his wife and three children to New Mexico in 1975. He has been writing science fiction and selling it since 1951, fulltime since 1967. He has also been an Air Force enlisted man, an electronics technician, and a writer/editor at Encyclopedia Britannica, *to which he contributed the article on science fiction. His published fiction output now includes about 18 books and 50 short stories. With his family he enjoys travel, hiking, swimming, and going to conventions about once a year.*

There are a lot more
where this one came from!